RAVE REVIEWS FOR SUSAN PLUNKETT, WINNER OF THE NATIONAL READERS' CHOICE AWARD AND THE *AFFAIRE DE COEUR* READER/WRITER POLL FOR BEST TIME TRAVEL OF 2000!

Ms. Plunkett exhibits "creativity and genius for characterization . . . unparalleled poignancy and an intimacy of both heart and soul."

—*Booktrees*

"Susan Plunkett . . . will entertain readers and make her mark as a true star of the genre."

—*Romantic Times*

"I have found a new, buy-on-sight, must-read author!"

—*Bookbug on the Web*

"Susan Plunkett distinguishes herself, moving into the field of the elite."

—*Booktrees*

"Ms. Plunkett has created a new dimension to the genre that must be developed further."

—*The Literary Times*

"Ms. Plunkett you are the BEST!"

—*Bell, Book and Candle*

"Ms. Plunkett writes some of the best sensual romance sandwiched between two covers."

—*Under the Covers Book Reviews*

"WOW! Ms. Plunkett knows how to draw readers into her story and keep them there until the end."

—*Old Book Barn Gazette*

300

For Kathleen Rehm with admiration.

A LOVE SPELL BOOK®

April 2001

Published by

Dorchester Publishing Co., Inc.
276 Fifth Avenue
New York, NY 10001

Cover art by John Ennis.
www.ennisart.com

ISBN 0-505-52434-1

The name "Love Spell" and its logo are trademarks of Dorchester Publishing Co., Inc.

Printed in the United States of America.

Visit us on the web at www.dorchesterpub.com.

SUSAN PLUNKETT

Alicia's Song

LOVE SPELL NEW YORK CITY

INTO THE WOODS

The man towered over her, his imposing mien similar to that of the timber giants protecting the nearby wildflowers from the elements. Strength and vitality radiated from his unyielding hands, which were still holding her. Silky hair as dark as a moonless night curled around his ears and fluttered across his forehead. The man had thunderclouds for eyes.

Alicia's gaze roamed the perfect arch of his dark eyebrows, then down his straight nose to linger on his lips. They were slightly parted, inviting lips. Sensuous lips. Whoa! Where had those wild thoughts come from?

Unsettled, her gaze snapped up to lock on his eyes. Something in their gray depths made her incapable of movement. It was as though he saw beyond the cool, practiced defenses she'd cultivated. He was peering directly into her soul and counting her vulnerabilities. The forest air grew still, close and humid, like before a spring storm.

The sinuous glide of his hands over her shoulders ignited small fires in her. His thumbs stretched around her arms, the knuckles grazing the sides of her breasts as his hands slid to her elbows, then up, lingering where her breasts were fullest. The long-dampened fires of passion flared within her, propelling a foreign, pent-up desire through her veins.

The man's head lowered, bringing his lips within inches of hers. The temptation to rise on her tiptoes and taste them was overpowering.

Prologue

The only cloud in the late afternoon sky drifted away from the town of Drexel's small cemetery. Digger Phelps, the caretaker, waited at the top of the stepping-stone path.

He mopped his weathered brow with a stained red bandanna, then stuffed it into the pocket of his overalls. Worry deepened the creases of his leathery face, old before its time and showing the rewards of hard work and harder living.

"You girls don't need to be singin' for this one. She were a strange one, livin' in them mountains by herself all them years. 'Tweren't natural. Some said she was a witch. . . . There ain't no tellin' what'll happen iffen you do your Christian-like service."

Digger barred the iron gate with his thin body in a gesture to protect the James girls from themselves, the alcoholic tremors in his hands increasing as his grit-encrusted fingers dove into the big side pockets of his baggy overalls.

"People have been scaring each other with those old rumors for years," Alicia assured him.

"Yolanda D'Arcy deserves the same consideration and reverence as anyone else, Digger," Bethany said in her most persuasive schoolteacher voice.

"She don't deserve nothing from you three."

"Yes, she does. You may as well step aside." Caitlyn slipped her small purse into the pocket of her tunic-length jacket and stepped forward. Although the youngest, she towered over Bethany by nearly half a foot, and had an inch on Alicia. In the stiletto heels she loved, Caitlyn's six-foot height intimidated even Digger.

A summer breeze stirred the trees. Alicia brushed errant strands of hair from her face, patiently waiting for Digger to move.

"Your mama wouldn't never have sung fer that one," Digger insisted.

Mama was the very reason for their graveside services. The daughter of a minister-turned-mortician, Lisette James had believed everyone should depart this world with a song celebrating the good things in life. For that purpose, she had cultivated her daughters' singing voices. In the process, she'd taught them the value of finding and cherishing the goodness in people, regardless how elusive it often was to the untrained eye.

"If she were here, Mama would sing with us now," Alicia reassured the old man. "You know she never allowed anyone to pass on alone."

"Well, I ain't stayin'. I don't want nothin' to do with this." Shaking his head, the old man reluctantly opened the gate and stepped aside.

The James sisters filed through, heading for the fresh grave of Yolanda D'Arcy in the far corner. Digger closed the gate after them with the finality of a slamming door.

"He sure was spooked," Bethany murmured, turning to watch the caretaker shuffle hurriedly down the stone steps to the parking area.

Alicia caught Caitlyn's wrist and checked the time. "Let's get this show on the road. I have to work tonight."

"Again? Darn it, Alicia. Leave your darn plants to themselves. I went to the trouble of making lasagna and lemon meringue pie." Caitlyn adjusted her watch.

"You mean you put a frozen lasagna in the oven and set the auto-bake," Bethany chided with a laugh.

Unperturbed, Caitlyn shrugged. "I made a new kind of salad and found a tart raspberry dressing for it."

"Uh-oh. She's been to the health food store again," Alicia teased as she stepped over the stone border of the Wagner family plot.

"It sounds terrific. I can't wait to eat," Bethany said. She had never been able to just let Alicia's teasing go; she always had to temper it with her own enthusiasm.

Well, maybe that was why they still were all so close. Because they balanced each other so well, were parts of a greater whole. Alicia spoke as they walked: "Save some pie for me. I'll be over after I finish my report."

Clad in a straight skirt and heels, and walking awkwardly on the grass, Caitlyn brought up the rear. She took her position on the right. Bethany stood in the center, her long skirt billowing in the breeze and as shapeless as the flowing blouse and linen vest hanging almost to her thighs. Alicia, who'd worn her favorite lemon-colored pantsuit to brighten the occasion, stepped into her place on the left. The bright sun and warm air made her wish she'd worn a cooler blouse.

While growing up, the girls had fallen into the habit of taking turns. And just as it was her turn to fix dinner after the service, it was also Caitlyn's turn to lead them in prayer. Together they would pray that Yolanda D'Arcy found harmony and happiness in the hereafter, something she had never found in Drexel.

As Caitlyn prayed, Alicia wondered about the dead woman's family. Had she sisters? Brothers? If so, where were they? Alicia's own sisters were the most precious blessings in her life.

The time had finally come, as she had known it would one day, when she had to make the decision between career and family. She only hoped she made the right one . . . whatever it might be.

At her far right, Caitlyn ended her prayer abruptly with

a puzzled expression, but before Alicia could ask whether something was wrong, her sister's pure soprano rose into the first notes of "Ave Maria." Alicia relaxed and joined Caitlyn in song.

A soft breeze whispered through the cottonwood centurions at the iron boundary of the graveyard, but the Jameses' melodious three-part harmony rang out sweet and clear. Their sound, Alicia thought proudly, even rivaled that of the mountain songbirds echoing through the Tetons.

After they'd finished, Bethany began "Amazing Grace." Then it was Alicia's turn to lead, her throaty alto upbeat for "Climbing Up the Mountain."

The buzz of insects faded into stillness.

The birds silenced.

The breeze died, the final note of their song hanging on the still air.

A relentless gray mist swept over the land, hugging the summer grasses and caressing the headstones.

The sky darkened from a sunny afternoon to a cloudy twilight.

The final note of "Climbing Up the Mountain" faded into a discordant quaver.

Fog swirled over Yolanda D'Arcy's grave and engulfed Alicia and her sisters in its warm breath. A sudden foreboding sent Alicia's heart racing. Good grief. She'd never been scared in a graveyard. Not like this.

She looked at her sisters. The growing cottony mist almost obscured them.

"I, uhh, think we ought to go. I'm not sure I set the oven to turn off." Caitlyn's voice dropped, and Alicia could tell she was afraid.

"What's happening?" asked Bethany. "Where did this fog come from? We weren't due for a front—"

"Who cares? We kept our promise. We're done here. Let's go." Alicia's apprehension was growing in proportion to the density of the eerie fog.

"What if Digger were right? What if Yolanda—"

12

Alicia didn't let her sister finish. "What if we get in the car and get the hell out of here?"

"I'll second that." Caitlyn's fingers reached through the pall and touched Alicia. "Lead on, Mountain Woman."

Alicia found her bearings and began to slowly wend her way through the forest of headstones.

"We're right behind you," Bethany called, then chided, "Don't lag, Caitlyn." Her voice seemed to come from a great distance behind.

"Don't worry. I'm right here."

Caitlyn's voice reassured Alicia. Like a blind woman navigating a familiar room—she'd been in this cemetery hundreds of times—Alicia snaked around the obstacles and found the gate.

"This is creepy." Her sister's pronouncement put Alicia at ease. They were together. Together, they could handle anything. Hadn't they already proven that by overcoming the horrible trauma of their parents' sudden death two years ago? Hadn't they seen Bethany through, too?

"Stay close," she insisted. She couldn't let them get separated. "Good grief, I can't even see the stepping stones." The hair on the back of her neck rose in eerie warning. "Here, Bethany, Caitlyn, hold hands so we don't get separated."

She groped the thick, dark mist. "Bethany? Caitlyn?"

She turned in a low, cautious circle. "Damn it, you two! This isn't funny! Answer me right now!"

Nothing.

There was only silence and fog.

Chapter One

Alicia batted at the last tendrils of fog, which clung to her with the tenacity of sticky spider web filaments, and blinked rapidly to clear the veil from her strange surroundings. As the last streamers dissipated, Alicia's hands stilled.

"What on earth . . ." Stunned, she gasped a lungful of clear air, then exhaled sharply. It tasted wrong.

Instead of cottonwood trees, giant hemlock and spruce towered overhead; their boughs gracefully lolled in a breeze barely reaching the ground. The scent of a coniferous forest, verdant green growth, and a hint of the sea filled her nostrils. A prickly sensation ran along the back of her neck and stretched down her spine.

The longer she looked, the more the strangeness of her surroundings seeped into her reality, the faster her heart beat.

"Bethany! Caitlyn!"

High in the trees, birds answered with unfamiliar songs in strange keys. A small animal skittered in the brush, startling her. She jumped back as it scurried deeper into a wall of ferns. Panic rose, clogging her throat.

Where was she?

More important, where were Bethany and Caitlyn?

She fought panic. Seeking something, anything logical, she forced her concentration on the giant trees.

Once, forests like this spread across her native western Wyoming, but nowhere did they flourish to such proportions as along the mountainous coast of the Pacific Ocean. The heavy scent of conifers intoxicated her.

"What is this place?" she said to herself.

Caught between a burgeoning terror and scientific amazement, she shook her head in an attempt to clear the confusion scattering her thoughts. For a moment, only the fearful staccato of her racing heart filled her ears.

Too pragmatic to deny the obvious change in her surroundings, she tried to summon an objective assessment, but even her scientific training failed her. She could think of no explanation for her situation.

Turning in a circle, she called for her sisters again. The urgent, panicky cry of their names ebbed into hopelessness.

Where was she?

Either the world had moved and she had stood still, or she had moved while the earth had spun off center. The prickly sensation she'd experienced in the fog-shrouded cemetery returned with fresh vigor.

A memory struck with the force of a thunderbolt. This place, these trees were part of a prophecy Yolanda D'Arcy had made years ago. There was more to it than a pristine forest, but the details eluded Alicia in her muddled state.

How had the old woman known this would happen?

Maybe she'd been a mystic, or a seer . . . or something not quite explicable, like the townsfolk of Drexel had implied. Like Digger Phelps had warned.

Don't be silly, Alicia told herself, the old woman hadn't caused this bizarre change. But she had prophesied something about pine trees and fog . . . and a river . . . and Alicia finding her future somewhere alone.

15

The old woman had known and tried to warn her of something.

Was this it?

"Why didn't I listen to her?" Alicia moaned. "Why didn't I write down what she said?" Because her heart had been broken and her life in the proverbial outhouse.

No, she would not consign this weirdness to a prophecy she couldn't remember. She hadn't believed in Yolanda's power years ago, why should she now?

And even if she did, then what?

That line of thinking led nowhere. There was a good, solid scientific explanation for the phenomenon ensnaring her. All she had to do was gather the facts, analyze them, then form a hypothesis. The logical solution would be obvious.

Alicia swallowed the lump in her throat, her mouth as dry as sandpaper. The dreadful certainty rose that her sisters were beyond reach. A wave of terror at the separation passed through her.

She started walking, though with no particular destination. Bleak isolation made each foot weigh a thousand pounds.

If she wasn't where she should be, where was she?

The question hung in the cool, humid air.

As a botanist, she could determine her general location from the fauna and flora. But how had she gotten here?

Good grief, nevermind that! She'd sort it out later. Right now, she had to deal with the facts as they were, not how they *ought* to be or the way she *wanted* them.

Still, she couldn't help feeling like the prize white rat in a lab experiment. All she wanted to do was find the cheese and the exit.

In a small clearing lit by a single finger of sunlight, deerberry bloomed. The first signs of its fruit were forming from spent white flowers. Broad, green leaves protected the stems. Nearby, reddish-purple coral root poked leafless spears from the humus, pink and red flowers clinging to the naked stalks. Beyond, a patch of Bluebells of Scotland bobbed on thin green stems sheltered by graceful grasslike leaves.

Head arched back, Alicia gazed at the canopy of foliage rolling in the breeze above her. A loon issued a forlorn cry that reflected the sentiments of her floundering spirit. She turned, steadily creeping backward, trying to catch sight of the bird.

The heavy weave of branches hid a formation of Canada geese calling back and forth above the swaying giants surrounding her. Her heel struck a rock. She stumbled, arms windmilling for balance—

Something reached out and caught her just before she tumbled to the ground. Arms flailing, feet scrambling, she righted herself and spun around. Her heart leaped, thudding against her ribs so hard and fast she expected it to pop out of her chest.

The man towered over her, his imposing mien similar to that of the timber giants protecting the nearby wildflowers from the elements. Strength and vitality radiated from his unyielding hands, which were still holding her. Silky hair as dark as a moonless night curled around his ears and fluttered across his forehead. The man had thunderclouds for eyes.

Alicia's gaze roamed the perfect arch of his dark eyebrows, then down his straight nose to linger on his lips. They were slightly parted, inviting lips. Sensuous lips.

Whoa! Where had those wild thoughts come from?

Unsettled, her gaze snapped up to lock on his eyes. Something in their gray depths made her incapable of movement. It was as though he saw beyond the cool, practiced defenses she'd cultivated. He was peering directly into her soul and counting her vulnerabilities. The forest air grew still, close and humid, like before a spring storm.

The man's eyes were consuming. They devoured her in silence, and a parade of expressions imparted loneliness, tenderness, and hope—more clearly than any words could ever do. Then he tilted his head slightly. The hunger in his eyes increased, an undefined yearning.

The sinuous glide of his hands over her shoulders ignited small fires in her. His thumbs stretched around her arms, the knuckles grazing the sides of her breasts as his hands slid to her elbows, then up, lingering where her breasts were fullest. The long-dampened fires of passion flared within her, propelling a foreign, pent-up desire through her veins.

The man's head lowered, bringing his lips within inches of hers. The temptation to rise on her tiptoes and taste them was overpowering.

"Please, let go of me," she heard a cool, logical voice say. It was her own.

He complied so abruptly, she had to take a step forward. Reflexively, she pressed her hand against the middle of his chest for balance. The muscles beneath his blue-and-green plaid shirt were as unyielding as the surrounding trees. The thatch of dark chest hair peeking through the open top two buttons of his shirt begged for stroking.

Alicia jerked her hand from his chest as though she'd touched a hot stove. The image of running her fingers through that silky mat had left her shaken. Embarrassment flooded her cheeks and neck with color. It had to be her strange surroundings making her have these wild thoughts! Certainly it couldn't just be this man who evoked this kind of reaction.

She busily smoothed her suit jacket and adjusted the purse slung over her left shoulder.

"Are you lost, ma'am?" His voice was velvet, the tones of a bass drum.

"I-I guess I am." She made the mistake of glancing at him, felt her heart skip, then forcibly tore her gaze away. The stormclouds of his eyes had turned to pewter, and the window into his soul had closed. The realization struck her with regret and relief.

"What are you doing wandering around these woods alone?"

Damned if she knew. Suddenly irked by the whole impossible situation, she retreated into her shell. "What does it look like I'm doing?"

The rub of his callused fingers over the black stubble

18

on his chin made a rasping sound. "It looked like you were walking backward in search of a good place to fall."

Expressionless, she blinked. "Don't be ridiculous. There is no such thing as a good place to fall. I was trying to get my bearings."

"I see." He dropped his hand from his chin. "Did you?"

"Did I what?"

"Get your bearings?"

"Well, not exactly."

He pointed over his shoulder. "That way is north."

She wondered whether he was telling the truth. How could anyone know which way was north in this dense growth? Her own directional instincts were nothing short of exceptional, and she had no idea.

"Are you sure?" Belatedly, she noticed the moss on the trees, then chided herself for not thinking of that sooner. Moss always grew on the north side of trees. Right?

A flicker of irritation furrowed his brow. It fled just as quickly. "Of course I'm sure. This is my land. I know every tree on it. That way is north."

Perhaps north meant something special, but she couldn't be sure. She hated asking another question whose answer should be obvious. However, Paul Bunyon, landowner in residence, didn't seem the type for volunteering information. "Would I be correct in assuming there is a town to the north of us?"

"Sitka is a couple of miles north by northwest. Isn't that where you came from?"

"No," she snapped. "I came from Wyoming."

Sitka. Sitka.

Her mind searched frantically for a reference. The only Sitka she knew was in southeast Alaska. Which wasn't possible.

Was it?

Stunned, she knelt and examined the ferns and wild-flowers' at the base of the ancient trees. The flora did match what she would expect of the indigenous vegetation of the islands forming Alaska's Inside Passage and Western Canada.

What had Yolanda said? Something about trees and rivers.

How had she gotten from Drexel, Wyoming, to Sitka, Alaska?

"Wyoming, huh? I read women have the vote there. Some folks here never thought Washington would accept them into the Union because of it." His head tilted and he gave a long, slow inspection of her attire. "Did women give up dresses down there, too?"

Of course women had the vote. They'd had it for years. Wyoming became a state over a century ago. Why in 1990, the entire state celebrated its centennial. "You're definitely not a historian. What are you? A fashion consultant?"

Perplexed, he shook his head and folded his arms across his chest. "Long trip, huh?"

The man had a gift for understatement. "Yeah, straight through the Twilight Zone. Do not pass Go. Do not collect two hundred dollars."

"Two hundred dollars in the twilight zone?" He squared his shoulders and reared back, obviously not following her side of the conversation.

"Yes. You know, Twilight Zone. Outer Limits. UFOs. Unsolved Mysteries." She walked away, muttering. "Damn, maybe I'm an X-File."

"What the h— What are you talking about? Are you running a fever?"

She spun around, and there he was towering over her again. She hadn't heard him move. The sincere concern drawing his eyebrows down heightened her pique. "No. I just hate not knowing where I am." *Or how I got here. Or how I get home. Or what happened to my sisters.*

"I just told you where you are. Unless you can sprout wings and fly, you need to head for Sitka." He chuckled. "It's the only town on the island."

"Thanks." She studied him, her eyes squinting in concentration. Unlike her, he belonged in this forest. His wide shoulders and muscular legs suited the strong, enduring forest around them. Quiet and unmovable, he exuded an untamed kinship with the whispering giants that surrounded them.

"Am I going in the right direction?" she asked, reluctantly tearing her gaze from him. She dared not ask his name. It might spoil her fantasies . . . the ones she knew she'd have. Knowing his name would make him somehow more . . . real. And the reality of him was the last thing Alicia needed. He disintegrated her reason with his probing gray eyes. He saw past her barriers and into her most private secrets. That made him dangerous.

Prudence dictated she never see him again. So why did she feel disappointed by his anticipated absence? Mentally, she shook herself, sure she'd lost her mind as well as her way.

"I'll lead you out of here and show you the road. Stay on it and you'll reach Sitka. Wander off it, and you'll end up as lost as you are now."

Before she could respond, he took the lead and wound a path through the ferns and stately trees. The yoke of his shirt strained under the motion of his powerful shoulders, the fabric threatening to burst if he moved too quickly or stretched the seams another fraction.

Maintaining the pace he set demanded all Alicia's considerable energy and concentration. The man moved with the lithe grace of a cougar, and it rankled her that he made no noise, while she sent small creatures scurrying for the underbrush and birds into flight with her passage. The sling-back pumps slipping against her damp feet provided scant protection and slid on the moist grass and detritus of the forest floor.

He stepped over a deadfall covered by moss and ferns. Alicia's shorter stride forced her to climb it. She barely mounted the top and stood when she began to slide. Arms stretched for balance, she fought to keep from tumbling.

Her forearms slammed down on his shoulders as he turned to catch her in his arms. The impact of her bone against his hard-muscled flesh reverberated along her frame to her toes. Her arms swept around his neck for stability. The silken mane of his hair filled her hands.

21

Effortlessly, he lifted her from the slippery deadfall. As her feet dangled above the forest floor, the molten heat of his body penetrated her clothing. A sudden rush of fire in her lower abdomen and the hardening peaks of her breasts crushed against his chest answered it.

In that instant, Alicia understood soul-searing lust for the first time. She had never been so aware of another human being in her entire life. She bit her lip to maintain control. Denying the impulse to lower her head the scant inches separating their mouths made her dizzy.

"You'd best let go of me, lady." The man's rasping tone sounded pained.

Staring at him, Alicia caught her breath. His lashes were incredibly long. She released his hair and relaxed. The massive arms forming a warm vise around her ribs lowered her, erotically sliding her down the full length of his body. The slow, calculated journey revealed every plane, every bulge—the most surprising of which was the one pulsing against the confines of his twill trousers. Apparently, he felt their sexual magnetism, too. She turned her head and avoided his gaze.

"How the hell did you get up here in the first place?" he muttered. Not waiting for a reply, he again struck out through the forest.

Thank heaven he didn't expect an answer. The same question plagued her. How could she explain what she failed to understand? Shaken by the potency of her experience in his arms, she plodded along behind.

As she walked, the first glimmer of comprehension flickered in the back of her mind. This spark, this thing that had passed between her and the man ahead was what her marriage had lacked. She and Chet had known each other since kindergarten. They'd planned and replanned their future a hundred times. It just hadn't turned out as they'd hoped.

Was this glimpse into the face of base desire what Chet had found with Betty Kroft? The memory of walking into her bedroom to find Chet and Betty sweating, panting, and undulating, crying out in encouragement and ecstasy, still burned in her mind. She and Chet had never shared such wild abandon. Maybe after all those years of growing up at each other's elbows, they had been too much like brother and sister for the fires of passion to burst into a carnal blaze.

The woodsman stopped at the crest of a hill and pointed. "There's the road."

Alicia snapped out of her reverie and looked around. A thin path snaked through the grasses and brush. She looked to the side and saw trees, then turned in the opposite direction and saw the same.

"*Where's* the road?"

The way he glared at her made her feel foolish. With the patience a loving parent might show a recalcitrant child, the man shook his head. He walked down the hill, his pace deliberate and slow to accommodate her slippery-soled shoes. Alicia followed, grateful for his restraint. At the bottom of the grassy, tree-dotted slope, she stopped and glanced around expectantly.

"You are standing on the road to Sitka."

"You're kidding." This wasn't a road. It barely qualified as a double-rutted path. Only a four-wheel drive vehicle could make it through.

"Continue walking in that direction and you'll reach town." The man's head dipped in the direction he wanted her to take.

Alicia looked up and down the ruts. Incredulous, she glanced back at her guide. He was serious.

"*This* is the main road?" Had innovations like concrete, asphalt, or blacktop never reached these people?

"Would you like me to escort you into Sitka?"

"No," she answered quickly. "I can find my way."

He hesitated. "Stay on the road. Don't linger." His eyes narrowed sharply and dropped to her mouth. "In case you hadn't noticed, it's dangerous for a woman to be alone out here."

Oh, she'd noticed . . . and the danger had nothing to do with wild animals or fallen timber. She took several quick steps toward town, then paused. "Thank you."

When he didn't respond, she glanced over her shoulder. The "road" was empty, as though he'd been a figment of her imagination. But she felt those enigmatic gray eyes on her as she picked her way down toward town, and she couldn't help wondering why he continued watching her.

Chapter Two

Exertion and emotion had made the afternoon warm. Head down, wary of rocks, weeds, and heaven only knew what else lurked in the forest, Alicia continued down the road.

Her first glimpse of Sitka stopped her short.

The primal beauty of the tree-tufted islands and tall-masted sailing ships dotting a harbor beyond the quaint town reminded her of a painting. A volcanic peak dominated one of the islands, though a solid growth of trees marching shoulder to shoulder down its slope indicated eons of dormancy.

Her gaze slid lower over the buildings and caught on an onion-domed Russian church. The landmark stood out from homes constructed with materials ranging from logs to fine brick, stone and finished siding, complete with porticos and gingerbread. On an adjacent hill, a fortlike building overlooked the sea. It contrasted sharply with an actual fort nearby, touting canons she could make out by squinting. In short, it was the oddest, most eclectic, most old-fashioned town she'd ever seen.

Her initial shock deepened. No automobiles traversed

the roads—not even four-wheel-drive trucks or SUVs. Nor did she see telephone lines or power poles running along the paths between irregular back yards or business fronts. Horse-drawn conveyances and saddled horses provided transport for people dressed in clothing straight out of a movie wardrobe warehouse.

Alicia's shoulders heaved in relief. That was it. They were filming a movie. Any moment a man peering through a camera would rise on the end of a crane and someone would shout, "Action!"

She waited, her feet throbbing in her sling-back pumps.

As the minutes ticked away, the magnitude of her situation settled like a rock dropped into a well. Her brief optimism faded. Her eyes closed. Her spirits plunged.

This was no movie set. No cars or motorbikes would come screaming down this rutted path overgrown by lush grasses and tiny seedlings, following the path of the sun. More than just her location had changed. Judging from the town waiting below, she had stepped back in time.

Had Yolanda mentioned a wrinkle in time?

No. A river of time, wasn't that it? Not that the woman's prediction explained anything; Alicia still didn't know how she'd managed to get wherever she was.

She drew a heavy breath and waited for the full impact of her predicament to knock her down. If she were ever going to have an anxiety attack, now was the time.

It didn't come. As usual, she was too pragmatic to indulge in escapism.

Instead she worried about her younger sisters. What fate had befallen Bethany and Caitlyn?Where were they? Had they remained in the graveyard? She'd always looked after them, always led them. What would they do without her?

A sudden thought came, sad but true. For now, she needed to concentrate on her own survival in this place and time.

She opened her eyes.

Nothing had changed, except the puffy high clouds rolling over the distant island volcano. She put one aching foot in front of the other and tried not to think about anything but descending the last of the rutted slope into town.

The first people she encountered gawked, she imagined because of her clothing. Some seemed amazed, others curious, about her Evan Picone pantsuit. She avoided all their eyes, hoping none possessed the temerity to question her. But glancing at the grass and mud stains on the fine, lemon-colored linen blend, she imagined the picture she presented.

Pitiful.

Judging by the variety of garb those she met wore, she assumed she could find something acceptable to change into at a general merchandise store. Although she'd prefer a mall, she settled for searching out an emporium. Dressed as she was, she stuck out like a sheepherder at the Drexel Cattlemen's Association.

Every little town had a main street, and finding Sitka's proved easy enough. Locating a clothing store was only slightly more difficult.

As she entered the store, she walked straight into a small woman in her midforties.

"I'm sorry, we're closed. I was just locking the door." The shopkeeper's eyes widened as she assessed Alicia's stained, outlandish clothing. "Goodness," she breathed.

Alicia's shoulders sagged. At this point, she'd accept sympathy, pity, anything. "I really need some clothes." She glanced beyond the shopkeeper at the barrels of dry goods, racks of harnesses, canned goods, lanterns, and yard goods, to the corner where several plain dresses hung beside a shelf stacked with folded merchandise.

"That's only partly true," Alicia confessed, dragging her gaze back to the woman. "I need some help." The admission stung her pride.

The shopkeeper nodded slightly. "It appears you do. Well, you're not likely to find it anywhere else. Come. Let's see what we can find." She reached around Alicia and locked the front door, then lowered the store windows' shades. "You're new to Sitka, aren't you?"

"I just arrived from Wyoming," Alicia stated in a matter-of-fact tone, as though it accounted for her difference.

"Wyoming. Oh, yes. Women have the vote there. And it seems they enjoy a number of other freedoms, judging from your dress. I doubt trousers on a woman will ever be accepted in Sitka."

"I gathered as much." Well, at least she'd found a continuity of thought concerning Wyoming as a trendsetting state.

"I'm surprised someone didn't apprise you of that on the ship before your arrived." The shopkeeper skirted the last barrel and led Alicia down an aisle of men's boots and heavy clothing.

"I'm afraid my other clothing sort of . . . got lost on my way here. This is all I have to wear."

"Those shoes are fit for a dance, not walking." A finger tapping her chin, the woman contemplated Alicia's pumps with an eagle eye.

Ten minutes later, Alicia's blistered feet luxuriated in comfortable stockings and sturdy shoes a smidgen large under normal circumstances, but suitable for now. She tucked a white four-point, cotton-blend blouse into a long, gored skirt patterned with thin brown and tan stripes running to the hem.

"How much does what I'm wearing cost?" Alicia asked darkly. She hadn't even given any thought for compensation. She had what she needed, or at least a start: Her new clothing and contrasting overjacket wouldn't draw attention on the street like an open wound drew the swarms of mosquitoes buzzing around her on the trail.

Edna Roth, the shopkeeper, tallied the bill aloud on her way to the counter.

Frowning with worry, Alicia joined Edna at the counter and opened her purse. She had a checkbook, credit cards, and plenty of money. The trouble was, none of it was any good.

"Will you consider bartering for the clothes?" Alicia asked. She glanced up.

The shopkeeper met her hopeful expression with a sigh. "You have no money? No gold? Wyoming currency is good, now that they've been admitted to the Union."

"I have lots of money. It just isn't any good here."

"I'm reluctant—"

"Please. As you can see, I'm in dire straits." *Desperate* straits was more like it. She looked squarely into Edna's pale eyes. "Look, I really need these clothes. I'll work here—sleep in the back—until they're paid for."

"I wish I could help you, but we don't need any help. My sons and I run the place just fine." Without warning, she threw her hands up. "Let me see those dancing shoes."

"They'll clean up with a damp rag and a little polish," Alicia encouraged.

"Maybe." As a test, Edna spit on a rag and rubbed the damp area over the toe of the shoe. The treated leather wiped clean. "All right. I'll trade the shoes straight across. Someone is bound to want these for a satisfactory price."

"They won't have to worry about anyone else having a pair like them," Alicia said. "They're unique." *In many ways.*

"What else did you have in mind?" Interested now, Edna eyed Alicia's purse.

Clutching her purse in both hands, Alicia leaned across the counter. "As a woman, you must appreciate how advanced Wyoming is. I mean, where else in the world do women have a vote in government?"

Edna's eyes flashed with amusement. She shook her head.

"We're on the cutting edge of fashion, too." Slowly, watching the shopkeeper's reaction and body language, Alicia withdrew a compact cellular phone from her purse.

Forget roaming charges. She was definitely "out of the area." Thank heaven she'd read the instructions for changing the ringing options.

An arpeggio tinkled from the small speaker.

"Oh my goodness! How did you do that?" Delight erased twenty years from the elder woman's face.

"This is a solar music box."

"A what?"

"See this little window?" Alicia pointed out the recharging cell. "It's the latest thing. The sun charges a little gizmo inside this so you never have to wind it."

An electronic rendition of "Dixie" followed by "Home on the Range" convinced Edna she had to have the ingenious item. Alicia traded the cellular phone for the skirt, petticoat, and stockings.

Next, she dug a dozen latex-coated paper clips—in a variety of colors—from the bottom of her purse.

Edna's curiosity had her dancing from one foot to another as she examined the treasures. "What are these?" she asked as she selected a red paper clip.

Alicia demonstrated their function by binding a stack of papers together.

"How marvelous! I've never seen anything like these."

The negotiator in Alicia launched into a dissertation on the merits of the latex coating in damp weather. Under different circumstances, she'd deem taking advantage of this woman shameful. However, the law of supply and demand moved the market—and these products were just as unique as Alicia was desperate. She touted the merits of every treasure she withdrew from her purse.

By the end of their haggling, Alicia had traded her shoes, the cellular phone, her Evan Picone suit, all the paper clips, and her ATM card (with its hologram). In return, she got the clothing on her back, some additional underwear, and a second outfit.

A few minutes more, and her lighted lipstick case and the sunglasses she'd forgotten she'd dropped into her purse were turned into ready cash.

Both women beamed in delight at the end of the exchange. Alicia threw in some breath mints as a bonus. Edna reciprocated by sending her three doors down to find a good meal.

Light hearted, Alicia collected her purchases and made her way to the recommended restaurant.

Only three other customers sat at tables in the cafe, and

they appeared nearly finished with their meals. A chalk-board at the door listed the daily fare.

Seeing the prices, Alicia realized it wouldn't be long before she ran out of cash . . . and things to trade. She had to find a job.

Hungry and desperate for a jolt of caffeine, she ordered coffee and the least expensive item on the menu: a bowl of soup.

She ate the soup and wondered whether she'd see her sisters again.

She glanced around. Only the proprietor remained in the cafe. Bolstered by the caffeine, Alicia turned to the next item on her survival agenda—a job.

The cafe proprietor wasn't hiring. However, he did offer the use of a current newspaper.

Alicia thanked him, then stared at the masthead. *June 3, 1895.*

The pit of her stomach plummeted to her toes. She drew a deep breath and swallowed hard to keep down the soup and coffee she'd just eaten. Every logical cell in her brain balked at what seemed an irrefutable truth.

Mustering her courage, she started looking through the newspaper. The printed date negated any uncertainty about her circumstances. She was definitely in trouble. Deep trouble. Her situation was worse than her scariest nightmare. *How did one go home from the past?*

The deep breath she'd drawn escaped with a sigh. Whatever had brought her would have to show her the way home. If indeed Yolanda D'Arcy's prediction of change was true, there might not be a way back. The notion of never seeing her sisters again thrust an invisible, hot lance through her chest.

"Did you find anything worth checking on?" asked the cafe proprietor. He wiped his meaty hands on a clean towel.

Alicia lowered the paper and gathered her wits. "Not yet."

"Try the board." He gestured toward the door, by which a kiosk held notices of all types and sizes. "Folks affix things up there all the time. Messages. News."

Intrigued, Alicia folded the newspaper and laid it on the table. Perusing the kiosk messages and ads—six jobs for fishermen, four for lumberjacks, and three others for what sounded like backbreaking labor on the docks—her heart sank, but just as she was turning away, a notice nearly obscured by a flyer for a new barber caught her attention. She parted the papers and took the ad.

Governess Wanted. Must have rounded education, even temper for tutoring small child. References required. Room and board furnished. Apply in person. Caleb Marker.

"Who is Caleb Marker?" she asked the proprietor.

"Ach. Caleb's been around longer than some of the trees on Baranov Island. He's a lumberman who owns the sawmill just south of town." The proprietor glanced over her shoulder at the ad. "He's a fine man. There isn't a fairer one to work for, young lady."

Alicia smiled at him, then introduced herself.

He took her extended hand and shook it warmly. "Otto Kratz. My wife and I own this place." He drew a watch from his trouser pocket, checked the time, then removed his apron. "She and my daughters are waiting. It's story night, and the babies have little patience."

"Oh, forgive me. I don't want to keep you, Mr. Kratz. You've been very helpful. If you don't mind giving me just one more minute, perhaps you can tell me how to find Mr. Marker."

"That's easy." He gave directions, all the while drawing a map on a scrap of paper.

Thanking him profusely, Alicia headed for the door, noting how quiet the streets of Sitka were in the late afternoon. Of course, if all the businesses closed as early as the general store and the cafe, there was little point in anyone milling about the town's walkways.

"Good luck, young lady," Otto Kratz called as he closed the door behind her.

When she looked over her shoulder, a shade filled the cafe window. A lopsided CLOSED sign dangled against the glass. "I'll need it, Mr. Kratz," she murmured. "I've always hated dog and pony shows. Now, I'm going to have to fast dance for the privilege of a baby-sitting job. Where's unemployment compensation when I need it?"

Squaring her shoulders, Alicia consulted the map. Her sore feet just might make the trek to Mr. Marker's home. She swatted a mosquito. Instantly, three dozen relatives appeared seeking vengeance.

Alicia lowered her head and embarked at a brisk pace down the road by which she'd entered Sitka. "Carefree Highway, my foot," she grumbled. "Give me a car and I-80 any day."

Chapter Three

Caleb Marker rubbed the final coat of wax into the finish of the school desk he'd built for Mariah. Crafted of hard maple, the surface would withstand anything the little girl could inflict until she outgrew the desk in a few years.

He completed the polishing in short order. His encounter with the disoriented wood nymph had incited a physical restlessness for which he'd found no outlet. It had been years since he'd looked at a woman and felt his entire body leap with readiness to bed her. Not even Margaret had affected him on such a primal level.

No, he mused, slinging the desk over his shoulder to carry it out of his wood shop. Nothing in his life had rocked his emotions and sent his blood racing like the woman in the forest.

Even remembering the way her curvaceous body slid down his stirred him. If she had held on to him a second longer . . .

He opened the mud porch door behind the kitchen.

What the hell had she been doing wandering through his woods? She was no innocent fresh from a schoolroom;

she was too mature. Nor had she looked to be a professional from one of the wharf-side taverns. So where was her husband? Any young, fresh, desirable woman had to have a man nearby.

"Wyoming," he muttered, setting the desk down where Mariah would see it in the morning. "The vote's one thing, but dressing like men? What next?"

He'd trailed the woman into town through the trees, just in case she'd detoured and become lost or encountered an animal. Even now, the memory of the way her trousers had defined her long legs warmed him. He recalled how the fabric had tightened when she bent to empty a rock or dirt out of her flimsy shoe. The trousers had stretched across her exquisite bottom, leaving little to his imagination. The clear image stirred the aching heat in his loins.

Caleb poured a drink. Out of habit, he arranged a stack of books on the table beside his favorite chair near the darkened fireplace. He picked up a volume on architecture. As one of his latest interests, he expected the topic to clear his thoughts. Instead, the book's words lay flat and dry on the page.

The last thing he needed was a female distraction, regardless of how delectable. Absently, he scratched his dog Nero's head. Part husky, part wolf, the beast lapped up the attention.

"Too many irons in the fire, boy. I haven't even got time to visit whorehouses."

Accustomed to his master's ramblings, Nero adored him with pale blue eyes. His tongue dangled over his teeth, fangs set in powerful jaws capable of snapping Caleb's thick wrist. Head cocked for full enjoyment of his master's scratching, the wolf dog only blinked in response.

"I know. I can't fool you, can I, boy. There's nothing on the waterfront worth risking—"

A timid rap on the front door stopped him short.

In a flash of gray and white, Nero shot across the room

and stood by the threshold, his fangs bared in silent warning.

Caleb heaved out of the chair and glanced at the clock in the corner. At this hour, a visitor boded ill. He crossed the room, wondering what mishap had occurred at the mill or the lumber camp. Resigned for yet another problem, he opened the door.

He froze.

Outside, the wood nymph gazed up at him in wonderment. Astonishment turned Alicia's mouth into an O. The last person she'd expected to encounter loomed before her. All the scenarios she had diligently rehearsed during the long, uphill trek from Sitka vanished. Good Lord, confined by the doorway, the woodsman appeared caged, but larger and even more potent than among the giant trees.

A bone-chilling sound drew her attention lower. Teeth. Big teeth. Reflexively, her hand rose to protect her throat. Afraid to run, afraid to stand still, she retreated in slow, shuffling steps.

"Stop."

Had he yelled or whispered? She didn't know, but she obeyed, then risked a glance at the woodsman.

"Another step and you'll trip over whatever it is you have on the porch behind you."

Focusing on the animal's bared teeth again, she didn't dare breathe. If she bent and retrieved her new belongings, she'd be an even easier target for the snarling monster.

The woodsman's hand descended over the beast's lips, drawing them down over all but the tips of its fangs. "Nero, go to the kitchen."

Alicia would have sworn the creature looked disappointed as it skulked off into the interior of the house. When her gaze shot back to the woodsman, she almost wished the beast had remained. Almost.

"What can I do for you, miss?"

Alicia tried to calm her thundering heart and recoup some of her earlier enthusiasm for this mission. "I, uh, I . . ."

"Are you lost again?"

"Uh, no. I came here on purpose."

His perfectly arched eyebrows rose. "Why?"

"I was told Caleb Marker lived here." Feeling totally inadequate, she gazed across the veranda at the long shadows consuming the tattered edges of sunlight from the clearing. "Please, don't tell me I made a wrong turn."

"You didn't. I'm Caleb Marker. Why are you looking for me?"

She fumbled in her pocket and found the ad from the message board. She unfolded the advertisement, then thrust it at him.

"I came in response to your posting for a governess. Has the position been filled?" From Otto Kratz's assessment, she'd expected a much older man. Someone benevolent, almost grandfatherly.

In a day filled with surprises, there was no reason for the sun to set without dealing one more sharp twist.

"No. The position is still open." He handed the notice back to her. "Do you have any qualifications? References?"

"Well, yes and no."

"Look, Miss . . ."

"James. Alicia James." Out of habit, she stuck out her hand as part of the introductory greeting.

Awkwardly, he took it, then dropped it as though her flesh were on fire. The sizzle of his contact warmed her. Color blossomed up her neck and into her cheeks. Maybe this wasn't such a good idea. The man meant trouble, and she had no time to sort it out. But the governess position was the only available and respectable job in town.

She drew in a deep breath, then let it out slowly. "If this is an inconvenient time for a discussion, perhaps we can set up an appointment for tomorrow."

"This is as good a time as any." He retreated, opening the door wider, then gestured her inside.

Alicia had considered the rambling stone and log home impressive from the main road. Upon closer inspection, the pristine tidiness of the grounds, house, barn, and two outbuildings evidenced the care Caleb Marker lavished on his property. Such organization appealed to her pragmatic side.

She retrieved the battered canvas carryall Edna Roth had given to her, then crossed the threshold.

The house interior exuded an unexpected warmth. Polished wooden floors gleamed in the muted glow of a lamp on a side table. Diffused outdoor light reached through fine lace curtains at the windows. The hour chimed. The rich sound drew her attention to an ornately carved grandfather clock. In the fading light illuminating the corner, she saw the exquisite workmanship of its cherrywood cabinet.

"That's a magnificent clock," she mused. The cabinet seemed to enrich and reverberate the tone of the chimes, making her momentarily forget everything else. Ten o'clock. How could it be so late?

The color drained from her face as realization dawned. "Oh, dear. I'm so sorry, Mr. Marker. I'd forgotten the daylight and time difference." No wonder every muscle in her body pleaded for a place to lie down and sleep.

"You're here. I see no point in your leaving before we talk." He motioned to an overstuffed sofa upholstered in soft bleached deerskin.

Certain she'd blown the interview before it started, Alicia perched on the edge of the sofa. She refused to lean back. Fatigued by the day's emotional strain and physical demands, she might blink too long and fall asleep.

She watched Caleb Marker settle into a chair designed for his more-than-six-foot height and his wide, muscular shoulders. His economical movements denoted a comfort with his strength and size. All the places her body had met his in the woods prickled with a delicious, dangerous yearning.

No. She wasn't likely to drift off while in the same room with him.

"May I see your references?"

"I don't exactly have any with me."

"Let me rephrase the question, Miss James. Do you have references?"

Alicia tamped down her strange reactions to him and focused on his question. "Probably not as you interpret the meaning of references. However, I'm anticipating the arrival of my younger sisters. They would vouch for my nurturing abilities." The answers she'd practiced en route flowed forth easily, and she hoped they held some grain of truth. If she'd been sent through time, her sisters—

"Your sisters," Caleb said in a flat voice.

"Yes. Both are excellent judges of character. We're all well educated in our own fields . . ." Her voice trailed off. The explanation was nothing short of lame.

"And would tell a stranger anything you wanted them to say," he finished.

Although the lamp on the table beside him brightened the room, she couldn't read even a hint of emotion in his stony features.

"Bethany and Caitlyn wouldn't lie to get a job for me. We weren't brought up that way." Her words were indignant, but she reminded herself that she needed employment and forced what she hoped was a congenial smile.

"Are you married?" he asked.

The smile evaporated, the question sparking a reflexive response. "No, I'm not. Does it matter?" Good grief, was he going to conduct an inquisition? She reined in her annoyance. This was 1895. Employers had liberties regarding personal information that she'd escaped providing in the twenty-first century.

"I won't tolerate even a hint of impropriety around Mariah," he warned, "regardless of how innocent it may seem."

"I'm not interested in finding a husband or dating."

For a long moment, only the ticking of the clock filled the room. Though his gaze never left hers, it seemed he peered through her clothing in search of a reason. Even more disconcerting was the uncharacteristic pleasure the sensation evoked.

"What did you do before you came to Sitka?" The soft-spoken question was unsettling; it reminded her of all she wouldn't be doing.

"I worked as a botanist."

"A botanist." Confusion flickered in her inquisitor's steel-gray eyes.

"Yes." If he didn't know what a botanist was, he'd have to ask. She wasn't going to volunteer a definition.

"What kind of educational background do you have?"

"Four years of college. I graduated fourth in my class rankings and first in my field." She relaxed, ready to discuss things more appropriate to her request for employment.

Caleb's left eyebrow twitched. "Impressive. Higher, formal education is a rarity in this country." He folded his hands over his chest and regarded her for a long moment.

Alicia met his gaze, determined to hold it until he looked away. Peering into the dark gray depths piqued her curiosity. If he had a wife, why did he need a governess? Or maybe he didn't have a wife. . . . For reasons she immediately attributed to the disorientation of her circumstances, she found the notion delightfully intriguing.

Caleb Marker held her gaze. "Tell me, Miss James, how does being a botanist relate to caring for a child? I don't see the connection."

Alicia perked up, ready for the question. "On a philosophical level, the care and nurturing of a child requires the same kind of patience and attention as tending to young plants. With proper guidance and devotion, a child, like a plant, will thrive and grow up to his or her full potential. Instead of pruning and staking, a child needs the surety of order, routine, and a firm but gentle hand when discipline is required."

"Is that so?" He blinked twice without changing his expression.

Undaunted, Alicia continued. "I'm not in favor of corporal punishment. There are other ways of getting a child's attention and winning her obedience."

"Hmmph. You mean bribe her or be her friend?"

Alicia shrugged and suppressed a faint smile at his sarcastic humor. "In part, but without abdicating authority.

Most young children treat their friends abysmally, until they learn how to be real friends."

He apparently weighed her response, while her discomfort expanded to fit the void of his silence. When he finally spoke, she sat on the very edge of the couch.

"Why do you want this position, Miss James?"

Caleb Marker didn't appear the type of man to be dazzled by creative explanation. Direct honesty seemed the best course. "I'm new in Sitka and need employment. Your ad was the only job on the message board I knew I could do and do well. I like children and I'm good with them."

"You make this interesting. You have no references, no recommendations, and, if I interpret your answers correctly, you have no experience as a governess. Please don't give me another far-fetched comparison between pruning children and nurturing plants. That logic doesn't qualify you for any position other than as a boarding school gardener.

"I need specifics for why I should entrust you with Mariah. Tell me why, in spite of your lack of credentials, you think I should hire you. Other than because you're a botanist who is good with children." His eyes narrowed as he leaned forward, his elbows braced on his knees. "And what does that mean—good with children?"

Until he'd punched holes in her carefully constructed logic, she'd thought she was doing pretty well with the parallelism between governess and botanist. Despite the fact he'd benefit greatly from a Dale Carnegie course on "How to Win Friends and Influence People," he was right. No viable connection existed between botany and child rearing. Abandoning her planned responses, she spoke from the heart.

"I've worked with children at the Women's Shelter in Drexel, Wyoming. Some of those kids were physically and emotionally battered. Some were abused in reprehensible ways. Some were happy, normal children curious about life and eager to learn. All shared a common hunger. Attention. I gave it. They required boundaries. I set

41

them. They thrived on encouragement and education. I provided those.

"Children need someone to listen to what they're saying, then decipher the meaning. I listened and decoded their messages. Most of all, they require a parent's unconditional love. But that's your job, Mr. Marker."

He regarded her for so long she began to fidget. The electric charge in the room reminded her of the Wyoming air right before a thunderstorm. Whatever private thoughts he struggled with, he did so silently. Still, he had not rejected her outright.

She tried to contain her urge to examine him, meeting his enigmatic gaze. However, in the periphery, she was aware of the way his trousers hugged his thighs as he sat with his legs parted. Heat rushed up her neck when she noticed the stretch of the fabric across his crotch. She'd never paid attention to such intimate things on a man—until now.

Alicia turned her head. The fireplace ashes were a duller but far safer sight.

"All right, Miss James, I'll take a chance on you. Though not because of the parallel you drew between botany and child rearing," he added quickly. "You're educated. You have a quick, inventive mind, and you can think. What's more"—the ghost of a smile softened his features—"you're the only serious applicant I've had for the job.

"Tomorrow I'll introduce you to Mariah. I'm at the lumber camp for days at a time during the summer. If things work out, you'll stay here with her—providing she likes you. I won't leave Mariah with anyone she doesn't like. So I guess we'll see just how *good* you are with children."

Amazed by his reasoning, Alicia sat a bit taller and tried to act professional. "Tomorrow—if she and I like each other—I'll have a few questions of my own." She rose and slung her carryall handles over her left shoulder. He rose, too. "How old is Mariah?"

"She turns six in October."

Alicia smiled, noting a softness when he spoke of his child. "A wonderful age. I'll look forward to meeting her. What time?"

"After eight and before ten. Naturally, I'll pay you for your time tomorrow."

Her meager resources didn't afford pride or refusal. "Very well." She extended her hand. "Thank you, Mr. Marker. I'll see myself out."

He shook her hand briefly, then plunged both fists into his trousers pockets.

Halfway to the door, she caught sight of his beast watching her from the shadows. This time she was ready for it. Because she was determined to take advantage of the opportunity Caleb Marker handed her, she accepted the animal as part of the job package. "He looks part wolf."

"He is. I'm gone a lot. He's protection against two- and four-legged predators. Does he frighten you?"

"He's in the house. You must allow him to be around Mariah, so I doubt I have anything to fear. Do I?"

"No, you don't," he agreed in a disturbingly soft voice. "Only uninvited guests have anything to fear."

She'd read that pets and owners often resembled one another in looks, temperament, or both. Glancing over her shoulder at Caleb Marker, she suddenly understood. It was certainly true of these two. Each posed a danger. At least she understood the one from the pet. Considering the maelstrom of inexplicable sensations Caleb incited in her, he might be the more dangerous.

Without another word, Alicia left, softly pulling the door shut behind her.

Caleb stared at the door long after Alicia James's footfalls faded from the porch. Nero ambled to his side and nudged Caleb's hand until he resumed stroking the dog's head.

Neither he nor the James woman had handled the interview well, and he hadn't been entirely honest with her. His reasons for giving Alicia the opportunity to meet his daughter were more numerous than he'd stated. Her eyes had intrigued him; he'd seen the honesty of her motives in their exotic, violet depths. Also, she needed employment and his posting was the only one suitable and available.

Caleb returned to his chair.

In truth, he was as desperate for competent care for Mariah as Alicia was for the job. Thus far, the local applicants had consisted simply of women seeking a way out of making their livings on their backs. Only two could read and write. Barely. A third had sought to compensate for her illiteracy by offering to share his bed.

Alicia possessed an education he envied. His own came from studying the library he'd accumulated. As a self-taught man, he often questioned the validity of what he interpreted from his reading.

And even his own self-education had slowed. Since assuming Mariah's care five years earlier, Caleb had foregone his sojourns to San Francisco. He missed the abundance of culture and the easy exchange of ideas that flowed in the club drawing rooms and parlors of his learned acquaintances.

At times, he wished he had married. However, he'd already learned the hard way that few women had a temperament adaptable to being a lumberman's wife on isolated Baranov Island.

Caleb patted Nero's head and rose.

Mariah had brought joy and laughter to his life. And though her presence also reminded him of loss and his own loneliness, he considered it an equitable trade.

He doused the lamps and headed for his room with an inexplicable combination of anticipation and dread for the morning.

"Why the hell did I tell her to come back?" he muttered to his dog.

Even as he spoke, an answer became apparent. The woman exuded an honesty he prized. Her quick mind would challenge both him and his daughter. Also the earnestness of her stance on punishment assured him she would be gentle with the girl.

He ignored his burning desire to explore the woman's delectable body and the hungry hope he might have the opportunity.

"No fires here," he warned, closing his bedroom door.

If Mariah liked Alicia, he would keep his distance. But that might be even more difficult than the seemingly impossible task of finding a competent governess willing to live on his remote lands.

Chapter Four

The long shadows cast by the setting sun blended into the trees. Lingering clouds glowed pink, red, and gold. In the east, the first evening star twinkled.

Alicia hurried down the steps of the Marker veranda. Regardless of how fast she walked, she'd never reach town before dark. Even if she did, she had no idea where to find a hotel or the cost of a night's lodging.

For an instant, she considered knocking on Caleb Marker's door and explaining her predicament, but her pride and self-confidence had taken enough of a beating for one day. Asking for his help now was tantamount to begging for his hospitality and waving a flag to draw attention to her shortsightedness.

"Stupid," she muttered, "just plain stupid. All you had to do was check a clock before leaving town. Now where are you going to sleep tonight?"

At the junction of the worn paths connecting the Marker barn with the main road, Alicia paused. Behind her, an unseen force beckoned. She turned back toward the residence, the pristine simplicity of the sprawling place twisting something in her heart. The contour of the stately trees encircling the homestead defined the boundaries, as though they relinquished the cleared land to Caleb Marker willingly. As well they should; his very presence and demeanor personified the trees—straight, tall, powerful, and rooted to the land. A few of the old Wyoming ranchers she'd grown up around epitomized those same admirable traits.

All the same, Caleb Marker scared the hell out of her. Simultaneously, he fascinated her in the same indefinable manner, for reasons she hesitated exploring.

The dull glow radiating from the windows over the veranda wall winked out. Images of the lumberman retiring for the night evoked a number of conflicting thoughts. The most dominant was an unreasonable jealousy. He had a bed, while she'd have settled for a pillow and blanket and called it luxury.

Although the house was out of question, the barn might provide shelter for the night. The solid walls promised warmth from the growing chill seeping through her clothing. Even the increasing whisper of the wind in the trees encouraged her daring.

Lured by the possibility of a safe place to lay her head, she started down the path leading to the barn. The last fingers of sunlight gilded the clouds with color, the waning twilight bidding her hurry before full darkness descended.

She explored nearly the full length of the barn before locating a small door. A glance to the right assured her that all within the silent house slept. A rope with a tattered, oversized knot dangled from a hole in that door.

She pulled on the rope. The sound of a latch lifting filled her with satisfaction. The door swung open on well-greased hinges. Quickly, she ducked inside and pulled the door shut.

The smell of animals and hay filled her nostrils. It wasn't the fetid stench of decay, but rather was fresh and clean. It reminded her of the barn on the James ranch where she'd grown up. As such, it imparted a sense of home.

She fumbled in her purse and found the lighter she carried for working in the lab. The massive darkness of the barn's interior swallowed the meager flame's light.

Alicia found a lantern hanging on the wall. Growing up on a remote Wyoming ranch had benefits she'd never expected to appreciate. In seconds, she had the lantern glowing and the lighter back in her purse.

The barn interior was as meticulous as she had anticipated. If Caleb Marker ran the rest of his business with the same attention and care as the homestead, he deserved respect.

Across the rock and plank floor, a cow mooed and shuffled in a small pen. Alicia chuckled at the familiar sound. A horse nickered in response, which fortified the wisdom of her decision. Here, she'd sleep well. She raised the lantern overhead and glanced around. To her right, a fixed ladder led to a hayloft.

Alicia grabbed the back hem of her skirt, pulled it through her legs, and tucked the edge into her waistband. Securing her purse and carryall on her shoulder, she approached the ladder.

The loft was heaven, pillowed in mounds of fresh hay. She hung the lantern on a peg jutting from the vertical support beam. A horizontal support ran the center length of the barn and disappeared into the far wall.

Just as she was ready to douse the light and collapse in the hay, she heard the door latch lift. She wheeled around and peered over the edge of the loft. Heart thumping, she wondered how angry Caleb Marker would be over her imposition. She surrendered to the inevitable— though just once in her life, it would have been nice to get away with something. She slumped against the post and awaited judgment.

Instead of Caleb, a beast similar to Nero crept through the open door. Its eyes glowed in the dark shadows, their focus directly upon her. Steadily, the animal approached the ladder.

Alicia didn't become worried until the beast started pawing the rungs. She'd never seen a dog or wolf climb a ladder, other than on television. Feral snarls that weren't quite barks or howls were issuing from its mouth.

She was no match for those big teeth.

Frantic, she glanced around. The beast on the ladder, getting closer every second, was between her and the only way out.

Wild-eyed, she gazed at the twelve-by-twelve-inch beam running the length of the barn. The floor below suddenly seemed very far away.

The animal snarled and snuffled, continuing to climb with a terrifying relentlessness. The clack of its nails against the wooden rungs was growing even more terrifying.

Alicia made her decision as his snout cleared the floor. Those big teeth could rip her leg right off her body—providing she kept him from her throat that long. She swung around the lantern on the support post.

Stepping onto the beam, arms spread like a tightrope walker's for balance, she inched away from the loft. As though sensing a threat nearby, the cow below initiated a steady protest. The horses—there were several, not one—whinnied displeasure.

Panting shallowly, Alicia continued along the beam. The only resting spot lay at the wall in front of her. There she could at least hold on until . . . Oh, God, until when? Morning? Would someone come out to milk the cow? How long would the wolf dog keep her cornered?

Given the creature's tenacity, it would keep her pinned on the beam until someone called it off. Undoubtedly, that *someone* would have to be Caleb Marker.

She glanced over her shoulder. The wolf dog paced the loft and eyed the beam. As its icy blue-gray eyes locked on hers for a split second, Alicia nearly lost her balance. The beast wanted to kill her. No doubt about it.

An ear-splitting cry, something between a howl and a bark, echoed through the barn. All the small hairs on Alicia's body shot up in attention. She was paralyzed by fear.

Below, the horses kicked at their stalls and whinnied. The cow bellowed. Another sound mingled with the chaos—a pig? A squealing pig. Only the chickens were silent in the coop at the back of the barn.

Alicia looked down on the Barnyard Hell and wondered what terrible sin she'd committed to deserve this.

Abruptly, the wolf dog silenced, though the animals below did not. Their protest was building to a frenetic pitch.

Alicia took a cautious glance over her shoulder. And nearly fell. The wolf dog was tentatively trying to join her on the beam. Arms windmilling, she recovered her balance.

If her heart didn't give out before the beast figured a way to cross the distance between them, he'd have her cornered.

Alicia's hysterical laughter pierced the cacophony of shrieking animals. Cornered. If this wasn't cornered, what was?

The side door flew open and banged against the wall, the distraction freezing Alicia in place. If she so much as looked away from the shadow-shrouded wall ahead, she'd fall.

"What the hell . . ." Caleb Marker's booming voice rattled the fillings in her back teeth.

Instantly, the wolf dog launched into its eerie howling bark. A second joined it from near the door. The penned animals in Barnyard Hell below followed suit.

Alicia closed her eyes and felt her head spin. Not only had she lost the one place where she might grab a few hours' sleep, now she'd lost any chance for the job she needed, too.

"Caesar. Back off. Come."

Were there any sweeter words in the English language, or a more welcome voice than that of the beast's master? Perched on a joint of a crossbeam, she waited, neither looking away, nor moving as the wolf dog retreated down the ladder. Not until she heard Caesar cross the floor to his master did she venture a brief glance down.

Flanked by two of the most vicious looking critters known to woman, Caleb Marker glared up at her. She wasn't sure which to fear more, the two-legged man or the four-legged beasts.

"I, ah, guess you're wondering why I'm here," she said in a voice as shaky as her knees.

"That question does cross my mind." .

He sounded calm. Too calm. Staring at the wall again, feeling the fatigue of the day wash away the last of her reserves, she attempted an explanation. "It was almost dark when I left your house. I wasn't sure I'd make it back to town. Besides, I don't have a hotel room there. So . . . I didn't think you'd mind too much if I slept in your hayloft."

Silence filled the barn. Even the animals were quiet.

"Actually, I hadn't planned to tell you I spent the night in your barn," she admitted. It couldn't get any worse than it was right now. Maybe he'd let her borrow a lantern for the long trek into town. But then what?

His silence held, adding to her certainty that he thought she was crazy.

Alicia sighed wearily. "The best made plans . . . I thought your wolf dog was in the house. It never occurred to me that you had two, let alone a ladder climber."

"Why didn't you say something about needing a place to stay?"

He sounded irritated. She refused to look at him, knowing she would only find censure. "I thought I already seemed enough like a ditz, which I am not. This has just been the most bizarre day of my entire life. All I wanted to do was—"

He cut her explanation short as he approached the ladder, his words surprising her. "Look, I apologize. This is my fault. I should have made sure you had transportation waiting. In these parts, we don't send women off to fend for themselves at night. It isn't safe. Hell, you're not even armed, are you?"

"No. I'm afraid I left my rifle in Wyoming." *Along with my life and everything familiar.*

"Can you come down by yourself, or do you need help?"

The ridiculous notion of just stepping off the beam and floating down to the floor in front of him flashed through her mind. She laughed, a bit hysterically. "I think I can manage a descent."

"I was hoping you'd use the ladder. Do you need help, Miss James?"

"No. I'll just back up."

"I wish you wouldn't. Walking backwards doesn't seem one of your strengths. Stay there, and I'll come and get you."

"No!" God, tired as she was, if he touched her up here, she'd melt and they'd both fall. Biting her bottom lip, she began a slow turn. A twelve-inch beam might seem like a football field to a gymnast, but she was no Shannon Miller or Amy Chow.

Concentrating on the beam, she put one foot in front of the other until she reached the vertical support post. There she wrapped both arms around it as though it was a life raft in a storm-tossed sea. After a deep, cleansing breath, she fetched her carryall and purse, slung them over her shoulder, then retrieved the lantern she'd borrowed.

Descending from the loft required an inordinate amount of ungainly maneuvering, as the ladder extended only one rung above the elevated floor. Somehow, she managed. But as she reached the last rung, her foot slipped. She fell backwards.

When strong arms caught her, it was all she could do to keep from turning into their protective shelter and losing herself.

"Sorry," she said quietly. "Guess I didn't see the last one."

Caleb steadied her, holding onto her upper arm when she tried to pull away. "You look like hell, Miss James."

"Well, Mr. Marker, sometimes looks *aren't* deceiving.

You called it well. I feel like hell, or forty miles of bad road, whichever you prefer."

"My housekeeper, Mrs. Crowley, has a room set up for Mariah's new governess. I see no harm in you using it for the night."

Alicia regarded him as though he'd just offered her the world. "Oh, I do thank you from the bottom of my heart."

He took the lantern from her, doused it, then hung it back on the wall from where it had come. A hand signal brought Caesar and Nero to his left side. "Take my arm. I don't want you tripping on anything," he said.

She quickly acquiesced. If a rock were indeed protruding from anywhere, it seemed likely she would trip over it. In the span of an afternoon she'd gone from a cool, organized professional to a complete, incompetent freeloader. "Ah, Mr. Marker. Just so we can keep the slate even, regardless of how tomorrow goes with Mariah, I don't want you to pay me. A warm, safe place to sleep tonight is payment enough."

Ahead of her, Caleb tripped on the back stair.

Chapter Five

Caleb led Alicia through the mud porch and into the kitchen. Watching her as he lit the lamps, guilt stung his conscience. He'd known the late hour when she arrived, known she was unfamiliar with the island, and he'd known she was alone.

What the hell had he been thinking when he let her walk out of his house? He wouldn't send Jeremy—Maude Crowley's son—into town on foot after sunset.

"Have you eaten anything this evening, Miss James?"

Whatever protest she prepared withered with a dismayed frown when her stomach growled.

"Sit." He pulled a chair away from the sturdy worktable at the side of the kitchen. "There's no excuse for my lack of hospitality earlier. I don't know how it is in Wyoming, but here people lend a hand to strangers and friends alike."

"Out on the ranches and in the back country, it's the same," she replied, dropping her carryall on the floor. "Do you mind if I wash up?"

Caleb led her through the house to the bathroom. The

54

modern innovations it offered were a source of pride to
him. They provided genuine convenience, particularly in
the cold winter months.

While she washed up, he heated the stew his housekeeper had prepared before going to visit her daughter in
Sitka.

Alicia James was an unusual woman. During their earlier interview, he'd sensed an agile, quick-witted mind.
However, seeing her balancing over the center of the barn,
Caesar raring to take a bite of her, that attested to something more important in the rugged country.

She had survivor instincts. Had she fainted at the sight
of the dog's approach, Caesar would not have treated her
kindly. Caleb would have had to deal with that and repost
his notice at Otto Kratz's cafe.

Relieved he'd arrived in time to avoid any such grue-
some scenario, he muttered a curse and a prayer of thanks
for Nero's bark. It had given him time to get out to stop
Caesar. The sight of Alicia on the crossbeam had damn
near stopped his heart. She had courage; more than that,
she was downright plucky.

"It smells wonderful."

He glanced over his shoulder in time to see Alicia settle
at the table. For an instant, their gazes locked. Damn, she
possessed an ethereal beauty he hadn't seen the like of in
years. . . . Not since Margaret.

Faint shadows formed crescents beneath Alicia's eyes,
but Caleb was taken by their color. He had never seen
eyes the violet shade of twilight. Captivated, he stared
until she lowered her lashes.

He stirred the steaming contents of the pot. "It is good.
Maude is an excellent cook."

"Is Maude your wife?"

Caleb chuckled. "Maude Crowley is definitely not my
wife. She's more my mother and my conscience. She's
been my housekeeper and cook for the last what . . . going
on seven years."

Caleb dished up the stew and gathered a spoon and
knife.

As soon as he met Alicia's curious gaze, she looked away.

"Eat. I'll get some bread."

She raised a hand. "This is plenty. Really. I don't want to be any trouble."

At the first sign of protest, he cocked his head, then shook it slightly. "If you eat and sleep well tonight, I won't feel like such an"—he searched for a term acceptable outside the lumber camp—"insensitive boor for letting you leave without making sure you had somewhere to go and a way to get there."

He fetched bread, butter, honey, and a couple of plates. While she ate, he snacked on the bread and honey. A raw, sensual excitement was rippling through him, the crest of each wave nearly as potent as the comfortable sensation of domesticity. Alicia appeared at home across the kitchen table. At the moment, it would be easy to convince himself she was born for the singular purpose of gracing his home with her feminine presence.

There was a sedate homey side to that image, but that wasn't what he envisioned. With every fiber in his being, he wanted to bed this fascinating woman seated at his table. As though sensing his desire, she met his gaze.

"Is there something I should know about your offered hospitality?"

The softness of her voice reminded him of velvet gliding across satin skin. "Like what?"

"You're looking at me as though you expect something. Do you?"

"No."

Liar! He saw the accusation etched into the slight narrowing of her eyes. But she was as wrong as she was right. He didn't *expect* anything from her, but he wanted to make love with her more than ever. Damn, was he really so lonely? So hungry for female companionship?

"You're pretty blunt for a woman," he said. He wasn't sure, but he thought he appreciated that.

"I suppose so. It saves a lot of confusion."

"I find it curious you didn't rent a hotel room in Sitka.

Was it because you didn't have enough money? Why did you leave Wyoming if you were so low on funds?"

For an instant before she blinked, then lowered her gaze, Caleb thought he saw a tear brim on her lower lashes.

"I don't want to talk about it."

A new dread welled up. Given his history of picking women, he'd better learn all he could about her up front. "Are you in some kind of trouble, Miss James?"

"No. I swear on my life and the lives of my sisters, none of us is in any trouble with the law or anyone else. We're so conservatively conforming, we're downright boring."

Boring? He found nothing even remotely boring about this woman. Intriguing, exciting, yes. Boring? Never. Although her table manners and demeanor were those Caleb associated with a well-bred, society-schooled lady, her speech and candor baffled him.

"Tell me about your sisters. When do you expect them?"

Silence ensued. It ended when Alicia pushed away from the table and carried her bowl to the sink. "My sisters and I got separated when I left Wyoming. I'm not sure where they are." She scrubbed the bowl and laid it on the counter. "It's been a long, trying day, Mr. Marker."

The way she shut down any probing into her life led him to believe there was a great deal more to her terse explanation. If she lasted through tomorrow, he'd discover her secrets.

No surprises, he promised himself.

"I'll show you to your room." He rose from the table and ushered her out of the kitchen.

In the glow of the lamp Caleb lit beside the bed, Alicia marveled at the exquisite headboard, armoire, and nightstand appointing the room. The wood surface of each was beautifully carved in smooth, fluid strokes, but it took a moment for her to recognize the scene: the Sitka harbor as viewed from the last hill cresting the city's main road.

"You know where the bathroom is, so I'll say good-night, Miss James."

Alicia reluctantly abandoned examining the meticulous detail in the furniture. "Thank you, Mr. Marker."

The door closed softly, leaving her alone in the middle of the room. An oversized patchwork quilt covered the bed, its blues, yellows, greens, and soft reds blending with a calico flower print. Heavily lined draperies hung at the windows.

Alicia undressed and climbed into bed. Tired beyond belief, she stared at the ceiling.

Bethany and Caitlyn had been right behind her in the fog. Not more than a few feet. What had happened? Were they now lost in the big Alaskan forest, looking for each other and her, or were they still in Drexel wondering what happened to her?

The first tear slipped from the corner of her eye. She'd never felt so alone, incompetent, or helpless in her life.

Not one to indulge in self-pity, she sniffed and held the torrent of tears back. If she started crying, she might not stop. Besides, she reminded herself, she didn't have any tissues.

How had she ended up in Sitka, Alaska? Waffling between anger and confusion, she found no answers. At last, the toll of the day caught up with her and she slept soundly.

The eerie howling bark of one of the Hounds from Hell woke her. She was already sitting up when she opened her eyes.

"Good grief. What happened to a rooster alarm clock?" she asked herself with a small grin. She stretched, then got of bed.

Twenty minutes later, scrubbed, dressed, and her hair combed, Alicia opened the bedroom door. Nero got up from the spot in front of her door and trotted toward the kitchen, his nails clacking on the polished wood floor. Heart thumping a lively pace, Alicia followed at a discreet distance.

"She's here," came a child's loud whisper from the kitchen.

The infectious excitement in the girl's voice brought a smile. "Good morning," Alicia said as she entered the kitchen.

A flour sack dishtowel hung from the waistband of Caleb's trousers. He picked bacon out of a frying pan with a fork. "Good morning, Miss James. I hope you slept well."

"I did. Thank you."

A little girl with raven hair and eyes the color of storm clouds regarded her from the table. A fine sprinkle of freckles drifted across the bridge of her nose.

Alicia smiled. Mariah smiled back, revealing a pair of deeply set dimples and the absence of a top front tooth. There was no mistaking the resemblance between father and daughter.

"Good morning. I'm Mariah." The girl scrambled from her chair, then waited expectantly.

"Hi, Mariah. I'm Alicia James."

"From Wyoming," Caleb added, bringing the bacon to the table. "Can you fry an egg without breaking the yolk?"

"I don't like broken yolks," Mariah confided solemnly.

"Sure. How many do you want? Six?"

Mariah giggled and shook her head.

"Ten?" Acting distressed, Alicia focused on Caleb. "You'd better go squeeze those chickens if she wants ten eggs. There won't be any for you."

Mariah laughed aloud and pointed at the egg basket. "Daddy says there's a dozen. That's twelve. Isn't that enough for me to have ten?"

"Sure. Ten for you, two for the cook. That's twelve. Count it on your fingers." She dropped onto her haunches and counted out numbers and fingers with the child. When Mariah ran out of fingers, Alicia used hers. "See? These two fingers are my eggs, right?" She wiggled them back and forth.

"Uh-huh."

"Those ten fingers are your eggs. Okay?"

"Uh-huh."

"So, no more eggs left for anyone else."

Mariah grinned. "What if I give Daddy some of my fingers?"

"Oh, Mariah, they won't fit his hand. Besides, he already has a fistful."

Mariah giggled and held up on finger. "I only want this many eggs."

"Okay. So if I get two and you get one, how many is that?" Alicia held up her two fingers.

Mariah counted the fingers. "Three."

"In that case, there will be some left over for him."

"Oh, good, 'cause he eats a lot for breakfast. Mrs. Crowley said so."

"Well, we'd better get cracking egg shells, then." Alicia stood and regarded the stove. It sure wasn't the Jenn-Air in her condominium. On the other hand, the big wood stove was a giant step up from an open campfire.

"Here." Caleb offered her the dishtowel apron. "You might want this."

Alicia flicked it open with a quick wrist motion, then tied it around her. "Since there are twelve eggs, does that mean I get twelve tries at cooking one without breaking the yolk?"

Mariah giggled and nodded.

"Only if you can eat seven of them," Caleb answered.

Alicia cracked the first one into the bacon grease. "So far, so good."

A short while later, the three of them sat at the table eating eggs, bacon, and bread with honey and butter.

"A few hash browns, and we could open a restaurant," Alicia said, wiping the corner of her mouth with her napkin.

"What are hash browns?" Mariah asked, imitating the napkin action.

"Grated potatoes fried in butter or a little olive oil."

"What's olive oil?" the girl pressed.

"Oil squeezed from olives." She considered the span of

a century of progress, then continued, "I believe it's imported from Greece."

"I know what grease is. How do they get oil from that sticky, gooey stuff?"

"That's a different kind of grease. This Greece is a country in the Mediterranean Sea, a very long way from here, where olive trees grow."

"Can we grow olive trees here?"

"No, Mariah. Different plants and trees require different kinds of soil and climates. The beautiful spruce trees surrounding us outside wouldn't grow in Greece, either. Plants, like people, have their favorite places. That's where they tend to do best."

"Do you have a favorite place?"

Drexel, Wyoming. Her heart lurched at the loss of her former life and the absence of family. "Everyone has a favorite place. For right now, here is good, too."

"My favorite place is the big chair near the fireplace where Daddy reads me stories."

For the first time, Alicia afforded Caleb a glance. She'd felt his scrutiny of her every movement and word. "Your Daddy's chair is a good place for a little girl to be."

"Are you gonna read me stories when he goes to the lumber camp?" Mariah's small hand rested on Caleb's arm. "She can sit in your chair, can't she?"

"—Of course," Caleb agreed.

"No."

They spoke simultaneously, leaving Mariah glancing back and forth in confusion.

"Your Daddy's chair is special for you and him. You and I will find our own special niche. And yes, we'll read. I'll teach you to read to me, too."

"Am I old enough?" Her gray eyes sparkled with expectation.

"Do you want to learn to read and write?"

"Yes."

"Then you're old enough, Mariah." Alicia lifted her coffee cup and took a sip. Caleb Marker made excellent coffee.

"Oh, goodie. Can we keep her, Daddy?"

Alicia nearly choked.

"We'll see. The day isn't over yet."

Alicia refused to meet his unrelenting gaze, though color brightened and warmed her face. "This is a two-way street, Mr. Marker."

"Yes, ma'am, it is, but there's no telling how the rest of the road is just from the first mile or two, is there?"

Rocky, she figured, unsure why his demeanor had become distant and guarded. "No, Mr. Marker. There may be some things we both have to take on faith. I hope mine won't be misplaced."

Mariah's confusion manifested in her furrowed brow. "Are we going on the road to town?"

Alicia tore her gaze from Caleb and smiled at Mariah. "I sure hope not. I thought you might show me around today and we'd talk about what we expect from each other."

"Will you be the boss of me when Daddy is gone?"

"If I'm here tomorrow, yes, Mariah, I'll be the boss of you when your Daddy is away on business." Alicia couldn't help grinning. Regardless of the time difference, Mariah was very much like dozens of little girls she'd encountered at the Women's Shelter and less spoiled than most.

"Show Miss James your room, Mariah." The sudden wink and smile he gave his daughter amazed Alicia even more when he turned his attention to her; all traces of tenderness evaporated.

Disconcerted, Alicia began gathering the dishes.

"Leave them, Miss James. Your job includes meals, not dish washing. Our thanks for making the eggs."

Mariah slipped her hand into Alicia's and led her from the kitchen. Alicia forgot all about Caleb's unpredictable mood as soon as she glimpsed the child's room. It was easily more spacious than the master bedroom in a large house, and bookshelves lined the back wall mostly still awaiting filling. A brightly embroidered spread covered the bed. A swan, the Snow Queen, a mermaid, and a cobbler holding a pair of shoes, each was carved into one of the four posts.

"Fantastic," Alicia breathed, gradually comprehending the source of the masterful woodworking evident throughout the house. She ran her fingers along the finely etched feathers of the swan's back.

"This one's the Ugly Duckling. It's one of my favorite stories," Mariah said from across the room. "Daddy made me this bed for my birthday last year. Mrs. Crowley said he worked very hard on it."

"I assure you, he did, Mariah. Your daddy is very talented. You're a lucky girl." Awed by the level of detail evident in each carving, she marveled at the sensitivity and strength required to create such a masterpiece. In the flicker of a heartbeat, she imagined those hands on her and shivered.

Alicia turned, her amazement increasing. The far side of the bedroom was a schoolroom with a teacher's desk, replete with matching chair. A smaller student's desk and chair faced the larger one. A globe, a chalkboard, and shelves of books awaiting the first class flanked the desk. One thing was very clear. Caleb Marker's love for his daughter knew few bounds, if any.

The potency of the realization added depth to her assessment of the man. And even more questions.

She cleared her throat and crossed the room. "Come. I'll show you where Greece is and where we are."

Movement outside the window caught her attention.

Caleb stood outside, watching.

Chapter Six

The simplicity of five-year-old Mariah's outlook had a seductive power Alicia enjoyed. The child had a curious, open mind and lived in the moment, something Alicia had never accomplished. The demands of ranch life and the responsibility for her sisters at an early age had forged her personality. But if Alicia lived in the moment now, the magnitude of the changes and losses over the last twenty-four hours might not overwhelm her.

If she lived for the moment, she wouldn't be worrying about why she hadn't done so earlier, either. The catch-22 of the situation made her crazy.

Talking all the while, Mariah poured four little cups of tea. A teddy bear sat on her left, a doll on her right, and Alicia sat on the floor across from her.

The child kept up a steady conversation between the doll and the bear. Alicia posed questions, made comments, and bit back laughter at Mariah's animated expressions when the doll and bear disagreed.

Of all the things Alicia questioned, not once did she wonder about the instant rapport between herself and Mariah. If magic existed in the world, it came from a child's smile and the generosity of a heart seeking love and acceptance. Clearly an easy child to love, Mariah had obviously been raised admirably. By Caleb alone? Alicia couldn't help wonder about Mariah's mother.

As Caleb had predicted, Maude Crowley and her son, Jeremy, returned from Sitka early in the afternoon—in time for supper.

Maude's neat silver-brown bun and all-seeing brown eyes indeed reminded Alicia of a mother or grandmother, right down to the wire-rimmed glasses that kept sliding down her nose. A couple of inches shorter than Alicia, Maude's ample build attested to her enjoyment of her own cooking.

The housekeeper served the meal in the dining room. In preparation, Alicia helped Mariah don one of her good dresses and shiny patent leather shoes.

"You look very pretty this evening," Caleb told Mariah. His daughter grinned with delight at the compliment.

"Miss James helped me fix my hair." Mariah sat up straight and beamed at her father. "Can she teach me to ride a horse?"

Caleb's eyebrows rose in surprise. "I don't know. Can she?"

"Oh, yes. She was born on a horse."

Alicia laughed. "I didn't mean it in a literal sense, Mariah. I learned to ride very young."

"You had your own horse when you were as big as me?"

"Yes. However, I also had to help take care of her. That meant shoveling out the stall, even during the cold winter months; making sure she had water and feed; and grooming her. There's a responsibility attached to having your own horse."

"But I just want to ride Daddy's."

Caleb shook his head. "Not until you know how to ride very well and are quite a bit bigger. Vesuvius is temperamental and not inclined to make allowances for little girls."

By way of explanation, Mariah addressed Alicia. "He erupts."

Alicia laughed. "You seem to have a proclivity for the historical, Mr. Marker. Caesar, Nero, and Vesuvius."

Caleb shrugged. "Since you ride, Miss James, how about joining me on horseback after we eat? You and I have a few things to discuss and some decisions to make. I realize you haven't had an opportunity to make other arrangements. Plan to spend tonight here, too."

Dealing with Caleb thrust her back into the realm of complexity; it was a change from the simplicity of his daughter. Alicia nodded and turned her attention to her food. She'd forgotten she didn't have the job yet. It seemed so natural to be in the Marker home, sharing the table with the other four.

"I'll look forward to the ride. Please tell me that my mount's name isn't Krakatau."

The wry smile he cast accompanied a congenial nod. "How did you guess?"

"Woman's intuition." And little girl chatter she added silently, relishing the coming confrontation. In preparation, she ate sparingly.

An hour later, she saddled a spirited dapple-gray stallion, then led him into the yard. Caleb's voice sounded behind her.

"You'll need a jacket."

"I don't have one."

"Buy one while we're in town tomorrow. Even in summer, you don't ride out unprepared. The weather can turn on you without warning." Caleb reined Vesuvius toward the mud porch at the back of the house.

"Thanks for the advice."

Just like that. Go buy one. Spoken by a man unconcerned with trivial things like employment, finances, lost relatives, or where to live after someone said, "Thanks, but no thanks."

"Find Edna Roth's General Store or Hamilton Traders, and put it on my tab." He dismounted and disappeared inside the house for a moment.

"Right," she told Krakatau, then slipped her foot into the stirrup. She mounted the magnificent gray to check the tack setup. "The man is out of his mind if he thinks I'll further obligate myself. If I want a jacket, I'll buy it or trade for it."

"Here." Caleb interrupted her tirade, tossing a jacket at her from the top step of the mud porch. "It'll be big for you, but it's warm."

She dismounted, satisfied with the stirrup placement, and secured the lent jacket with rawhide ties behind the saddle's cantle. "Go ahead. I'll catch up."

Instead of immediately remounting Krakatau, she petted his head and spoke quietly, continuing to familiarize him with her voice and scent. While saddling him, she had done the same thing, rubbing him down with her hands. At last, she was ready to ride. Caleb waited for her across the clearing. She took her time, using her legs and knees to check the horse's responses. Before reaching the treeline, she determined that someone, probably Caleb, had trained the horse very well.

The trail they took wound among the trees. At times, the heavy forest growth obscured the path. Enjoying her horse, the forest domain, and the island of solitude, she took her time riding.

Ahead, Caleb waited beside a giant spruce, his expression unreadable, his eyes unblinking.

"Is something wrong?" she asked, halting Krakatau beside Vesuvius.

"I don't know. How much of your interaction with Mariah is genuine, and how much is what you think I wanted to see?"

Alicia bristled, bringing Krakatau's head up. "With me, what you see is what you get. I don't like pretenses. They have a nasty way of biting back unexpectedly." She gave Caleb a pointed look.

"However, Mariah is losing her teeth, so her bite isn't likely to hurt. She's a delightful child. Bright. Curious. Eager to learn. You're doing an admirable job raising her. But there are a few things that puzzle me."

Caleb led them into the trees and rode in silence for a while. "Ask. I'm listening."

Alicia urged her horse over a deadfall, noting the easy power with which he took the obstacle. "Who cared for her before? Mrs. Crowley?"

"Her daughter. But Jane married three weeks ago and moved into town." He pointed, reining Vesuvius in the direction of a swale. "Maude has her hands full with cooking and housekeeping. Sometimes her arthritis gets so bad, she has trouble going up the porch stairs."

Alicia nodded thoughtfully. "Five-year-olds can move like lightning."

"Mariah needs an education, too. Maude only learned to read a few years ago. She doesn't feel confident teaching Mariah."

"Did you teach Maude?"

He nodded.

"And Jeremy? Has he gone to school?"

"He'll be leaving in the fall for Gonzaga University in Spokane. His uncle teaches there."

"Maude will miss him," Alicia said.

"Yes. She will. Fortunately, Jane and her husband are staying in Sitka. Family is important."

He sure didn't need to tell her that.

The trail narrowed, forcing them into single file. The question burning on Alicia's tongue leapt free. "Speaking of family, most children talk about their parents. What about Mariah's mother?"

Caleb's shoulders squared with tension. "Her mother died in a fire a few months after giving birth."

The door on that subject had slammed shut so hard it echoed in the forest. Alicia didn't try to force it back open. "I see."

"You probably don't, but it isn't necessary that you do. We don't discuss her mother. Nothing can change the past, so let it lie."

His furious unwillingness to elaborate fueled her curiosity, but she knew she shouldn't pry. Later, if she were still around, she'd indulge her inquisitiveness. "Is there anything else I should know about Mariah?"

Caleb halted his horse at the edge of a clearing. Alicia joined him and forgot everything beyond the fringes of the world before her. Wildflowers splashed blues, whites, yellows, reds, and pinks across the meadow. Most dominant were the shooting stars, Indian paintbrush, and buttercups. On the far side, a black-tailed deer regarded them warily.

" 'Migod, this is gorgeous." She drew in a deep breath of the perfumed air. The profusion reminded her of Yolanda D'Arcy's garden, although the difference in climate, soil, and altitude precluded the rationality of any such similarity.

When she dragged her gaze to Caleb, a shiver of awareness danced through her. He stared, as though he were able to read her soul as easily as one of the many books tucked into the nooks and crannies of his home.

Dangerous desire radiated heat from him, his gaze lowering to her mouth. Good grief, he wanted to kiss her. She felt the exciting certainty in the marrow of her bones. Heaven help her, she wanted him, too. He exuded a sensuality that lured and frightened her in the same heartbeat. The palpable attraction denied the foolish notion of a single, simple kiss. He would want more. The new, strange emotions he'd awakened in her begged for the freedom of exploration.

"Tell me about yourself." His words—not what she wanted from his lips—were harsh.

Alicia tore her gaze away to contemplate the serenity of the meadow. Its pastel flowers soothed her rapid pulse and restored a semblance of order. "What do you want to know?"

He took his time before asking, "Are you staying, or are you going back to Wyoming?"

For an instant, she didn't think he was asking with Mariah's interests at heart. "I'll stay as long as I can." *As though I have a choice.*

"How long is that?"

"As long as it takes to do what I need to do here."

"What do you need to do?" Although his words were softly spoken, there was an anger surrounding Caleb.

She wished she knew the answer to his question. "It's personal," she said instead. Summoning her best corporate demeanor, she squared her shoulders. "You and I don't know one another well enough to share confidences."

"I need a long-term governess for Mariah, not someone looking for a position of convenience."

"Believe me, Mr. Marker, since arriving in Sitka, nothing has been convenient. I'm not in the habit of making commitments I can't keep. Mariah is a delightful child. It's impossible not to love her. For her sake, I won't leave you high and dry."

"But I should keep looking for a governess even if I hire you, is that what you're telling me?"

Exasperated, Alicia shook her head. "I'm not going to take off in the middle of the night." Unable to hold still any longer, she urged Krakatau along the edges of the clearing. "My middle name is responsibility."

Yet she couldn't know when or how she might be summoned back to the present, if ever. How could she promise anything? She hadn't realized what a heavy burden freedom was.

Caleb urged his mount up beside hers. "What about your family? Your sisters?"

"My parents are dead. My sisters are my family." Even though they aren't born yet. Her head spun. Technically, she hadn't been born either. This entire conundrum tied her logical mind in knots.

"And they're in Wyoming. Voting. And wearing trousers. Right?"

She turned sharply, causing Krakatau to snort. Her flash of pique melted when she saw Caleb's half-smile. "Actually, I don't know. I was going to ask people in town. If no one has seen them, I'll assume they remained in Drexel." *Beyond my reach, beyond the sound of my voice.*

"You speak of them as though they need looking after." Caleb nudged Vesuvius so close his right leg brushed her left knee. "Are they children?"

"Bethany is twenty-four and Caitlyn is twenty-two."

"Why aren't they married?"

The question stunned her, then made her laugh. "I don't see where their marital status has any bearing on you hiring me."

"Are they ugly?"

Aghast, she finally looked at him, then laughed at the teasing twinkle lighting his eyes and the hint of a smile on his perfect lips. "Not hardly, but that shouldn't make any difference. Physical beauty is only skin deep. It's fleeting."

"Do your sisters look like you?"

Alicia shook her head. "Other than our eyes, and maybe the jaw-line, we don't resemble one another much."

"They have eyes the color of mountain violets?"

She glanced at him, feeling the hunger she'd effectively tamped down lurch back to life. "Yes. It's a family trait from our mother's side."

"In that case, if they followed you to Alaska, they'll be easy to find. No man would forget eyes like yours."

Wary, she regarded him for a long moment. "Is that a come-on?"

"A what?"

"A line, like 'what's a nice girl like you doing in a place like this?'"

He appeared utterly baffled. "I was speaking the truth. As for your line, I've been wondering why you're here since meeting you in the trees yesterday."

"That makes two of us." Uncomfortable with the conversation, she inclined her head to the farthest point of the clearing.

"Let's see what you can do, Krakatau." She kneed the horse into action. Ready to run, Krakatau responded with a restless energy of his own. When he hit his stride, Alicia was in synchronization with him, sharing the freedom of open land and speed. The powerful stallion turned gracefully with the pressure of a knee. Not until she completed a second turn did she realize Caleb had disappeared. She glanced over her shoulder and saw him gaining, then urged Krakatau on.

It took another full minute before Vesuvius was at her flank. Sensing the approach, Krakatau unleashed a burst of speed and pulled ahead. Triumphant, Alicia's laughter mingled with the thunder of racing hoofbeats.

They circled the large clearing a third time before Caleb eased off. Alicia followed suit, feeling the labored breathing of the horse beneath her. She slowed Krakatau in stages, softly praising him for his efforts and stroking his neck.

Caleb pointed at a break in the trees and trotted off toward it. She followed, exhilarated by the cool air and the prime horseflesh carrying her through the wildflowers.

"He's a magnificent horse," Alicia told Caleb as she caught up. As though to substantiate her claim, Krakatau flung his gray head up and down. Caught in the moment, she laughed and patted his neck.

"You ride him very well. In fact, you ride better than most men I know."

"Thank you." She grinned. "I ride better than most men I know, too."

"Your humility is staggering."

"Better to profess honest pride than false humility, Mr. Marker."

"Is that what you aim to teach Mariah?"

"Honesty? Yes. Pride in accomplishment after diligent practice? Yes. Demur, false platitudes for soliciting more compliments? No." She scrutinized the terrain. The spruce mingled with giant hemlocks, alder, black cottonwood, and lodge-pole pines. Dwarf dogwood stretched above thorny devil's club.

She fell behind Caleb and kept Krakatau well away from the spikes. The diversity of the land beguiled her. She'd read of such places and studied the plants and their properties, but it wasn't the same as moving through a pristine forest virtually untouched by man.

Caleb led them to a small pond fed by a waterfall pouring out of a sheer granite cliff where ferns clung for life in the cracks. The pond fed a gurgling creek racing for the sea over angular rocks. Blueberry, salmonberry and deadly poisonous bright red baneberry lined the sides of the creek and the far side of the pond.

Alicia watched Caleb dismount. If ever a man was born for living in the heart of the forest, it was this one. Despite his size, he moved with the grace of a willow in a gentle breeze. The breadth of his shoulders embodied the solidity of the three-foot-wide Sitka spruce trunks. The way his trousers stretched over his legs reminded her of sculptured burls of wood instead of muscle. Her breath caught in her throat at the direction her thoughts wandered as she stared at his tight buttocks.

As though sensing her inspection, he turned and patted Vesuvius on the rump, sending the horse to water for a drink. Then she saw only his eyes, smoldering yet icy and as volatile as an Arctic storm rushing over the mountains. The conflicting hunger and wariness, roiling like those same storm clouds ready to nourish and drown the arid terrain of her soul, seemed to ask a question.

Shaken by her physical response, a powerful ache, she dismounted and led Krakatau to the edge of the pond. "Drink up, boy. You deserve it."

"Miss James."

She spun around and nearly lost her footing, Caleb was so close. His strong hands gently steadied her shoulders. Other than the ripples of electricity stemming from his fingers, she felt only her pounding heart.

His head lowered, bringing his mouth mere inches from hers. If she stood on her tiptoes, she'd find out whether his lips were as warm and hard as the rest of him, or gentle and giving with a promise of sensual bliss. The motion of his thumbs along the inside of her arms just below her breasts intensified the pulsing desire to stretch that little bit and find out.

If she faced temptation another second, she'd succumb. "You, ah, you haven't told me yet," she stammered, turning her head to the side. The magic flared, then ebbed as he released her. Keen disappointment—whether with him

73

or herself, she didn't know—swept through her.

"Haven't told you what?"

"Whether you're hiring me."

His long silence forced her to look at him again. Guilty color rose in her cheeks. She winced, fearing he knew his effect on her and had decided to use it as a reason for denying her the position. She couldn't blame him. He wanted Mariah protected from all forms of questionable behavior, particularly that of her governess and father. She knew their attraction made it a difficult situation, but she needed the job and genuinely enjoyed Mariah.

"There can be nothing but an employer-employee relationship between us." The distant quality of Caleb's voice left her confused as to whom he was speaking, her or himself.

"I consider this a professional, not a personal, association, Mr. Marker. Mixing the two would become too complicated." Hearing the truth pour from her mouth banished any thoughts in the opposite direction.

"Then you'll do. All I ask is, if you decide you want to leave, you'll stay until I find a replacement." The reluctance with which he had released her showed in the flinch of the muscles around his eyes, the deepening of a frown. "Do we have a deal?"

"Not so fast. Let's discuss salary, benefits, days off, and what sort of compensation you're offering if you find someone you like better and decide to let me go without notice."

"You don't get any days off when I'm away from home. I'll pay you well. You'll have all your meals, the room you stayed in last night, and full run of the place." He pushed Krakatau away. "I'll leave the horse for you, too. But you will have to make friends with Nero and Caesar. One of them will accompany you wherever you go when I'm not home. The other stays with Mariah, so most of the time you'll have them both. Will having a dog that's half wolf following you be a problem?"

His predatory gray eyes were slightly narrowed with intense concentration. Somehow, he seemed more formidable than either wolf dog. If she weren't careful, he'd wound her in the most painful, invisible place she possessed.

Her heart.

After their ride, Caleb watched Alicia groom Krakatau as he worked on Vesuvius. She obviously understood horses and knew how to win their respect and affection. The way she always moved a bare hand along the big gray's hide while brushing it kept the horse docile.

If she ran her delicate hands over his body the same way, stroking and petting, Caleb would be anything but docile.

What the hell was wrong with him? For two days, a woman without enough sense to find her way out of the forest had dominated his every waking thought. She was the most desirable creature he'd ever encountered, and she had a straightforward, yet subtle manner. Hell, it didn't make sense. No one was both. Not at the same time. Except Alicia James from Wyoming, the only state he knew of where women wore pants and voted.

Recently, not much of anything made sense. During his objective moments, which seemed to have become fewer and farther between, Caleb wondered what had possessed him to hire her. For that matter, why had he even allowed Mariah to meet her?

True, she was well educated. Any fool knew that after watching and listening to her. But Caleb knew virtually nothing else about her. She had no references. No luggage.

Tomorrow or the next day, he'd check out newly arrived ships. Perhaps someone knew something about her sisters or the fate of her trunks. No woman traveled such a tremendous distance without at least one or two trunks.

"Mr. Marker?"

His head shot up, and he peered at her from over Vesuvius's back. "Yes?"

"Mariah wants to learn how to ride. It's probably a

good idea in this country. Have you given any thought to it?"

The hopeful concern in her big, violet eyes melted the agitation shrouding all Caleb's questions regarding Alicia. References or not, she'd won Mariah's affection in a single day. Come to think of it, that was just about the amount of time it had taken him to lose his senses.

"I don't want her on the stallions," he said. "I'll start looking around for a pony. Meanwhile, she can ride double with you, if you're willing to handle it."

"Oh, I can handle it. I can teach her a lot before we put her up alone."

The sparkling smile she flashed sent a bolt of satisfaction through him. This woman took every restriction he handed her and turned it into a liberty. "Fine. We'll start tomorrow and see how you get along on Krakatau. She can ride with you when we go to town."

Alicia led Krakatau toward the open barn door. "Why are we going to town?"

"We've a few things to take care of, including asking about your sisters."

Her back became ramrod straight as she halted in her tracks. "You'd help me?" she asked, not turning.

Caleb patted Vesuvius on the rump and sent him into the barn. "Sure. Why not? Worst case, I'll add on to the house so they're comfortable until they find husbands."

A throaty sound came from deep inside Alicia and shook her shoulders. When she opened her mouth, her laughter filled the air.

Watching her leave the shadows and walk with Krakatau into the barn left him completely in the dark. What the hell was so funny?

Chapter Seven

Alicia was a sorceress. Caleb was convinced of it. Nothing else explained the spell she'd cast over every member of his household.

Or had he lost his objectivity along with a good portion of his senses?

Sunny skies favored their journey into town. Mariah rode in front of Alicia on Krakatau. Their saddle, one crafted for him, easily accommodated the small child and the enchantress.

She was also a thief. She'd robbed him of sleep by plaguing his dreams, and last night was one long on fantasy and short on rest.

Years ago, he'd dreamed of life with Margaret Bronson as his wife. She'd accepted his engagement ring and his heart. God, how he'd loved her. He'd have walked through fire for her—and did when she jilted him.

Last night, for the first time in years, the woman he cherished in dreams had Alicia's face, not Margaret's. In the netherworld of fantasy, she laughed with him. Love shone in her violet eyes. Upon his approach, her lips

77

parted, eager for his kiss, his touch, and his lovemaking.

The memory sent a shiver through him in the cool morning air. He'd learned a painful truth all those years ago. Dreams were not safe to believe in. They were wishes for the impossible. He knew better now, was smarter than to reach for what he couldn't have. The kind of woman he wanted, one like Alicia, wasn't likely to see beyond his burly build, callused hands, and self-acquired learning. The monetary rewards of his business wouldn't compensate her for the lack of societal interaction, the isolation of his home.

His life had changed irrevocably when he'd fetched baby Mariah from San Francisco five years ago. That journey had been his last voyage south. And yet, despite his regrets, he wouldn't trade a day of his daughter's company for the companionship of his city friends.

He smiled at Mariah. She'd insisted on wearing her hair down, like Alicia's. The little girl's long, raven locks fell in curls and waves to the middle of her back. In contrast, Alicia's straight brown hair bobbed at the nape of her neck.

As though sensing his warm appraisal, both looked at him. Mariah's jack-o'-lantern grin made him smile. Her gray eyes, reminiscent of those he saw in the mirror each morning when he shaved, blinked unevenly.

He winked back.

She used her forefinger to draw one eyelid down.

"I've been practicing. Miss James says I can do anything if I practice enough."

"I'll bet you never heard that before."

Mariah giggled. "You told me lotsa times, but look." Eyes squinting in deep concentration, her left eyebrow twitched independent of the right.

Caleb's laughter boomed into the trees. "You did it. You wiggled your eyebrow!"

Mariah laid her head back and gazed up at her governess. "Can you do it?"

A warm sense of satisfaction flowed through Caleb as Alicia tried the maneuver. He wasn't sure why her inability to wiggle one eyebrow at a time delighted him.

"Looks like I'll have to practice," Alicia told Mariah.

"Can you wink?" Mariah tried winking again, this time without the finger. Her left eye squinted as the right one closed.

Alicia winked with her right, then her left eye.

"Not bad, Miss James," Caleb complimented, chuckling.

"I'm a woman of many hidden talents."

That, he didn't doubt. Before his mind wandered into forbidden territory, he asked, "Such as?"

She adjusted Mariah and straightened the girl's skirts. "I speak another language. Pig Latin."

Uncertainty melted Caleb's grin into a lopsided smile. "Never heard of it."

"Listen closely." Alicia cleared her throat, then spoke. "Oo-day oo-ya eak-spay ig-pay atin-lay?"

"Again." He listened intently, sensing the simplicity. Upon repetition, he caught the gist. "Ery-vay owly-slay."

"Marvelous, Mr. Marker," she exclaimed. In Pig Latin, she asked him to buy a pair of riding trousers for Mariah.

"Why?"

"Leather burns bare or stockinged legs," she told him in Pig Latin.

"What are you saying?" Mariah demanded. "Teach me. Please."

"Most certainly, I will. We can work it into a phonics lesson. In no time, you'll be speaking Latin as well as any pig."

"Oink, oink," Caleb mimicked, sending all three of them into gales of laughter. The camaraderie drew them closer as they crested the final hill before Sitka came into view.

Alicia reined Krakatau to a halt and stared at the vista below.

Caleb shook his head at Mariah when she started to speak. The way Alicia's arms enfolded his daughter's small shoulders made his heart ache. Her rapt expression betrayed her awe at really seeing Sitka as though for the first time. He doubted she'd noticed the beauty of the town the other day. She'd been too busy emptying dirt from her flimsy shoes and watching the trees for predators, of which he'd begun to suspect he had been, and still was, the hungriest.

Riding along the streets of the town, Alicia wondered how she'd managed to miss the profusion of flowers overflowing window boxes along the boardwalk. The mixture of Russian, Tlingit, and American influence everywhere she turned intrigued her.

Wearing a brown cotton skirt and Alicia's yellow suit jacket, Edna Roth leaned on her broom and waved as they guided their horses to a rail in front of her General Store. "Hello Mr. Marker. Mariah. I see you found employment, Miss James."

Edna's friendly, familiar greetings and welcoming smile put Alicia at ease. "Yes, and I believe it will work out just fine." She handed Mariah down to Caleb. Her heart skipped a beat at the emotion shining in his eyes and the question his slightly raised left eyebrow posed.

Alicia dismounted, then straightened her skirt, longing for a pair of jeans in which to ride. She wished it hadn't been necessary to trade the linen slacks matching the yellow jacket Edna now wore. "The jacket looks marvelous on you, Mrs. Roth."

"Thank you, dear. I believe it's the most unusual, yet elegant, piece of clothing I've come across." She set the broom aside and ushered them into the store.

By the time they were ready to leave, Caleb had tucked a pair of denim overalls for Mariah among his purchases. "I'll need these, too," he told the shopkeeper.

"Fine. You might check over at Hamilton Traders for the other item you mentioned," Edna suggested.

Caleb thanked her and escorted Alicia and Mariah onto the boardwalk. "Alicia and I need to speak to a number of people concerning her sisters."

"You mean it will be boring."

"Maybe, but I'm sure you'll be the perfect lady, even if you're bored."

The gentle way Caleb imposed his high expectations on Mariah reminded Alicia of her own parents.

In this strange land and time, Alicia possessed only the faintest notion of going about the task of finding her siblings. For the first time in her life, she was out completely out of her element. And as uncomfortable as it made her, she appreciated Caleb's help.

On the way to Hamilton Traders, they encountered the store's distinguished owners. Alicia quickly learned they were the equivalent of Alaskan royalty.

After the introductions, Caleb glanced at Alicia. "Miss James and her sisters became separated on their journey."

Ransom Hamilton was a striking man with eyes the color of a tropical sea and thick silver hair. Silver also threaded his wife Felicity's dark hair. The woman's coat-dress and hat were the latest fashion, and she regarded Alicia with an expression that appeared to be friendly interest.

Lying was difficult. Alicia was by nature a stickler for the truth. But in this case, the truth was too far-fetched for anyone to believe. The trouble with weaving a lie was keeping all the little threads straight. It took a more scheming mind than hers. "I'm not sure how it happened, but my sisters and I became separated during an . . . unexpected journey."

"Ah, you're the young woman from Wyoming, aren't you?" Felicity asked, her gloved hand taking her husband's.

"Yes." Forget the Internet, radio, or television. Small-town gossip was the most efficient mode of news dissemination.

"When were you and your sisters separated?" Ransom Hamilton asked.

"June third." *Approximately four-thirty in the afternoon.* She'd have to do better than that or the foot in her mouth would choke her. "I mean, June third is when I arrived. Here, that is. In Sitka." Where was that dratted magic fog when she needed it to hide her from her own faux pas?

81

"I see." Ransom gave his wife a look Alicia couldn't interpret. "Did you take the train from Cheyenne, then a ship from San Francisco?"

In a silence where her heart beat like a bass drum, Alicia met Hamilton's gaze. For a split second, she'd have sworn he knew her secret. His eyes had an inscrutable look to them.

Stress was making her crazy. "Umm, yes. That would be the normal course of events." How she wished she would have paid more attention in her high school Wyoming History class.

"I hope the noxious stench of whale bones drying on the San Francisco piers didn't deter your sisters." Ransom Hamilton smiled knowingly. "It can be overpowering at times."

Whale bones? Good grief, what did Fisherman's Wharf look like *before* the 1906 earthquake? The gulf between the times yawned wider.

"Alicia? Are you feeling ill?" Caleb asked.

"Uhh, no. Just trying to remember."

"Of course being separated from your sisters is upsetting," Felicity soothed. "Perhaps it will help to tell us a little about them. What are their names?"

The understanding in the elder woman's voice soothed Alicia's mounting panic. By devoting her attention to Felicity, she managed to relate names, ages, descriptions, and provide a snippet of each of her sisters' personalities.

"Tell you what," Ransom interjected. "If you'll write up what you've just described, I'll have it copied and sent out with my ships for posting."

Alicia didn't know whether to laugh, cry, or grovel in gratitude for the Hamiltons's help and guidance. "Oh that would be so good of you. Thank you. I'll get it to you tomorrow." Then, the specter of doubt reared its head. "Of course, they may not have left Drexel. . . ."

Felicity touched her arm. "I'm sure you'll find your answers. In time." Her smile bolstered Alicia's confidence and forced a return.

"We're meeting Joseph, so we must be going. Drop the

descriptions off at the shipping offices or our home, Miss James, and we'll hope for the best." Ransom and Felicity Hamilton made their good-byes and continued down the boardwalk.

"Alicia," Caleb said when the two of them and Mariah were alone again. "Is there something I ought to know?"

"No." She looked down the street, unable to meet his gaze.

They resumed walking, Caleb's gaze boring holes into her. However, true to his earlier word, he proceeded to introduce her to what seemed half the town.

She described her sisters and the fabricated story of their separation during the journey from Wyoming. This time, she added the element of the train, starting in Cheyenne.

Her delivery improved with each telling. By late afternoon, she didn't care if anyone believed her. The townsfolk would watch for her sisters. Her mission was accomplished.

In subtle ways, Caleb had even helped her clarify the contradictions and inconsistencies in her story.

However, that meant eventually he'd demand answers.

A rain shower extended their stay in town a bit longer than intended. Caleb took advantage of the delay by treating them to dinner.

It was near Mariah's bedtime when they started for home. Caleb and Mariah had made the day memorable for Alicia. Because of him, the townsfolk would watch for her sisters. She couldn't ask for more.

Holding Mariah against her, Alicia kissed the top of the weary girl's head. Softly, she began singing a lullaby her mother had sung to all three of her children. As always, singing the song soothed her. When it ended, she felt Caleb watching her.

"Don't worry. If your sisters made it this far north, they'll turn up. Write your letters, and I'll see they get to the towns across the water as quickly as possible."

She nuzzled the top of Mariah's head. The child shifted,

her sleeping body limp as a dishrag. "How did you know I was thinking of them?"

"Your song. You have a beautiful voice, Miss James. You're as good or better than any I heard at the San Francisco Opera. And a voice that mirrors the emotions can reveal more than its owner intends. You sang as if you were remembering another time and place."

His perceptiveness amazed her. Few people heard beyond a song's words and melody. "Thank you, and yes, I was thinking about them. My sisters and I sing in three-part harmony. They're the ones with the excellent voices, especially Caitlyn." Alicia met Caleb's relentless perusal and discovered a wistfulness that tugged at her heart. "Sometimes when we're singing, the purity and power of Caitlyn's voice gives me goose bumps."

"I'd like a front-row seat for the performance."

His sincerity coaxed a smile from her. "If they show up, I'll make sure you have one," she whispered, doubting it would happen.

"Will you sing another song?"

As the easy melody flowed through the air, she imagined Bethany and Caitlyn harmonizing. Her voice strengthened, the perfect pitch of each note and word shaming the birds into silence. As they approached the house, she felt an unexpected peace.

Caleb dismounted and pushed Vesuvius toward the barn. "Hand her down and I'll take her inside. Jeremy will tend the horses."

Together, they maneuvered Mariah into Caleb's arms. The child snuggled against him and murmured, "I heard an angel," then yawned and went back to sleep.

The warm look Caleb bestowed on Mariah, then turned on her, heated Alicia's bones. In her own century, no man had seen so deep into her guarded heart. Not in her disastrous marriage, and certainly not after. She'd never allowed more than friendship or professional cordiality. In a matter of days, Caleb Marker had penetrated her defenses.

Her growing tenderness toward him suddenly concerned her. If she weren't careful, he might wheedle his way into her affections. That would be a grave error.

"Thank you," she murmured.

"For what?" he asked, following her up the veranda steps.

She opened the front door and held it for him to slide through with Mariah. "Today. Your help and patience." She closed the door, then hurried ahead of him to Mariah's room.

Together, they prepared the child for bed and tucked her in. She roused enough for a good-night kiss from Caleb, then reached for Alicia.

Touched by the honest affection, Alicia hugged and kissed the little girl, knowing without a doubt events and emotions were sucking her into a deliciously comfortable realm. She had to remember that, even if she wanted to belong here, it was probably not possible.

Watching Caleb place a final kiss on Mariah's forehead, Alicia realized how near the edge of entanglement she already skated. During her brief marriage with Chet, she hadn't wanted children. After the divorce, she had indulged her maternal instincts with the children at the Women's Shelter. That had been enough.

"Mariah is an easy child to lose your heart to," she said without thinking. From the first day, she and Mariah had meshed.

The raven hair tangling about Mariah's face framed an innocence seldom evident in the children Alicia had worked with. No gang wars, drive-by shootings, or nuclear terrorists plagued this time. Yet nor was there Disneyworld, Sesame Street, or pink bicycles with white fringe at the ends of the handlebars.

Not a bad trade for a little girl, Alicia decided. But was it an equitable trade for a *woman?*

Caleb closed the door softly, then guided Alicia to the kitchen.

She fetched a glass of water. "I'm beginning to understand how you've managed to raise Mariah into the sweet child I see now."

Caleb shrugged. "It's her nature. I do what I can, though. I read books on child rearing and the popular methodologies by so-called experts."

The sudden disdain in his tone intrigued her. "And?"

"Some of what I read was useful. Some was horse manure. Mariah's bright. She should have an education in whatever interests her, not just subjects that make her a good conversationalist. She's as smart as or smarter than any boy her age."

His defensiveness made Alicia smile. She sat at the table and took a cookie from the plate in the center. "I couldn't agree with you more. She may want to follow in your footsteps. She doesn't need brawn to run a business, just brains."

Caleb scowled. "Brawn helps if your business is timber. I'd send her to the States and let one of those fine ladies' schools mold her into a useless piece of social fluff before I'd let her take over this business. A lumber camp is no place for a woman. I want her respected. That wouldn't happen if she spent any time at a lumber camp or sawmill."

Alicia leaned back and regarded him thoughtfully. "It sounds to me like you're shopping for trouble before it's on sale. Mariah's a happy child. Believe me, that's a treasure. Who cares what path she follows fifteen years from now if she's happy?"

"I do."

Alicia chuckled and broke the cookie, then offered half to Caleb. "Have you already picked out her husband, too?"

His head shot up, his eyes stormy. "No, but I expect to provide her some guidance when the time comes. I don't want her marrying a rough timberman." He accepted the cookie and bit into it emphatically.

"She could do worse, Caleb. Besides, she may have her own ideas when the time comes. Young people usually do."

"Are you speaking from experience?"

The challenge in his tone was unmistakable. Her stomach did a flip-flop and her fading smile disappeared. "I've already stumbled through my share of mistakes. The last thing I'm interested in is a husband. I don't have enough trust left in the male of the species to even consider it."

He nodded. "Does the reason behind your mistrust have anything to do with your . . . explanation about losing your sisters?"

"No." She finished her cookie and carried her water-glass to the sink.

She felt, rather than heard or saw, him stand and move up behind her. Heart accelerating from the electricity of his nearness, she turned around slowly. The urge to run her fingers up his chest and over his expansive shoulders made them tingle in anticipation. She balled them into fists and pressed them into her thighs. Rather than meet his eyes—she dared not see the emotion blazing in them or the temptation of his mouth—she stared at the third button of his shirt.

"Is something wrong?" she asked. The tremor in her voice disappointed her.

Caleb's voice did not tremor. "Forget this afternoon. What's going on here, Alicia?"

His tone reminded her of distant thunder rumbling from the mountain tops. "I don't know what you mean."

"Look at me."

The force of his command lifted her chin. Her heart pounded like a jackhammer. Her gaze fell upon his lips and faltered, and she wondered what his kiss would be like. Big, solid, and tall, this man could easily crush her with one arm. Yet the loving way his hands caressed Mariah or lingered upon a piece of furniture he'd built promised an ecstasy Alicia had only begun to comprehend.

Finally, she met his gaze. Her breath caught. A desire that went beyond burning need radiated from him. The hunger in his eyes left no doubt he would devour her body and feast on her soul.

"What's happening here?" he asked in a husky voice.

"Absolutely nothing." She could not bring herself to give in to this, no matter how badly she wanted to.

"Am I the only one who feels the pull between us?"

Alicia turned her head aside and lowered her gaze. "No . . . but nothing good can come of it. Let it go."

"Damn it, I know I should." He paused. "Sometimes I look at you and wonder whether you're the best or worst thing to happen to us."

"I don't want to be either one, Caleb. It's too complicated."

When next he spoke, his voice was fraught with emotion. "I want to know everything about you—all your secrets, Alicia. But I won't press. I don't want you to be uncomfortable. Quite the opposite, though I'll be damned if I understand why. I damn sure know better."

She risked a look up, then rose on her tiptoes before catching herself. "One of us is scaring the hell out of me."

"I hope it's you," he whispered, then brushed his lips across her forehead.

The sweet sensation of his mouth and the warmth of his breath begged for her response. Instead, she dug her nails into her palms and kept her wrists firmly pressed against her thighs. The heat of his kiss forced her to close her eyes.

Then he was gone. The back door to the mud room closed with a click and she was alone in the kitchen. What did he want from her? Why couldn't she tell him that she couldn't give him her lips without giving him her heart? A little voice inside of her promised that if she remained in the Marker home, the master would own her heart, and her body. Panic welled up as she considered where she might run.

Chapter Eight

Caleb spent the afternoon cutting and sanding cherry planks. Alone in the yard with a couple of sawhorses, he stripped off his shirt. The warm day and the vigor of his efforts sent rivulets of perspiration down his back.

Making a hope chest for a five-year-old might seem premature, but he damned well had to do something to smother the unholy urges consuming him. The reason for his restlessness was one neat, complicated package: *Alicia*.

And this physical activity was a perfect distraction . . . except when he thought about the purpose of the chest.

One day, this cedar-lined cherry box would hold the treasures Mariah saved for the day she left her father for another, more important, man.

Had Alicia filled such a chest in Wyoming? Had she saved woman-soft silks and satins for her wedding night? Lace that dripped over the gentle curve of her breasts? Had she gathered the things a woman needed to build a new home with her husband? If so, where were they now?

Was there a man waiting somewhere?

Probably. The way she exuded sensuality was bound to have left a string of men pining and panting.

A slow rage charged him as he imagined her bedding one of them. Yet, given the right circumstances, he'd be under her skirts in a heartbeat.

The current arrangement was anything but *the right circumstances*. She was Mariah's governess.

And she had deep, perhaps dangerous, secrets. The way she avoided any discussion of her life before her mysterious arrival bothered him. Despite her assurances and denials, regardless of the pull of his heart and loins, he couldn't shake the nagging feeling something was out of kilter.

God help her if she'd lied to him about her situation. God help them all.

He'd done his best to keep his distance, both physically and mentally. Trouble was, staying away didn't allay the sense Alicia was hiding something. Neither did it calm the raging fire of lust burning him from the inside out. Nor did it lessen his sudden certainty that she was the right woman for him.

The sawmill in Sitka had consumed most of his time over the past week. Thus far, both the lumber camp and the mill were ahead of schedule.

Caleb mopped perspiration from his chest with his shirt, then tossed the shirt aside. When he assessed the hope chest's wooden surface, he noted with satisfaction that the planks fit together seamlessly—the way Alicia's body would fit his.

Disgusted for seeing a sexual equivalent to even the roughest chores, he fetched his shirt and pulled it on. He waved off Maude's call for dinner, strode to the barn, and saddled Vesuvius. Moments later, he warmed the horse into a hard trot leading up to a full gallop.

From the veranda, Alicia watched Caleb ride away, wishing she could ride, too, only in the opposite direction.

"Where's Daddy going? He never misses dinner." Mariah slipped her hand into Alicia's. Caesar caught up to Caleb at the treeline.

"I suspect he's gone shadow-chasing," Alicia mused without thinking. She had chased more than a few shadows herself, sometimes on horseback, sometimes by driving her pickup truck over remote Wyoming roads for hours on end. Funny how those shadows always caught up.

Throughout dinner, Alicia chatted with Maude, Jeremy, and Mariah, but she kept an ear out for Caleb's return. When the hour grew late, she helped Mariah with her bath, then tucked her in with a bedtime story.

Alicia understood Caleb's disappearance, although the rest of the household did not. The man was a victim of the same amorous tension disturbing Alicia's sleep with intense, erotic splendor. For a week, she'd awakened from her dreams perspiring and short of breath.

It almost seemed she and Caleb were soul mates. If so, denying fate was as futile as trying to hold back the ocean with a sandcastle moat. Yet, with so much uncertainty clouding her life, she had to do just that. If she gave in to temptation . . . if she made love with him . . .

What a sweet temptation.

What a recipe for disaster.

She bid Maude and Jeremy good-night. Nero accompanied Alicia to the great room where she curled up on the leather sofa with the Charlotte Brontë classic *Jane Eyre*.

The story distressed her. The parallelisms of Jane's helplessness, Rochester's male dominance, the deceit, Jane's lack of alternatives were all suddenly a bit too real.

Like Rochester, Alicia's sins were of omission. No doubt, Caleb would disbelieve her time-travel explanation and her transportation to this 1895 Baranov Island. He'd think her an imaginative liar. After all, there were no books or articles on the subject of time travel.

Jane Eyre forgave Rochester his deception. Caleb would not.

Silence, and distance, and absolutely, positively *not* making love with him was her only viable option.

She tossed the book aside and scratched Nero around the ears, an act guaranteed to turn the beast into marshmallow.

"Hedonist," she accused. "You live to be petted, scratched, and coddled, don't you? And what do you do for me in return? Slobber on my hand. Lucky me." She laughed softly as Nero cocked his head, then laid down on his back so she could scratch his tummy. "You like that, huh? Scratch, pet, then pat, in that order. I've got your number. You guys are all alike. Lie on your back and revel in the pleasure of it all with your tongue hanging out."

"Some of us manage to keep our tongues in place." Caleb's voice came from behind her.

Startled, she bolted upright, sending Nero to his feet in response. The fickle wolf dog nudged his master for attention. The big hand didn't move.

She met Caleb's gaze. Awareness of their shared desire shot through her with the force of lightning. Oh, dear God in heaven, was she strong enough to protect them both?

"Perhaps I'd better turn in for the night," she suggested, rising from the sofa. *Distance. Willpower. Survival.* The words rumbled through her doubt-filled mind.

Caleb blocked her retreat. They stood inches apart, neither speaking nor moving. Alicia's heart thundered so loudly, she was sure he could hear it. The focus of her gaze remained fixed straight ahead. Instead of the usual shirt button at her eye level, she stared at the thick mat of his silky black chest hair. The familiar scent of him blended with the outdoor freshness of horse and green trees.

Until this moment, she had never considered the aroma of perspiration wrought from hard labor appealing. A part of her marveled at the things that became an aphrodisiac once the full charge of lust subverted logic.

"Tell me you don't want me."

The intensity of his words wrung a small moan from Alicia. Fearful of betraying the shortness of breath his nearness caused, she swallowed and repeated his words in a monotone. "I-don't-want-you." They were the hardest words she'd forced out of her mouth in her life.

The feather-light touch of his curled finger under her chin was like an electric charge. Her head lifted with reluctance, and her gaze met his. The brief contact sent her pulse racing.

"Tell me eye to eye."

Don't do this. Please don't make me do this.

"Tell me, Alicia."

"I . . . I . . ." After licking dry lips and swallowing the ball of sandpaper in her throat, her heart slowed enough for her to speak. "I don't—I don't want—"

"Don't want what?"

"You," she breathed, hating the lie on her lips.

"You're a lousy liar."

"I know." The storm in his eyes calmed into a sad satisfaction. He knew she wanted him. What he didn't know was that it was the depth of her desire that frightened her. Nothing in her life had prepared her for the raw need she felt, driving her to commit unspeakably brazen actions even for a twentieth-century woman. Thank God for self-control! It stood between her and disaster.

Unfortunately, it was crumbling.

"I'm leaving in the morning. Distance ought to help us both."

He was a better liar than she. When he returned, they'd be right where they were now. Perhaps it *would* be better . . . for a little bit. Then, maybe it would be worse. She suspected the latter.

"And if it doesn't?"

"We'll cross that bridge when we come to it."

"Did you put up a new posting for a governess?"

"No."

"Maybe you'd better."

"Do you want to leave already?"

Alicia shut her eyes and shook her head. "No. God help me, I don't." Given a choice, she'd never leave the Marker household. She hadn't chosen to leave her home in Drexel. But if whatever brought her here decided to return her, what then?

Either way, she faced heartbreak. Still, she could minimize the heartache for Caleb and Mariah.

But, if she never returned . . .

If she remained here for the rest of her life . . .

Oh, why wasn't anything simple anymore?

"Then we'd better find a way to deal with whatever is happening here," Caleb said. "It's goddamned uncomfortable all the way around."

Alicia resumed staring at the silky chest hair curling around the placket of his open shirt. She didn't dare look down, already aware of the discomfort to which he alluded. Fortunately, her own desire couldn't be seen. It was easier to hide, though just as wild.

"Have you eaten?" Perhaps changing the subject might ease some of the tension between them.

"I'm not hungry. Not for food, anyway."

She swallowed hard. "Mariah was worried about you. She said you never miss dinner."

"What I wanted for dinner wasn't on the menu," he rasped, then turned so abruptly that Alicia had to grip the side of the sofa for stability. Mute, she watched him depart, her fingers digging into the soft deerskin upholstery in a subconscious rhythm.

"I'd better kiss Mariah good-night," he said over his shoulder. "I don't want her worrying."

Alicia stared at the floor, wondering what she might have done had she met Caleb in her own time.

His raw, almost violent, sensuality seethed from every pore. It invaded her defenses in ways she was still discovering. He never pushed, nor did he make her feel anything less than honorable for not giving in to him. He respected her control.

Yet Caleb did everything with passion, from telling Mariah a story to sanding boards. She'd watched him work. As he did, he'd repeatedly halt to ensure that the process was done with microscopic precision.

She remembered the look of him toiling in the sun without his shirt. Rough trousers and even rougher gloves and boots were all he wore.

Her pulse raced when she closed her eyes and imagined him, muscles bunching as he worked. The sun turned the perspiration running down his back into glistening diamonds melting at his waistband.

Alicia shook herself. "Stop it," she seethed, then started toward the kitchen.

She had the table set by the time Caleb joined her. Without a word, she retrieved the meal Maude had left in the warmer.

"You don't have to wait on me, Miss James."

"I know. Don't expect it on a regular basis." She settled across the table from him, noting that he'd taken a bath. His wet hair swept straight back and dripped on the yoke of his shirt. "So, you're going to the lumber camp tomorrow. Tell me about how you harvest trees."

"Harvest trees? We don't harvest them. We cut them down, take them to the sawmill, then rip them up into beams and boards." He severed a hunk of venison with the side of his fork.

"You don't mean you clear-cut the entire area?" The possibility dismayed her.

"What's clear cut?" A spark of genuine interest kept his fork hanging in midair.

"Clear-cutting is when you take every tree."

"Of course we do. That's why we're there."

Alicia shook her head, wondering how to explain the devastation such practices wreaked on the land. She pulled his plate away from him, then took his dangling fork.

Painstakingly, she mounded the potatoes into a cone-shaped formation. "This is a hillside."

"No it's not. It's mashed potatoes," he growled, reaching for his plate.

"Give me a minute." She stayed his hand and turned the plate. "For now, pretend it's a hillside." She cut and arranged bits of meat and vegetables along the potato slope. "Now, if you leave a few trees and plant new ones after you cut, what happens when it rains?"

"Nothing."

She ladled gravy over the mound. Despite some sagging, the little mountain held fast. "See?"

"All I see is gravy running down potatoes."

"Okay." She scraped the meat and vegetables from the slope, leaving it bare. "Now, this is the hillside. It's clear-cut. Not a tree left." She dipped a ladle of gravy and poured it over the potatoes.

The mound weakened, sagged, and turned to a sludge of potatoes and gravy running into his meat and peas. "See what happened to the potatoes? The same thing happens to the hillsides.

"You strip them of the trees, and there's nothing to hold the top soil. It ends up in the streams, then the ocean. You need the topsoil to grow new trees, bushes, and grass. By leaving, say, every tenth tree, you keep the slope intact so it can grow more trees for you or your sons to harvest in twenty or thirty years. That's good business."

"If you're through playing with my food, I'll eat it before it all becomes an iceberg."

Flustered by the realization she'd literally taken the food from his mouth for the demonstration, she pushed the plate in front of him with an apology. While he ate, she elaborated on the ecological effects of clear-cut logging.

Caleb's attention remained on his food through the last bite. When finished, he cleared the table and washed the dishes. Finally he asked, "Where did you learn about lumberjacking? From the college you attended?"

"Partly," she answered, relieved that he had listened after all.

"Show it to me in a book."

The simple request stopped her cold. The books containing modern forestation practices and logging studies were decades away from publication. "Just because something is in a book doesn't make it accurate."

His left eyebrow rose a fraction and his gaze turned to steel. "Excluding fiction novels, I have almost always found my reading to be accurate."

Nonplussed, Alicia stared at him for several heartbeats. Never had she met anyone who actually believed all information in books was true. "Caleb, you're an intelligent man, a lumberman for what . . . nearly twenty years? You live among the trees. You've seen the effects on the land that was clear-cut years ago. Think about it. You can change that."

He set the plate on the countertop without making a sound. "Show it to me in a book." The coldness of his voice and the rigidity of his shoulders promised moving a mountain would be an easier task than changing his mind about the sanctity of the printed word.

"I can't."

He turned away. "If it's not in a book, it's not real, just a figment of imagination. Or a lie."

She rose and caught his upper arm. "Are you so closed to new ideas?"

"Let's say I prefer tried-and-true methods. I don't waste my time reinventing the saw when the one I have works fine."

"What if you could improve something you're doing so it would pay big dividends in the long term?"

"Men have brought down trees since they discovered fire. Finding a better way than skids and oxen to get the timber to the sawmill might be worth experimenting with—even if it weren't in a book. But not which timber to cut."

"So when someone publishes an article or writes a book about improved transportation methods, you'll jump on the bandwagon, but not until then?" The man exasperated her.

"Look, damn near everything I know about lumbering, building, farming, even raising kids, I learned from a book. If you can't show it to me, as far as I'm concerned, it doesn't exist. I don't have time to experiment with new-fangled ideas that might not pay off. I can learn from what's been done—which *has been written in books*."

Alicia retreated a step and folded her arms across her ribs. "I don't believe you."

Annoyance narrowed his hard gray eyes. "I don't see where it matters what you believe. This is my business and my beliefs we're talking about. I'm not trying to change your way of thinking. You're trying to change mine. You talk a good story. Back it up. Show me in a book where my methods of logging are wrong or harmful. Show me in a book where it says your way is right. Or are you saying you know something no one else has even figured out?"

Reminded of the gulf between them, Alicia shook her head. "I'll do better than show you it in print."

"You can't."

"When you go to the lumber camp this time, go visit some of the slopes you've clear-cut several years ago. Look at the erosion. Really look. Forget your books. Forget everything except the trees and the land. You love them both too much to remain blind to the destruction. Think about it, please."

She started out of the kitchen. "Good-night, Mr. Marker."

"You're a busybody, Miss James. Your job is Mariah, not my trees."

She paused at the door and risked a backward glance. "But you'll think about it, won't you?"

His words were both grudging and amused. "Considering the source, I don't have a choice."

Chapter Nine

"If those logs sit there another hour, they'll sprout roots," Caleb shouted at the bullwhacker. "Get your beasts down the damn mountain!"

"Have some coffee, Caleb," Kyle Larsen, the crew's foreman, suggested. "You've been meaner than a wounded bear. Take the edge off."

Caleb wheeled on him, ready for a fight, then caught himself. Kyle was right. He was behaving like an ass. The nights he normally spent in exhausted sleep had been broken by erotic dreams of Alicia, and it seemed he had a constant ache in his groin. Yet, as uncomfortable as that was, he could survive it. Worse, was the yearning in the core of his being. This woman was everything he desired. She exuded a combination of personal strength, confidence, and tenderness he hadn't thought possible.

But despite all the enticing qualities Alicia revealed, Caleb couldn't escape the fact she harbored deep secrets. The day they'd gone into Sitka he'd practically spoon-fed her the answers to the townsfolk's questions about her barely believable tale. While she probably really didn't know where her sisters were, the story she'd concocted about confusion in the Cheyenne rail yard and her vague descriptions of San Francisco only added to his suspicion she was hiding something important.

By her own admission, she didn't trust men. Was she running from an old lover? A husband? She'd denied both, but he'd been lied to before. Given the way she looked at him with as much desire as he felt, Alicia was no naïve virgin.

Although he shared her reluctance to open the wounds of the past and show a little trust, one of them was going to have to take the risk. Soon. He knew the bitter taste of betrayal and disappointment. He wasn't keen on getting a second dose.

His mind's eye summoned a recent dream with Alicia as the star. She sat in their warm home. Children surrounded her. Her children. Their children.

He cleared his throat with a harsh oath.

Indulgence in fantasy was lunacy. A strong, intelligent, educated woman like Alicia needed far more than he could give her. Hell, he wouldn't move into town. It was too crowded. And he'd yet to meet a woman, other than Maude Crowley, who loved the isolation of the Marker lands as much as he.

"I'm ready to check on the slope you talked about," Kyle said.

Caleb returned to the present. "Then let's go." He saddled Vesuvius and led the way toward the two-year-old cut Alicia had maligned.

"What are we looking for?" Kyle's sharp, green eyes surveyed the trail with a knowledge of dangers unseen by men of lesser experience.

"Mashed potatoes," Caleb mumbled.

"What'd you say? Sounded like smashed taters."

"Never mind."

The demonstration with the gravy had left him as cold as his food had become. The passion of her entreaty, wrought from deep conviction, had swayed him into doing as she requested. She'd seemed so damned sure whatever he was about to see on the old cut site would change his mind.

Vesuvius skirted a boulder obstructing the trail. Caleb waited to speak until he and Kyle rode together. "You've worked these trees for a long time."

"Not as long as you." Though both men were nearly the same age, Caleb Marker had been working the lumber camps since he was old enough to walk, and cutting timber before he was old enough to shave.

"Yeah, but I've only worked my trees. Or before that, my father's trees. You worked around before settling here. In all your experience, have you ever known of an operation not to cut down every tree when it was logging a sector?"

Kyle rubbed the sandy-colored two-day growth on his chin thoughtfully. "Can't say that I have. Why?"

"I heard a theory, I guess you could call it a business argument, for not taking all the trees."

"Why the hell would you leave any? What would be the point?"

Caleb proceeded to explain the rationale Alicia had put forth so vehemently. "We're going to take an honest look and see whether the argument holds merit. I damn sure don't want the land destroyed or made useless for a long time." Something deeper nagged at him as he continued. "We have to leave it in good condition for the next generation of loggers."

Kyle straightened in his saddle and slid a curious, narrow-eyed stare at Caleb. "Are you getting married?"

Caleb's head snapped around, and he scowled. "What the hell put an absurd notion like that into your head?"

Kyle shrugged but continued scrutinizing his boss. "Well, you're mean as a polecat in heat. I've never seen you like this, Caleb. And now you're talking about saving things for the next generation. Hell, only a woman makes a man do those things. A serious woman. When did you find time for courting?"

"I'm not courting a woman." Damn, but he wished he was.

"You're not, huh?"

"No."

"Then do us all a favor. Go visit Flossy or one of her ladies before you come up here again. Your short fuse is hell to live with."

Caleb swore under his breath. He wasn't good at hiding his feelings, and he was even worse at not pursuing what he wanted. The frustration of doing both had overflowed without any way of stopping it. The men didn't deserve his wrath. No one did. His trouble lay in finding an outlet for the mounting tumult surrounding Alicia.

The terrain had grown harsher and steeper. They rode single file, now. The sounds of the forest and their horses picking their footing across the rocky mountainside passed as conversation. The journey relaxed Caleb. The land had a way of straining the volatile foam from the cauldron of his festering sentiments.

Caleb halted Vesuvius on a rocky ledge overlooking the clear-cut terrain. Fissures created by two spring snow-melts scored the steep slope. The debris of the logging operation crisscrossed the land like giant, decaying tooth-picks. Exposed boulders acted as dams for deadfalls, rocks, and soil rushing toward the base of the slope with the melting snow. Only in the sheltered places did the first real signs of new growth reach for the sun.

How the hell had she known this?

Kyle whistled and tilted his hat back on his head. "Looks pretty bad. This was a steep slope. It'll be a while before the forest closes in."

"Yeah. Maybe if we'd left some trees on it . . ." The words died in his throat. *How the hell had she known?*

"If you're looking for regrowth, there might be something to this theory you read. What do you know, one of those books you're always carrying around finally paid off." Kyle dismounted and stretched. "Looks pretty bad."

Caleb ignored the reference to a book. Like most others, Kyle assumed books were the source of his ideas and innovative changes. Until Alicia, that had indeed been the case.

Damn it. She was right. He couldn't walk away from the disaster before him. "We need to start looking at trees like a crop."

"Hell, Caleb, we aren't farmers. We're loggers. What do you mean, a crop of trees?" Kyle whipped off his battered felt hat and finger-combed his sandy hair.

"What we are is responsible for the land, Kyle. We hurt it here. Badly. I don't want us doing this again. I need to think this over. Figure out how to leave some trees and seedlings for the next crop."

"We aren't farmers."

"No, damn it, we aren't. We are timbermen. But as such, we're also businessmen. It's good business. Free reforestation for the price of a few trees and a faster reestablishment of growth."

"Which means a quicker cut, excuse me, harvest of the next batch. I see where you're going." Kyle nodded thoughtfully. "You are one shrewd son of a bitch. Mariah's husband is going to inherit an empire of trees." Kyle turned sly and regarded Caleb for a moment. "Unless you're lying to me about a woman and plan on having a couple of boys to cut timber with you."

Caleb leaned on the saddle horn and gazed over the defiled land. "I'm afraid my chances for marriage and a family are about as fertile as the land down there."

"In that case, maybe you ought to do something about it."

"Like what?"

"You worry too much, Caleb. Let me run the camp and leave Larry alone at the sawmill. Hell, if we've got a problem we can't solve, we'll let you know. You don't have to cut timber. And you damn sure don't have to do topping anymore." Kyle shook his head. "I'm asking you as a friend and as the foreman of this camp, don't do anymore topping. It's too damn dangerous. If something happened to you, I couldn't tell Mariah her daddy isn't coming home. You gotta think of her, too."

"I do. All the time," Caleb growled, his anger boiling. It was true. But he no longer thought about Mariah without Alicia. And when he thought of Alicia, one thing led to another. All the questions about her past, her odd choice of words, and a dozen other things he couldn't dismiss. Ruthless desire washed away his reservations and left him aching.

"The trouble with you is, you don't know how to handle prosperity. Damn it man, you're a financial success. Hell, even by stateside standards, you're a rich man. Do you live like one?"

"I live the way I like. Back off, Larsen."

The warning made Kyle pause for a full minute. "If you were living the way you like, you wouldn't be ripping people's heads off for no apparent reason." Kyle climbed onto his horse. "Let's go. We've learned something, and that's good for the future, if not for the land below."

"Go ahead. I'll be back before dark." Caleb reined Vesuvius away from the ledge. "I'm going down there."

"Don't stay too long." Kyle headed back to the lumber camp.

Caleb maneuvered Vesuvius down the slope. He studied the scarred bank, his heart growing heavier. Next to Mariah and his home, he loved the land best. In the midst of its harsh, unpredictable moods lay an unequaled peace and beauty. He felt himself a part of the serenity found only in the heart of the forest.

Big raindrops plopped from the dark clouds above the trees. He whipped out his rain gear from the saddlebags and pulled it over his head. As the rain began to beat down harder, he let Vesuvius find shelter in a dense canopy at the edge of the scored land.

As he watched, the fissures carved into the slope filled with water. Rivulets ran around the sea of tree stumps. The edges of the fissures crumbled, widening the scars on the slope. Another layer of soil washed away.

"How the hell did you know, Alicia?" he hollered at the hillock, his heart heavy.

"And how do you know *me* so easily?" he whispered into the rain.

* * *

As long as Alicia stayed busy, she managed to hold thoughts of Caleb at a distance. Idleness, even a momentary lull, opened the door with his name on it. Each time he intruded, shutting out the emotional chaos rushing through her became more difficult to control. He'd been gone a week. One moment it felt like an hour, the next it seemed a year.

Maude poked her head into Mariah's room. "Jeremy has the horses hitched. Are you ready?"

"Oh, yes," Mariah answered with glee, her gray eyes sparkling with excitement for the adventure ahead.

"Are you certain Mr. Marker would approve?" Alicia asked, hoping she wasn't making a mistake. Mariah was her responsibility, no one else's, during Caleb's absence. He'd made that very clear.

"I'm sure, Alicia. You worry too much." She winked at Mariah who giggled and winked back with near perfection. "If worry could solve the woes of the world, you and Caleb would be its saviors."

"Then won't he be—"

"He'd let her go," Maude insisted before Alicia finished the question. "Jane and her husband are leaving in two days. They're turning a business trip into a belated honeymoon. We won't see her for months. Not to worry, Alicia. Jeremy and I will be with Mariah tonight. Besides, she's visited Jane's new home before. It isn't strange to her."

Alicia nodded. She was being foolish. Overprotective. The Crowleys were a greater part of Mariah's life than she. Two weeks were nothing when compared to the five years the little girl had spent with the Crowleys.

"Would you feel better if we took Nero and let him sleep in Mariah's room tonight?"

Relief dampened some of Alicia's agitation. Nothing would harm Mariah with Nero nearby. "Yes, I would."

"All right. But you bring Caesar in the house, or I'll worry about you being all alone out here."

"Me, too," Mariah added solemnly. "I wish you were coming."

Alicia knelt in front of the girl and adjusted her coat. "This is your special time with Jane. She and I will have plenty of opportunity for getting to know each other when she returns from San Francisco. I know you'll be a little lady and make your daddy proud."

"Oh, I will." Mariah hesitated, then flung her arms around Alicia's neck. "I love you, Miss James. Don't ever leave us."

A lump formed in Alicia's throat. "I love you, too, baby." God help her, she did love the child and would do anything for her. She kissed Mariah's smooth cheek, then straightened her hat.

A few minutes later, Alicia waved good-bye from the veranda as Jeremy drove the carriage out to the main road. She watched until they were out of sight. Caesar nudged her hand. Absentmindedly, she sat on the top step and petted the beast.

A fine mist coated the land. She watched the clouds roil along the treetops. They mirrored her churning emotions. To avoid thinking, she twisted and leaned against the porch post, then sang. Caesar put his big head in her lap and watched with half-closed eyes. His ears shifted with the melody of her songs.

Alone and unconcerned over references to things from her own time, she sang whatever came to mind. The words created mental visions of a different time and place. One without Caleb.

She left on a jet plane, rode a motorcycle into hell and back, lived the good life Latin-style, and danced a last dance with Mary Jane.

As fog descended into the trees and the mist became a drizzle, the tempo slowed. While singing about the power of love, the drizzle increased into a steady rain typical of the island world. Content at last, she patted Caesar and pushed to her feet before her skirts became soaked from the splatter dripping off the eaves.

Her hands pressed into the small of her back, she stretched.

Caesar bolted to his feet, tail wagging and big tongue

dangling over his fangs. Alicia followed the line of his expectant gaze. The tenuous peace woven by song and flights of fantasy fled.

Caleb was home.

Chapter Ten

"Sing it again. Please."

The request reached through the rain. Luminous gray eyes regarded her from within the shelter of the hat pulled low on Caleb's brow. Water dripped off the brim and ran down his slicker. Impervious to the whether, he reminded rooted like a giant spruce in the yard halfway down the veranda.

All the yearning Alicia had sought to divert through song returned. Joy at his return burst through her senses. She smiled hesitantly. An unreasonable urge to embrace him and shower him with kisses until he rewarded her with one of his smiles that made her heart skip a beat forced her along the shelter of the veranda.

Facing him, she halted, realizing the folly of such actions. Her fingers gripped the railing as though anchoring her from impulses with disastrous consequences.

"Sing for me, Alicia."

Powerless to deny him, she drew a breath and let her voice soar into the rain. The darkness of the thunderclouds of his eyes swallowed her.

The lyrics of the song she chose conjured two sated lovers entwined and whispering affirmations of their love amidst tangled bed sheets. When Alicia closed her eyes, she imagined herself and Caleb in just such a way. In her fantasy, the phantom thunder of his heart rolled across the space between them. It matched the thrum of rain spilling off the eaves and creating a veil of unreality shimmering between them.

Much as she craved making the image a reality, holding his body against hers and hearing him whisper passion in her ear, she knew she could never trust this man. Not wholly. Oh, she could love him, and perhaps she had already fallen prey to her own weaknesses.

But to admit it, to succumb to the strange, potent desire he incited with a look . . . Her heart couldn't withstand the pain it would cause when he heard the truth and called her a liar.

Her voice rose with the song's chorus. Despite all her mind's logical warnings, she wanted to be Caleb's lady and lay claim to him for all time. But her only reward would undoubtedly be heartache.

She became as lost as the woman in the song, bereft from all that was familiar, all that she loved. A keening loss flowed through her and into the emotion of the song.

She opened her eyes and met Caleb's smoldering gaze. The sharp talons of her fear loosened on her heart. The vortex of her desire for Caleb grew.

He'd filled her thoughts from the moment they met. The distance between home and the lumber camp or Sitka couldn't diminish the vigor of his presence. Everywhere she turned, each time she closed her eyes at night, he was there. Waiting, just as he waited now and listened with intensity that permeated all her defenses and laid her heart bare.

When she repeated the chorus of the song, she almost believed she was his lady. Her grip on the rail relaxed. Unbidden, she reached toward him.

Her emotions hurled her down an unfamiliar path even

109

more perilous than the one from the Wyoming fog bank to the spruce forest. Falling in love with Caleb didn't frighten her—it terrified her.

She sang, the lyrics reflecting the yearning in her soul. In the fleeting instant of *now* the rest of the world seemed light-years away. Her pulse beat so loudly that her temples throbbed.

When the song ended she continued staring at him, mesmerized. If he moved toward her, she'd fall over the rail and into his arms. Her fingers clutched the narrow beam, stopping her.

"Thank you." His voice echoed the longing in his eyes. They narrowed, as though he peered through a crack in her defenses and read the truth of her emotions. It was electrifying.

"It—it's just a song."

"You sing from the heart, Alicia. It wasn't just a song." He turned, breaking the connection.

Quaking like an autumn leaf, Alicia watched him gather Vesuvius's reins and disappear into the sheets of foggy rain. Shaken, she rested her head against a railing pillar. "Dear God, what am I going to do?"

How long she stared into the rain sorting out her feelings for Caleb, she didn't know. When the ache in her lower abdomen subsided, she heaved a sigh and went into the house. Caesar followed after a glance in the direction of the barn.

Intent on occupying herself, Alicia set about preparing a meal for Caleb. Undoubtedly Caleb would be cold as well as wet when he came into the house. She set the table and put out the meal Maude had left in the warmer. It seemed the least she could do for Caleb. Besides, her appetite had disappeared with the butterflies in her stomach upon seeing him watching her in the rain.

Satisfied everything was prepared, Alicia readied her escape. She did not intend to spend a moment in the same room with the man. Alone as they were, she didn't trust either of them. Worse, if he asked her to tell him *no* again, she doubted her tongue could do it, regardless the consequence.

Her mouth went dry at the memory of forcing the words out: *I don't want you.* No way could she look him in the eye and lie like that again.

But if he asked again . . .

Disaster waited on both roads. She pondered for a moment, then left the kitchen.

The great room suddenly seemed too small. Needing space, she grabbed a shawl and returned to the veranda. As she settled onto the swing hanging from the rafters, the fog thickened, pressing in from all sides. She pushed her foot against the floor and sent the swing into motion.

Watching the fog, she tucked the shawl tightly around her arms and slouched in the swing. The moody mist reminded her of the fog that had spirited her from Drexel.

It retreated to the treeline, leaving her to scale the mountain of questions.

What if she took what Caleb offered? Whom would it harm, other than herself?

The answer was clear. When Caleb sent her packing or pressured her departure, the consequences of her folly would fall heavily on Mariah.

"Unacceptable," she breathed into her steaming coffee.

In the isolation created by the fog, she heard Caleb moving around in the house. He'd wanted her to know he was there, or he would have gone about his business as quietly as he'd entered the yard. Big and solid as a mountain, he could still move as silently as a cloud.

He could split a log in a single blow and soothe the tears of a skinned knee with a caress and tender kiss.

"Caleb Marker doesn't have a mean bone in his body," Maude had told her just this morning.

No, perhaps he wouldn't mean to break her heart. But it would happen when she left him.

She sipped her coffee, wondering how long until the next weird, time-shifting fog sent her home to Drexel.

"Where is Mariah?"

Startled, she swiveled around on the swing and gazed

up. Caleb stood nearby and worry formed a pale line around his lips.

"I let Mariah go with Maude, Jeremy, and Nero to Sitka for the night. Jane is leaving in a couple of days. They'll be packing and . . . I didn't think you'd object." All her earlier misgivings crashed down. "If you like, I'll go get her. There's enough daylight."

"She'll be asleep by now."

Distressed, Alicia lowered her eyes. "I keep forgetting about how late the sun shines here."

"Don't tell me you're going to sleep as long as it's dark in the winter. If so, you may as well hibernate in your bed."

Fleetingly, she envisioned doing just that with him. She shook away the image and stood. "No. I'm not the hibernating kind. Just out of curiosity, how long is the longest winter night?"

"I've never timed it, but sunset to sunrise is about seventeen and a half hours." He punched his hands into his pockets and raised an eyebrow. "You sent Nero with Mariah?"

"Well, yes. I thought he'd be a good deterrent for any trouble." Suddenly, she felt very foolish. "I know she's safe at Jane's. Maybe I was overcautious because I don't know what kind of latitude you allow with Mariah."

"Damn little." The stark expression hardening his features melted into a half smile. "But I'd have let her go, too. She and Jane like each other a great deal."

Alicia exhaled in relief. "That's good to know. That you would have let her go, I mean."

"Why are you on edge?" The soft timbre of his question increased her jitters, kindled the fire leaping through her. "Is it the isolation of being so far from other people?"

Alicia laughed softly. "This? Oh, Caleb, this isn't isolation. Isolation is a ranch in Wyoming twenty-five miles from anyone, in the dead of winter, after a Northern drops several feet of snow." She went to the rail and set her cup on top, then hugged the post with her right arm.

Gazing at the mist-laced trees through the drizzling

rain, she continued. "What you have here is priceless in its uniqueness. You've built a paradise replete with the comforts of home and the freedom of open land and wild nature. The beauty of the mountains and trees touches my heart in an inexplicable way.

"Most people need other people around to divert themselves from what's inside of them. There's a big difference between being lonely and being alone. I've been the loneliest in a crowd. I'm seldom lonely when I'm alone." She cast a backward glance at him.

The warmth of his hand on her shoulder radiated through the marrow of her bones, weakening them.

"You're trembling. Are you cold?"

"No." Quite the opposite.

"Do I frighten you?"

"More than anyone I've ever known."

"Why?"

She shook her head, unwilling to explain the desire burning her veins and contracting her lower abdomen. "This isn't smart, Caleb."

"Tell me you don't want me."

The caress of his warm breath against her ear sent a thrill over her skin. "This is trouble," she warned, unable to stop from brushing her cheek against his, then leaning into him as his arms folded across her collarbone. His erection pressed against her tailbone and the small of her back. The flames of her desire leaped higher. A delicious tingling hardened her nipples and made her gasp.

"You want me as much as I need you, Alicia." The soft caress of his lips along her jaw sent her head back, exposing the slender column of her neck.

"It doesn't matter. If we give in to what we want you'll send me away."

"No, I wouldn't. I promise you I won't. God help me, something about you has me breaking damn near every rule I've lived by for years."

Her breathing became short. Concentrating on her last fragmented thread of sensibility became more difficult with each heated caress of his mouth on her sensitive neck. "Right now, we'd promise each other anything. Tomorrow . . . tomorrow it will be my fault. It's always the woman's fault."

"Who told you that nonsense?" His teeth closed on her earlobe.

"I read it in a book, so it must be true."

He rested his chin on her shoulder for a moment. "Really? Can you show me." Without warning, he released her.

His abrupt absence had her clinging to the post for support. Silent yet desperate disappointment trilled through her tattered nerves.

"Turn around, Alicia. I won't touch you." A ragged sound that might have been a laugh followed. "You're safe."

Was that what she wanted? To be safe? After drawing a steady breath, she faced him. The tensing of his jaw betrayed his silent struggle. Hunger and disappointment shone in his eyes.

"I don't know how to handle this situation," she whispered.

A sad smile eased the tension in his face. "I'd say you're doing better than I am. You're unique. I've never met anyone like you, Alicia." His gaze devoured her. "I do, or I used to, get to Seattle and San Francisco regularly. I'm not a total isolationist."

"Then that is where we differ. I *could* be, given the right circumstances. Which I guess you've provided me with here. For now."

"Why are you so certain I'd ask you to leave if we made love?"

"You'd want"—*the truth about where I came from*— "things I can't give you. It would get complicated, uncomfortable. Mariah would be caught in the middle. Children always are. We wouldn't want it that way, but that's how it would end up. It's human nature. I want to see you when you're here and spend my days with Mariah, not put it all at risk. I love her, Caleb. How could I not?"

"Could you ever love me, Alicia?"

A dull pocketknife carving her heart from her chest might inflict less pain than his question. "I'm not a masochist. Good-night, Caleb."

Trembling, she walked around him and entered the house. She didn't stop until she had reached her room and closed the door. In the near-darkness of the room, she sat on the edge of the bed.

A tear spilled over her lashes, followed by a second. The flow quickened, uncontrollable.

"Could you ever love me, Alicia?"

Not willingly, but she'd begun to doubt she had a choice.

"We can't avoid being together without Mariah or Maude around for much longer," Caleb told Alicia three evenings after their encounter on the veranda.

Alicia plunged her garden trowel into the dirt. "I know. I've been thinking the same thing." She wiped her hands on her apron and stood.

She might have been thinking it, but she damn sure wasn't changing anything. She looked everywhere except at him, which made him wonder what else occupied her thoughts.

"You don't have to landscape the place." Damn, the woman worked as hard as a logger. And she didn't complain.

"I enjoy it. So does Mariah, I'm pleased to say."

"What are you planting? They look like weeds."

Like her singing had, her unexpected laughter lightened the dark cloud hanging over him.

"In some parts of the world, they're considered just that. Weeds. Here, we'll call them herbs. Some are for cooking, others have medicinal properties. Mariah is learning the difference as we plant them and monitor their growth. The best prevention against misuse is education. Already, she can identify the medicinal herbs by name. That child has a mind like a sponge and excellent retention abilities for her age."

Alicia picked a clump of dirt from under her fingernail.

"I was wondering if you'd mind parting with the scraps outside your wood shop."

"Sure. What do you want them for?"

"Flower boxes. Some of the herbs need drier soil." She gestured at the elaborate, tiered herb garden she and Mariah had fashioned on the south side of the house. "This is the driest place I could find, but not all of these will survive here. If I put them in boxes where I can control the soil moisture, they'll do better."

"Tell me what you want. I'll build it." Why hadn't she said she wanted planters? Chagrined, he knew why. She didn't want to ask him for anything. The same big, violet eyes that had been haunting him, awake or asleep, flashed up at him. She reminded him of a baby bird venturing out of the nest for the first time.

"Oh, I don't need anything fancy. I can do it. I've built lots of flower boxes and seedling flats," she answered offhandedly.

What she wanted and what she'd settle for seemed two different things. "Come on," he said taking her wrist.

"Where are we going?"

He'd marched her halfway through the mud porch before she balked.

"Let me take my shoes off."

"Next time you're in town, get some mud boots to garden in. Consider it an expense on my part for Mariah's education in horticulture." He waited while she unfastened her shoes and set them next to the kitchen door.

"Wash up, Alicia. Then you're going to sketch out exactly what you want. Not just what you need, but what you want. Tomorrow, I'll build it."

"Caleb, this isn't necessary. You've got so many demands on your time."

To shut her up, he turned her toward the sink and gently gave her a push. "Wash."

She scrubbed her hands and face, then brushed back her hair. He handed a towel to her, wishing she'd let him kiss away the water beading on her pink cheeks and lips.

"Really, you don't need to bother. Mariah and I can

build the boxes. A few boards, nails, a hammer and saw—"

"Yep. That's what I'll use, too." He tossed the towel on the table and gestured toward the door with a bow. "My office. After you, Miss James."

Resigned, but reluctant, she led the way to the farthest corner of the house. He reached around and opened the door for her. After a couple of steps, she stopped short. If he hadn't been watching so closely, he'd have run into her.

"What's wrong?" Anxious, he glanced around for a field mouse or spider brave enough to invade his private domain.

"My God!" Her hand covered her mouth. Her astonishment grew as her gaze roamed the bookcases, tables, chairs, and desk before seeking him out. The awe shining in her expression heated and unnerved him at the same time. He'd give all he owned for her to look at him that way after they had made love.

"Alicia?" he asked, uncertain what had affected her so profoundly.

"You did all of this?"

He glanced around the familiar surroundings. The wood chosen for each piece reflected his mood at the time. The room reflected his personality. He nodded. "Not in one day, or even two."

At the desk she dropped onto her stockinged knees. The reverent homage of her slender fingers running over the carving of San Francisco tightened his entire body. Briefly, he imagined her exploring him with the same degree of interest.

"Magnificent." She bent closer to examine a detail of a cable car. "This must have taken years."

"Months, actually. Before Mariah, I spent a couple of the winter months every year traveling. That still left plenty of long, dark evenings to fill. A house can only hold so much furniture. Carving takes longer. The house fills up slower."

"Your wife must have prized your work." She stood,

dragging her fingertips along the glassy finish on the desktop.

"I've never been married," he admitted softly. "Have a seat at the table. I'll get some paper and pencils."

He felt her eyes following him and knew she was bursting to ask questions. Though he'd answer anything, she held her curiosity silent. She sat at the table and ran her fingers along the scrollwork edge. He watched her intently and lamented that he wasn't the towel, the desk carving, or the scrollwork. Some of his hunger must have been evident because her fingers halted. When he met her gaze, the uncertainty was back.

"Explain what you want, and sketch it at the same time." He placed materials in front of her.

"What I want, not what I need?" She picked up the pencil and adjusted the paper.

The challenge in her tone made him smile. "Nothing less, unless you think the task beyond my capabilities."

"I don't think there's much in this world beyond you, Caleb. Though it might be prudent if you didn't get any ideas about weeding my herb patch." The pencil in her hand flew over the paper with lines and dimensional notes.

Her knowledge of precision planning fascinated him. He wasn't much with a pencil and paper without a ruler, compass, and protractor. The dimensions and landscapes for his carvings appeared in his head, then manifested in the wood without a pencil mark on it.

Alicia drew two views of a four-tiered box garden. "If you put it on big wooden wheels with brakes, I could roll it along the veranda as the daylight changes over the months."

"What is this piece at the bottom?"

"A catch-all tray. Any dripping water will accumulate there instead of wherever we park the planter." As she elaborated on the purpose of each part of the design, she visibly relaxed.

Finally, Caleb pushed the plans aside. "I'll build it for you tomorrow. In the afternoon, take Mariah and go to Hamilton Traders. Pick out some paint for your flower box." He rapped the plans with his knuckles. "Any color you like. And mud boots. They're essential here. If you don't believe it, just wait until it starts raining."

Laughter bubbled through her startled expression. "I thought this was the rainy season."

"Nope. August through October we get a lot of rain. You'll get used to it in a year or two. I don't suppose you have a slicker, do you?"

"Of course not. I'll buy one with my first month's wages," she promised.

"Save your money. There are extras in the barn. Make sure you take one with you if you're going anywhere for very long." One way or another, he'd provide for her welfare. Pride was good, but stubbornness could lead to trouble.

"I understand the dangers of weather catching me by surprise." She smiled at him. "Or people who do the same."

"Me? How did I surprise you?" She was the surprising one with her conversational twists weaving on and off safe ground.

"You don't know anything about herbs or container gardening, yet you're willing to spend the time building this." She fingered the paper with puzzlement drawing her brows closer.

"Because you want it, Alicia. I don't have to know anything about anything else."

"I don't understand you, Caleb. Why would you do this when you know I won't, well . . ."

"Make love with me?"

Her lower lip disappeared between her teeth as she nodded.

"One has nothing to do with the other. Furthermore, I'd be damned disappointed if you believed they did."

She rested her chin in her hand and regarded him with a twinkle dancing in her eyes. "So, if we made love, you wouldn't build this for me?"

"Yes, ma'am." Enjoying her humor, he winked.

She winked back, then grinned and mischievously raised her left eyebrow.

Grinning back, he matched the movement, following it by raising the right one.

Alicia laughed. "Practice, practice, practice. The right one is more difficult."

"I've heard tell if you want to do anything badly enough all you need is patience and practice." He wiggled his right eyebrow again. "Mariah believes it."

"Sort of like the way you've created all of this?" Her gaze followed her hand sweeping the room. "Do you know you've created masterpieces?"

He followed her motion around the office. "I like bringing out the secrets hidden in the wood. Some trees beg to have their images set free. The Tlingits believe trees are witnesses to history. They free the stories by carving away the layers hiding these stories. It's the tree's destiny to tell a tale. . . . Then it, too, becomes history."

"What is your destiny, Caleb?"

"To raise Mariah into a young lady as beautiful inside as she is outside. I'd be pleased if she turned out like you."

Long lashes fell over eyes so sad that Caleb winced. Despite his determination not to touch her, he did. "What is it?"

"I want more for her. I want her to be wiser."

The soft skin of her cheek glided under his callused fingertips. "Then she will be. You'll see to it. I won't ask what happened before to make you so skeptical and afraid of me. God knows, I'm no prize and maybe it's just something about me, my size or the color of my hair that puts you off."

"If I ever could trust a man again, it would be you, Caleb. There's nothing wrong with you. Not your size, the color of your hair, or your proclivity for isolation. It's me."

She gazed out the window. A melancholy radiated from the depths of her being and raised the fine hairs on the back of Caleb's neck. "And there's something else that has nothing to do with men, or trust, or anything you can imagine."

"Does it have something to do with your sisters or why you came to Sitka?" Mentally, he held his breath in the hope she'd confide in him.

"What if I'm the only one who . . ." She drew a sharp, ragged breath and sat a bit straighter.

"Who what?" The agony in her voice pinched his heart.

She stared beyond the distant trees blending in the shadows of a long twilight.

Certain she'd withdraw if pressed, he held back his questions. The secrets she harbored exacted a cruel toll.

"Thank you, Caleb." She rose and examined the carvings of various trees along the sides of the bookcases. "You are an amazingly talented man." She paused at the door. "I'm privileged to know you." Without another word, she left, closing the door behind her.

He had the strangest feeling she hadn't been referring to his woodcarving.

Chapter Eleven

"We had a happy time buying paint." Mariah settled into her chair at the dinner table. Her elfin features glowed with exuberance. "Mr. Wagner made us laugh and laugh. He can be so silly."

"I didn't know Kendrick Wagner had a sense of humor," Caleb said, hoping it had been Kendrick, not his brother, Joshua, behind the counter at Hamilton Traders.

Mariah rolled her eyes and giggled. "Oh, Daddy, not Mr. Kendrick Wagner. He never makes me laugh. Mr. *Wagner*, his brother. He knows all about everything in Mr. Hamilton's trading post. He showed us herbs from China. And then he invited us to eat dinner with him. He was so much fun, I wanted to stay, but Miss James said you'd be waiting for us." Mariah's curious eyes narrowed on Caleb. "Were you waiting for us?"

At least Alicia had declined. That should have taken the edge off his irritation at Josh Wagner's interest in her, but it didn't. "Of course, I'd miss you. If you hadn't come home for dinner, the food Maude prepared would have gone to waste. Maude and I can't eat this much alone."

"But we would have tried," Maude chimed in. "I imagine it won't be long before half the young men in Sitka ask you to dinner, Alicia."

"If Mr. Joshua asks you to dinner again and you go, can I go with you?" Mariah asked.

"No," Caleb muttered. An image of Alicia and Joshua Wagner talking and laughing across an intimate dinner table popped into his mind. Something twisted inside of him.

Alicia paled and set her fork aside. "I don't have time for dating," she answered flatly.

Caleb watched her closely, realizing her reticence wasn't only regarding him. She truly had no interest in being courted by any man.

Mariah swallowed the food in her mouth, then asked, "What's dating?"

"Courting," Caleb answered. Alicia had used the word the night he interviewed her. He'd thought it odd then, but understood its meaning from the context. "Dating is a term used in Wyoming," he added, watching Alicia's expression change from alarm to relief.

"Oh." Mariah accepted the answer easily. "Well, we saw Mr. Nelson, too. He said something to tell you." Her brow furrowed, and she beseeched Alicia for help with an exasperated expression. "I don't remember what he said."

"It wasn't important, Mariah. He was making conversation," Alicia assured her with a forced smile.

The slight shake of Alicia's head when she glanced at him fueled Caleb's agitation. Damn. Was every buck in Sitka standing in line to sniff her skirt?

"Like the soldier?" Mariah asked.

"What soldier?" The harsh question was out before he thought twice. No longer hungry, he pushed his half-finished meal away.

"The one we had hot chocolate with. At Mr. Kratz's cafe. He knows Miss James, too." Mariah took another bite of her meal.

She was the only one eating. Jeremy had already finished and appeared relieved he wasn't part of the evening conversation. Maude's fork remained poised over her plate. Behind her clear, round glasses, her brown eyes sparkled with amusement. Alicia met Caleb's ire with her chin outthrust in indignation.

"Who? The soldier or Otto Kratz?" An unfamiliar heat crawled up his neck. The dinner he'd eaten curdled in his stomach.

"Mr. Kratz." Alicia's gentle answer belied the irritation flashing in her violet eyes. "I found your posting for a governess on the kiosk at Mr. Kratz's cafe. At the time, he was very helpful and kept the place open while I sorted through the notices. As for the soldier, he was probably lonely. He inquired about the weather."

Alicia's voice turned sugary, but her piercing glare conveyed the depths of her offense. "At no time was Mariah exposed to anything questionable, and I resent innuendo by word or attitude hinting otherwise."

She pushed away from the table. "I'll get the dessert, Maude."

Unaware of the tension, Mariah continued, "Mr. Kratz told the soldier if he was new in town he shouldn't be bothering strangers. Does that mean he can't talk to anyone 'cause he doesn't know anyone? How's he gonna make friends if he doesn't talk?"

Seething, Caleb watched Alicia disappear through the kitchen door. He cleared his throat to answer his daughter. "He can talk with the men he's billeted with, Mariah. The proper way is for two people to be introduced by a third party they know." With effort, he kept the pique out of his voice. It wasn't Mariah's fault that every revelation regarding Alicia further angered him.

Mariah's gray eyes clouded with puzzlement. "What's a topper?"

"Who said anything about a topper?" Caleb asked slowly, noting Maude had stopped eating again, and stared at Mariah.

"Mr. Kratz did. He told the soldier if he stayed around

too long you'd turn him into a topper. Or something like that. But I liked hearing the funny way he talked. Miss James said he was a Southerner. Do people talk that way in Seattle? That's south, isn't it?"

"I meant a Southerner from the United States," Alicia answered, placing a berry pie on the table. "That's very far away."

"Farther than Wyoming?"

"Yes. After dinner, I'll show you the southern states on the map."

Although he contributed little to the rest of the dinner conversation, Caleb grudgingly admired the way Alicia directed Mariah's interest. Inwardly, he fumed at himself, Larry Nelson, Joshua Wagner, and every other man in Sitka who'd noticed her.

When Jeremy, Alicia, and Mariah left the table, Maude rounded on him with a vexation of her own. "What's gotten into you? Alicia James is the best thing that's happened to this home in a long time, Caleb. She likes it here. If you go asking questions about every man she talks to in town, I can tell you right now, she isn't going to put up with it. Or you. And what're you going to do if she leaves without—"

Maude quit speaking as though the words froze on her tongue. She leaned forward, her ample bosom spilling over the edge of the dining table. "You got feelings for her, don't you?" She gave him a pointed look. "Well, don't just sit there fuming and feeling jealous. Do something about it, Caleb."

"Mind your own business, Maude." Caleb stormed away from the table.

Two near-serious blunders, Alicia berated herself as she closed Mariah's bedroom door for the evening. She'd slipped earlier in Caleb's office when wondering aloud. Fortunately, she'd caught her lapse before revealing anything Caleb could latch on to. Even more fortunately, he hadn't pressed for clarification.

Or perhaps he had truly chalked up her blunders to idiosyncrasies peculiar to Wyoming folk.

Still, no such vagaries existed about his behavior at the dinner table tonight.

Feeling again the anger aroused by his innuendo, she resolved to search the house for him. In the kitchen, Maude consulted a recipe surrounded by cake pans and ingredients.

"Do you know where Caleb is?" Alicia asked, searching the yard visible through the kitchen window.

"He's sulking in his wood shop," Maude answered. Her words were sweet and drew a sharp glance from Alicia.

"Thank you," she said. Hands balled into fists, Alicia marched out the door and across the yard. Without knocking on the open door or announcing her presence, she stormed inside.

Caleb was bent over an elevated worktable, mating two pieces of wood to form a dovetail joint. A lock of raven hair tumbled against the bridge of his nose as he slid the pieces together. He seemed oblivious to the rest of the world.

"Mr. Marker. I'd like a word with you." Hands on hips she awaited his response.

"I apologize," he murmured, undeterred from his task. A second set of joints slid together, and he reached for a third.

How dare he apologize before hearing her complaint, then ignore her? "Your apology is not accepted."

That got his attention; he looked up. The hunger blazing in his taut features made Alicia question the wisdom of her refusal. Caleb radiated the coiled restlessness of a cornered panther.

"Why? You think I should make a bigger ass out of myself and argue with you? I was wrong at the dinner table. I had no cause to question who you talk with in town."

Most of Alicia's fight evaporated. "I'd never expose Mariah to anything unsavory or the slightest bit questionable."

"I wasn't concerned about Mariah. I trust you with her." He assembled the fourth joint, then wiped his hands on a rag.

"Then—Why were you so angry with me?" Alicia found herself at a loss. If she lived with this man until Mariah was old enough to leave home, she still wouldn't understand him.

"I wasn't angry with you." He closed the distance between them. The glint in his eyes heightened the predatory feel of him. "I was angry at the whole damn world because you're more comfortable with a stranger than you are with me, Alicia."

"That's not true," she whispered.

"Are you comfortable with me now?"

The fresh scent of wood and soap filled her nostrils. Her eyes drifted upward from the buttons of his shirt. The pulse hammering in the hollow of his throat beat as rapidly as her own.

"No," came her barely audible admission. "But that isn't your problem." All she had to do was touch him, lift her face, and stand on tiptoes. She moistened her dry lips, and slowly raised her head.

"The hell it isn't."

Without warning, he embraced her. Any thought of protest died when his mouth descended on hers.

Caution fled.

Reason wilted.

The power of his massive arms cradling her against the hard wall of his body scattered her senses. He held her fast without crushing her. A small cry died in her throat along with any notion of struggling.

On their own, her arms lifted in a return embrace. The freedom of holding him and the restrained pressure of his kiss banished her fears. For just a moment, she'd indulge in the delicious feel of him and the sensual glory of his lips.

He eased away, not quite departing, not quite kissing her. The urgency of disappointment sent her arching on tiptoes, her hungry mouth open.

Caleb accepted the offering with restraint, and she could feel him quake against her. Her hands greedily roamed the rippling landscape of his back, drawing him closer. The sensation of his heavy arousal pressing into her lower abdomen wrenched a groan from them both.

Alicia gave over to the firm, yet reverent caress of his big hands along her spine and shoulders, and when his tongue swept into her mouth, she lost all ability to think. Every drop of blood in her body boiled and screamed for the sweet joining of their bodies. She drew his tongue farther into her mouth, stroking it with her own hunger.

Emboldened by her response, Caleb cradled the base of her neck and head in one hand and cupped her buttocks in the other. Alicia locked an arm around his neck, never wanting their kiss to end. Her pebbled nipples burrowed against the stone wall of his chest with each rapid, ragged breath.

Oh yes! her entire body screamed.

As though answering her silent summons, Caleb's fingers moved from her neck to close around her breast. Alicia slanted her mouth across his, delighting in his feel and taste. All the while her hips grated sinuously against him, treasuring the erotic slivers of lightning his body sparked in the deepest part of her.

Surges of desire cascaded through her with increasing intensity. Want became need. Hunger became starvation. Caleb held the promise of nourishment. She had to know . . .

He broke the kiss with a harsh groan.

Stunned, Alicia gaped at him. Her shattered senses lay in pieces at her feet. As awareness overcame her, surprise became disappointment, then embarrassment. It was she, not Caleb, who wouldn't stop with a kiss. In the mindless passion of the moment, she'd never have ended the soul-quenching kiss.

"Caleb." His name flowed with a whisper of breath from her kiss-swollen lips.

The tortured desire in his eyes glistened behind a curtain of thick, lowering lashes. He enfolded her at the shoulders and held her close. "Sweeter than I'd imagined," he whispered in her ear.

A trembling that started in the core of her being ran through her limbs. She held him tightly until it ebbed. "Don't ever tell me to say I don't want you. I do. So much, it terrifies me."

"You have nothing to fear from me."

For a second, she almost believed him because he believed himself. But he would change.

"Sh-h-h," he soothed. "I know you don't believe it. Not yet."

The feel of his jaw gliding against her cheek soothed the protest on the tip of her tongue. She wished it were possible to believe him.

"One day, Alicia, you'll trust me."

She obviously couldn't trust herself to maintain any sort of restraint concerning him. Right now, when she should be putting distance between them, her arms tightened. If she didn't release him soon, she'd turn her head and capture his mouth again. The temptation nearly overwhelmed her.

Caleb saved her by kissing her forehead, then taking her shoulders and retreating a step. A short, sad laugh burbled from his throat.

"I don't think this is funny," Alicia managed, bereaved by the sudden absence of his sensual heat.

"It isn't. Letting you go now is either the stupidest or noblest act I've ever done."

She suspected the latter. She'd been the stupid one by becoming the aggressor when he'd have been content with one sweet kiss. "I don't know why I did that. It seems I'm the one who owes an apology."

Darkness roiled across his face. It hardened into an unreadable mask. "Are you sorry?"

"Yes." *Liar. You wanted him. You* still *want him. That was the most exciting kiss ever.*

"I mean, no," she stammered. *Fool. He'll betray you. Then what?*

"I don't know." The man watching her wasn't Chet. He

couldn't betray her. They'd made no promises, taken no vows.

But it was more than broken marriage vows responsible for her divorce from Chet. If she had satisfied his needs, he wouldn't have looked elsewhere. She had failed at the marriage, too.

Gazing at Caleb's controlled expression, her heart skipped a beat. Wanting him with a depth that flourished with each touch increased her vulnerability.

"Would you like to see your herb planter?" he asked softly.

Alicia swallowed the lump in her throat and nodded. Why did he have to be so perceptive and generous?

"I'll put the first coat of paint on it tonight." He led her toward the back of the wood shop.

Alicia stared, dumbfounded. In a single day, he'd built exactly what she'd drawn in his office. The four-tiered garden cart moved on oversized wooden wheels with clamp brakes at the back. A handle extended from the sides and across the front for leverage.

"You're a wonder, Caleb. It's marvelous. Thank you." No one had ever built anything for her, let alone asked what she wanted. Of course, she'd never so much as hinted when she needed something. She'd always done everything for herself. "I don't know what else to say."

"There isn't anything more you need to say, Alicia. I enjoyed doing it. The appreciation on your face makes it doubly satisfying."

"I can paint it. That's the least I can—"

"No. I like to finish what I start."

Alert, her eyes flashed at him. She wondered at a double meaning.

"Some things take longer to finish than others. Patience isn't one of my strengths. You'd best leave now."

The softly spoken dismissal sent her turning on her heel. She paused at the door and glanced over her shoulder. "Thank you, Caleb. For all three."

"Three?"

"The cart, the warning . . . and the kiss. Good-night."

Though she ached to remain, to close the door and let free the wild tumult clamoring in her nerve endings, she forced herself outside. There, she strode quickly toward the house, lest she change her mind. The scent of a storm as volatile as the one inside her rode the gathering wind.

Caleb left on Vesuvius before breakfast the next morning. Lunch passed without his return. By the time Alicia and Mariah finished the lessons for the day, the sun had warmed and dried the night's rain from the island world. Cotton-ball clouds drifted in a blue sky and played peek-a-boo with the slow traveling ball of fire.

Alicia spread a blanket on the ground and lay down with Mariah cuddled in the crook of her shoulder. "What do you see up there?"

"Clouds," the child answered.

"Well, I see a unicorn." She pointed at a formation with a spike trailing into blue sky. "There's his horn. His mouth."

"I see it!" Mariah pointed at the ever-changing cloud-scape. "I see his mane, too."

"I think he's magical," Alicia whispered conspiratorially.

"Why?" Mariah whispered back.

"Because he can shape-shift. There are Indian legends where I come from that speak of that."

"What is a shape shipper?" Mariah turned her head to look up at Alicia who met her inquiry with a smile.

"Shape-shifters, sweetheart. According to Indian legends, they're magical men who can turn into wolves, or owls, or ravens. They do things a man never could or would do as a man, like fly."

"If I could change into a bird, I'd be an eagle and fly in the clouds."

Alicia pointed to the disintegrating unicorn formation. "Look, the unicorn is changing. Now, it looks like a giraffe."

"It doesn't have any spots."

Alicia chuckled at the disappointment in Mariah's

voice. "Blink your eyes real fast and it will."

Mariah obeyed, giggling. "Now everything has spots."

"Good. We'll look for a leopard then."

"But what if we find a tiger? How can I give it stripes?"

She tapped Mariah's right temple with a gentle forefinger. "Up here, Mariah. Use your imagination. Look at the clouds and let your mind see whatever it can. The more you learn, the more your mind will open and your imagination will grow."

"Does looking at clouds open my mind?"

Alicia laughed softly, enjoying the freedom of doing nothing more than watching the clouds roll by with Mariah. "If you let it. Your turn. Find something you recognize in the clouds."

Mariah scanned the sky for several moments. "I see trees." She pointed at a cluster banked just above a stand of hemlocks.

Alicia tilted her head. "I see them, too. They look like giant oaks. Can you see anything living in them?"

Mariah squinted, slowly pushing up on her palms. "Yes. Yes. Look." She pointed at a smaller shape. "It's an owl."

"Looks like an eagle to me," came Caleb's voice from above their heads. "May I join you?"

"Oh yes," Mariah gushed. "This is fun. We're opening up my mind."

Alicia's heart beat faster as Caleb settled onto the blanket opposite of Mariah. For an instant, his gray gaze met hers and revealed a hunger as deep as her own.

"What do you see, Daddy?"

Alicia noted the power and ageless strength of the man's profile against the whispering green summer grasses flanking the blanket. Without warning, his fingers brushed the back of her left hand, then captured it within their electrifying grasp. Instead of pulling away, she relaxed and let her fingers lace with his.

Lying with Mariah and Caleb on the sun-dappled yard felt right. It was as though the world stood still, giving her a glimpse into life as it could be. The child nestled against her had won a piece of her heart. If she weren't careful, she'd lose the rest of it to the man holding her hand.

They picked out shapes and debated the features hidden in the clouds. Mariah's imaginative description of the numerous shapes emerging in the gathering gray and white puffs sent the trio into peals of laughter.

"I see a totem pole." Caleb pointed at a spiral of clouds with vague shapes piled atop one another. "But I can't read it."

"I can," Mariah whispered. "It says a lady came to our house and stayed. I loved her and she became my mama."

A shiver ran through Alicia. What if the sole reason she were here lay beside her on the blanket?

"I don't need to be your mama to love you, baby." Caleb's grip on her hand tightened, then set her free. Alicia's fingers stretched to recapture his and closed on air.

Head rocking, Mariah squinted at the clouds lolling across the sky. "Uh-uh. But I don't ever want you to go away."

"She doesn't have her bag packed," Caleb assured his daughter.

"But if your sisters come—"

"Don't worry. I'll build rooms for them, and they can all stay here." Although he spoke to Mariah, he met Alicia's unwavering gaze.

She had no objections. Living in the Marker home with her sisters, the Crowleys, and Mariah and Caleb was a nice fantasy, but it wasn't going to happen.

"Meanwhile, I guess I'll have to content myself with throwing up a new stall in the barn before winter," Caleb said in a lighthearted voice.

"Is Jeremy getting another horse before he goes away?" Mariah asked, still scanning the sky for images secreted among the clouds.

"No. We'll need it for the pony I brought home today."

"A pony?" Mariah bolted upright. "You got a pony? Can I see it?"

"She's waiting in the barn."

The man was full of surprises, and even the largest he revealed with a subtlety that kept the focus away from himself. Alicia sat up and smoothed her skirt. "Does the pony have a name?"

"Of course. Her name is Edgecombe. We can call her Edgy." Caleb stood and offered a hand. Alicia took it.

"I should have guessed. At least Mount Edgecombe is dormant. Isn't it?" Alicia cast an eye westward. Though she couldn't see the peak from here, she knew the looming cone was doing its share in cloud molding today.

"It is." Caleb caught Mariah, flipped her giggling, squirming body over his head, and set her on his shoulders.

Alicia shook out their blanket and folded it as they crossed the yard on the way to the barn. She listened, grinning, as Caleb described Mariah's duties and responsibilities concerning Edgy.

An excellent judge of horseflesh, Alicia examined the pony with a critical eye. The Welsh pony was seven years old and had a docile temperament.

"Will your saddle fit her so I can ride?" Mariah danced beside the placid beast.

"Is she ready to ride alone?" Caleb asked Alicia.

"She's as ready as she can get riding with me. I've let her have the reins on Krakatau. She has a lot of natural ability. I'd put her up."

"Looks like all you have to do is change clothes, young lady. I'll saddle her for you."

"Oh, goody! I get to wear my trousers. Oh, I'm happy. I'm so happy." Heels kicking like a sprinter's at the wire, she raced toward the house.

Alicia laughed, enjoying the child's infectious glee. "Which makes her happier? The pony or wearing the trousers?"

"It's hard to say, isn't it?" He tossed a saddle blanket over Edgy's back. "Does wearing trousers make you that happy?"

"I prefer them to skirts," she conceded.

"Besides finding your sisters, what else would make you happy, Alicia?"

The sudden seriousness of his tone melted the mirth from her lips. A few weeks ago, she'd have answered going home to Drexel in her own time. Today, she knew that if she did, she'd long for everything she'd discovered on this isolated, pristine homestead on Baranov Island. Despite the familiarity of Drexel, there was no Caleb Marker making her blood boil with desire then, nor was there his sweet, gray-eyed daughter brimming with love and affection.

"I don't know, Caleb. I'm quite content here." Content, she realized, was akin to being at peace. The past was gone. Here, only the present existed. Ironically, the woman who planned for everything and everyone had no real plans for the future.

Watching him lift the saddle from its tree with two fingers, she wondered what kind of a future they would have if they made love. If she left him as unsatisfied as she had Chet, she'd never have to worry about telling him how she got here. He wouldn't care.

"Content? For how long? Until you go back to Wyoming?" He put the saddle on Edgy then lifted onto the balls of his feet to thread the cinch.

"No. There's nothing in Drexel. Not yet."

She caught the sudden jerk of his head, then felt the scrutiny of his probing gaze. "What do you mean, not yet?"

Damn, she'd slipped again. "I meant now. Why are you so sure I'll be leaving? Do you want me gone?"

He leaned across Edgy's saddled back. "I don't want you gone. I don't want Mariah crying her eyes out. And it's not just my daughter. My reasons for wanting you to stay are selfish, but you probably know that."

"Look, Caleb—"

"You like directness, so I'll be direct." He continued as though she hadn't spoken. "The way I see things, there's a strong pull between us. I've read about love at first sight and don't believe in it. Lust is another matter."

The veiled reference to her behavior in the wood shop

reminded her it was he, not she, who possessed the restraint. "You believe in lust at first sight?" The surrealism of the conversation made her head spin.

Nodding, he drew a deep breath. "Yeah." A bone-chilling seriousness was stamped into his features.

"What are you getting at?"

"We have a serious predicament here."

"Go on."

"All right," he said, his sharp gaze never leaving hers. "Can we agree there is a strong probability we'll repeat what we started in the wood shop last night?"

"Do you mean kiss?" A mix of anticipation and embarrassment warmed her neck.

"Yes. . . ."

When he didn't continue, she grew more uncomfortable. "Your point is?"

"You know my views on compromising any part of Mariah's—"

"Yeah, yeah. I lose either way." Irritation heated her face and cheeks.

"We'd all lose, but that's not the point."

"What is?"

He straightened, his gaze still pinning her in place. "We get along well enough. You seem to like it here. Being this far from town doesn't seem to bother you. That gives me hope you'll last through the winter without sailing to Tacoma or San Francisco."

Barely daring to breathe, she said, "Yes, I like your entire household, the ranch, farms, or whatever you call your home. And neither Tacoma nor San Francisco hold any appeal."

"Is there anything I should know about you? About your life in Wyoming? Your involvement with anyone or anything of question?" He leaned a little farther over Edgecombe's back. "Any potential surprises waiting down the road?"

The inevitable moment she'd dreaded had arrived. No amount of preparation had readied her. She didn't blink, just kept looking into his eyes. Part of her spun on a precipice.

Leap or retreat? Ought she tell the truth and gamble he'd believe her wild tale of prophecy and time travel? How could she explain what she herself didn't understand? And could he ever believe her story? It certainly wasn't something she could back up with a book.

She retreated, knowing her denial would hurt him. "There is nothing in my life that can hurt either one of us, Caleb." *Except falling in love with you.*

He regarded her for a long time, his expression unchanged yet unreadable. "I can provide anything you want or need, financially speaking, Alicia. You want to stay. I want you to stay. It's only a matter of time until we make love. I don't want you leaving later and carrying away my child when you go."

"Child?" In so many ways, Mariah had become the child Alicia had refused to have with Chet. While she'd thanked heaven she'd listened to her instincts, she'd often wondered what life would be like with a child to care for and love. Mariah's sweet presence was one way for her to know.

"Child?" she repeated. "Your child?" The notion rocked her. She groped for the stall post.

"If we made love . . . If we had a child, it would stay here. With me."

Horses had thrown Alicia with less impact. "You know, Caleb, I don't know whether to pick up a shovel and bash you over the head or laugh. If you think for one minute—"

"What I think isn't as simple as what we want at the moment. There are consequences to our actions. Responsibilities to—"

"I'm going for the shovel."

"Bashing my head won't change a damn thing, Alicia. If you stay, you know as well as I do that we're going to make love. Maybe not today or next week. Maybe not until winter. But it is as inevitable as winter ice.

"When that time comes, we'll have to consider something permanent. I'm leaving for the lumber camp in the morning. Think about it while I'm gone."

She felt like she'd just stepped through the time fog again. The unreality swarming her senses forced her to reach for the stall post again. A near hysterical laugh bubbled from her throat. "Do you honestly think—"

"I'm ready," Mariah shouted, running into the barn at full tilt. "Can I ride her now?"

The electricity between Alicia and Caleb crackled, then disintegrated as he turned his powerful stare away. Every nerve in Alicia's body burned with her sudden comprehension.

Mariah.

Oh, God! Was that what had happened before? Had he loved a woman only to have her leave with his child? If so, why? Because of the isolation of this island? He'd said Mariah's mother died in a fire. Where? And how long had their separation lasted before death had claimed her?

Alicia cleared her throat and squared her shoulders. She'd be damned if she waited until he returned from the lumber camp to conclude this conversation.

Chapter Twelve

Alicia sipped a second glass of burgundy as she swung on the veranda swing. The friendly cotton-ball clouds of the afternoon had merged into a darker thunderhead that matched the turmoil churning in her stomach.

For a little while this afternoon, she'd forgotten about Caleb's confrontation. Watching and helping Mariah ride Edgy had made them all laugh. In a few days, Mariah might even be ready to solo on Edgy as far as town.

"She fell asleep before I left her room." Caleb's voice interrupted her musing. He closed the front door, then leaned against the jamb. "She's exhausted."

"So is Edgecombe. Where did you find her?" The amazing little pony seemed appreciative of Mariah's aptitude. The girl's accommodating demeanor had been the reward for the preliminary work Alicia had done with her on Krakatau, and it had been well worth it.

"Walk over to the wood shop with me and I'll tell you on the way." He offered a hand.

"All right." The pony was the least important topic she intended they discuss, and the wood shop offered the privacy needed to continue where they'd left off this afternoon. She rose from the swing.

"Your garden cart needs a final coat of paint. If I get it on tonight, it should be dry and ready to use in a day or so." Instead of releasing her hand, Caleb tucked it into the crook of his elbow, then held it in place on his left forearm.

On the way to the wood shop, she tried freeing her hand, but he held fast. "Is there some reason you need my hand more than I do?"

"Yes, but we were speaking about Edgecombe." His thumb ran over her knuckles, and she no longer wanted to pull away. "A friend was looking to sell Edgy. His son was ready for a horse."

Watching his stern profile, the sudden appearance of Caleb's smile nearly caused her to stumble.

"It was convenient because I was in the market for a pony. You were right. Mariah should learn to ride; it's a necessity in this country. In the cities, young ladies ride for pleasure . . . though they ride side-saddle."

"I never learned to do that."

"Why not?"

"It's dangerous, particularly when one is rounding up cattle."

"You think skirts are dangerous."

"They are. And impractical in this country." She paused at the wood shop door. " 'When in Rome, do as the Romans.' "

"If we were in ancient Rome, would you wear a toga?" His left eyebrow rose a fraction. Amusement glittered in his eyes, suggesting he was more than a little curious.

"If I had to. What about you? Would you be a gladiator and wear one of those little leather skirts?" She hesitated at the door.

"Depends. Would you cheer for me or the lions?"

The hope in his voice tugged at her heart, reminding her of what she needed to discuss with him. "That would depend on whether or not you had my hand trapped."

"If I let you go, you'd cheer for the lions?"

The softly spoken question made her flinch. Whether from the wine or from the macabre joke about being swept back in time, the game lost its appeal. "Probably not. Mariah would be lost without you."

"And you, Alicia?"

The muted glow of long twilight poured through the windows along the south wall. The rays seemed to collect in Caleb's silver eyes. She couldn't tell him she'd miss him every day for the rest of her life if something happened to him. Why, the mere thought of it caused a hitch of anguish in her chest. "I would mind."

"Because of Mariah?"

Alicia flexed her fingers on his arm, sensitive to the warm strength beneath the silky skin. "What do you want from me?" she asked at last.

"Honesty in all things. Trust."

"Anything else?" *Like my heart, soul, and body?*

He straightened. Suspicion hardened the furrow along the bridge of his nose. "Are you married, Alicia?"

"I told you the night you interviewed me, I'm not married." She gave him a look. "I also told you I had no interest in romantic involvement."

The palpable hunger roaring between them made it more difficult to stand her ground. Alicia sipped her wine and swallowed it with the ball of emotion clawing its way up her throat.

"I remember," he whispered. "But you can't fault me for questioning something too good to be true."

"I don't understand."

His arm formed a brace effectively barring her from leaving. "There I was, walking in the woods, wondering how I was going to care for Mariah and my business. You appeared out of nowhere, like an angel answering a prayer, looking for a position. You're educated. You and Mariah took to each other like ducks to water. You fit into this household. Hell, you even seem to like the isolation." The turbulence had returned to his eyes, along with a frown.

She held her breath and her silence.

"It's perfect. You're perfect. There has to be a catch, something you're not telling me."

"I'm many things, Caleb, but not perfect," she said evenly, then took another sip of wine.

"What ship did you arrive on?"

"The *USS Fogbank*."

"Never heard of it. When did it arrive?"

"As my employer, just how much of my privacy do you think you're entitled to invade?"

"Whatever it takes to understand why a beautiful, educated young woman would settle in a place distant from civilization with a little girl and a self-educated man who disappears for half the summer." It was an earnest plea to understand, and that replaced the turmoil in his eyes.

"Explain it to me, Alicia."

Outside, long shadows blended with the roiling clouds that consumed the edges between light and dark. Mist descended through the trees, threatening to swallow the entire world in gray. In its frothy embrace, nothing was right or wrong, black or white. Things merely were. Like her failures. Her inadequacies. Her shortcomings. Holding the wineglass in both hands, Alicia walked into the darkness of the wood shop and stared out the windows.

"I was married once. It didn't last a year." There, it was out. Like a demon released from the shackles binding it to her heart, the past hovered around her, taunting. "From the time we were ten, Chet and I knew we'd get married someday. We met when we were both five—about Mariah's age. We grew up on neighboring ranches. We saw each other every day at school. We went off to college together. During the summer between our final two years, we were married."

The sting of old memories forced a pause punctuated by another sip of wine. "My parents were alive then. My father gave me away. My sisters were my maids of honor. Betty Kroft was my bridesmaid. She and I shared a room for two years at the university."

As she spoke, she realized the betrayal had lost its sharp edges. Was it time, or understanding . . . ? More than anything, Alicia sensed it was the sensual pyre Caleb had ignited within her that had fostered her newfound enlightenment.

"Chet and I were friends who could tell each other almost anything. What he couldn't tell me, and what I didn't know at the time, was how lacking I was as a wife. We were great at planning and executing plans for the future. We enjoyed the same literature, the same . . ." She caught herself before adding movies, songs, actors, and videos.

"We had a great deal in common. Everyone thought we had the world by the tail, including me. We'd finish school, work for a while, then buy a ranch near town. We'd settle down, and have half a dozen kids. We'd grow old and rock on the porch, and count our grandchildren and the cattle, experiment with the plants growing in the greenhouse, and spoil the grandchildren."

How unrealistic, naïve and distant the dream she'd embraced for a dozen years now seemed. Nothing was so simple or clear cut. Not even in Drexel.

"What happened?"

The whisper in her ear and heat of Caleb's body a hair's-breadth behind her jolted her back into the present. She lifted her chin and stared into the descending fog masking the early twilight.

"I found Chet in bed with Betty." A sad mixture of laughter and sobs burst from her throat. "What really vexed me was that they were enjoying it in a way I never had. They were having a good time. I mean, a *really good* time.

"I was hurt. Furious. So jealous. Every bone in my body vibrated with rage. My own inadequacies sickened me. Chet and I shouldn't have married. We were better friends than lovers. But I trusted him."

She sipped her wine again, then tilted the glass and finished it. "Ultimately, we all lost. I filed for divorce the next day."

"I'm not Chet." Though barely a whisper, his proclamation reverberated in the marrow of her bones. No, he *wasn't* Chet. She'd never desired Chet the way she did Caleb. The difference was as great as holding a paper match against the power of a wind-driven forest fire and comparing the heat.

She had trusted Chet, and he'd betrayed her. That had hurt her terribly. If she followed her heart and trusted Caleb, he could do more than hurt her. He had the power to destroy her.

And if the river of time doubled back and returned her to her life in Wyoming, her heartbreak would stretch through time. Heaven help her, she wanted to stay here with Mariah. With Caleb.

"I thought we agreed upon an employer-employee arrangement," she managed. "For Mariah's sake." Opening the bandage covering the past had exposed scars she'd thought faded long ago.

"We agreed for reasons separate from Mariah. You get under my skin and scare the hell out of me, Alicia."

The steady glide of his hands on her shoulders lured her away from the window and toward him. A quiet understanding softened the worry creases etched into his weathered face. The laugh lines around his eyes melted into the grayness of the dwindling light. His lips, tender yet strong, passionate yet gentle, hungry yet restrained, remained slightly parted and inviting.

She wanted to stare at the safe familiarity of the third button on his shirt. Of their own accord, her traitorous eyes sought his. The window of his soul yawned open for her scrutiny.

"Keep your secrets, Alicia. I have no desire to cause you pain. Trust works both ways. Perhaps you'll give me yours one day." A slow, ironic smile tugged at the corners of his mouth.

Her head shook slowly, sadly. "I can't give you what you want."

"Yes, you can." His hand slid behind her neck and cradled the back of her head.

Before she realized his intent, his lips brushed hers,

shattering her fragile, hard-won calm. The second delicious brush ignited a flashfire in her veins.

Dazed, then eager, she reached for him. Lord, how she wanted to experience the culmination of the ecstasy rampaging through her each time his arms enfolded her. He held her as though she were a precious treasure.

The sound of the wineglass shattering on the stone floor froze her, though her lips were seeking his.

"It's nothing," he breathed against her mouth. He nipped lightly on her bottom lip, then soothed it with the tip of his tongue.

And she let him, entranced by the sensual lure stealing her resolve. The bulwark of her defenses crumbled, then disappeared like paper butterflies cast into a gale.

Her arms tightened around his neck. Breathless, her body melted against him, savoring every granite ridge and valley.

He toyed with her mouth: suckling her lip, testing the texture, dancing the tip of his tongue against hers in growing desire.

"Shall I kiss you, Alicia?" At last his hands moved, one across her shoulders, the other gliding down her spine, and pressing her against his tumescence.

"No," she breathed, teasing and testing him the way he explored her. So close to him, she lost all ability to protect herself against the ravages of the aftermath. It seemed inhuman to want another person with the intensity that now seized her body and absorbed rational thought.

"All right. *You* kiss *me*." The playfulness of his voice suggested a lighthearted, but dangerous, game. The sinuous rocking of his hips increased the wild need ripping through her. His hand cupping her buttocks became a fire stoker.

Each pulse heightened the flames burning her from the inside. If she weren't careful, the frivolity he suggested would wind up as a fatal folly.

"One kiss."

Even as she agreed, it seemed someone else spoke the words. Desire drowned the distant voices warning of disaster in a sea of fire. Her fingers threaded through his hair and drew him closer.

He met her mouth, then took possession of her entire being though the kiss. Tender one moment, voracious the next, she let him taste her every way possible. Meanwhile, he explored her hips and buttocks, drawing her closer until he molded her to the hard contours of his body. She flowed against him willingly. The endless excitement of holding Caleb close mirrored the tumult of her heart and fueled her need to know more of him.

When he broke the kiss, both of them were breathing raggedly. He held her close and stroked her hair. The wild pulse of his heart hammered in her ears and blended with the thrum of the blood surging through her veins.

"Heaven help me, Alicia, I want you more than I thought a man could want a woman."

"Then take me," she whispered. Oblivious to consequence, she lowered her arms and threaded them through his. Sure of only one thing, her desire for him to be where he wanted to be, she fumbled his belt loose. The dull clink of the metal tongue flopping against the buckle sent a fresh shiver of excitement along her spine.

His hand stilled her efforts. "If we make a child, you'll have to marry me, Alicia."

She froze for an instant. "It's the wrong time of the month." *Thank heaven.* "I wouldn't take that kind of risk for three minutes of sex—even with you."

Caleb left her long enough to close the door and bolt it.

Heart thundering from desire and bravado, she hiked her skirt and released her drawers.

Three minutes? In his state of arousal, it took several heartbeats to comprehend her meaning. If she thought they'd make love for no longer than three minutes, she was mistaken.

Watching her in the near darkness, he realized that was exactly what she'd meant. True, the harsh environs of the wood shop offered a poor substitute for a bed where he'd linger and take his time exploring every delicious inch of her body. But three minutes?

"What are you doing?" she asked.

"Lighting a lantern so I can see you."

"No! What if Maude or Jeremy looks in the windows?"

The panic in her voice stayed his hand. He glanced at the windows and doubted anyone would look in. If they did, the high panes allowed little visibility inside the structure.

Seeking to allay her concerns, he gathered her in a loose embrace. As she drew near, his hips arched, thrusting his erection straining the confines of his trousers into the soft folds of her skirts over her belly. In the fading rays of twilight, he thumbed an errant lock of hair from her forehead.

"You're trembling."

Her head dipped briefly.

"I won't hurt you."

"I know."

He felt the warmth radiate though the fabric of her blouse. Damn, she was frightened. But of what? "Do you want to change your mind? Go back to the house?" His heart sank as he spoke. The thought of leaving in the morning without having known the sweetness promised by her kiss gnawed at him.

The delicate movement of her hands sliding up his forearms was her answer. The way her fingers explored and glided over his exposed flesh made him wish he was naked.

"Kiss me so I don't have to think," she whispered.

He drew her closer and complied with her request by laying a slow, deliberate siege to her senses. He cupped her chin in the web of his thumb and forefinger. Ever so lightly, he kissed her forehead, then each of her temples.

"I want you to think when I kiss you," he breathed against her ear. "Think about me, Alicia."

With the softness of a hummingbird's wing, he kissed her eyes, all the while massaging the back of her neck and gauging the tension in her taut muscles.

"Think about what I do that you like." His lips moved down her nose, then laid a trail back to her forehead to start over. "Tell me what pleases you . . . or if I do something you don't like," he whispered between kisses.

Tiny tremors vibrated from her fingertips, which traced all the places on his face that he kissed on hers. His foray broadened across her cheekbones. He caught an earlobe between his lips, then nibbled and gently nipped it with his teeth. The scent of clean, warm woman filled his nostrils with heady impact.

Lost in the captivating thrill of her fingers exploring his face, he heard the song she'd sung to him in the rain echo in his head. Those frozen moments in time had changed his world. Now, he felt the power of the caged passion within her. With every fiber of his being he wanted to free her from whatever she feared, fly with her in ecstasy, and experience the bliss. Her generous heart promised more than he'd ever dared to dream. And he wanted it all, starting with her delectable body.

Savoring every touch and kiss, he sipped at the corners of her mouth. Her warm breath smelled of wine. He knew the taste of her and craved it again. Yet he took his time and traced the line of her jaw and chin with restrained kisses.

"Caleb," she whispered as he brushed his mouth against hers.

"Did I do something you didn't like?" The tip of his tongue explored the corner of her parted lips, then slid across to the other side.

"No. I . . ."

He knew what she wanted, but he held back, determined their first time wouldn't be a mindless coupling. His other senses exalted in his wise determination and restraint. He wanted to drown in her essence, to glory in pleasuring her.

The delicate fingers wound in his hair closed tightly, drawing him closer, directing his mouth to hers. The rapacious hunger of the beast within him lunged for the nectar of her kiss. The tethers restraining him slackened as her tongue invaded his mouth. For a moment he indulged the need to experience her on all levels, then drew the reins of his desire tight.

Breathing raggedly, Alicia explored his mouth, her aching breasts pressed against the wall of his chest. The desperate need to be part of him incinerated all but the wildest, errant thoughts. The power he commanded over her senses fed her rampaging desire.

Then his hands were moving over her shoulders and back, sliding along her ribs. Shock waves of anticipation shot through her each time he neared her breasts.

Without warning, his hands closed around her hips and lifted her. A small cry escaped as she broke the kiss and clung to his neck and shoulders. He carried her a short distance, then set her on the edge of a workbench. With deliberate slowness, he eased her thighs apart and moved into the breach.

As the shock ebbed, she laughed, burying her face in the crook of his neck and shoulder. The trace of her fingers over his cheek told of his grin in the darkness of the room. "Am I your project now?"

"Most definitely, my lady. My workbench, my project—our pleasure."

She wished she could see his face and the emotion reflected in his eyes. The anonymity of darkness hid her craven desire from his scrutiny. In the light, he might see the love burning in her heart.

She let her hands drift along the broad ledges of his shoulders, then lower. One by one, her trembling fingers slipped the buttons of his shirt free. From watching him work on the building he constructed in the yard, she'd memorized every muscle, cord, and sinew of his chest and back. The tingling sensation that plagued her fingers on those occasions returned. At last, she was free to touch, explore, and taste him.

Cloaked by darkness, she grew brazen. The tails of Caleb's shirt slipped easily from his waistband, and palms flat, fingers splayed, Alicia's hands crept up from his abdomen. Silken chest hair slithered through the webs of her fingers. The small nubs of his nipples protruded from the thick mat heaviest over his pectorals. Awed by the magnificence of him, she explored higher, forcing the shirt over his shoulders. A tremulous smile curled her mouth when he shrugged off the garment and let it fall into the dark abyss surrounding them.

"You're like a granite fantasy heated by the summer sun. But you feel like satin and velvet," she marveled, running her hands over his shoulders and down his upper arms.

"Don't stop," he whispered.

She doubted that she could. Her hands had assumed a mind of their own. Her passion overtook her senses as it had threatened since their first meeting; the need to know him completely banished all caution. It stripped away her reserve.

"I watched you work in the yard," she whispered, part of her shocked by the admission. "I wanted to touch you like this a thousand times."

He groaned, fumbling with the last button on her blouse.

With two fingers, she traced the pattern of his chest hair as it narrowed along his abdomen. The waistband of his trousers rebuffed her foray, sending her upward. Dimly, she felt her will no longer belonged to her. A powerful force had robbed her reluctance and disintegrated all caution. In place of the self-conscious control freak fearful of her inadequacies with men, a brazen woman lacking inhibition flourished and strengthened. Alicia reveled in the newly discovered aspect of herself emerging in the darkness. Once, long ago, she had known this side of her nature.

The cool brush of her blouse inching down her arms caught her attention. She relinquished the garment, all the while trying to see Caleb's face in the night. The ties on her chemise released with a gentle tug.

The throb in her breasts blossomed into an ache. Her breath quickened and her hands moved faster, more deliberately across the planes of his chest. The contagious urgency cast a fine sheen of perspiration across his shoulders.

He caught her wrist and helped her ease her arm through the chemise. When it lay around her waist, he lifted her wrists to his shoulders.

All the breath rushed from her lungs as he drew her into his iron embrace. The pounding of his heart against her sensitive breasts infused an unexpected completeness to her existence. Being so close to him, so near the joining that made them one, imparted a sense of righteousness.

Unbidden, her legs locked around him. She kissed his shoulder and tasted the salt of his perspiration. A faint trembling in his arms reverberated along her spine.

She whispered his name, then met his mouth in a thought-devouring kiss. As though he couldn't get enough, he slanted his mouth repeatedly over hers. She greedily met his entreaty and demanded more.

A cry of delight escaped into his mouth when his hands closed around her breasts. The marvelous glide of his thumbs skimming her hardened nipples sent her back arching and her hips squirming. The press of his erection in the cleft of her womanhood showered the pyre raging in her with fuel.

To her dismay, he broke the kiss, then delighted her by creating a trail of fire along her neck with his mouth. Her head arched back. The sublime excitement of her nipples being rolled between his thumbs and forefingers set her back on her palms, her breasts jutting toward him in blatant expectation. And he didn't disappoint her. She bit her lip to stifle a cry of pleasure when he captured a nipple in his mouth.

"You are even more beautiful than I'd dreamed," he murmured.

The reverence in his voice crested a wave of satisfaction over her pleasure. "You can't see me," she whispered.

"Oh, but I can, Alicia. I can." His hands closed on her ribs. With an artist's touch, he sculpted her abdomen, carefully measuring and weighing her breasts and giving special attention to the pebbled nipples basking in the adoration he lavished so freely. "I see you with my hands. I could sculpt you with my eyes closed."

"Carve me later. Just don't stop," she breathed, intoxicated by the flurry of sensations he created.

A soft chuckle vibrated his lips against her sensitive flesh. "There is no stopping now, my lady."

He abandoned her breasts for her legs. She loosened her hold on him, then reveled in the sinuous glide of his hands under her skirts. He moved like lava, hot, permeating, and inexorable in pursuit of his goal. And she relished each movement, feeling the leash on her desire strain as he reached the apex he sought. The quaking in her intensified.

"I want you, Caleb."

"You have me."

"Inside me."

"Soon. Very soon," he promised, bowing his head to her chest.

The pleasure of his mouth on her breast and his fingers exploring the cleft of her femininity sent her arching back with a muted cry of delight. Captivated by the mounting spiral of need and pleasure he created, Alicia felt something foreign building in her. Before she understood, he abandoned her breasts, scooted her to the edge of the workbench, and lowered his mouth to the gate of her womanhood.

Thought ceased. Sensation ruled. She wanted. Needed. Something. Something beautiful and building with the force of a typhoon.

Barely able to catch her breath, she cried out Caleb's name. It was magic. Real magic. Like a bubble filled with sweet scented colors, it expanded, ready to explode.

Suddenly, everything hung in suspension. He had stopped weaving the magic.

"Alicia," came his raspy demand.

The next thing she knew, he was gathering her to him. She went eagerly, clinging, needy. The elusive bubble was just out of reach, but still there.

He entered her slowly, groaning as she buried her face against his neck. The bubble floated closer. As though to keep it, her legs locked around his waist. She surged against him, drawing him deep inside.

"Reach for it," he urged in a strained voice, his hips driving him into her with an increasing intensity.

She reached.

The bubble exploded, showering her with a rainbow of bliss, lifting her higher and higher into the heart of the shower. She cried out his name, then savored the ecstasy twinkling in every nerve ending she possessed.

When she floated down to awareness, she felt him hot and trembling, barely breathing in the stillness surrounding them. She held him and languished in his powerful arms.

"I didn't think I was capable . . ." she admitted before the sound of her confession brought her firmly back to herself.

"You're going to do it again. This time with me."

His promise sent goose bumps along her body. In terms of real experience, she'd never known such an intimate or complete loving.

The slow, shallow pace he set ignited fires she'd thought quenched. The thunder of his heart sent her blood roaring. His passion became hers.

Hungry kisses and deeper, quicker strokes built their mutual need. They became one entity, breathing, moving together. Alicia sensed the bubble of pleasure again rising and gasped for breath. As though to hold it and draw it closer, she felt the walls of her body tighten around Caleb.

"Alicia," he gasped.

The agony in his raspy whisper doubled the size of the bubble and sent it dancing with sparkling lights in every color she'd ever imagined.

"Oh, yes," he ground from between his teeth. "Stay with me."

Then he was with her. The bubble burst in slow motion, lifting them, showering them with joy, rainbows, bliss, and a million delicious kisses of light.

153

She held Caleb and basked amid the euphoric glow. In his arms for that moment, she knew she'd seen heaven and had, in fact, been there. How long they clung to each other, she neither knew, nor cared. Pure contentment cloaked her being as he stroked her hair and occasionally kissed her.

Eventually the night chill settled on them. Without a word, they helped each other dress. Caleb lit a lantern, then retrieved her drawers from where she'd let them fall.

A tinge of awkwardness settled on Alicia. "What does one say after such an incredible experience?"

"Figure it out and let me know when I get back."

She closed her eyes and swallowed, suddenly very tired. "That's right, you're leaving in the morning."

"Think about me while I'm gone." He kissed her forehead, then released her.

She started toward the door. Not daring to look back, she headed for the light Maude had left inside the mud porch. If she weren't careful, Caleb Marker would destroy every concept she valued. Not that she objected to him destroying the myth of her inability to achieve orgasm.

At the back porch, she paused and looked back. Light from the lantern glowing in the wood shop outlined Caleb with the ethereal glow of a halo. He stood at the door, watching. Waiting.

Chapter Thirteen

The crisp morning cast a fond light on the memory of the previous night's passion. Alicia struggled to concentrate on Mariah's lessons. In resignation, she gave the girl a piece of chalk and set up a penmanship exercise on the chalkboard.

She wandered outside to the wood shop. The structure appeared the same as it had yesterday morning, or the morning before that. Had she expected it to change because of what transpired between her and Caleb?

An invisible wave thrilled her from the tip of her toes to the crown of her head whenever she thought of the wondrous feelings he'd stirred in her. Part of her sighed in relief each time. Perhaps the man made the difference. In a bright morning sun almost as brilliant as the afterglow of their intimacy, there was nowhere to hide from her feelings for Caleb.

She had loved Chet. In retrospect, she admitted that if she'd had a brother, she'd have wanted him to be like Chet. And perhaps therein lay the crux of the problem: He had been her friend and the brother she'd never had.

155

The passion reserved for a lover had never awakened. For either of them, she realized.

Caleb evoked no such fraternal emotions. To the contrary, he exuded a raw, pulsing sexuality. He made everything in her sing.

With her tug on the latch, the wood shop door swung open on well-oiled hinges. She closed her eyes and breathed deeply. Whether by force of will or imagination, she recaptured the perfume of their passion amid the lingering aromas of wood and paint.

Of all the places on his land, none held his essence more than the wood shop. Last night, he'd created her as a whole woman here. As his project, he had placed her on his lowest workbench and sculpted her raw, wild, fearful emotions into something more beautiful than could be imagined. He'd freed her from herself like he freed the images hiding in a piece of wood.

Remembering the ecstasy and quiet intimacy afterward curled her lips into a satisfied smile. Caleb couldn't possibly know the magnitude of the gift he'd given her. For the first time, the passionate side of her soul had soared. Gone were the oppressive doubts, the inhibitions, and the self-condemnation she'd known too long.

"Thank you, Caleb," she whispered. He'd given her a precious gift no one could take away.

Opening her eyes, she wandered to the workbench where they'd made love. In the fingers of sunlight poking through the windows, she saw the memento he had left for her. A simple wooden ring bound the stems of two sprigs of forget-me-nots.

"Oh, Caleb, when did you find time for this?" she whispered, blinking back sudden tears.

Turning the flowers in her hand, she slipped the ring off the stems. *Alicia Marker* was carved inside the polished circle.

"Not marriage," she repeated. "You don't know me, either."

Nor could she afford telling him more than he already knew about her life in Wyoming. If things were different, she'd consider taking the leap of faith and trusting him with her heart.

But things were the way they were. He'd never believe, and therefore, never trust her if she told him the only explanation for her presence lay in a prophecy she couldn't remember. How could he? Some days, she struggled for belief, too.

She slipped the ring into her pocket. When he came home, she'd return it.

"What are you doing?"

Mariah's innocent question startled her. She spun around and forced a smile. "Checking."

"On what?" Mariah came to her side and wrapped her arms around Alicia's waist. "Your garden-thing Daddy built?"

"He painted it last night. He thought it might be dry by tonight. Tomorrow morning we'll move it and fill it."

"I miss him when he goes away. I wish he didn't have to leave so much." Big gray eyes turned up to Alicia. "Do you miss him, too?"

"I suppose so." Her smile became genuine. "He's easy to have around the place, isn't he?"

"I guess so." The child's brow narrowed. "What does that mean?"

Alicia laughed softly and hugged Maria. "It means he's a nice person whom you enjoy being with."

"Oh, yes. I love him. Do you love him, too?"

Focusing on the entwined flowers, Alicia's smile faded. "Your Daddy is a good man and very thoughtful." Regretfully, she placed the forget-me-nots back where she'd found them. "What say we saddle Krakatau and go for a ride. When we get back, I'll put you on Edgy."

"Oh, yes. I'd like that."

"Then let's do it." There was only one place Alicia wished to go. She needed a bastion of purpose against the turmoil testing her convictions.

A short while later, flanked by Caesar and Nero on the road to town, Alicia let Mariah take the reins.

"Are we going to Mr. Kratz's?" Mariah craned her head back to encourage a positive answer.

"We might. Have you ever been to a cemetery, Mariah?"

Her gray eyes grew wide. "Un-unh. Everybody's dead there," she whispered.

Alicia smiled patiently. "The cemetery is where their bodies rest. Trust me, they were dead before they got there."

"Is that where we're going?" The excitement had faded from the little girl's lips.

"If you don't mind. However, if you're uncomfortable or would just prefer not to, we'll ride somewhere else." What had Caleb told the girl about death and the hereafter? Anything?

"How come you want to go there, Miss James? Did someone you know die?"

Alicia shook her head and gazed down the road. "No. It's not that. Ever since I was a little girl, my sisters and I used to sing at the cemetery in Drexel. It was sort of a tradition handed down to us by our mother."

"Your mama sang to cemeteries?"

The awe in Mariah's voice made Alicia smile. It did sound a little odd explaining what might be perceived as macabre by a five-year-old. "Mama was a wonderful, kind woman who looked for the goodness in people. She didn't believe anyone should leave this life without a song of celebration for the joy they had experienced and created while alive. Some folks have more joy than others. And most don't realize you have to make your own happiness."

Funny she should remember that now. How could she make herself happy here? Yet, how could she leave the Marker home and find happiness anywhere else? What a dilemma.

"So you and your mama sang for those people?"

"Yes, we did."

"But how could they hear you if they were dead?"

Alicia laughed aloud. "Some people believe the body

158

dies, Mariah. The spirit that makes you, you, and me, me, keeps on living. You can't see them. But at night, if you look up at the stars, you can see all those spirits looking down and smiling with a twinkle."

"Honest?"

Again, she laughed. "Did your daddy tell you about the cycle of life?"

Solemnly, Mariah shook her head. "No. I just learned about the cycle of summer and winter."

"The cycle of life is sort of like that. If you watch the land, you can see the young plants sprout from seeds in the spring. They bloom in the summer and set out their seeds for the next cycle in the fall."

"In winter, they die, don't they?"

"Some do. People seasons are different from those of plants and trees. Some people live many seasons. Others, only a few." She leaned forward and caught a glimpse of Mariah's contemplation.

"So when a person doesn't have anymore seasons," the child asked hesitantly, "she becomes a star and comes back in the spring?"

Alicia bit her bottom lip, knowing she was on shaky ground regarding the child's beliefs of reincarnation and religion. "Some people believe that," she said. It was definitely time to switch gears. "Regardless, it's best to look for goodness rather than worry about the bad in people. Which is not to say there aren't bad people. There are, Mariah. Your daddy, Maude, and I will try to help you tell the difference. Meanwhile, you'll have to trust us to know what's best."

"Oh, I know you're a good person, Miss James." The little girl touched her heart and tilted her head back to see Alicia. "I feel it here."

Alicia placed a kiss on Mariah's forehead. "That's what you should listen to, sweetheart. The rest will take care of itself." But as she spoke the words, she wondered. Following her own heart's desire promised disaster.

"We should sing at the cemetery," Mariah said softly. "Will you teach me the songs?"

"Absolutely." Alicia took the reins and guided Krakatau off the road and over the ridge.

She and Mariah dismounted and approached the deserted graveyard with Caesar and Nero ambling alongside.

Alicia held Mariah's hand and closed her eyes. For a moment, she was back in Drexel holding Caitlyn's hand and standing between Bethany and their mother. She began to sing, her voice gaining strength and power. The pure notes reverberated across the aged grave markers. The brief, familiar link with her old life soothed her worries. Peace settled over her.

Although fate separated the James sisters, singing among these headstones and hearing their voices weave with hers in her memory felt right to Alicia. Each of them had to find her own destiny. They could not live one anothers' lives, and had perhaps leaned upon each other too long.

Alicia opened her eyes, content. Ready or not, the time of living for herself, by herself, was upon her. The challenge seemed enormous. The excuse of responsibility for her sisters was no longer hers: The molding of her destiny rested in her hands alone.

Reflecting on the changes, she marveled at how little she missed her job at United Growers. A short time ago, her life had revolved around the lab. The suspicion that United Growers was where she had hid, not where she had lived, settled uncomfortably upon Alicia. She cast it aside for more important matters.

Why am I here? she wondered again.

Mariah squeezed her hand.

In a flash of insight, she understood. This little girl needed her almost as much as Alicia needed to nurture and love her in return.

And what of Caleb? How would she resolve that dilemma? Or did it have a satisfactory resolution? Not every question has an answer, she reminded herself.

When she glanced around, two women regarded her from the far side of a fresh grave. Watching them, she sang a final song for the loved one they obviously grieved for.

"Thank you," said the more elderly of the two. She was clad in a black shawl drawn over her head.

"God go with you," Alicia answered, then took Mariah back to Krakatau.

As the horse carried them down the hill, the child took Alicia's hand and kissed the back of it. "I want to learn to sing like you. I bet the stars all twinkle very brightly tonight 'cause you sang for them. Don't never leave us, Miss James."

Alicia swallowed the lump in her throat. "I'm not planning on it, sweetheart." She squeezed the girl's hand. "You know, I'll bet Mr. Kratz has some ice cream. Shall we find out?"

Mariah nodded. "I love ice cream, but I think I love you more."

"More than ice cream? My, but that's a whole bunch, isn't it?" She leaned down and whispered conspiratorially, "I love you more than ice cream, too. So, since we have each other, let's have ice cream, too."

"And you'll teach me to sing?"

"I'll do the best I can," she said, hoping the child had a voice to train.

"At the graveyard, so we can have—what did you call it?"

"Tradition?"

"Yes. Then I can pretend you're my new mama even if you don't like my daddy more than ice cream."

The trouble was, she did like him more than ice cream, and damn near everything else.

Everything was going to hell. Caleb felt it in his bones. Problems at the lumber camp had kept him away from home longer than anticipated. The three days he'd calculated turned into five, then seven. Although anxious to return home, he had visited Norm Slidell in Sitka first. Even a seasoned, careful logger like Norm couldn't have foreseen the treetop that sent him crashing when it snapped unexpectedly.

Norm would be laid up for the rest of the summer, but at least he'd mend as good as new. After Caleb paid the doctor, he dropped in on Otto Kratz's cafe.

"I heard about Norm Slidell," Otto said, shaking Caleb's hand. "Too bad he got hurt. Guess it leaves you short-handed up in the trees."

"Norm will be laid up for a while. There are a couple of loggers interested in joining the crew. Meanwhile, I'd like to take care of Norm's meals for the next couple of months." Caleb dug into his pocket.

Otto stayed his hand. "I'll run a tab. Greta will deliver the food. Not to worry."

"Thanks, Otto."

"You need coffee."

Tired and dirty, Caleb nodded. "Yeah, I do. Strong as you have."

"I don't care what you say. It ain't right," intruded a sharp voice with the sting of a wasp. "It's improper for her to drag that little girl into a cemetery and force her to sing."

The pitch of the woman's voice grated on Caleb's nerves. He tried ignoring the rest of the patrons, but the woman's companion responded with equal vehemence.

"As much as that girl laughs, I doubt she's tied with a rope and dragged up the hill. What's wrong with singing in a cemetery?"

Caleb hunched his shoulders and reached for the coffee Otto set before him. Normally, he disregarded the conversations of gossips, but . . . a woman and a child, at a cemetery, singing? An unsettled feeling nagging what little remained of his patience prodded him. "What are they talking about?" he asked Otto.

"Miss James and Mariah. Miss James is teaching Mariah how to sing. Sarah Frost doesn't approve of anything anyone does, unless they do it how she pleases."

Caleb's blood ran cold, then burned. Alicia was taking Mariah to the cemetery? To sing? What the hell was wrong with teaching the girl to sing at home? The damn cemetery?

The lump of ire slid down his throat with a slug of hot coffee. "Miss James has her own way of doing things and Mariah is benefiting from it." His statement, spoken louder than he'd intended, carried a confidence he didn't feel.

"Your little girl worships the ground Miss James walks on, Caleb. You're a lucky man to have found her for a caretaker. Bet you didn't think you'd ever find anyone you'd approve of for Mariah." Otto motioned at his nearly empty cup. "More?"

Caleb shook his head and popped a coin onto the table. "Thanks, but I'm going home. Tell Greta thanks, too." He rose and started for the door. "By the way, Norm eats a lot."

Otto lifted his hand in acknowledgment. "Never knew a logger who didn't."

With a final glance at the women arguing at the table near the window, Caleb departed. All the way home, he tried to convince himself there was a logical explanation for Alicia's actions. But what?

"Daddy! You're finally home. I'm so happy!" Mariah bolted upright in bed.

Startled, Alicia leaped to her feet and whirled toward the bedroom door. Alarmed, she clutched the bedtime storybook against her breast. Caleb's raven hair swirled in a disheveled fashion around his ears and forehead, nearly hiding the distinct arches of his eyebrows. The look he gave Alicia warned of an anger barely held in check.

The surge of joy she derived from his presence froze in her chest. The mouth that had lavished unspeakable pleasure remained pressed in a line of hard, unreadable emotion.

Shaken, Alicia dropped her gaze to the child eager for the reassurance of her daddy's strong arms.

"How's my girl?" Caleb asked Mariah as he crossed the room.

"I missed you." Mariah's outstretched arms and wiggling fingers closed around her father's neck. As though to prove it, she showered his face with giggling kisses.

"Careful. I haven't shaved for a week," he warned with a chuckle.

"But your whiskers are soft." Mariah's small hand stroked Caleb's cheek.

Alicia wished she could do the same and wondered whether his beard was as soft as it looked.

Each hour of the four days he'd been overdue had stretched into eternity. Now, studying the condition of his clothing and boots, she knew Caleb had ridden hard to get home. Yet, his aloof demeanor hinted that fatigue wasn't the sole reason for his rough appearance. Had he also done some hard thinking this past week?

A sudden emptiness opened in Alicia. "Would you like to finish Mariah's bedtime story?" she asked, unable to tear her gaze from him.

Caleb kissed Mariah's cheek, then tucked her in. "Yes."

"You must be hungry. I'll see if Maude can find something for you." She offered the book to Caleb, then smiled down at Mariah.

"Do that. And join me." He grasped the book, then held it until she met his commanding gaze. "Please."

"All right," she agreed, noting the sharpness of the lines running along his temples and framing his mouth.

"Thank you." Dismissing her, he focused his attention on Mariah.

Alicia departed, wondering what had delayed him at the lumber camp and darkened his usually good humor. So much remained unspoken between them.

Perhaps he'd realized he'd jumped the gun by carving a wedding ring for her to find. Perhaps he'd found himself in an uncomfortable predicament he felt honor-bound to resolve.

As tenderhearted as he was, he'd probably struggled with how to tell her. But he should have. Lord knew, she had experienced the awful punishment of being trapped in a relationship for the wrong reasons.

She'd make it easy for him to state his change of mind—and try not to offend him by exposing the ambiguity flowing through her like sunshine and storm clouds.

Convinced he'd come to his senses, Alicia helped Maude prepare a plate for Caleb. When the housekeeper retired for the night, Alicia set about pouring a cup of coffee.

"Would you pour one for me, please?"

The unexpected sound of Caleb's voice startled her. Hot liquid sloshed over the rim of the cup and onto her hand.

He took the coffeepot and the steaming cup and quickly set them on the sideboard.

Alicia rinsed the scalded area with cool water, then patted it dry. Wordlessly, she fetched a knife and left the kitchen. Caleb followed her through the house and out the front door.

"What are you doing?" he demanded.

"Just getting some aloe. Fortunately, Mrs. Hamilton grows it in her solar. Someone told her I tried ordering aloe plants through Hamilton Traders. She sent a plant there for me. I brought it home and planted it in our little garden on wheels." She sliced through the top of the largest spike on the plant. "Too much water rots their roots, and they can't survive a hard freeze."

She smeared the gelatinous moisture squeezed from the plant onto the reddened area of the scald. "This will help."

"A kiss from your oozing plant makes it better?" He smiled at her for the first time since returning home.

"Yes." The urge to run her fingertips along the uplifted corners of his mouth made her forget the sting of the burn. "It's an old, natural remedy."

"Come." With the command, he took possession of her arm and guided her to the veranda swing. "Sit."

She complied, watching him cautiously.

"Stay."

"I'm not Nero or Caesar," she said to his retreating back.

"You sure as hell aren't, and I'd never confuse you with them."

Before she could fling the retort on the tip of her tongue, he disappeared into the house. He'd shaved before he'd come down. Well, life was full of surprises. Maybe some other time she'd get an opportunity to find out how soft his whiskers became with what had to have been a week's growth.

She examined her hand. It wouldn't blister, but it would smart for a while yet. She heard Caleb return and didn't look up. Maybe it would be easier for him if she didn't seek his gaze.

A cup half-filled with coffee moved into the field of her vision. "If you want more, I'll get it."

"I thought you were going to eat," she said, offering him a reprieve.

"I'm not hungry. What I'd like to do is talk."

"I'm not going anywhere." She sipped her drink and stared into the cup. "You were gone longer than we expected. I hope everything worked out for you."

"It will. In time." He pulled a chair around and sat with one foot braced against the seat of the swing. "Sometimes things don't happen the way you plan."

"Oh, I understand perfectly. The less said, the better, on those occasions." He didn't have to elaborate on the reasons for changing his mind. Moments of lucidity struck even the craziest person. Not that Caleb was crazy. However, the notion of them getting married lacked the rationale of sanity.

"When not enough is said, surprises can stop you in your tracks."

Apparently, he needed to state his reasons. "I don't like surprises." Or did she? The last one had brought her here. But at what price? Her sisters. The realization lacked the sharpness it had possessed before the first day at the cemetery with Mariah. The mother hen in her had freed her chicks. Now they, like she, must fend for themselves.

"I've given a lot of thought to what you said the night before I left."

The odd strain in his voice forced Alicia to steal a glimpse of him as he studied the contents of his coffee cup. So he had listened after all. That should have made it easier to see the wisdom of the conclusion he'd obviously drawn.

"And?" Go for the heart, she decided. Let him say it and get it over with for both of them.

"You're right. There's a great deal I don't know about you."

"I know even less about you, Caleb."

"That isn't relevant."

Alicia bristled and glared at him. "Excuse me? Not relevant? Would you care to elaborate on that statement? Or just plain retract it?" Did she look like a one-way street? Even in 1895, people must have told each other something. After all, there wasn't any TV or radio. No phones. Lord, they had to talk to one another—in the winter, at least.

"I thought I knew what I needed to know about you concerning attitudes, beliefs, and habits. You never revealed any unusual behavior in my presence." His gaze when he met hers sent a chill down her spine. "And I watched. Closely."

"How could you possibly think you know all there is to know about me? I've only been here since June, and you've been gone a lot of that time." Did he think there was so little to her? No, no, her logical side crooned. *He's thought things through and realizes we're playing with fire. Let him go. Free him, and yourself.*

"However, you're right," she conceded lightheartedly. "Sometimes re-evaluation and reflection can clear the air. Quit beating around the bush, Caleb. Say what you have to say. It really is all right. We'll forget it ever happened."

Caleb set his coffee cup on the porch and cocked his head. He stared at her for a long moment in open bewilderment before asking, "What the hell are you talking about?"

Men had no appreciation for a woman's insight. With an exasperated sigh, she determined to end the jousting.

"I'm talking about you deciding it was a mistake to leave a wedding ring for me to think about. I'm trying to tell you it's fine. I haven't changed my mind about marriage for any reason, so let's forget it."

Caleb balanced his chair on its two back legs and cradled his coffee mug over his abdomen. "It wasn't a mistake, and I haven't changed my mind, either."

The blood drained from Alicia's cheeks. She felt it sink to her toes, and her skin turned cold and pale. "You haven't? Then . . . then what are you talking about?"

"I was talking about you and Mariah."

Mariah? How could she have been so wrong? And what did Mariah have to do with anything? "Mariah?"

"I heard you've been taking her to the cemetery."

"What's wrong with that?"

"I don't want her there. She's too damn young. She doesn't understand death or grieving, even though she's had more than her share for a child her age."

Slowly, the heart of his objection penetrated her confusion. His reasons dawned with startling clarity. "Because of her mother?"

"If you want to go, do so on your time off, or leave Mariah with Maude when I'm gone. Work it out between you, but don't take Mariah to the cemetery again."

An odd twinge of disappointment forced her gaze across the yard to the stately trees pushing the evening breeze inland. "You'll explain it to her?"

"Yes."

"I see," she whispered. "If we pretend it doesn't exist, she won't have to face death even though it's part of life. That way she can be as lost as most adults are the first time they bury someone they love."

"She's not going to bury anyone," he insisted, letting the front legs of his chair thud onto the porch.

"She already has. And she knows it. She doesn't speak of it, but she knows it. How can she not, Caleb? She's so hungry for a mother and permanency. . . ." Her voice faded into a hushed stillness. She'd brought them back to square one. How had this happened?

Alicia cleared her throat and set her cup on the rail as she stood. "We've read every name in the cemetery. Do you know what Mariah uses the crosses and markers for?"

Caleb met her question with silence.

Undaunted, Alicia continued in a serene tone that hid the tumult roiling inside her. "She uses the markers as notes. She wants to learn the songs I sing the way my sisters and I learned.

"We learned in a graveyard, Caleb. Each marker or cross represents a note. When I point to one, Mariah sings that note, just as we did. She wants to do this because it was a tradition my mother started with us when we were Mariah's age. She wants to be part of something she can pass on, because it's a legacy of love. Maybe singing in a graveyard isn't your idea of an appropriate tradition handed down or perpetuated among people who love one another. I understand that. But before you speak with Mariah, you'd best know there is more involved than you see at first glance."

Alicia heaved a sigh. "Do you really think I would have *forced* her to go with me to a cemetery?" She glanced over her shoulder at him.

"No. But you wouldn't have to. She'd do damn near anything for you."

"And you think I'd let her do something that made her uncomfortable in order to please myself?"

"I didn't look at it that way."

"Well, give it a try, and let me know what you come up with. Meanwhile, I think we'd better say good-night." Angry and hurt, she snatched up her empty cup.

"Did going to graveyards with your mother help you prepare for death?"

Recalling her mother and father's graveside service, she stiffened. "Nothing prepares you for the loss of both parents. Nothing prepares you for the fact that the drunk who forced them off the road at sixty miles per hour is walking around and breathing the same air you are. But it did help with closure on accepting they were gone. Every time I sing at a graveside, I think of my mother. How can I not?

169

Sometimes, I can almost feel her standing beside me and hear her voice in my memory."

Caleb rose and pushed the chair back with his legs. The grating noise marked a change in the stormy aura surrounding him. "I don't think I understood part of that. How does a drunk force people off the road? Nothing goes sixty miles an hour."

Alicia closed her eyes and swallowed hard. This time, he'd caught her slip and called her on it. "It doesn't matter. It's just a colloquialism from Wyoming. It means they're dead and the man responsible for their deaths isn't. Life isn't fair, but sometimes a little justice would be appreciated."

"I see. About Mariah . . . I'm willing to consider your opinion in this," Caleb murmured. "We'll talk again before I speak with her."

Sensing there was nothing more to say on the subject, she reached into her pocket and withdrew the wooden ring he'd left for her. "This is yours."

"Keep it." He folded her fingers around the ring in her palm.

"I can't."

"Then throw it in the kindling basket."

"I won't. You made it." She removed her hand from his and turned the ring over in her palm. "I can't imagine when you had the time. And the flowers—" She shook her head, still amazed by the thoughtful gift.

"Regrets, Alicia?"

"Many, but not for making love with you," she whispered. "I'm too selfish to regret the magic you created."

"Thank God," he breathed. Visible relief eased the rigidity from his shoulders.

"It would be wise if we didn't repeat it. It seems when it comes to sex, those who don't want children usually end up with them, while those who are desperate to have children go wanting. All things considered, we belong to the first category."

Caleb exhaled sharply. "I've never heard it put like that, but I suppose it's true."

She mustered the courage to meet the heated gaze warming her face. "Neither one of us wants to bring a child into this world under these circumstances."

His silence spoke louder than any words.

"I've never gotten away with much in life, Caleb. *I* don't want to have a child now. *I* don't want to be pressed into a difficult situation. *I* don't want to choose between leaving and having a child on my own or a marriage both of us aren't comfortable with." Color rose into her cheeks.

Sorrow and some unfathomable emotion glittered in Caleb's eyes. "Do you truly believe we won't make love again, Alicia?"

The softly spoken question struck at the heart of her desire and doubts. "I'll try not to think about it."

"But you do, don't you?"

"Caleb . . ."

"You think about it in the middle of doing something during the day. The nights are worse, aren't they? You dream about what led to the little piece of heaven we found together. You don't want to dream about it, do you? The desire builds, waiting for the next time. You can't help it any more than I can."

"I think about a lot of things. I don't act on them."

"While you're thinking about what you don't think we should do again, think about me thinking how sweet the magic was and how much I want us to experience it again."

He closed her fingers around the ring he'd made her. "Do you realize how backward this is?"

"It's not backward. Women have borne the responsibility of keeping a clear head and saying *no* since Eve."

"I'm talking about the marriage part of it. Women use sex to get a proposal. More than a few men have fallen into the trap."

"I don't want to trap you, Caleb."

"You've made that very clear. I won't bring the subject of marriage up again. At least, not without a reason."

The relief she expected didn't come.

"But I won't stop wanting you, either. I doubt it's possible. Still, I'll try to keep my distance if that's what you wish."

Head bowed, Alicia murmured her appreciation. She didn't look up until he'd left the veranda. Inexplicable sorrow descended as she watched him cross the yard in the direction of the wood shop. Each time she even glanced at the building, she recalled every vivid detail of their lovemaking.

Tonight, she'd won an easy victory over Caleb's logic. Her path was sane, sensible. So why did she feel like she'd lost something precious?

Chapter Fourteen

Alicia padded through the mud room door and into the night. On the porch, Caesar begged for attention with a nudge against her leg. She scratched between his ears, her thoughts on Caleb.

Beyond the confines of the Marker walls, the world loomed enormous and clear. Overhead, low clouds scudded across the half-moon. A cool summer breeze swept up from the sea. The cloudy mist rode along and darted among the treetops in a game of night tag. The wisps mirrored the tumult racing through her mind. Nothing slowed long enough for her to grasp.

The crisp air penetrated her flannel nightgown still damp from the perspiration of a dream too vivid to fade with wakefulness. She reached inside the door and grabbed Maude's shawl off the peg. With a small shiver, she wrapped it tightly around her shoulders. For the moment, not even the cool summer night would drive her inside.

Caleb's proximity, so near, yet so far, heightened her reaction to the nightly visitation of sweet memories. When the intense dream woke her this time, she'd fought with every grain of self-restraint to remain in bed until the unreasonable desperation to run down the hall to Caleb's room dimmed.

If she knocked on his door, he'd greet her with a kiss that would melt her into a puddle of wax. Then he'd make love with her, just as he did in her dreams.

A shiver ran through her as she gazed to the wood shop across the grass billowing in the moonlit breeze.

In her mind's eye, the walls disintegrated. She sat upon the altar of Caleb's workbench and relived his passion. Ghostly echoes of each exciting, marvelous touch he lavished upon her love-starved body flooded through her.

Unable to endure the torrent of breathtaking memory, she walked away from the house.

Fat blades of damp grass caressed her bare feet and wrapped around her ankles. Fine rocks poked at her soles. The gentle swishing of her nightgown against the dewy grasses dampened the hem.

She picked her way across the yard until the house was well behind. Facing the giant trees, she halted and gazed at the moon playing peek-a-boo with the low clouds. Like the lingering excitement of her dream, tendrils of mist reached from the clouds and teased the treetops unmercifully.

The memory of the brief hour she and Caleb spent in his wood shop had destroyed all misconceptions that making love with him would quench her desire. To the contrary, the physical astonishment she'd experienced haunted her. Even more potent was the sensation that something rare and marvelous had passed between them. The elusive emotion defied all attempts for understanding. The nightly remembrances had robbed her of sleep during his absence. With his return, her memories assumed a potent vigor she wasn't sure she'd survive if they continued.

Absently, she dragged an errant lock of wind-blown hair from across her eyes and tucked it behind her ear. Her shoulders lifted as she drew a deep, cleansing breath. The longer she watched the clouds dance with the moon and trees, the easier it became to lose herself in the beauty of the night. However, she was not the Goddess of the Moon. Nor was she the Princess of the Forest. She was nothing special, just Alicia James from Drexel, Wyoming. And, like millions of people the moon shone its light on, she wanted what she couldn't have.

A small laugh escaped her, bringing Caesar's cold, wet snout against her hand. Hunkering onto her heels, she petted the wolf dog with both hands, then scratched behind his ears.

The century between her origins and the present formed a mountain of reasons for limiting her involvement with Caleb Marker. Already, he had caught and questioned two serious gaffes on her part. If she told him the truth, his rigid belief that all things possible lay on the pages of books would seal her fate. She hadn't seen a copy of H. G. Wells's *The Time Machine* on his bookshelves—not that Caleb would accept early science fiction as gospel.

Even now, it would break her heart if Caleb asked her to leave Mariah, and him. In their own ways, each had found gaping rents in the other's armor. Just thinking about Caleb's censure, should she reveal her origin, sent a fist of anguish squeezing her heart.

When the fist eased its horrible grip, she stood tall and strong in her purpose. For her own self-preservation, her love for Mariah, and the tender, frightening feelings she bore Caleb, she would be strong. The mind controlled the flesh. Surely, her iron will would rise to the occasion and enforce the necessary restraint.

Scratching Caesar a final time, she started for the house.

How foolish to allow a man control of her dreams. Leaving her warm bed and racing out of the house just to put distance between them bordered on ludicrous.

She mounted the steps to the veranda. When she glanced at the front door, she saw Caleb in the shadows. Fickle moonlight slashed across his bare chest and left shoulder. His face remained hidden by shadows. She willed him to stay there. If he stepped into the light, the familiar hunger in his eyes and the slight frowning twist of his mouth would erode the underpinnings of her resolve.

To her chagrin, Caleb moved out of the shadows. A line of mercurial moonlight illuminated his face.

All her carefully built resolve threatened to bolt into the night wind and hide in the flimsy mist. Her step faltered.

A sudden, severe ache for his touch shot through her with the force of a bullet. Whether bravery or weakness lifted her chin until she gazed directly at him, she didn't know. Her thundering heart skipped a beat when she met his eyes. For the briefest instant, she saw into the core of him and felt her heart exposed in return.

He would love her, cherish her. . . . He offered all of himself now. She saw the totality of the gift he wished her to accept in his eyes. The responsive chord he struck in her heart left no doubt. The heat radiating from his half-naked, aroused body promised rapture when she accepted.

Alicia yearned to run her fingers through the soft, silken whorls of chest hair glistening in the moonlight. Unbidden, she reached out, then caught herself mere inches away. She did not have to touch him to feel the rapid beat of his heart. The pulse in the hollow of his throat raced in harmony with hers. Mesmerized by raw need, her hand rose. The heat rolling off him seared her fingertips. Her breath caught in her throat.

If she touched him, she'd make love with him. She lacked the strength to turn away. And if they made love again, how much closer to disaster would they move? Love demanded trust. Honesty.

And open honesty was out of the question.

Her fingers curled into a fist she cradled between her breasts for protection.

Caleb's sharp intake of breath bespoke his disappointment.

Dry-mouthed, she felt the change in him.

Her breasts grew tender with expectation as his powerful chest expanded. A dull ache rode low in her abdomen and swelled as moisture seeped from the core of her.

With the last shred of willpower at her command, she broke the spell of his torrid gaze by closing her eyes. She released a ragged breath and tried to gather the wild emotions holding her in place. The scorching heat of his desire wilted her determination. Before it gave way, she lowered her head and lunged toward the door, bidding her reluctant feet to carry her the distance.

Strong fingers curled around her upper arm. She flinched. Her heart leaped into her throat, and her legs stopped working. Determined to remain strong and hold the crumbling line of her only defense against total devastation, she kept her head bowed. If she gazed into his eyes and again saw the depth of need in his soul, she'd be lost. She'd offer her body and her heart without regard for the price she'd pay later.

Better to love him at a distance and deny the intimacy they both craved than risk losing him completely. If he knew the truth, she'd see the disbelief, betrayal, and finally the censure that would kill the tenderness and longing she now saw in his eyes.

She forced her legs forward another step.

Caleb's hand slid down, leaving a fiery wake over her elbow and forearm.

His next move brought her up short. He captured her hand and held it. The phantom trail of his fingers permeated the sturdy fabric of Maude's shawl and her nightgown with the heat of a forbidden promise. Beneath, the slight pressure of his hand quaked against her skin. The blistering effects raced through her veins like a narcotic. The reflex of her fingers taxed her hard-won control.

The fight raging between her desire and her future filled her eyes with tears.

With an awareness tuned to his very heartbeat, she felt him shift. Unable to withstand yet another assault of her weakening determination, she raised her head and looked over her shoulder.

Tears blurred him against a wave of moonlight racing across the yard. More than anything she ached to throw herself into his arms and let tomorrow take care of itself.

She blinked. A line of crystalline regret spilled over the dam of her lashes. The gentle movement of his thumb across the back of her knuckles loosened a second cascade of tears.

When he lifted her hand to the hot, firm press of his lips, she opened her mouth in protest, but no words escaped.

She felt his resignation. His release of her hand left her bereft. Unable to withstand the potent swirl of emotions and the palpable desire churning between them, Alicia forced her legs to carry her into the house. She did not stop until she was closing her bedroom door.

She stared at the ceiling until the sun rose. The hall floorboards alerted her of Caleb's approach. He paused at her door, then continued. She wasn't sure why disappointment turned her face to the wall.

During the three days Caleb spent at home, neither Alicia nor he mentioned the episode in the moonlight. Caleb respected her desire to keep a distance and not be alone with him for more than a few moments. Mariah's oblivion to the tension between them softened the awkward moments. Only in Mariah's innocent presence did Alicia's heart smile with delight and a rare joy she cherished.

The morning of his return to the logging camp with a new topper, Alicia rose early. Loneliness enshrouded the relief she expected at his impending departure. In the early hour, the house flaunted silent reminders of him everywhere she looked.

She entered the kitchen to make the morning coffee. The aroma of a freshly brewing pot assailed her in welcome. She glanced toward the stove. Caleb stood near the sink and gazed out the window.

"Good morning, Alicia," he said, his back to her.

Alicia murmured a greeting, then poured a cup. "Have you told her?"

"Told who what?"

"Have you explained to Mariah why she can't sing at the cemetery?"

Caleb shook his head, then faced her. Fatigue deepened the laugh lines around his quiet eyes. "No. I'm remiss on that score. I'd prefer not to tell her, then leave."

She lowered her gaze, afraid he would see the depth of her feelings for him and destroy her paltry defenses with a gesture or word. "I appreciate that. While you're gone, will you think about accompanying us to the cemetery just once?" Before he could protest, she placed her cup on the table and approached him. "For your sake, Caleb, see what you're denying her before you do it."

This time, he looked away. "It means that much to you?"

"It means that much to her." Mentally counting the seconds of the ensuing silence, she turned away. When he did not answer, she started out of the kitchen.

"Alicia."

She paused in the doorway.

"I'll think about it while I'm gone. We'll resolve it when I get back in a few days. Can the two of you stay clear of the cemetery until then?"

She nodded, relieved yet amazed he'd considered reversing his dictate. "Yes, I can manage my end of the compromise."

"That's not all we're going to settle when I return."

"Wh-what else is there to address?" Her knees locked in place.

"You know damn well what's unsettled between us," he murmured from behind her.

The warmth of his breath raised the fine hairs at the nape of her neck. "It *is* settled, Caleb. Should I be looking for another job?"

"Do you want to leave?"

The sudden acceleration of her pulse made her distrust her voice. She shook her head.

"Alicia."

He embraced her shoulders with a reverence that made

179

her want to cry. Small tremors ran through her knees, which were still locked and holding her in place.

"You're all I think about, whether I'm here or at the lumber camp." His heat flowed through her. "When I sleep, you're with me in dreams." The weight of his forehead against the crown of her head increased the burden weighing heavily on her heart and conscience. "I've never cared for a woman the way I do you. I thought I knew what it was to be in love. But this is different. It makes no damn sense."

Alicia whirled. She covered his mouth with the fingertips of her right. Head shaking, every fiber in her trembling, she silenced him. "Don't say that. Please, Caleb. Don't. I couldn't . . ." *stand it when I tell you the truth and you think I'm insane or a liar.*

He held her wrist and kissed her fingertips until she formed a fist. "I don't have to say it. You know the way of my heart regarding you."

"Don't . . ." Head shaking in denial, she wanted to flee. The electric pulse of his hands on her wrist grounded her in place.

"Tell me what you fear," he whispered.

Staring at her hand, she searched for the right words. "I'm not for you, Caleb."

"You *must* be. You make me laugh. You frustrate and torment me until I could rip the trees out of the ground bare-handed. You planted more than the seeds of green plants here, Alicia. From the moment I saw you, I wanted you so badly I couldn't think straight."

"You—you're still not thinking straight. We have no future together. Not the way you want." The scent of his shaving soap became an exotic, tantalizing perfume. For half a heartbeat, she almost dared to believe the impossible.

"We do, and I intend to make you believe it as surely as the books in this house contain words." The soft kiss he pressed on her forehead slowed the effects of his statement.

Books. Words. Truths.

The pages of her truth were blank, the preposterous words forever elusive. The realization gave her the strength to pull away.

"You read too much, Caleb. Life isn't as simple as the precious words in your books make it seem. There are truths not written on those pages. Truths so fantastic no one writes them down. There are things on the brink of reality no one mentions, let alone owns with a pen and paper."

The anguish of rejecting him roiled within, giving her an odd strength. "What is impossible is you and me being anything more than employer and employee."

His words were entreating. "Even if you tell me Mariah is nothing more to you than a job, I would not believe you meant it. The two of you worship each other."

"Mariah is my job," she repeated. Gathering all her courage, she dared a glimpse of him. The torment pinching his features made her flinch. Hot coffee sloshed over the lip of her cup. Absently, she dried her hand on her skirt. "But you are right, I do love my job. Still, nowhere in my job description does it say I'm obligated to have any personal feelings for my employer."

"I want nothing in the way of obligations from you."

Shaking, she retreated. "You want what I can't give," she said. She kept her back to him, unwilling for him to see the tears threatening to spill down her cheeks. If she were smart, she'd take Mariah into town and search the kiosk for another job as soon as Caleb left.

Chapter Fifteen

A strident rapping on the front door startled Alicia. Over the clouds of flour rising from the bread dough Mariah was helping Maude knead, the two reflected her surprise. She glanced at Mariah, then at Maude.

"Were you expecting anyone?"

"No. Would you answer it?"

"Of course." Alicia quickly pushed away from the worktable and hurried across the kitchen. *Please. God, don't let anything have happened to Caleb.*

Nero waited beside the front door, his fangs bared. She ordered the dog back and waited until he complied before releasing the door latch.

The desperate force of the visitors storming the house ripped the heavy door from Alicia's hand. It hit the wall with the impact of cannon fire.

"Get out of my way! Let me in! Wolves!"

A flurry of green rushed inside.

Instinctively, Alicia lunged for Nero to keep him from tearing the intruders apart. The power of the beast dragged her to the floor.

Amid ear-piercing shrieks and fur and fangs straining against her arms, Alicia got her knees under her. The strength of Nero's attack stance barely let her move.

"Mortimer! Shoot! For God's sake, kill it!" the woman shrieked, then collapsed directly in front of Alicia.

Caesar bounded through the open door. Alicia barely had time to throw an arm around his neck and shout a command to still both wolf dogs. Sprawled on her knees with her arms locked around Caesar's and Nero's necks, she lifted her head to a froth of green and white frills.

Nero loosed a sound low in his throat.

Caesar strained against his training, which was all that held him from getting rid of the noisy interlopers.

Alicia batted away the yards of petticoat in her face, and glanced at the woman's companion. The nattily attired gent fumbled for something inside his coat pocket. Fear shot through her. "If I see a weapon, I'll give them the command to attack. They'll tear out your throat before you raise your arm another inch."

Mortimer froze. Other than his slick, sable mustache, all color left his face.

"Who are you people? And why would you force your way into a home protected by wolves?" Holding Caesar and Nero, Alicia scrambled for her footing without tripping on her skirts.

The man who had crashed through the door opened his mouth, but no sound emerged. His blue eyes froze on the wolf dogs and horror filled them.

Collecting her wits, Alicia squared her shoulders and ordered the dogs to sit, which they did. Slowly.

The hard patter of running feet preceded the slamming of Mariah's bedroom door.

Alicia dispatched Nero to check on the child. If anything were amiss, the dog would let her know.

"I asked a question. Who are you people, and why are you busting down the door to Mr. Marker's home?"

The woman on the floor moaned.

"Hold on to that vile beast." The man found his voice

as he hunkered beside the woman obscured by billowing petticoats and yards of material.

Determined to learn the identity and purpose of the intruders, Alicia folded her arms and waited beside Caesar. A low muttering drew her attention. Nearby, Maude vigorously wiped her hands on a towel and strode down the hall to Mariah's bedroom. En route, she afforded a single, disdainful glance at the woman on the floor.

Alarm prickled through Alicia. Whoever these people were, Maude and Mariah weren't happy with their presence.

"Fetch a cold compress for Miss Cunningham." The male intruder cradled the woman's head and removed her disheveled hat. Golden curls draped across his sleeve and onto the floor.

"I suppose I could." A hand signal kept the ever-vigilant Caesar in place. Alicia walked around him to get a better view of the woman. A skilled application of cosmetics accentuated the woman's natural beauty. Her high cheekbones and a fine jaw reminded her of someone.

"Oh, Mortimer, did you kill them? Are we safe?" What started as a plaintive moan ended as a whine.

"Of course he didn't kill them," Alicia answered, drawing both their eyes. "For the last time, who are you people?"

"Are you going to ask silly questions or fetch a compress? Can't you see how distraught she is?" Mortimer demanded.

The mile-wide stubborn streak in Alicia asserted itself. "No, I'm not going to *fetch* anything." She cocked her head at Caesar. "He won't fetch for you, either."

"Where is Caleb?" Color suffused the pale features of the woman on the floor.

"He's not here at the moment." Alicia caught the glances exchanged by the intruders and the small twist of a triumphant smile on the woman's delicate lips. Instant distrust made her retreat a step.

"I'm sure he'll be disappointed to have missed our visit."

"No doubt." Alicia surveyed the flow of green serge dipping from the high neck of the collar to a point below the woman's tiny waist. From the fashion books at Edna's store, she recognized the dress as the latest sophisticated style.

"Mortimer, be a dear and assist me."

"Are you sure your constitution is strong enough for you to rise, my dear?"

"Oh my, I am a bit lightheaded, but I believe I'm recovered enough to be about our business."

"Whatever you say, Constance."

The graceful maneuver Mortimer used to bring the woman to her feet smacked of a well-rehearsed Fred Astaire and Ginger Rogers dance sequence. Either he escorted women who fainted frequently or the pair possessed a familiarity that exceeded the propriety dictated by the times.

Whatever their business entailed, Alicia suspected she wouldn't like it. The two of them reminded her of con artists from a seedy black-and-white movie shown on television after midnight.

"Caleb will be back soon," she said. So it was a little white lie. In this country with limited roads and no transportation beyond the stamina of a horse, *soon* was an ambiguous measurement.

"We will wait for him," the woman said, smoothing the fall of her skirt so the broché cream figures fell evenly.

Alicia signaled for Caesar. The wolf dog joined her before the couple could move. "Fine. If you'll be kind enough to leave your names, I'll inform him you wish to see him when he returns." The congenial smile she mustered belied her wariness.

"You have wolves in this house. With a child," the woman stated the obvious with an accusatory tone that promised the death penalty.

"Only half-wolf. The dogs serve as protection."

"Protection?"

"Against unwanted visitors." Alicia met the woman's icy glare. In utter amazement, she watched the woman

185

soften and tilt her chin as though assuming a different persona. Silently, Alicia reminded herself that a rattlesnake with clipped rattles was still lethal.

Mortimer cleared his throat. "Those creatures gave us a terrible start. Please accept my apology and forgive our poor manners. This is Miss Constance Cunningham, and I'm Mortimer Palmer."

Alicia shook her head. The importance his tone bestowed upon their names eluded her. "My name is Alicia James."

"Are you Caleb's new . . . housekeeper?" The saccharine dripping from Constance's voice contrasted sharply with the stinging rake of her gaze. For an instant, Alicia wondered whether the woman was a rival for Caleb's affections.

"No, I'm not." The brief response left an uncomfortable silence.

Jeremy crossed the veranda and paused in the open doorway with his hat in hand. Whatever he wanted to say stayed locked behind pressed lips when he saw the visitors.

"Why Jeremy, how you've grown. You're turning into a handsome young man. I'll bet the young girls swoon when you go into town." Constance flashed a brilliant smile as she approached him.

"Miss Cunningham," he acknowledged, his gaze flickering to Alicia.

"Young man, would you be so kind as to see to the horses?" Mortimer asked.

"I'm sure he would, but he isn't going to tend your horses, Mr. Palmer. You and Miss Cunningham need to return to Sitka." Alicia motioned toward the door. "I'll send word when Mr. Marker returns. I don't expect him tonight."

"When do you expect him?" Constance demanded. "The man has no sense of responsibility to go off and leave Mariah with strangers in this godforsaken country."

Alicia's left eyebrow shot up at the mention of Mariah. "Strangers?"

"You, Miss James, are a stranger. Of all the things I believed Caleb capable, I didn't think he'd resort to bringing his backwoods entertainment under the same roof as Mariah. She deserves better than that. She deserves—"

"I'm Mariah's governess and tutor, Miss Cunningham." Anger softened her voice to a whisper. "I think it is time you and Mr. Palmer leave."

"I'm not going anywhere until I speak with Caleb. This matter is settled. I'm taking my niece back to Tacoma."

"Your niece?" The woman was out of her mind if she thought Caleb would part with his daughter. "I doubt Mr. Marker will allow you to take her across the yard. He's very protective of Mariah."

"Of her money, you mean." Constance took her hat from Mortimer. "He has less claim on Mariah than I. As a woman, I should be raising our niece. It's positively indecent for a young girl to grow up in the wilderness with men and animals."

Dread congealed into a lump in her stomach. Her mind stumbled over Constance's words. Mariah was whose niece? Constance and Mortimer's? Or Constance and . . . no. Mariah was Caleb's daughter. Wasn't she?

"Constance, perhaps we should refrain from discussing this with Miss James," Mortimer chided softly.

Constance shot him a fulminating glance. "If Miss James requires employment, I'll entertain continuing her position as Mariah's governess—after I evaluate her, of course. It would certainly simplify things until I arrange a place for the girl at an appropriate school."

Constance looked around, her gaze lingering on Jeremy. "Where is the dear child?"

"She's not feeling well today." Alicia felt the seeds of revulsion blooming around Constance Cunningham.

"Well, I shan't see her then. I dislike being exposed to noxious childhood maladies. Still, if her uncle Caleb possesses an ounce of genuine feeling for the girl, he'll not fight my taking her back to Tacoma."

The double whammy of hearing Caleb was Mariah's uncle, not her father, and the realization the irritating Constance Cunningham might actually take the child kept Alicia silent.

"I believe I'll stay and oversee Mariah's care. One cannot be too diligent when it comes to a child's health." Constance glided toward the living room in a haze of green froth. "I cannot believe the man still makes his own furniture. How base."

Alicia closed her eyes for a moment and envisioned a hundred talons descending on Constance. Mariah wouldn't survive a week with the woman.

And Caleb . . .

A slow anger glowed in the pit of her stomach that he had not seen fit to reveal the true nature of Mariah's parentage. Why hadn't he told her? Why had he let her think Mariah was his daughter?

"Have you a room for Mortimer?" Constance asked from nearby the soft, deerskin upholstered couch.

"No," Alicia managed. "We don't have one for you, either."

"Oh,. I don't mind sleeping in Caleb's bed. I'm sure Maude will freshen the linens for me."

"No one invited you to stay, Miss Cunningham. Under the circumstances, you had best accompany Mr. Palmer into town."

The sweet smile Constance gave Alicia dripped venom. "You fail to comprehend the situation, Miss James. That makes me question your effectiveness as Mariah's tutor. You see, I am family. My late brother-in-law would turn over in his grave if you refused me Caleb's hospitality. So, Miss James, I stay if I so choose. And I choose to remain near my dear niece."

Never in her life had Alicia taken such an immediate dislike to anyone, but there was a first for everything. Despite her feelings, she conceded Constance's victory in this surprise skirmish. "If that's the case, I doubt Mr. Marker would turn you away."

"And you'll find a place for Mr. Palmer?" Constance cooed.

Alicia smiled. "Mr. Palmer may have his choice of the

barn, where Caesar here sleeps"—she ruffled the dog's furry head—"or the hotel in Sitka."

"I meant in the house."

"Oh, no. Mr. Marker has made his wishes very clear. An unattached man may not spend the night under this roof unless Mr. Marker is in residence."

Constance folded her hands in front of her. "Well, I'd call Jeremy an unattached male, wouldn't you?"

"Yes," Alicia answered, glancing at the young man. "But Jeremy has his own apartment behind the barn."

"Well," Constance pressed with a forced patience that turned her blue eyes as brittle as glass, "couldn't Mr. Palmer stay there?"

"Absolutely not. There is only one bed, and it belongs to Jeremy. There's nowhere for Mr. Palmer to sleep."

"Jeremy wouldn't mind sleeping in the barn, would you, Jeremy?"

Before the young man could answer, Alicia shook her head. "Out of deference to age, he would undoubtedly do as you suggest, Miss Cunningham, but I will not ask him to do so. This is his home. This is where he works. Neither you, nor Mr. Palmer, have any right to displace him for your convenience, and I'll not allow it."

"Who do you think you are, Miss James?"

"The one in charge until Mr. Marker returns. Whatever I do to make you unhappy you may take up with him." A quick hand signal sent Caesar to the guard post beside the kitchen door. "Mr. Palmer, at this point you may stay or return to town. However, you will not be spending the night in the house."

A grudging respect showed in the hint of his smile. "I understand perfectly, Miss James." He nodded at Constance. "I believe it best if I return to Sitka. Jeremy, would you mind following and bringing back Miss Cunningham's luggage?"

Alicia nodded at the question in Jeremy's expression.

"Yes, sir." Jeremy practically fled the doorway.

Considering the matter settled, Alicia summoned Caesar. The animal assumed a sentry position at the hall entrance. Constance had won the battle of hostile occupation, but the hounds of war would continue roaming the battleground and protecting the allies huddling in Mariah's room. As Alicia approached the door, Nero shifted, allowing her passage, then resumed his post.

Inside, Maude and Mariah hugged each other on the edge of the poster bed. Two pairs of teary eyes looked up at Alicia.

"The man's going back to town. Miss Cunningham insists on staying." Guilt replaced her anger at Constance and Caleb as the modicum of hope in their eyes soured.

"I'm sorry." Their misery made the apology more inadequate in the face of a volatile situation she didn't fully comprehend.

"There's no help for it, Alicia. Just like flies swarm on a piece of pie, Constance can't resist the lure of Mariah's trust fund." Maude patted the child's back, comforting them both.

Alicia ran her fingers through her hair. "I don't understand. She's been here before?"

"She comes to Sitka every year. This is the first time she's come before August. When she's here, Caleb takes Mariah into town to see her. This is the first time she's been at the house. After the first visit, he hasn't allowed her to come here."

Fury and embarrassment warmed Alicia's cheeks. "Well she talked her way into staying this time. She isn't going to leave willingly, and I don't have the leverage to throw her out." Outfoxed because of ignorance. Why hadn't Caleb warned her? Another black mark on the man's score card. Thanks to his silence concerning Mariah's parentage and the battle over some trust fund, this conniving woman wrangled a place in the heart of Marker territory.

Mariah sniffed and brushed tears from her cheek with the back of her hand. "I heard her. Is she gonna take me away this time?"

Alicia crouched in front of her and opened her arms. The little girl rushed into them and hugged Alicia's neck.

"Not if I can help it. I love you, little one, and I'm not giving you up."

"I wish Daddy was here. He could make her go away."

Alicia hugged Mariah tightly and met Maude's knowing brown eyes. Caleb wouldn't be home for days.

Chapter Sixteen

"I'm not waiting around this wilderness until Caleb decides to wander out. Three days is the extent of the courtesy I'm willing to extend him—even for the sake of family harmony. If he doesn't return today, I want you to pack Mariah's things. I'm taking her to Tacoma. I'm sure Caleb will find time to visit us there and carry out his responsibilities.

"Mortimer has checked the docks for sailing schedules. The *Carpathian Queen* departs for Tacoma tomorrow afternoon. He assures me the accommodations are suitable." Constance glided away from the front door, shot a disdainful glance at Caesar, and continued into the parlor. The animal bared his fangs, but remained seated.

Alicia pressed her lips together. The acerbic retort on the tip of her tongue begged for freedom. "Why on earth would you think I'd help you separate Mariah and Caleb Marker?"

"I'm doing what's best for her."

"Kidnapping a child from her happy home is your idea of what's best for her?"

The radiant smile lighting Constance's classic features when she turned sent chills along Alicia's spine.

"Please don't be dramatic. All I'm asking of you is that you perform your duties. Taking the poor, neglected child to Tacoma is nothing as nefarious as kidnapping, my naïve governess.

"A judge in Tacoma has awarded me temporary guardianship until he can reexamine Mariah's situation. Fortunately, he agreed she requires a civilized, structured environment and proper education. You may accompany us. Your presence will no doubt make her more manageable until she settles into her new home and school."

Each encounter with Constance brought one unpleasant surprise after another. All along, Alicia suspected the smug, saccharine smile Constance assumed whenever she caught Alicia staring at her hid something bleak, if not sinister. Now, she wasn't sure whether the woman was baiting her with talk of the judge, or had finally dropped the other shoe.

Either way, this latest twist upped the stakes of Constance's game. Suddenly, Alicia felt cornered. Any way she turned the situation, Mariah lost. The question became one of damage control.

Alicia approached Constance. "Do I understand correctly? You have a court order to take Mariah from Mr. Marker?"

"Of course." Glee filled her sudden laughter. She withdrew an envelope from a pocket hidden in the voluminous folds of her skirt. "You certainly don't think I would rearrange my social calendar to venture into this wilderness without being assured of the outcome.

"After my visit last year, I just couldn't bear the thought of making this arduous journey on an indefinite basis. Have you any idea how disruptive these visits are to one's social life? Spending a month up here in this"—a wave of her hand indicated the expanse outside the window—"isolation?"

"May I?" Alicia reached for the envelope.

Shrugging, Constance placed it in her hand. "As you

193

can see, I'm well within my rights to take the child."

Alicia unfolded the document. The decree held all the *whereases* and *therefores* characteristic of court orders. Her heart sunk with the realization Constance had obtained temporary guardianship.

Why, oh, why hadn't Caleb told her about Constance?

Surely, he had taken steps to ensure his position as Mariah's permanent guardian. All Alicia's instincts screamed he wasn't the sort of man who let something this important slip through the cracks. No, he was much too detail oriented for such an oversight.

He'd fight Constance for Mariah—if he knew the battle was underway. Tacoma was Constance Cunningham's territory. In this day and age, Caleb didn't have a snowball's chance in hell of retaining custody.

The thought dangled like a poisonous snake hanging from a tree limb.

Seeing the direction of Constance's plan, Alicia felt like David sent out to slay Goliath without even a sling or rocks.

The seal at the end of the document gave it an official designation she couldn't ignore.

A thousand questions begging for answers raced inside her mind. She didn't dare ask Constance and reveal her ignorance. Though Caleb might deserve the consequences, Mariah did not.

Constance sighed, turning away. "After I leave with Mariah, Caleb may reconsider his obligations concerning his family. After Mariah starts school, he won't be seeing her unless he agrees to my terms."

Dread turned the blood in Alicia's veins into the consistency of cold gravy. "Why? What does school have to do with it?"

"Don't be foolish. You know yourself that the best education and social connections for young ladies come from the eastern boarding schools. The sooner Mariah adapts to the place in society we Cunninghams have cultivated for generations, the easier a time she'll have of finding a satisfactory husband. Connections are everything, you know."

"Husband? Good grief, she's five years old!"

Offended, Constance lifted her chin as she snatched the papers from Alicia's hand. "I know we're starting late, but it couldn't be helped."

Alicia thought she'd witnessed the aftermath of the worst traumas a child could endure when she'd volunteered at the Women's Shelter. She recalled the fearful faces of battered women and children with their self-esteem in tatters around their ankles. Any one of them would have given their last crust of bread—and risked stealing more—for the kind of love and tenderness Caleb showered on Mariah. The notion of plucking Mariah from her mountain home filled with love and placing her into the setting Constance painted with an admiring, glowing brush screamed of wrongness.

She couldn't let Constance take Mariah without a fight. Yet, she had nothing to fight with, no designated place on the battleground.

Desperate to do something to save Mariah, Alicia needed a plan. Maybe if she escalated this war . . .

Memories of playing Risk with her father and a couple of the ranch hands who wintered in the bunkhouse rose from a dusty corner of her mind. It was a game of strategy and war, and she mentally laid out the territory and assigned colors. She was blue, the color of a Wyoming sky in summer. Caleb became green, the color of the trees that suited him so well. Constance . . . Constance was black with armies in Tacoma, Sitka, and the Marker homestead. Black suited the woman.

"Constance, won't you please reconsider and wait for Caleb?" Alicia asked.

"No. I've waited three days. Obviously, he does not consider Mariah important enough to spend time with her, or he'd be here."

"Of course he does. He loves her deeply. They are like father and daughter. If not for him, consider the consequences for Mariah if she doesn't have closure by saying good-bye to him."

"She'll adjust." Constance tucked her court order into her pocket and turned toward the hall. "Have her ready in the morning. I'll tell her the wonderful news at supper."

Agitated and hating the helplessness stealing over her, Alicia watched Constance disappear into Caleb's room. When the door closed, she retreated to the kitchen where Maude and Mariah awaited the outcome of this latest confrontation.

"Ladies, we have plans to make." Alicia ruffled Mariah's hair. She wasn't going to passively hand the girl over to Constance and let her sail to Tacoma behind Caleb's back. Heaven help her, regardless of how angry she was at the man for letting her walk into this hornets' nest without a can of Raid, she couldn't let Mariah be the pawn of retribution. Not hers. Not Constance's.

The plan germinating in her fertile mind sprouted as she eyed the wine cupboard. "Mariah, do you trust me to do what's best for you?"

"Oh, yes."

"Good," Alicia said slowly, her plan blossoming. "Go take a nap." She picked up the child and kissed her nose. "No matter what is said at supper, I want you to be cool and quiet. I'll take care of you. Okay?"

Mariah hugged her neck. "I'm not sleepy, but I'll try to take a nap. How do I be cool? It's warm in the house at supper time."

Alicia nuzzled the girl's cheek. "Just pretend nothing Constance says upsets you. If she's talking about something unpleasant, quietly practice your Pig Latin." She kissed Mariah's cheek, then put her down.

"Take Nero." She watched Mariah depart, then fetched a bottle of wine. "We've got a lot of work to do before dinner, Maude."

Of all the practical applications Alicia knew for plants, this was the first time she considered drawing on her expertise for unsavory purposes.

* * *

"Was I cool?" Mariah pulled on her gloves, her expectant gaze shining in shared conspiracy.

"You were the coolest." Alicia secured Mariah's rain slicker. "Now, my little mountaineer, we are going to be as quiet as church mice."

Maude's head poked through the doorway. "Jeremy is ready."

Alicia took a deep breath, then exhaled and shouldered a pack crammed with clothes for herself and Mariah. Glancing around the room bedecked with tokens of love reaffirmed the rightness of her decision. Drugging Constance's wine had ensured a long, sound sleep and sufficient daylight for a clean escape. Now, the only path lay ahead. Caleb Marker waited at the end. Just thinking about the list of grievances he had to answer for warmed her ire.

"Let's go, Mariah." She took the girl's hand and followed Maude through the house.

Jeremy plucked Mariah off the ground and set her securely in the saddle. "You let us know when you get tired. We've got some hard riding to do before we make camp for the night."

"I took a nap, so I won't get tired."

"Good. Got your feet settled in the stirrups?"

"I'm ready."

Alicia tied the sacks Maude handed across the porch to the saddle. "Are you sure you're going to be all right when Constance discovers we've gone?"

"Phew, yes. What can she do to me?"

"I'd feel better if Nero stayed with you."

Maude shook her head. "Take them both for protection. You may need them against a four-legged devil. This one," a thumb jabbed toward the house, "has claws and a sharp tongue, but no stamina. She can't cook, so she needs me."

Alicia gave Maude a quick hug, then mounted Krakatau.

"Let's head 'em up and move 'em out." Already the shadows of a long summer day showed the lateness of the hour. They wouldn't make Caleb's lumber camp by nightfall.

Once beyond the clearing, Jeremy took the lead; Alicia brought up the rear and kept a sharp eye on Mariah. Caesar and Nero trotted beside the child, occasionally running ahead or lagging behind to check the trail.

After a couple of hours, the full moon lit the trail as the evening shadows thickened. Their progress slowed. All the while, Alicia seethed at Caleb for putting her into an untenable position when he could so easily have prepared her with the truth.

She'd not feel guilty about withholding anything from him again. No, sir.

Considering the court order she read, when she returned, her next home would likely be a small, dark cell in Sitka with an up-close and personal view of the wharf derelicts.

"Miss James?"

"Yes, Mariah?"

"I think Edgy's getting sleepy," Mariah answered through a yawn.

Alicia brought Krakatau alongside of Edgecombe and stuffed her jacket between herself and the saddle horn. The small space just accommodated the child. "Why don't we lighten her load and you ride with me for a while?"

Jeremy turned his horse and collected the pony's reins. "We'll go a few more miles before we make camp."

Alicia nodded agreement, then lifted the child into the saddle.

Within minutes, Mariah slept.

They made camp in a small clearing lit by brilliant moonlight. Jeremy built a strong fire while Alicia tucked Mariah into her blankets. Nero and Caesar took turns scouting and hunting; one of them remained beside Mariah at all times.

Alicia sipped water from her canteen, then capped it. "How long until sunrise?"

Jeremy glanced at the sky. "Four hours."

"How long until we reach Caleb's camp?"

"Another two hours if the weather holds. Longer if it rains."

"I'll take the first watch."

"Miss James, I can't let you stand watch."

Alicia shook her head. "Jeremy, forget I'm female. There are two of us. We'll split the night."

"Have you ever stood watch in the wilderness?"

Alicia laughed, recalling many nights on the open range with her father during roundup. "Yes, and I don't panic easily."

"Things sure must be different in Wyoming."

"I assure you, they are." Very different, and she doubted she'd see Wyoming again.

A steady drizzle coated the forest before they broke camp. Under the dripping arms of towering evergreens, Jeremy forged a trail. With Mariah tucked inside her slicker, Alicia followed on Krakatau. Edgecombe ambled behind on a long tether. Moisture collected and formed tiny streams that sluiced down Alicia's rain hat and changed course on her slicker. Holding Mariah close, she nudged Krakatau over a deadfall.

"Daddy will be surprised to see us."

"I'm sure he will be," Alicia murmured. *And just as delighted as I was to spend three fun-filled days in Constance's presence without a roll of Tums.*

"Is he gonna be angry we came up here?"

"Not at you, Mariah." *And his anger will pale in the face of mine when I get him alone. If anyone has a right to explode, it's me!*

"Oh, I don't want Daddy to be angry at you, either."

Alicia squeezed her upper arms in a hug. "Don't you worry about him being angry at me. I'm sure he'll agree coming up here was best after I have a few words with him."

Mariah shifted in the tight fit of the damp saddle they shared. "Are you mad at Daddy?"

"I'm not particularly happy with some of his actions of late, but there is nothing for you to worry about."

Mariah took a deep breath, her small body tensing. "Does that mean you don't like him better than ice cream?"

Resignation twisted Alicia's grim mouth into a near smile. Like most children, Mariah had a one-track mind when it came to wanting something beyond her small sphere of control.

"Did you pack some ice cream? What flavor?"

Mariah giggled. "I couldn't bring ice cream. It would melt."

"Well, with no ice cream around, I guess your daddy has an edge."

Mariah gripped the saddle horn as Krakatau navigated a boulder in the middle of the faint trail.

Resigned, the child shrugged her small shoulders against Alicia. "I like riding in boy's trousers instead of dresses."

Satisfied at the new direction of conversation, Alicia tugged at Mariah's hood to shield her face. "They're more practical in this country."

"We're so lucky we're girls."

The little wiggle that escaped with Mariah's proclamation made Alicia smile. "What makes you say so?"

" 'Cause we can wear boys' trousers and girls' dresses. Boys can't wear girl clothes for anything."

Alicia hugged the child, loving her simplistic approach to the world and treasuring the innocence of her viewpoint. No matter what she had to do, she'd not let Constance Cunningham take Mariah to Tacoma, the East Coast, or anywhere else.

"We're almost there," Jeremy called. "Let's keep Nero and Caesar close. We don't want anyone to get nervous and mistake them for wolves."

A chill that had nothing to do with the cold, damp breeze sent a shiver through Alicia. Her whistle called the animals to opposite sides of Krakatau.

True to Jeremy's prediction, as they crested the ridge, the logging camp became visible through the thinned trees. The little settlement consisted of three large tents and a smaller one. All bore mud stains and rain streaks.

A fourth large tent had two sides rolled up. A long table flanked by benches filled most of the interior. Crates, barrels, and various dry goods stood in neat stacks perched on logs in the sheltered corner. A cookstove vented a steady plume up the stovepipe chimney extending high above the tent roof. Beyond a line of trees, Alicia made out a series of corrals fortified by wagons beside a small tack shed.

At first glance, the camp appeared deserted.

"Which one of these circus tents belongs to the ringmaster?" Alicia wondered aloud.

The freckles over Jeremy's nose spread with a sudden grin. "You'll think it's a circus when the men return for chow."

Alicia glanced at the mist hugging the treetops. "At least the rain has eased. Still, it seems . . ." Mariah fidgeted, reminding her to guard her worries. "Do they cut down trees while it's raining?"

"Caleb says logging is dangerous in any weather if a logger doesn't pay attention to where he is and where the timber is coming down." Jeremy dismounted near the cook's tent.

For a moment, Alicia studied him. Somewhere among the trees and harsh terrain, he'd lost the guise of youth and become a man.

The rain ebbed to a fine mist drifting from the gray veil slowly scrubbing the upper branches of the higher trees. The scent of damp forest, wood smoke, and damp wool filled Alicia's lungs.

Waves of nostalgia rippled through her. The instant she closed her eyes, the familiar smells conjured childhood memories. They flowed across her senses like a comfortable quilt on a chilly night.

For a brief slice of time, she returned to the high rangeland of the Tetons where cattle awaited roundup and branding. Any moment, her father would call her, Bethany, and Caitlyn. They'd check their gear, mount their horses, and then ride with Papa and the men to gather cattle from the high pasturelands.

Alicia opened her eyes. Jeremy and Mariah stared up at her in silent concern.

"Just remembering. The smell of the camp reminds me of roundup time in Wyoming," she murmured.

"Do you miss your family all the time?" Mariah's big, gray eyes regarded her solemnly.

"They're with me in memories." She lifted Mariah's leg over the saddle horn. "Down you go. Catch, Jeremy."

Jeremy swung Mariah from the saddle, then in an arching half-circle before setting her on the ground. "Get your legs steady."

Alicia dismounted, absently patting Krakatau's neck. "Let's see if we can find something to eat."

"And coffee," Jeremy added.

"And hot chocolate?" Mariah asked with a hopeful lift of her eyebrows.

"Jeremy! What in thunderation possessed ya ta bring a woman and Caleb's kid up here? Have ya lost all yer senses?" A balding man with a sagging halo of bushy gray hair rose from near the cookstove and hurried toward them. A faded apron protected a plaid shirt, its cuffs rolled up his beefy forearms. He was a stocky and thickset man, more muscle than fat. Heat flushed his rosy, cherubic cheeks, the only unlined territory on the road map life had etched into his face.

Jeremy engulfed the burly man in a hug. "It's good to see you, too, Corky." He clapped the cook on the back.

Mariah's hand found Alicia's. "Is he angry because we came?" she whispered.

Alicia managed a smile and squeezed the small hand in her own. "I'll bet if you smile your best smile, he'll smile back."

Clearly, the child knew Caleb did not want her in the logging camp. Yet, she had asked no questions concerning the reason for the trek. Doubt drew Alicia's mouth into a frown as she focused her attentions on Jeremy and the cook.

"Yeah, I'm glad to see ya, boy." Corky returned the bear hug. "You comin' to cut timber?"

"Nope, I'm needed down below. 'Sides, Ma feels like she just lost Jane, and I'll be leaving for Spokane in a few weeks." Jeremy released the man. "I brought Caleb a couple of presents." Jeremy's smile dimmed. "You know we wouldn't have come up here without good reason, which Miss James will explain to him personally."

Jeremy motioned to Mariah. "Corky, you remember our little princess, Mariah, the love of Caleb's life."

Corky bent and responded to Mariah's tremulous smile with a jack-o'-lantern grin of his own.

"Her lovely companion and governess is Miss Alicia James, a genuine lady with more backbone and patience than most men I know."

"Corky?" Alicia inquired, extending her hand.

"Yes, ma'am." Uncertain, he wiped his palm on his apron, then shook her hand, his grin broadening.

"I gather this is your domain." She nodded at the mess tent and caught a whiff of roasting meat.

"It most certainly is, ma'am. Can I get you something to eat? I just put on some coffee."

"Yes, we'd love whatever you have at hand. We've ridden steadily since we broke camp." Recalling an earlier request, she smiled at Mariah. "I don't suppose you have any milk and cocoa for hot chocolate to warm a little girl's tummy?"

Corky ran his fingertips over the gray stubble sprouting from his chin. "We got a cow, so I got milk. Seems to me, I might have some cocoa stashed."

"Oh, thank you so much. Can I watch you fix it?" Mariah released Alicia's hand and hurried after the cook.

"Corky?"

"Yes, ma'am?"

"When do you expect Mr. Marker?"

"Not until supper, ma'am, unless Jeremy wants to go looking for him."

"It might be best if you explained our presence here while the rest of the men work the trees," Jeremy said softly.

203

Alicia nodded. "After you have something to eat and a decent cup of coffee. You've got to be as tired as we are."

She headed for the metal cups stacked on a table beside the cookstove, hoping the right words surfaced when Caleb stormed into camp.

Alicia tucked the blanket around Mariah. Thus far, she hadn't shown any ill effects from the cold, damp night on the trail. The child's curiosity expanded with the vastness of the land around them. Between Alicia and Corky, they'd managed answers to most of her questions; however, Caleb was going to have his hands full when he returned.

Caleb.

Alicia took stock of the small tent with its amenities of a pot-bellied stove, two cots, and a trunk stuffed with spare clothing and blankets. A pair of chairs sat on opposite sides of a table laden with books, ledgers, maps, and assorted papers. A double chimney lamp in the center of the table glowed in the dimly lit tent barely admitting the gray light of late afternoon.

Alicia retrieved her slicker from the oversized hat tree beside the tent door. She donned it and slipped outside. Caesar and Nero afforded her a glance, then came to their feet, their attention piqued by something in the distant trees. Though mist no longer seeped from the low-hanging clouds, they appeared ready to weep at the slightest provocation.

Even from the distance Vesuvius closed at a steady walk, Alicia felt as well as saw the heat of the molten steel of Caleb's gray eyes. Her heart did a flip, then skipped a beat. Absently, she pulled the slicker closed over her breasts and held her ground.

"Where's Mariah?" Caleb asked in a voice too calm for the situation.

"Taking a nap in your bed."

"Good. Get on Jeremy's horse. We're going for a ride."

The order made her bristle. "I thought we had already established that blind obedience is not one of my virtues."

204

"Get on the horse, Alicia." The softness of his voice served as an additional warning. She chose to ignore it.

"I'm not one of your men to be ordered from one place to another."

"I would never make such an obvious blunder, Miss James. We're going to talk. Away from here, because one of us is going to yell and I'd prefer Mariah not hear."

The anger festering in Alicia since Constance Cunningham burst through the doors of the Marker home suffused her veins. She grabbed the reins from Jeremy and mounted. "You're damn right one of us is going to yell, Caleb Marker, and it isn't going to be you." From the saddle, she glared into his angry face for an instant, then reined the horse away from the tent. "Which way?"

Without another word, Caleb took the lead.

When her thoughts strayed to the masterful way he handled the horse around deadfalls and boulders dotting the rugged slopes, she recalled Constance Cunningham and stoked the pyre of her anger.

Caleb guided them into a ravine deepened by a quick-running creek, then dismounted.

Before he could make a move to help her, Alicia alighted from the horse and pushed it toward the creek for a drink.

"Why did you bring Mariah here? I made it very clear I never wanted her in a logging camp."

Although a couple of feet away, she felt the heat of his ire. Suddenly, her own anger surged, then simmered just below the eruption point. "Oh, you made it very clear, Caleb. There isn't anything wrong with your ability to articulate what you want me to know. You have the audacity to demand from me what you aren't willing to give yourself."

"I'm assuming you have a point?"

"Truth. Honesty. Trust. You demand it from me. But you—You hide behind omissions and reveal only what's convenient or beneficial to you. You wouldn't know the whole truth if it were screamed in your ear."

"I'm listening. But I'm not hearing anything that sounds like truth or answers, Alicia."

"I'm not the one who owes answers here, Caleb. You are!"

"What the hell are you talking about?"

Alicia tried to settle herself. She drew in a quick breath, then swallowed. "In two words—Constance Cunningham."

He became as still as the giant hemlock tilting over the creek as though eavesdropping. Finally, he blinked. "What about her?"

Alicia turned on her heel, head shaking in disbelief. "What about her? What *about* her?" She picked up a stick and whacked the closest boulder. The impact left a welt in the moss covering it. "I don't believe this. You have the nerve to ask *me,* what about her?"

"What is wrong?"

"You never mentioned her. You never mentioned Mariah had an aunt who wanted custody of her." She struck the boulder again, then spun on him. "No, why would you? You never even mentioned that Mariah isn't your daughter.

"Do you have any idea how incredible I find this?"

"Apparently not."

She took two quick steps toward him, her stick whipping the side of her leg. "You tell me I know everything important about you. But you don't even tell me Mariah isn't your daughter?" She gave him a look full of all her anger and incredulity. "Am I the only sane, rational person here? Or do you see something wrong with this little—what shall we call it? Omission? Oversight? Half-truth? How about lie? I think I like lie because that's how it feels, Caleb. You lied to me and left me to pick up the pieces of a disaster—"

"I didn't lie to you."

"You sure as hell did! You lied by contrivance. By omission. By letting me believe Mariah is your daughter."

"She is my little girl."

Frustrated fury seized Alicia in an iron grip. Her teeth

clenched, but the acrid words spilled out. "The only way she's your daughter is if you were sleeping with your brother's wife."

Caleb didn't so much as flinch. Silence followed; not even the branches of the giant hemlock dripped.

"Since I don't believe you to be the sort of man who'd sleep with his brother's wife, I'm left to assume Mariah is not your daughter. However, in recent days, I've discovered I don't know you very well at all."

She turned away, swinging her stick with a fresh energy born of disappointment. "Obviously, I'm not as astute a judge of character as I thought I was." A squeak between a scream and a laugh escaped. "God knows, when it comes to men, I'm wrong more often than I'm right."

Caleb walked to the edge of the creek, scooped up a handful of water, and drank. "I didn't expect Constance before August. That's when she usually comes."

Alicia froze. "I see. And when would you have told me about Mariah?"

"I don't know. I think of her as my daughter. I'm her father, the only parent she's known. I changed her diapers. Trained her. Walked the floor with her when she cried. Nursed her when she was sick. Answered her questions. For damn near five years, I've loved her more than life. She is my life, Alicia. Everything I do is built around her. She is my daughter."

Sudden, hot tears leaked from Alicia's eyes. Head hanging, she understood the emotion in his trembling voice. "Why, Caleb? Why did you let me think you'd had a lover who ran off with Mariah? Why was it easier to let me believe a lie than to tell me the truth?"

"Ah, Christ, Alicia, I never thought about it like that."

The curl of his fingers around her shoulders brought sobs from the deep well of her pain and disappointment. The man she loved—and God help her, she did love him—didn't trust her with a simple thing like the truth about the child they both loved.

She fought the wild tumult raging against her heart. The anger and hurt blended into a smoky ball of red angst even the vast forest seemed too small to contain.

"I'm sorry, Alicia, so damn sorry I didn't consider how you'd react. Trust has nothing to do with it."

"It has . . . everything to do with it." She sniffed, striving to quell her grief.

Caleb rested his forehead against the crown of her bowed head. "Did you come up here to tell me you're leaving?"

Alicia shook her head. Of all the things that had crossed her mind since the Pandora's box Constance Cunningham had opened, not once had she considered leaving. The hammer of truth felled its defeating blow. She didn't want to leave. Not even now when the impact of all her emotions was striking its hardest.

"Maybe to go to jail," she croaked, then cleared her throat.

"What do you mean?"

"Constance has a court order giving her temporary guardianship of Mariah. I read it in front of her the day I took Mariah away. Technically, I'm guilty of kidnapping at worst, defying a court order at best."

Caleb swore under his breath.

"There's more."

"Can it get worse?"

"Oh, yeah, it can, Caleb. I didn't want Constance to catch us when we left, so I drugged her wine at dinner. If God is kind, she'll think she drank too much bad wine and maybe not notice the aftereffects of the drug through her hangover."

Alicia gathered all her willpower and stepped away from the gentle vise of his hands, but she couldn't muster the gumption to turn around. "I couldn't let her take Mariah no matter how angry I was at you."

"Thank you."

The finality of his gratitude acknowledged the chasm widening between them.

Chapter Seventeen

Caleb prowled the foggy night. The snores of hard-working, tired men punctuated the nocturnal stillness. The flames in the center of the clearing sizzled as mist kissed the embers at the edge of the fire pit.

How was it that the best intentions wound up hurting the one woman he'd never wanted hurt? If some other man had inflicted the pain reflected in Alicia's violet eyes this afternoon, Caleb would have beat him into wood pulp. Even that realization seemed absurd since he always approached problems with his head, not his fists.

Right now, it would feel damn good to beat something into submission. In the physical frenzy, he might forget his unquenchable desire for Alicia for a moment.

He gazed at the tent sheltering his precious treasures.

Alicia had nailed him to a tree with her assertions.

He should have explained Mariah's parentage. *Parentage?* Hell, he hadn't known anything about babies when he'd brought Mariah from San Francisco as an infant. From books, he'd learned how to fix a bottle and what to feed her.

Somewhere between the first time he'd held her and now, he'd quit thinking of her as his brother's child and started believing she was his daughter.

But he knew better.

Like a winter blizzard, Constance Cunningham's annual visit was inevitable.

He'd lied to Alicia by omission, never considering the act a lie, or an act of deception.

Too many years of keeping his own counsel. Too many years of men turning to him for answers when there was no one else to offer guidance, not even him. The self-reliance cultivated since his father's death fourteen years ago hadn't allowed for the sharing of his secrets, his doubts, or his dreams.

"I'm beginning to understand why you're finally ready to turn this operation over to me."

Caleb tensed, then turned in the direction of a match flaring in the darkness.

Kyle lit his pipe. Each puff sent a new billow of smoke around his face. "Alicia James is quite a woman, Caleb." The man dropped the match and stepped on it. Kyle concentrated on the orange glow in his pipe's bowl. "Though I must be preaching to the choir on that subject. Hell, I thought the heavens would have to open and drop an angel on your doorstep before you trusted anyone with Mariah the way you trust Alicia. Whatever else is going on, those two are something to see."

The lumberjack laughed. "By supper, every man in camp regarded them as a Madonna and child. Even Corky couldn't do enough for them, and not a man complained when he showed them preference." He drew on his pipe. " 'Course if you had stuck around, instead of leaving it to me to watch over them, you'd have seen for yourself."

"Things aren't always what they seem, Kyle." He himself wasn't what he seemed; he wasn't Mariah's father in the eyes of the law, only in his own mind. Having that delusion broken cost a part of his heart.

"They seldom are, my friend. They're usually more."

"You're awful damn philosophical tonight."

Kyle chuckled and examined his pipe. "It's a helluva lot easier to be philosophical about a situation I'm not directly involved with than my own."

Caleb folded his arms and leaned against a tree. The tent he usually shared with the man filled his gaze. "How did you survive Prudence and Jackson's deaths, Kyle?"

The subject of the lumberman's deceased wife and child lay exposed in the darkness. After a long time, Kyle answered. "What makes you think I survived?"

Caleb studied his friend in the dim light; Kyle hadn't survived, he'd just kept breathing. He'd worked like a demon cutting timber from spring until the heavy snows blew in from the north. Like Caleb, he went into partial hibernation during the winter. Unlike Caleb, memories of his dead wife filled the house he'd built for Prudence near the sea.

Was that what life without Alicia's smile would be like? Memories of a fleeting time he'd squandered in silence? How long before she disappeared from their lives?

"What's troubling you, Caleb? The woman or her bringing Mariah up here?"

The simple eloquence that came so easily in Caleb's business dealings deserted him when expressing the profound ache festering in his soul. Thank heaven Alicia possessed the intelligence and gumption to rescue Mariah from Constance's greedy conspiracy. Her tirade had evaporated his anger on that score. He'd deal with Constance.

The greater issue of Alicia's perceived deception ate at him. Not knowing how to mend their fragile bond added to the sense of futility gnawing on his heart.

"Something is troubling that woman mighty deep for her to bring your girl up here." Kyle gestured with his pipe at the tent where Alicia slept.

"Yeah, something is." Caleb stared at the tent.

"Fix it."

"I don't think I can. Not all of it."

"Find a way."

"It's complex."

211

"Complex never daunted you before. Must be something you can do."

Caleb's eyes narrowed on the tent. Was she asleep on his cot? Did his blankets keep her warm as he ached to do? Did they caress her soft skin with the loving tenderness he wanted to give her? Did they—

He shut out the torturous conjecture. "It's too late. She thinks I lied to her."

Kyle puffed on his pipe for a moment. "Did you?"

Caleb nodded. The admission burned his eyes from the ache in his heart. "Guess I did. I let her think Mariah was my daughter. Constance set her straight."

Kyle swore under his breath and emptied his pipe on the ground. "I thought you bought that bitch off."

"So did I. Still, that doesn't change what's happened. It isn't Constance's fault I didn't tell Alicia the truth. It's mine. I can't turn the clock back and tell her what I should have confessed the day I hired her."

"Maybe not, but if you let her go without a fight, you're a fool, Caleb."

A fight. How the hell did a man fight for a woman's love, her trust, her very heart and soul? He wanted all of her for the rest of his life.

Kyle tucked his pipe into his shirt pocket. "Prudence dispelled me of the notion that love is fragile. Hell, it's stronger than these trees, stronger than anything I know. Even death. Find a way to win her trust and put this behind the two of you."

Caleb contemplated his friend and the dogmatic statement wrought from hard-won knowledge beyond his experience. He sure wouldn't find that advice on the pages of any book.

The trouble was, Kyle's logic supposed Alicia loved him back. She had never said she did. She'd shunned marriage . . . although she'd made love with him.

His heart skipped a beat.

Was her desire for him gone, too?

He could hardly be near her without aching to touch

her or draw her into his arms and make love to her until they lost their senses.

When he glanced beside him, the foggy night was his only companion.

During all the years he had lived alone, he'd known times of loneliness. Not until today had he felt the bleak, black infinity, the depths possible of such an emotion.

Not even the prospect of losing what he never really had tempered the sensation of his lungs filling with need until near bursting. He gripped a tree limb. The force of his restraint turned his fingers white. Bark dug into his callused palm. With every fiber in him, he wanted to cross the expanse to the tent, spirit Alicia into the forest and lose himself in her soft flesh. He craved her touch, yearned for the nearness of her feminine scent and the sweet taste of her mouth and skin.

Even more than the rapture of eroticism her body promised, he wanted her smile. Her laughter. Her loving violet eyes gazing on him with a happiness that made her glow.

Abruptly, he released the limb and turned into the forest. He wanted to howl like the wolves protesting their loneliness to the moon.

Accepting he'd brought destruction on himself revealed a new depth in the pit of his solitary existence. Not even Mariah's bright smile could light the part of his heart Alicia owned.

Alicia listened to the first stirrings of the logging camp. The snatches of troubled sleep she caught during the night had imparted no rest. On the cot beside hers, the slumber of innocence still wrapped Mariah in a deep cocoon.

The familiar sting of tears burned Alicia's eyes. Of all the situations imaginable, she'd never dreamed of such a convoluted set of circumstances. Sometime during the long night, a glimmer of understanding had crept through the maze of her chaotic thoughts.

Was it so wrong for him to consider the child his?

If only he had told her the truth . . .

But life was fraught with *if only's*.

If only she had known what she and Chet lacked, they never would have married.

If only her parents had left two minutes later, they might not have died on the highway.

If only she had held hands with her sisters in the graveyard, they might be together today.

If only . . .

It changed nothing.

As the morning brightened the tent ceiling, a new realization dawned with debilitating shame. She was a hypocrite, guilty of keeping the same kind of devastating silence as Caleb; and her motives embodied nothing as noble as unselfish love.

In self-defense, she tried to argue the unique difference of her circumstances. It was one thing for him to omit the facts of Mariah's parentage, and quite another to reveal that she had traveled across time and lost her sisters in the process.

"Oh, what a tangled web we weave, when first we practice to deceive!"

Unable to share the bed with the incriminating truth, she pulled on the skirt and petticoat she'd stuffed into her pack. Once dressed, she added a log to the stove. The radiant heat had dried the moisture from her boots. She pulled them on, then combed her hair.

She took three steps from the tent, then stopped. Caleb watched from beside the fire at the center of the encampment. Several men milled about on the far side of the flames with coffee cups in hand.

Her feet refused to budge when Caleb started toward her. The misery in his bloodshot eyes reflected her tormented soul. The shame of demanding honesty from him while harboring her own fantastic secret forced her to lower her gaze.

He offered the steaming coffee cup in his hand.

"Is this a peace offering?"

"It's a cup of coffee."

She took the cup and lifted it to her lips; the aroma

214

filled her nostrils. Maybe she could be semi-human after she drank it.

"I don't know what to say or do now," she murmured, again averting her traitorous gaze from the sorrow deepening the faint lines around his eyes.

"Neither do I. I never meant to mislead you. I'm sorry, Alicia." He shoved his hands into his trouser pockets. "Sounds pathetic, doesn't it?"

"If anyone is pathetic, it's me," she said. "Look . . . Caleb . . . there's something I should tell you. Something as incredible as it is important." The words died in her throat. Explaining the inexplicable defied her scientific training. She studied the ground for a moment. When she lifted her head, Jeremy joined them.

"Corky said you wanted to see me."

The unfettered cheerfulness of his smile made Alicia feel old and sullied.

Caleb's relentless stare bored into her heart.

He withdrew two letters with names neatly penned on envelopes from his shirt pocket. "Tell your mother we'll be home in a few days." The whisper of his callused thumb sliding across the heavy envelope sounded loud. "Take this one to Constance. She's leaving my house. After you deliver it, go into town and give this one to Patrick Brown. Tell him to get ready to do whatever it takes to get Constance out of our lives. For good."

Jeremy pocketed the letters, his smile gone. "Shall I ask Mr. Brown to have Constance removed from the house if she doesn't go?"

"No. If she isn't gone by the time I get home, I'll send her packing." He released a heavy sigh. "All things considered, I'd probably enjoy a good confrontation with her."

"Why do I get the feeling there is a great deal more to Constance's visit than the desire to see to her niece's custody?" Alicia asked.

"Because there is." Caleb turned to Jeremy. "Get something to eat, then go."

Jeremy nodded more in agreement than in obedience to an order. "On my way."

An awkward silence fell once they were alone again.

"You were about to tell me something of great importance," Caleb reminded.

"I . . ." Her bravado fled. A sudden dryness locked the words in her throat. Her palms began sweating in the cool morning air. She rubbed them against her skirt. *I can't tell him now when he's battling to keep Mariah.* Her heart sank. *I don't have the courage to tell him now.* When the admission formed, the constriction in her throat eased. "Is—is there a history of trouble between you and Constance?"

The discomfort she experienced under Caleb's scrutiny and her own cowardice forced her to look away.

"Is that what you want to tell me, or what you want to know?"

"What I want to know," she whispered, quickly sipping coffee to moisten her dry mouth.

The pressure of his fingers around her upper arm soothed her tumult. She accompanied him toward the warmth of the fire. "When Mariah was two, Constance paid her first visit to Sitka. Until then, she hadn't seen her niece since she and I battled over Mariah's guardianship in a San Francisco courtroom."

Alicia risked a glance when he hesitated, but held her silence. It hurt to look at his bloodshot eyes.

"Jed was my younger brother. After Dad died, I sent Jed East. Ransom Hamilton called in a few favors and helped me get Jed into Harvard."

Although Caleb spoke with little emotion, he avoided meeting her gaze. Years ago, he'd given the education he valued to his brother.

"Jed's heart lay in the West. After graduation, he went to San Francisco. I'd spend a couple of winter months there." He stared into the fire. "When he returned to Sitka it was for my wedding. He was my best man."

The revelation knocked the breath from Alicia. Marriage? In how many areas had he misled her?

"Margaret . . ." He cleared his throat, then turned and looked straight into her eyes. "It took meeting you to understand what happened with Jed and Margaret. They took one look at each other and nothing or no one else mattered. They eloped on the first ship out of Sitka."

The depth of his hurt and humiliation at the time must have been staggering. "Oh, God," she breathed, sinking onto a log.

He settled beside her, but no longer met her gaze.

"Margaret received a small inheritance shortly after they were wed. Through hard work, Jed's investing schemes turned it into a substantial amount of wealth. Fortunately, he knew how to protect it from Margaret's relatives in the event of disaster."

"The trust fund," Alicia said. At last, some of Maude's references and innuendoes were beginning to make sense.

"No. I set up the trust later. Jed and Margaret had devised a more formidable plan. In the event they died together, everything they had became mine—including their daughter."

"After they betrayed you?" The words escaped without thought. "I mean—"

"I know what you mean," he said softly.

"When Constance learned the conditions of the will, she fought it in the courts, but didn't win. Jed knew all the right people in San Francisco and made damn sure they knew he'd come back from the grave if his and Margaret's wishes weren't followed."

Alicia glanced at him. The barest hint of a smile reflected the pride with which he regarded his brother.

"I'm a timber man. I didn't know anything about wills or courts when I went to San Francisco. I sure didn't know anything about caring for a baby. I bought books on child rearing. I also got some good advice from the wives of Jed's friends. Meanwhile, his fellow barristers not only gave me assistance; they gave me an education in the law.

"I suspected when I paid Constance off last year, she'd be back again. I didn't expect it this soon."

Incredulous, Alicia slowed her step and gaped at him. "You paid her off? Why, if you have custody? What does she think she's going to gain?"

"Money. Constance is about money. She always runs out of it. I warned her there would be no more from me." He shoved his free hand into his pocket. "Jed and Margaret made it clear in their wills that I was the sole recipient of their estate. They didn't leave anything to Mariah. They knew I'd take care of her. I liquidated their real estate assets and put the money in a trust fund for Mariah. Dividing the estate may have been what drew Constance like a bear draws flies. She thinks if she has Mariah, she'll get control of the trust fund. In part, she's right, but I won't agree to giving her free rein to squander it."

Alicia listened with growing irritation at Constance's duplicity, and her own gullibility. "So she's using whatever she can to force you to pay her blackmail . . . or access to Mariah's money," Alicia mused. The unscrupulousness of the woman's nature ran deeper than she had guessed. "I detest users, and I abhor being used."

Caleb made a sound in his throat. "Constance is quite accomplished at manipulating a situation to suit her ends. My guess is she figured by coming early, she expected to gain the advantage."

"She succeeded." Alicia stopped near the fire and gazed up at Caleb. "I'm not familiar with court documents, but the papers she has authorizing her temporary custody look official. Can a Tacoma court undo what the San Francisco courts decreed?"

Caleb shook his head. "I don't know. Patrick Brown has the legal expertise to advise us."

"She can't have Mariah." The conviction in her statement came from the deepest part of her heart. "No one, particularly not money-grubbing Constance who will ship her off to an eastern boarding school, is going to take Mariah from us." Her words rang true, but sounded wrong. "I mean, from you, Caleb. She *is* your daughter . . . in every way that counts." Flustered, Alicia turned away.

"You were right the first time," she heard Caleb murmur as he headed for the horses.

Chapter Eighteen

The clouds drifted away during the evening meal. A sky so blue it seemed alive stretched over the logging camp already darkened by shadow. The clank and clatter of pots and plates took on a rhythm. Dimly, Alicia heard Corky hum a tune as he scoured the remnants of the evening meal from the plates.

"Can we grow some baby trees for Daddy to plant?"

Alicia smiled at Mariah. "I don't see why not. We can start them in flats on the mud porch."

Delighted by the notion, Mariah fidgeted on the bench. "Can we name the trees we grow, too?"

The enormous task of finding enough names for the number of seedlings required to replant the devastated hillside Kyle had taken them to this morning made her laugh. Like everything else during the last several days, the trek had filled her with conflict.

Her first glimpse of the eroded slope made her want to cry out in protest at the ecological devastation wreaked by clear-cutting the timber. The longer she stared at the expanse, the more detail crystallized. On the ridges packed by boulders and old, gnarled deadfalls, bits of color reached for the sky. The countless tiny sprigs of transplanted seedlings and several dozen drooping saplings touched her heart.

"This piece of mountain has become Caleb's project." Although Kyle had spoken to both of them, Alicia understood the explanation was for her benefit. "It seems he feels responsible for replacing every tree we took, and then some. He gets the men going in the morning, then skedaddles into the timber to dig up little trees and plant them here. He once told me he's sowing a crop for the next generation to harvest. Can you beat that?"

The sprouts struggling for life on the harsh slope made her want to cry. Caleb had not spoken about changing his methods of logging. Not once since her tirade about the horrific consequences of clear cutting had he mentioned the subject. Now, his actions spoke of his love for the land. More touching was the evidence that he had embraced an idea not found in any of his books.

The free-standing network of shelters and dams constructed into the scarred slope kept the rain from washing away the fragile green sprigs. As a caretaker of the forest, he sought to mend the blight he'd created.

"Can we?"

Drawn to the present, Alicia nodded. "We can give it a try. It will take a lot of names." She regarded Mariah, recalling the girl's diligent help in finding and transplanting seedlings earlier in the day. "Why don't we start by printing a list of all the names you can think of."

Mariah wiggled her fingers. "My printing fingers might have forgotten how to make all the letters. Maybe I can think of short names."

Stifling a laugh, Alicia helped the child off the bench. "Sounds like a good idea to me."

"I'm gonna go see what Uncle Kyle is doing with those sticks."

Alicia saw Kyle's head tilt at the mention of his name. "Maybe he'll whittle a pencil for you."

Mariah skipped across the damp ground to a beckoning "Uncle" Kyle.

Unable to remain motionless, Alicia joined Corky at a table set apart from the mess tent. The mounds of dishes he washed were part of his nightly routine. The next day's soup, consisting mostly of beans, onions, and venison, simmered on the cookstove.

"Ya don't have to do this," Corky said, handing a towel to her.

"I know. But this was one of my jobs during roundup before we sold the family ranch in Wyoming. Indulge me."

"Wyoming, huh? Women vote there."

"Yes, they do," she agreed with a smile.

Corky shrugged and sank his hands into the steaming water soaking knives and forks. He resumed humming.

Within minutes, Alicia sang with him. The clean-up slowed when they tried harmonizing in a soft duet, Alicia humming when she didn't know the words. Their laughter when one of them missed a key or word filtered into the trees.

The forest took on the guise of night, though the sun had a couple of hours until it dropped below the western ocean. Alicia and Corky finished before lamps became necessary.

Corky dried his hands, then poured a cup of hot chocolate. He snapped a damp towel over his forearm, bowed, and offered the steaming cup to Alicia. "Don't think I ever had such a good time washin' dishes."

Alicia laughed, enjoying the gallant play. She accepted the hot chocolate with a mock curtsey. "My pleasure, Sir Corky."

When she turned around, a sea of eyes watched from their log perches around the fire.

"Do you know any love songs?" one of the men asked.

His companion nudged him. "The kind of songs you know ain't love songs. They're drinkin' ditties."

A round of laughter broke the circle.

"I know a love song when I hear it," the lumberjack insisted.

"I'll bet you do," Alicia agreed. She sat on the sawed-off round beside Caleb who nestled Mariah on his thigh.

"When I was growing up, my sisters and I looked forward to roundup every year. It was hard word. Dirty. Tiring. The cattle were ornery. But, we loved it. At night we'd sit around the fire, listen to stories, and sing with the ranch hands."

"Corky there could pretend he's one of yer sisters, couldn't he?" offered another man.

Alicia laughed with them. "He doesn't have to. My sisters are here." She touched her head. "And here." Her water-wrinkled hand rested over her heart. "We'd love to sing at this fire."

An abrupt hush fell over the camp. Only the fire dared crackle a disturbance. "What would you like to hear?" She smiled at the man who'd made the original request. "A song for the lady love you miss?"

When he nodded, she drew a breath and sang an old Moody Blues favorite of her father's called "For My Lady." As the song unfolded, her voice rose and fell with the emotion of the words. Between stanzas, she imitated the background music flowing through her memory. Her voice trailed into a haunting hum at the finale. Through it all, her gaze remained locked on the man who'd requested it.

"Thank you, ma'am. That surely was the most beautiful song I ever heard," the lumberjack said, his eyes glistening.

The somber mood of the men made her uncomfortable with the realization of how seldom they saw their loved ones during the logging months. "Why don't we all sing something?" she suggested enthusiastically.

Fourteen lumberjacks instantly cowered in fear. Their reaction elicited a quick laugh. She might as well have asked them to dance nude on Broadway.

"I'll sing with you." Mariah extricated herself from Caleb's lap.

"Good! I have one brave little girl who will join me."

She handed her cup to Caleb, then pulled Mariah onto her lap. "What would you like to sing?"

"The song about the world holding hands and singing. I forgot the name."

Alicia straightened. Mariah followed suit.

Alicia raised three fingers, then counted down. The little song a beverage company adapted from an old 1970s hit emerged on-key. As Mariah grew confident, her eyes brightened with anticipation.

Alicia started an alternate round in a softer tone. Mariah followed Alicia's hand and held her part perfectly. When they finished, they hugged each other and laughed as though they were the only ones present.

"Where did a little princess like you learn how to sing so well?" Kyle asked, applauding.

"In a graveyard," Mariah answered brightly. Pride shone in her sparkling gray eyes.

"A graveyard?" Kyle repeated.

Alicia felt Caleb shift beside them. Yet another unresolved issue awaited debate.

"Uh-huh. I used the markers as notes. Mr. Kramer is high C. Mrs. Thorndyke is middle C. And Unknown Sailor is low C. Sometimes, there are notes between the graves. The ones at the foot of the graves are flats. The ones at the top are sharps. It's very simple. When I grow up and marry Jeremy, I'm gonna teach my children to sing just like Miss James taught me."

Alicia leaned back. This was the first she'd heard about Mariah's plans for Jeremy. She felt Caleb's discomfort growing by the minute.

"Jeremy?" Caleb snorted. "He's going to be an old man by the time you're ready to get married."

Mariah's eyes widened and her smile dimmed. "Oh, dear. As old as you, Daddy?"

"No," he muttered. "But old."

The restless shift of men trying hard not to laugh aloud whispered against the grating crackle of the fire.

"But you're not too old to—"

"Why don't we sing something else?" Alicia hurriedly

suggested. The direction of the conversation wasn't anywhere she or Caleb wanted to go.

"Do you want to sing 'Ave Maria'?" Mariah asked.
"We do that one good."

"Sure," Corky answered from across the fire. "We
could use an evening prayer once in a while."

The simple harmony of the song left the men silent,
almost contemplative.

"You taught her that much about music in a graveyard?" The disbelief reflected in the glow of firelight on
Caleb's features sounded in his voice.

"She has an excellent ear and near perfect pitch. For a
child as gifted as she is, the whole world is a classroom.
All she needs is a teacher."

"She has one, doesn't she?"

"Yes, Caleb," she whispered, knowing he was asking
about far more than Mariah's continued education. "She
does." Even as she answered, she felt the mire of unresolved problems and impossible secrets tug at her soul.
For now.

The sun had set by the time Alicia tucked Mariah in for
the night. With more determination than bravery, she ventured back to the fire. Most of the men had turned in for
the night. The rest drifted toward the large sleeping tents
and their cots. Caleb sat facing the fire. His forearms
rested on his knees as he fashioned a piece of wood with
a small knife.

Alicia settled beside him. "You disappeared on me this
morning and left Kyle to shepherd me and Mariah. Why?"

He glanced at her, then focused on the wood taking on
the shape of a little girl. "I thought you might want some
time away from me."

She did. And she didn't. The mountain of what needed
resolution seemed to grow with each passing hour.

"I see." And suddenly, she did see.

"Do you?"

Fate had put her on his doorstep. Love had invited her
inside. "Yes, Caleb, I do."

His hands stilled. Searching gray eyes peered into hers and refused retreat.

A small nod tilted her head. Gazing into his questioning eyes, her uncertainties evaporated.

"What do you want, Alicia? Time? Distance?"

The time for word games and evasions ran out. The battle she waged between emotions and logic, right and wrong, and desire and restraint abruptly ceased. In the void that descended, weariness swept over every front. All that remained in the unnatural stillness seeping over her turmoil like a velvet cloak was truth. "You," she whispered, offering as much honesty as the fragile internal truce allowed.

Caleb tensed. "Explain in words I can understand."

"I want you. You were right when you said we'd make love again. That I'd want to make love with you," she admitted in a shaky whisper, hardly believing the words escaped her deepest desires.

Confusion knit his brow. His head slowly moved back and forth. "You sure as hell know how to throw me off balance."

A small laugh escaped her. "Sorry. Sometimes I don't understand why I say some of the things I say. But I'm tired of fighting emotion with logic and denying what I feel."

"What is it you've been denying? Desire?"

Desire and a love she'd never thought to know and now feared losing. Eventually, she'd have to tell him the truth. He wouldn't believe it. Why should he? Sometimes she woke in the night unable to believe it until she opened her eyes. "Do *you* want *me?*"

"So damn much that if I stand up, I may take you right here."

She followed the line of his flickering glances. The strain of his trousers evidenced his answer. She swallowed hard, remembering the wood shop and the exciting beauty of making love with him. Feeling his hands on her skin. Exploring his hot flesh and the sensation of his muscles gliding like steel flowing beneath satin. With his love-filled heart thundering against her breast, he revealed an ecstasy she had lost all hope of experiencing. The brief instant when she felt his soul touch hers had changed her forever.

God help her, she wanted to experience the beauty of making love with him again. And again. And every night for the rest of her life.

"You want us to share our bodies, nothing else. Is that it?"

The teasing in his voice helped her collect her desire-ravaged thoughts and form a cogent answer. "It's complicated."

"No, it's simple. Yes or no."

Her heart skipped a thunderous beat. "I wish it were a matter of yes or no, but it isn't." She rose on shaky legs and headed for the tent where she'd stare at the ceiling for another sleepless night. "The last time I thought anything about life was simple, it was in a test tube."

The next night, Alicia scratched Nero's head and gazed around the lumber camp. Several men busied themselves with laundry. A few gathered near the cook's tent. The sporadic hum of their conversation blended with the sounds of the men settling down. On the far side of the camp, the bullwhacker groomed his oxen. The gentle praise he crooned contrasted sharply with the relentless stream of invectives he lashed upon them during the long workday.

She left Nero standing watch at the small tent. Mariah had barely kept her eyes open long enough for a quick clean-up and change into her nightgown. Alicia longed for the untroubled sleep of childhood. Since arriving at the lumber camp, she spent the nights staring at the canvas tent ceiling. Dreams steeped in questions and turmoil laced the few hours of exhausted sleep she managed.

The rustling sound of the tent door heralded Caleb's presence. He never missed an opportunity to tuck Mariah in and kiss her goodnight.

"We'll leave for home in the morning. Patrick Brown

will have seen the papers Constance filed and taken action by the time we get back," Caleb told Alicia. "Knowing Patrick, he enjoyed re-introducing himself to Constance and her attorney, Mortimer Palmer." He spat Palmer's name with unbridled animosity.

She wandered toward the fire. Jeremy had ridden down the mountain two days earlier. Since his departure, she'd often imagined Constance's wrath when he returned alone.

Alicia lingered at the edge of the jagged log circle around the fire. "Was Mortimer Palmer with her last year?"

"Yes. And in San Francisco, though I didn't know his role in all of this until she contested Jed and Margaret's wills."

She followed his gaze to the forest. If they ventured into the shadows, their conversation would be of a tactile nature. "Is Palmer that good in court?"

"He and Constance orchestrate an effective show. Neither one of them is concerned with integrity, law, or her sister's probated will.

"But Patrick can handle Palmer," he assured her. "You had the courage to make the most important move. You got Mariah out of her reach."

The sea of Alicia's need forced into patient waiting heaved in anticipation when Caleb took her hand. The simple gesture seemed so natural. Her fingers entwined with his. The caress of his thumb along the inside of her wrist teased the desire simmering in her veins. They continued toward the fringe of the encampment.

"Caleb . . ." She had to tell him before they headed down the mountain in the morning. "I, ah, I am different from the women you've known. Anyone you've known." The sudden thunder of her heart made her ears ring with the rush of blood surging through her veins. He thought her courageous. But she wasn't. She was a coward.

Caleb drew her away from the last glimmer of firelight leaking into the forest. The near darkness of the descending night above the trees formed a cocoon around them.

"I know."

He didn't know. He couldn't possibly know. The explanation begging for a voice was locked in her throat. Struggling for the right words and the ability to utter them, she accompanied him deeper into the forest.

"Caleb . . ."

He stopped abruptly.

Alarmed, she looked up at him. The moonlight straining through a break in the tree canopy illuminated the hunger reflected in his eyes. Instinctively, she touched his cheek.

The tightly restrained tethers of desire snapped.

Alicia neither knew, nor cared, which of them moved first. In the space of a single heartbeat, she held him, tasted his hunger, and savored the promise of ecstasy. A sharp breath carried the tang of spruce and the masculine scent of Caleb through her senses.

A strong hand gripped her buttocks through the layers of her skirts and lifted her against him. He backed her against a tree; his foot moved between hers. Gladly, she parted her legs, then tightened her arms around his neck. The thrust of his thigh between hers evoked a moan from her. Instantly, the ache and dampness of desire too long denied seized her.

With trembling hands, she cradled his face. Breaking the kiss was as anguishing as ripping out her own heart.

"Don't stop," she rasped.

In response, he caught her face between his hands. For the briefest instant, Caleb looked so deep into her eyes, she felt the heat of his gaze on her naked soul.

"You belong with me." The brush of his mouth against hers forced her onto tiptoes for a taste of him. "You know it." Another tantalizing brush brought the tip of his tongue over her lower lip. "I know it. Since the moment I saw you."

Without warning, his mouth descended on hers; his body, hard and ready, pressed her against the tree. Alicia's blood raced at a near violent speed.

The craving to touch him, feel his heart pound against

her naked flesh, enslaved her senses. She wanted more from him than sating the primitive drive of libido; she wanted the consummation where her soul touched his, their hearts beat as one, and any vestige of separateness disappeared. She yearned for the giving and taking until neither of them existed separately. The communion of spirit promised completeness with the union of their bodies, the mingling of their passion in glorious rapture.

He murmured her name between fiery kisses along her jaw. Her head arched against the tree, exposing her throat. The desire trembling between them threatened to burn them into the bark of the giant spruce.

Fire raced through her body when his hand closed on her breast. The eager anticipation of her aroused nipples prodded at the fabric of her chemise and blouse. Within a few heartbeats, he breached the barriers of her clothing and exposed her breasts to the heat of his callused fingers in the cool night air.

When he drew a nipple into the tantalizing moisture of his mouth, waves of delight crested against the lava of need building in her lower abdomen. The way he ravaged her with a near violent passion tempered by a lover's controlled gentleness drove her wild. She held his head against her breasts; her hips canted forward and rode high on his thigh. The urgency of his arousal pulsed against her hipbone.

He gathered her skirts and drew them up in impatient handfuls. A quick fumble released the button on her drawers. He braced a hand against her heaving abdomen as he sank to his knees. The straightening of her legs let her drawers fall around her ankles.

With the patience of a saint, Caleb removed her drawers, then stuffed them into his trouser back pocket.

"Caleb?" Though a question, she would do anything with him and allow whatever exploration he desired. But he needed to hurry. The wild passion he incited threatened a total disintegration of her senses.

As though reading her thoughts, Caleb raised her skirt to expose the delicate triangle of hair covering her femininity. The moisture of his breath against her sensitive skin wrung a small cry from her.

"Beautiful," he breathed against her curls. The back of his knuckles trailed up the inside of her thighs, teasing her legs apart. "Yes. That's the way. Let me in."

If Alicia's heart beat any faster, it would explode. It came very close when he slid a finger across the sensitive nub hidden by her feminine curls, lingering, testing, teasing, drawing her desire to a near frenzy that forced her to respond.

"Yes, sweet Alicia, show me your desire. Let me taste—" As though unable to wait even long enough to finish his thought, he replaced his finger with his mouth.

Alicia covered her mouth with the back of her hand. Surely no woman could survive the marvelous things he did with his mouth and tongue. The beautiful bubble of ecstasy she'd found swelled again with ever-brightening colors. Just when she thought she'd leave her body and fly to the moon, Caleb eased his fingers deep inside her.

The combined effect created bliss so carnal, so magnificent, she wanted to revel in the bountiful glow forever. Wave after wave of physical delight washed through her. God, how she loved him.

The fine trembling in her arms reverberated down her body. It took a while to realize the quaking came from Caleb. She held him tightly, savoring the gift of euphoria.

"'Migod, Caleb," she whispered, awed by his unrestrained worship.

He caressed her shoulders and lowered his head. The hot, moist desire raging like a blood fever kissed the side of her neck.

Alicia felt the price of his unselfish restraint. That he wanted her with such intensity stoked the tempered fires of passion. "Come inside me. Be one with my body . . . my heart . . . my soul."

With a groan of submission to a power far greater than either of them, Caleb swept her up. He carried her deeper into the forest to a moss-covered deadfall. The last strains of daylight gave the moss a velvet texture on the gnarled tree nature had sculpted into a throne.

In the near darkness, he lowered her feet to the ground and continued holding her. "You give new meaning to what I once thought was desire," he whispered, then kissed her temple.

Alicia raised her head as her fingers went to work on freeing his shirt buttons. "I have to touch you."

Caleb straightened, reluctantly easing the tight embrace pressing her abdomen against him. "Anywhere, everywhere."

The intoxicating invitation tightened the coil of excitement begging for the sweet bliss of becoming one with him. She freed the last shirt button, then brushed the fabric aside. A small hiccup escaped her throat. "You're beautiful."

"Beautiful? Men aren't beautiful."

The amazement in his voice made her smile. "You are. Inside and out."

The finger curling under her chin forced her to look up. "You like beautiful?" he asked.

In the dying light, she glimpsed his puzzlement and smiled seductively.

"All right, I'm beautiful. I'd be anything you wanted to see you smile like that." His fingers caught the hair at the side of her head and brushed it away from her face.

Eager to indulge in the uninhibited openness of his body, her fingertips trembled against his dark, silken chest hair. Given free rein, she followed the contours of his chest, splaying her fingers across his collarbone, then searching under the shirt hanging from his wide shoulders. Each movement sent delicious sensation along her arms and into the core of her desire.

"If I couldn't touch you, feel you against my skin, you'd be the best fantasy I could imagine." The hair at the center of his chest tickled her nose when she pressed her lips to his skin. A faint, salty taste teased the tip of her tongue. The violent pounding of his heart reverberated against her lips.

232

She broadened the range of her exploration. His belt gave easily. The dreamy abandon of experiencing as much of him as her desire-riddled senses could tolerate emboldened her. The pressure of his impatiently swollen flesh made the trouser buttons stubborn. When the last fastening slipped free, his hot, pulsing desire filled her hand.

Caleb stiffened with a sharp hiss of air drawn between his teeth and into the expansive chest growing hotter beneath her lips.

Driven by urges she didn't question, she flung her free arm around his neck and found his mouth. She met the wild invasion of his tongue eagerly. The raw passion of his kiss consumed her.

In a swift, sure move, Caleb caught her behind both knees. He settled on the velvet-moss throne, then drew her thighs around his.

Surprised, then delighted, Alicia threw her head back and laughed until Caleb captured a nipple with his mouth.

By bracing her hands on his shoulders, she kept her balance as she rocked from knee to knee. Grinning in response, Caleb tugged her skirts free. Finally, he settled her on his thighs, her skirts bunched around her waist.

Caleb lifted her at the hips, carefully positioning her over him. He held her, neither raising her nor lowering her, letting their scant contact intensify the need for more.

Alicia caught half a breath before lowering her mouth to his. The urgency of her kiss met a gentleness that returned her assault with tenderness.

Ever so slowly, he lowered her. Alicia cherished every pulse and nuance of their joining.

"Ah-h-h—Alicia," he whispered when he'd filled her.

The press of her breasts against his chest melded their savage heartbeats. This was what she craved in the deep abyss of her dreams. Caleb was the light of her soul, the fullness of her heart.

She murmured his name and rose as his hands opened. Only they did not release her, merely moved upward to caress her ribs, then encircle her breasts.

Amid the maelstrom of desire, Alicia felt the colors

of love wash through her. She lavished the unspoken ardor of her heart and luxuriated in the radiant love he showered on her with the brilliant colors of the sun.

She felt his raging hunger for the instant when their souls touched in totality. As though racing toward the promise, the rhythm of their lovemaking increased. She abandoned herself to craven wantonness. The first tiny tremors of her climax brought a groan from him.

"Come to heaven with me." She reached for the bubble of bliss surrounding her. His splayed fingers held the soft flesh of her buttocks and hips, guiding her, helping her.

In a wild burst of unleashed passion, he surged into her, claiming her with a ferocity that sent her soaring. They crackled and exploded like a pair of lightning bolts, the brilliance of their rapture marking their unity of spirit.

Gradually, the sounds of the forest intruded. Alicia nestled in the sanctuary of Caleb's powerful embrace. Her naked breasts were sensitive to the synchronous rise and fall of Caleb's breathing. The heady scent of their lovemaking blended with the tang of damp spruce and moist earth.

Caleb buried his face in the crook of her neck and shoulder. The reassurance of his hand gliding along her shoulder and back allowed her to bask in the afterglow.

"One day, we will make love naked, in my bed, with the lamps burning. I want to look into your eyes when the pleasure carries you away."

Emotion constricted Alicia's throat. Much as she yearned to, she dared not confess her love for him and further complicate matters. Such a completion of one's soul visited once in a lifetime, if a woman was lucky. To deny it, to cast it aside, tainted the beauty of the gift.

She bit her lower lip and reluctantly pushed away from him. "We'd better get back before we're—"

A tender kiss broke her words.

Caleb's hands cradled her face as he kissed her again, then released her. "You don't need to tell me this changes nothing. I can feel it in you with the same intensity as I feel myself inside you now."

Alicia swallowed. The flex of his hard masculinity buried in her deepest recess reminded her of what she shared with no other. He covered her breasts and fastened the ribbons of her chemise. "Caleb, there are things . . ."

"Sh-h-h. Take advantage of the moment when I'm not pressing you for an explanation. I want no angst or regret in the wake of what we've given one another tonight."

Her arms slipped around his neck. In the haven of his return embrace, she held him for a long time while her heart silently cried out her love.

Chapter Nineteen

Alicia stretched like a cat. The lower portion of the blankets slithered across her knees. A few tender spots remained from last night's marvelous lovemaking. She had anticipated the magic she shared with Caleb. The delicious satisfaction lingered sweetly.

Basking in the afterglow, her smile broadened with the realization of how well a few hours of solid sleep refreshed her. Faint stirrings from the direction of the cook's tent sharpened her awareness of what lay ahead today. She rose and straightened the cot, then quickly washed and dressed in her denims.

Mariah lay curled amid a snarl of blankets. One loosely fisted hand poked from the edge.

Alicia had almost finished packing their belongings when she heard Caleb's soft call at the tent entrance. She stuffed the skirt she'd worn last night into the bag, then hurried to the entrance.

She opened the tent door, then held it tightly to keep from hurling herself into his arms. For a long moment, she met his gaze as soft as a lover's kiss. In the span of a few heartbeats, his gaze evolved into a molten desire that heated her with its intimacy.

"Good morning," he finally said, then thrust his hands into his trouser pockets. Shirt cuffs rolled to midlength revealed the tension in his arms.

Behind him, streamers of lavender scored the eastern sky. Morning dictated a return of the distance they'd practiced successfully until last night. The perfect form of the mouth that gave her ecstasy captivated her for a long moment.

"Good morning, Caleb." She lowered her gaze slowly, drinking in the fit of his shirt across his shoulders and chest—the same chest she had explored and kissed. The brown and gray flannel hung over his abdomen, which became washboard rigid when he worked or made love.

Her fingertips tingled. She longed to close the scant distance between them. She gripped the door tarp as restraint.

Her assessment drifted lower. The buttons of his trousers strained from the pull of his fisted hands in his pockets.

"Are your hands cold?" she asked, wishing he were standing naked and they were the only two people in the world for just an hour. She'd settle for that, an hour alone and naked with the man she loved.

He withdrew his hands, then folded his arms across his chest as though he didn't trust himself. "No. Just aroused."

Alicia briefly drew her lips between her teeth as she inhaled. *And a magnificent arousal it is*. Staring, she felt the flush of desire rise across her neck and into her cheeks. A familiar dampness reminded her of how badly she wanted to know again what they'd shared last night.

"If you looked at another man the way you're looking at me, I'd pulverize him."

He spoke so softly she almost missed it. When the implications registered, she turned her head away. "Sorry. I was staring."

"Don't be sorry, unless you didn't like what you were staring at."

Flustered, Alicia faced him. "Tell me, are all men as pleased with what they have between their legs?"

Caleb grinned and relaxed. "Probably. It brings so much pleasure with the right woman."

The certainty she was the *right* woman for him was as undeniable as that of being in the wrong time. The realization cast a chilling perspective on her wild emotions. She reined them in, but they refused the caged sanctuary that kept both her and Caleb safe.

Alicia straightened her backbone in readiness for the long day ahead. "How soon do you want to leave?"

"Once Mariah wakes, we'll have something to eat, then go." Noise from the nearest barracks tent drew his attention. "I have a few things to take care of first. Why don't you grab breakfast? Corky has it ready."

She nodded, and held on to the door until he departed. After the men surrounded him, she left the tent. Instantly, Caesar and Nero vied for attention, which she lavished upon them.

Caesar accompanied her to the fire where she poured a cup of coffee from the pot Corky kept filled on a side grate. The wolf dog settled behind the log she sat upon and watched the tent where Mariah slept.

Alicia was glad for the early morning isolation.

Her sisters were who-knew-where. Her career was gone. Every material thing she'd worked for lay beyond her reach. Even what she'd thought she knew, she didn't.

This was 1895.

Everything was different. Society. The culture. Things that seemed so simple a hundred years from now were taboo.

How could she have been so stupid as to think she and Caleb could have any kind of intimate relationship? Each time they made love, they played baby roulette. Eventually, they'd win the jackpot. Then what?

"I didn't want that," she whispered.

"Didn't want what?" Kyle settled beside her. "Or am I eavesdropping?"

"Yes, you're eavesdropping," she managed in a kinder voice than the one decrying the interruption.

"Any good answers?"

Alicia shook her head. "Sometimes there are no answers. No acceptable ones, anyway."

"I've got a question for you, Miss James." The lumberjack rose from the log and stretched toward the fire. The lighted twig he brought to the bowl of his pipe danced as he drew the flame to the tobacco.

"Answers seem to be in short supply these days." Chin in hand, she studied the sandy-haired man for an instant. That was all it took to understand his green eyes saw far more than most.

A quick grin crinkled his day-old growth of whiskers. "Oh, you know the answer. The trouble is, I have no right to ask the question eating at my curiosity."

"What's your game, Mr. Larsen?"

"Game?" Perplexity pinched his brow.

The sincerity in his unwavering green eyes assured her that he did not play games. "Ask your question."

Kyle's eyebrows rose a fraction. "Before I ask, I ought to tell you that Caleb Marker's the most decent man I've ever known. Over the years, he's helped all of us some way or another. He deserves something other than trouble coming his way." Kyle drew hard on his pipe, then exhaled a cloud of smoke. "What I want to know from you, Miss James, is whether or not you're in love with Caleb?"

The question stunned her. Did it show? Did a neon sign light up over her head whenever someone spoke of Caleb? And if Kyle Larsen could read her deep feelings for Caleb, did the townsfolk see it, too? Would they know about the ceaseless desire they harbored for each other? And if they did, then what?

"You're right, Mr. Larsen. It's a very personal question." One she had no intention of answering.

Kyle ground his boot heel into the damp earth. "It was, and I thank you." A haze of aromatic pipe smoke seeped

239

from between his teeth clenched on the pipe stem.

"For what?"

"Answering."

Confused, she searched his expression and found a disturbing confidence. "I didn't answer."

"Sometimes what people don't say tells me more than what they do." He drew on his pipe, then exhaled slowly. "You couldn't have picked a better man." The sudden grin he bestowed took her aback. "Even if you had a choice about who you fall in love with."

Caesar popped to his feet.

Flummoxed, Alicia followed his line of sight. Nero stood at attention beside the tent entrance.

Glad for a reason to leave Kyle Larsen, Alicia stood. "Excuse me. Mariah is awake."

An awareness of Kyle's all-seeing gaze followed her to the tent. If he foolishly believed love conquered all, disappointment was bound to find him.

Love did not conquer all.

Caleb nodded farewell to Kyle. Years of working together allowed them to read each other without exchanging a word. However, Caleb failed to interpret the knowing expression lighting his friend's face this morning. The temptation to question him died quickly. The man revealed only what he wished someone to know, and in his own good time.

Caleb checked Edgecombe's saddle for the third time, then lifted Mariah onto it. "Let us know if you get tired." He checked the placement of the stirrups.

"I will." Mariah's solemn gaze assured him that she understood the importance of the warning.

He caressed the delicious roundness of Alicia's denim-clad hips as he helped her mount. A hint of the passionate memories they shared flickered in her smile.

The crisp morning seemed too cheerful for what lay ahead. A few clouds drifted across a brilliant blue sky that promised fair weather.

Caleb set a deliberate pace for home. Frequent backward glances at Mariah often met Alicia's vigilant eyes. His daughter's sure-footed pony negotiated the rough terrain with plodding diligence.

The myriad problems facing him melted into the single, imperative perplexity of Alicia. The intimacy they shared in the forest haunted him, tensing his body and firing his blood. Until the day he'd found her wandering in his woods, he'd made no distinction between having sex and making love—not even with Margaret. Unknowingly, Alicia had altered his perceptions.

Many of the countless books he'd devoured over the long Alaskan winters described the bittersweet consequences of falling in love.

Nothing within the pages of his books adequately described the fierce need to lose himself in his love's eager, passionate body. No imagination documented the heights to which they ascended during the communion of their lovemaking.

Her refusal to wed him defied logic. And she seemed so logical in all other areas. What secret could she harbor that was so dire as to deny them a life together?

Perhaps she did not love him.

The possibility chilled him in the warm morning.

No, she'd not have given herself to him without love, or at least tender emotion.

True, she was like no woman he'd met, not in Sitka, San Francisco, or during his brief trips to Tacoma. The intelligence and wisdom she exhibited outshone most men of his acquaintance. Were the qualities he prized responsible for the great secret she refused to share? What could possibly be so terrible she could not trust him with knowing?

She'd assured him the man she'd married and divorced had no interest in her, or she in him. He believed her.

Memories of her paltry expectations of their lovemaking in the wood shop made him smile. She had anticipated his disappointment. Hell, if that were the fabric of disappointment, he'd gladly suffocate wrapped in it.

After their first liaison, he knew he'd never get enough

of her, but he hadn't thought making love could get any better—until last night. Now, fantasies of having her naked in his bed, without concern for time and propriety, consumed him.

A couple of hours into the journey, a backward glance at Alicia, then Mariah, brought him out of his speculation. He called a rest and examined the pony while Alicia and Mariah visited the bushes.

Hearing the sweet music of their laughter made him smile. When they joined him, each carried handfuls of lavender and Alaskan violets. He watched in fascination as Alicia braided the delicate flowers into a crown for Mariah.

On the trail again, Alicia and Mariah sang, pausing only when the hazards of the trail demanded full concentration. Their music sent his heart on a whirlwind that carried him to the pinnacle of his hopes, then dashed them with the reality she did not want to share his life.

For their next rest, Caleb detoured through the trees to a swift-running creek. On the sun-dappled bank, they sat on boulders and consumed the simple meal Corky had sent.

When they resumed the journey, Mariah rode with Alicia. Soon, Alicia launched into an elaborate tale about talking animals rife with very human dilemmas. Caleb listened with growing admiration and an angst-ridden heart. Today, they were a family. Damn, but he liked the feeling.

"That was a very imaginative story," Caleb complimented at the conclusion of the story Alicia called *The Lion King*.

"But I don't understand," Mariah protested.

"What don't you understand?" Alicia asked.

"Why didn't the little lion tell his mother about what happened? Why did he have such a mean uncle? And was the uncle named Scar before or after he got a scar on his face?"

Alicia's laughter dispatched a flock of birds from their

roosting places in the trees. "I don't know, sweetheart. It's just a story."

"Well, I'd never run away from Daddy or you. No matter what. I'm never leaving home."

"What's the matter, Mariah?"

Caleb exchanged a concerned glance with Alicia, then drew his horse beside Krakatau.

"I don't never want to have to ever, ever leave you and Daddy." Tears brimmed Mariah's gray eyes when she looked up at Alicia. "Aunt Constance said I have to go live with her and go to school far, far away. Are you taking me back to her?"

"No," Caleb answered harshly. "You aren't going with your Aunt Constance."

Mariah blinked back her tears and gazed on him with adoring eyes. "Promise?"

"I promise," Caleb vowed. He angled his horse closer, then plucked her from the saddle, and carried her on his left arm. The small, trusting arms encircling his neck sought comfort he would always give.

He would pack her and Alicia up and light out for Anchorage or the Yukon Territory in the middle of the night before he let Constance take her.

Although he had warned her of his intent regarding Mariah earlier, in that moment Alicia understood the depth of Caleb's commitment to those he loved. Regardless what it cost him, what he gave up, or the consequences, no one would take the daughter of his heart. He'd take care of her, protect her, and lavish her with affection, then let go when she became a wife.

Alicia lagged behind under the pretense of checking Edgecombe's tether. She found it hard to breathe, despite the clean mountain air scented with summer flowers and conifers. She ached to tell Caleb that she loved him—and that she came from a time and place not found in any book he'd read. Even more, she wanted him to embrace both her love and the truth. It didn't matter that the story of her arrival on Baranov Island was incredible. What mattered was his acceptance.

While his capacity for love might seem limitless, the likelihood of him accepting the impossible was just that. Impossible.

"I see home," Mariah announced, then giggled and hugged Caleb's neck.

Home.

The Marker house possessed an aura of warmth and friendliness similar to the James family ranch before the death of her parents. Love had filled the rooms of the old ranch house. Serenity had embraced her there.

The condominium she'd bought in Drexel was convenient, but never felt like *home*. New when she bought it, the dwelling had remained sterile of emotional character.

Home.

Alicia longed to plant the roots of her future deep in the Alaskan soil Caleb cherished.

They crossed the clearing and approached the barn. Caesar and Nero raced ahead. Within minutes, Jeremy appeared from behind the barn. He wiped perspiration from his brow with the back of his forearm, then waved.

Mariah greeted him with enthusiasm.

Alicia shook off the bleak turmoil weighing her thoughts. There was much to do before dinner.

"Did you have any problems delivering the mail?" Caleb asked, handing Mariah down to the young man.

"Nothing unexpected." Jeremy swung Mariah through the air and grinned when she giggled. "Mr. Brown expects you'll want to see him shortly after Miss Cunningham takes up residence in Sitka."

Alicia dismounted and stood beside Caleb. "That sounds like we still have the pleasure of her company."

"Indeed, we do."

A palpable shift in Caleb's demeanor summoned a familiar tension present since Constance's arrival. He dropped onto one knee and cradled Mariah at the shoulders. "Would you help Jeremy with the horses?"

"Yes," she answered with a smile.

"Good. Take your time. When you're done, maybe he'll need help hitching up the buggy."

Mariah's eyes grew wide. "For Aunt Constance to go home?"

Alicia's heart skipped a beat. They had tried not to alarm the child, but she had known anyway. Sadly, Constance had made sure of it.

"Not home, but at least to Sitka." Caleb kissed her forehead.

Alicia gazed at the house, wondering whether she should remain with Mariah.

Caleb settled her uncertainty by resting his hand on her shoulder. "Shall we, Miss James?"

She headed for the mud porch off the kitchen. "Are you sure I should go in with you?" She wished he'd reconsider. The prospect of being privy to a confrontation between Caleb and Constance was as enticing as a root canal.

"Yes. Everything will be in the open. We'll present Constance with a united front."

"Are you sure that's wise? I mean, I don't want her to think there is more to our . . . our arrangement than business." Oh, heavens! What if Constance read the depth of their involvement as easily as Kyle Larsen had?

"Constance doesn't need a reason to sling accusations or bend a situation to what she perceives as her advantage. You spent three days with her. Surely you learned she has no regard for anyone beyond herself." He cupped her elbow as they mounted the steps.

Alicia heaved a sigh of resignation. "I don't want to antagonize her." If she had to bite her tongue until it bled, she vowed to remain in the background. This wasn't her fight; it was Caleb's. She had neither a right, nor an obligation to interfere. However, the battle lines had blurred the day she'd removed Mariah from Constance's reach. Undoubtedly, she'd incurred an enemy for life.

"Constance views anything keeping her from getting

her way as an offense," Caleb breathed, opening the kitchen door.

"I'm very glad you're home, Caleb," Maude said from the middle of the kitchen. She released the butter churn plunger and pushed her glasses up the bridge of her nose. Beads of perspiration dotted her forehead, though the kitchen felt cool.

"I apologize for the situation, Maude. Thanks for staying around. I expected you to visit in town for a while." He pumped water into a glass and handed it to her.

"And leave the hussy alone here? Not on your life! I locked your office and Alicia's bedroom. Didn't want the nosy woman going through every drawer in the place." Maude closed the subject with a curt nod, then sipped the cool water. "The shrew has no regard for anyone beyond herself."

The clench of Caleb's jaw revealed how offensive he regarded Constance's actions. "Thank you for watching over things, Maude. Where is she?"

"In the parlor. She expects me to bring her tea like she's some sort of English lady or royalty."

"Maude," Alicia started, feeling guilty for leaving the entire burden of the Marker house on Maude's shoulders. "Did she have any adverse effects from, you know, the wine?"

Maude shook her head. "Just complained about Caleb's poor judgment for wine. Truth is, she was so angry you took Mariah away, it's amazing she didn't choke on her own venom.

"She and her lawyer friend tried to get the law to go after you. Patrick Brown told that snake Palmer to take it up with the new judge."

Alicia felt the starch melt in her knees. Constance was a bulldozer swathed in silk.

"I'm a lucky man to have friends like you and Patrick," Caleb said.

Maude opened the top of the butter churn. "Luck has nothing to do with it." She pulled out the plunger. "Lift this up for me, will you?"

Caleb put the churn on the table sideways, then held it while Maude crammed a couple of towels around it to keep it from rolling. "She's found a new tactic. If she's successful, there will be drastic changes."

"She's desperate, all right. You do what you have to do, Caleb. I know it'll be the right thing for all of us." Maude used a wooden spoon to scoop the butter from the churn.

The rich tone of the parlor clock chimed four times.

Maude looked up from her chore. "Tea time. The queen awaits."

"By all means, let's not keep her waiting a moment longer. Alicia."

Appalled by the toll Constance had exacted on Maude, Alicia accompanied Caleb through the kitchen.

No sooner did they enter the parlor than Constance rose from Caleb's chair. A cloud of pink and white voile glided across the room with amazing speed. Alicia quickly jumped sideways.

Caleb remained rooted to the floor.

Constance's arms entwined his neck. The kiss she planted on his lips greeted him like a long lost lover.

Alicia blinked several times, sure the scene was part of a delusional episode brought on by prolonged stress. Each time she looked, Constance had her body pressed against Caleb and her mouth claiming his.

Alicia held the back of the couch to keep her legs from buckling. Obviously, there was something about their "history" she didn't know. Jealousy became an acid burning in the center of her chest.

"Caleb, my darling, it has been so long. I've missed you terribly. I just couldn't wait until August to see you," Constance gushed.

Alicia clenched her teeth to keep from ripping Constance off Caleb by the roots of her perfect blond curls.

Caleb grasped Constance's forearms. When she didn't release her lock on his neck, he tugged sharply and broke her hold. "Why are you in my house?"

Constance smiled so sweetly that Alicia bit the inside of her lips to ensure silence.

"Why, darling, I've thought it over, and I intend to live here. I've realized how foolish I've been, and I've decided to allow you to court me."

Good grief. Constance and Caleb? Alicia's stomach lurched.

"You're demented." Caleb wiped his mouth with the back of his hand.

Eyes downcast, her mouth drawn into a sad frown, Constance hung her head. "I know I hurt you. I was a child. Barely eighteen."

"What the hell are you talking about?"

"Why, Caleb, it was no secret you wanted me and settled for Margaret. Even Margaret knew; that's why she ran off with your brother. She hated being second."

The coy smile she bestowed on Caleb would have enticed any man. "I was a thoughtless child then. I've grown up. I know now what a marvelous life we could have together. What a comfortable home we could make for Mariah." She ran a fingertip along Caleb's jaw.

"This isn't about Mariah. It's about you. You quit being a child the day you started talking, but you've always been thoughtless, Constance." Caleb removed her hand.

"Oh, Caleb, I know you don't mean to distress me, and I do apologize for causing you a moment of hurt."

Alicia observed the exchange with the macabre fascination of watching two cobras vie for lethal weaknesses.

"What's the matter, Constance? Won't Mortimer Palmer marry you?"

"Oh, now Caleb, you know Mortimer and I are nothing more than business acquaintances. It's you I've decided to marry."

"Why? Are you pregnant again?"

Alicia froze. Pregnant *again?* Good grief, had there been something between them years ago?

Color surged into Constance's cheeks. Blotches of crimson stained her neck and the exposed flesh of her upper chest. The pink hue of her dress clashed sharply with her new complexion.

Alicia swallowed hard, barely breathing in anticipation of what came next.

"Of course not! What on earth would make you dare ask such an ungentlemanly question?"

Caleb stepped aside and gestured to the couch. "Won't you have a seat, Miss James? It has been a long, tiring ride."

And about to get worse, Alicia decided. She moved around the end of the couch and sat.

Caleb settled in his chair, rested his elbows on the arms, and laced his fingers across his chest. The steely confidence surrounding him assumed control of the game the two of them had practiced over the years.

"Is it your intention to ignore me, Caleb? You should ensure my comfort and offer me your chair. You certainly don't mean to relegate me to share a place on the couch with someone who smells like horses." Constance crossed her arms beneath her lush breasts. The action exposed more cleavage. "I know you can be very considerate when you choose to be."

Caleb's eyes narrowed. He took a moment before responding, then did so in a calm, calculated tone. "It isn't possible to be discourteous to an unwelcome squatter."

"I'll overlook your short temper, Caleb. I'm sure you must be tired after your long ride. When you've had time to consider, you'll realize I'm offering the best possible solution for Mariah. Just think of the doors we can open for that child. I have the wedding arranged. We'll be married in Tacoma." Constance counted her plans on her ringed fingers.

"Tacoma is, well, neutral and midway between San Francisco and Sitka. We have no bad memories there, do we?"

An ominous chill tiptoed up Alicia's backbone. The complex ruse took on substance. Constance had contrived to have it all—Caleb, Mariah, and control.

Constance moved to the next finger. "We'll live in Sitka

249

part of the summer so you can oversee your business." Her blue eyes scanned the ceiling. The subtle sway of her body in Caleb's direction accompanied a deep breath that accentuated her bosom.

"The rest of the year, we'll live in San Francisco. You can join one of those clubs you liked to frequent with your learned friends. You'll see, our marriage will be absolutely perfect for us and Mariah."

Caleb raised his eyebrows; the steely shards of his gaze never left Constance. "I have no intention of marrying you or living anywhere other than here."

"But Caleb . . ."

"Don't play your games with me, Constance."

"Think of the benefits to Mariah."

"The answer is no. To everything."

Constance crumbled to her knees, her hands gripping the muscle high on his thigh.

Alicia tilted her head for a better view of where Constance slid her hands and the direction of her gaze. The entire scenario made her feel like part of a virtual reality soap opera.

"Have you any idea what I'm offering you, Caleb?" The press of her breasts against his knee accompanied the seductive question.

"Nothing that hasn't been offered before. I didn't want it then. I don't want it now."

"But we spoke of marriage."

"Not *we,* Constance. You, my brother, and your sister spoke of marriage to give your child a name."

"You're a cruel man, Caleb. Far too cruel to raise my sister's delicate little girl."

As Constance rose, a slow, deadly smile spread across her fine features. "I'd hoped we could share her. I was even willing to do my duty as your wife." Constance heaved a dramatic sigh and gazed heavenward with the sanctity of a martyr. "No sacrifice is too great when it comes to my love for my niece. My conscience won't allow me to leave her in this desolate place without a mother or an adequate role model."

"What am I? Chopped liver?" Alicia blurted.

The disdain Constance conveyed as her gaze scoured Alicia's dusty boots, her stained denims, loose shirt, and uncombed hair proclaimed that was indeed how Constance regarded her. "You, I dismissed as totally irresponsible, unsuitable, and unconventional when you took that sweet child away. You haven't the sense to come in out of the rain. No, you dragged that baby into a storm and forced her into dangerous territory without protection. You, Miss James, deserve to be horsewhipped for your actions." Constance lifted her chin, then sniffed. "Not to mention the anguish and distress you inflicted on me. Why, I was so distraught that you would do such a thing, I was ill for two days."

Alicia pressed her lips together to keep the acrid retort on the tip of her tongue from escaping.

"Constance." Caleb straightened in his chair.

In response, she lifted her head and gave him one of her best smiles. "Yes, Caleb?"

"Get out of my house."

"Why Caleb, you can't really mean for me to leave. My darling niece just returned from that dreadful trip in the wilderness. I haven't even seen her."

"Whatever you don't have packed and out of my house in an hour, I'll throw into the pig wallow."

"You wouldn't—"

"I would. And I'd enjoy it. You aren't welcome here. You knew that and imposed upon my housekeeper and Mariah's governess in my absence."

"We're family. I have a right to impose if I so choose."

"We're not family, and you have no right to anything here."

"You're not thinking clearly, Caleb. Perhaps—"

"You have fifty-nine minutes of your hour left. If you're not out front for Jeremy to take into town, he'll unhitch the buggy and you can walk."

"Surely you aren't serious." The gemstones in her rings glittered as she wrung her hands.

"You've never known me to be otherwise." He rose

from the chair and used his towering height to intimidate her. "Now, get out of my house and don't ever come back."

Rage shattered Constance's facade. "I'll not be bullied by you, Caleb Marker. You owe me—"

"I owe you nothing!"

The boom of his shout turned Alicia's mouth dry. The man of infinite patience had just vented the relief valve on his emotions.

"Yes, you do! You took my niece away. You stole her in the courts. You greedily gathered every penny rightfully mine and Mariah's."

"Jed and Margaret didn't leave you anything."

"Well, they would have if you hadn't convinced them to leave it all to Mariah."

"I didn't convince them of anything. I live in the wilderness, remember? It's not as though I brow beat them into the conditions of their will."

"But Mariah—"

"Was left without a penny, too. Jed and Margaret gave her to me, Constance. They knew I'd care for her and protect her from greedy, grasping, conniving shysters like you and Mortimer Palmer."

Caleb squared his shoulders. "You have fifty-five minutes to get out of my house, or so help me God, I'll pick you up and throw you out."

"You'll be sorry, Caleb. I'll make you sorry." Chin high, she wrinkled her nose at Alicia, then stomped from the parlor.

Alicia had no doubt Constance would use every weapon in her considerable arsenal to do just that.

Within moments, the sounds of drawers slamming onto the floor burst down the hall and into the parlor.

Caleb raised his eyebrows and glanced at the ceiling, then smiled. "There is a God, and some days He likes me."

Chapter Twenty

The next day in Patrick Brown's office, Caleb wasn't as confident about the favor in which God regarded him.

"Are you telling me some judge in Tacoma can sign papers to nullify the decision handed down in the San Francisco courts?" His darkest fears unfolded before him.

"All I'm saying is that the papers are legal. Apparently, they convinced Judge Farrell to reopen the guardianship question. Like she initially asserted, Constance contends Mariah needs the female influence, preferably that of a relative." Patrick removed his thin wire glasses and rubbed the bridge of his nose. "We have two ideologies bumping heads here."

"Bumping heads. That's a hell of a way to determine Mariah's future." Caleb rose from the chair and went to the window.

Outside, life continued in quiet routine. Regardless of what happened with Mariah, little in Sitka would change. That was one of the reasons he loved the place. He thrived on the stability and peace of the island and the people who called it home.

"Until recently, the courts refused challenges to a man's right to raise his family or those under his guardianship the way he sees fit. Constance found the one judge in the country who takes a different view. Maybe Farrell wants to write a new law. Maybe he believes a child's interests are best in a same-gender household. Maybe his motives are of a more nefarious nature. Regardless, he's given Constance an opportunity to get what she lost in San Francisco. Mariah."

"She has no intention of taking a personal hand in raising Mariah. She'll send her off to a boarding school. Probably in Boston, where she thinks there are more opportunities for a rich husband."

"You don't know that," Patrick said.

"Yes, I do. She told Alicia James of her intent."

"We have to take the approach she believes it's in Mariah's best interest. There are some who support a boarding school education."

"Education has nothing to do with it. She's after the money it would require to support her in Boston or wherever she decides to send Mariah." Disgust left a sour taste in his mouth. "Of course, as her guardian, she'd have to accompany Mariah. The child couldn't be left alone in a strange city."

Caleb turned from the window and met Patrick's studious gaze. "Have you any idea of the financial ramifications of her demands?"

"Her objective is money, right?" Patrick pushed away from the expansive cherry desk.

"I've already tried buying her off. She probably used a portion of what I gave her last year to finance this latest debacle." He shoved his hands into his trouser pockets and approached his chair. "How do I end this, Patrick? She won't back off until she has every cent Jed and Margaret left and everything I have, too. This farce is nothing short of legal blackmail."

"You could refuse to give her any money."

Caleb shook his head. "And cast Mariah on the mercy

of a woman who has none? No, I couldn't. Constance knows I wouldn't."

"In that case, the only chance you have of raising the issue of Mariah's guardianship beyond Constance's reach is through marriage."

A shiver of revulsion rippled through him. "Marriage to Constance is not an option."

"Good God, man. I wasn't suggesting you cast yourself into the fires of Hell." Patrick circled one of his many doodles for emphasis. "I'd hate to defend you in a murder trial.

"What about marriage to Miss James? She seems an upstanding young woman. I've seen her with Mariah, as have most in town. There's no question of her loyalty to the child."

This wasn't the first time the thought of sharing his life, his bed, and filling the house with their children had crossed his mind.

When he didn't answer, Patrick continued. "I'd draw up adoption papers. The two of you could sign them after the wedding. Once filed with the court, Constance is powerless on all fronts. That would end it, Caleb. Forever."

So simple, other than the fact Alicia wouldn't consent to marriage. In time, she might weaken, but time wasn't on his side. "What other options do I have?"

"None as irrefutable as marriage and formal adoption." Patrick braced his forearms on the edge of the desk. "I hope you and Miss James can put the welfare of your niece ahead of any notion of marrying for love and go forward with a wedding. Palmer has broached the issue of an unmarried woman living in your home and the possibility of impropriety. The longer this drags out, the more likely Miss James is to suffer the effects of gossip that eventually touches all of you."

Caleb swore under his breath.

"They don't have to prove anything, just raise the morality question to bolster their innuendoes. Soon they'll start sounding like facts. Gossip requires no substance to do damage."

Caleb settled into the chair and thought for a long moment. "When does the new judge arrive?"

"Judge Wardel is in Juneau. He'll probably be here in a couple of days. We're on his docket."

"Can he nullify the court papers Constance procured in Tacoma?"

Patrick shrugged. "I don't know whether he will. Our job is to give him a reason to rule in your favor."

The odds seemed piled against him. He'd attempt to ensure Mariah's welfare in the courts. If they failed, he'd keep his promise. Constance Cunningham would not have Mariah as long he drew a breath.

Ready to tackle the problem at hand, Caleb gestured at the shelves of legal tomes behind Patrick's chair.

"Which of those books can show us what we need to do in preparation for the hearing?"

Alicia devoted the day to restoring routine to Mariah's schooling. As though sensing the great disturbance roiling under the veneer of normalcy, Mariah pored over her lessons. She asked questions only when Alicia's mind wandered and her explanations faltered.

In the schoolroom portion of Mariah's room, imagining the child anywhere else bordered on the fantastic. The absurd. The magnificent carvings on the girl's four-poster bed reflected the love and time Caleb lavished on the daughter of his heart. A judge need only speak with the child for five minutes to comprehend the wealth of values Caleb lovingly instilled.

Alicia whispered a prayer of thanks for the nurturing childhood her own parents had lavished on their children. Growing up in a family that thought it important to shower a child with love and guidance accentuated the injustice of Constance's intent.

Staring at the swan forming a bed poster, Alicia realized she had needed her sisters far more than they needed her. Since the divorce from Chet, her involvement in their lives had protected her from cultivating a personal life of her own.

Caitlyn had been right when she'd called her a coward for not dating. In her naïveté, she'd struck at the core of Alicia's secret. She was a coward, and had always been a coward. Anything she'd done she remotely construed as brave, she had done with her sisters.

She had married Chet, believing it would last forever. She'd never dated anyone else. Never considered the possibility of his infidelity until it happened. In her eyes, their safe relationship forged from years of familiarity would endure anything. Had she been brave enough to look around, perhaps to date another man, she might have realized what had been missing.

The perfect hindsight in the world of *ifs* and *should haves* became oppressive. The lessons gnawed at her. Distantly, she wondered whether the reason for her being in this time and place was to strip away the cloaks of security she'd thought she owned in Drexel.

She couldn't have it all.

Like traveling through time, the events crashing down on her and the others were beyond her control. And like falling in love with Caleb, there was no way to determine exactly where those events might lead. Nor could she have planned for the emotional roller coaster she rode since meeting him in the woods.

If she were a brave woman, she'd explain what happened to her and how she'd come to lose her sisters.

If she were a brave woman, she'd tell him about Yolanda D'Arcy's prophecy and how it had come true.

If she were a brave woman, she'd have no qualms about explaining her circumstances, regardless of whether she understood how or why they existed. Logic be damned. Caleb would have to accept the truth because she could not allow their relationship to progress until he did. Therein lay the rub.

If she were a brave woman and acted as a brave woman should, she'd also be unemployed and disbelieved by the man she loved.

Alicia heaved a sigh. Maybe it was a good thing she wasn't brave.

257

A small voice warned her that the time for secrecy was finite.

She nodded, knowing she'd face the inevitable when it came, just as she always did—with suppressed emotions and a thick hide. Only this time, even a titanium shield wouldn't protect her heart from the pain sure to follow losing Caleb and Mariah.

Drexel, Wyoming, Bethany, and Caitlyn never seemed farther away.

Shortly after tucking Mariah in for the night, Caleb joined Alicia on the veranda. The book he carried reminded her of his dogmatic belief in finding solutions to life's problems in the written word.

"We had almost given up on you joining us for supper tonight," Alicia said as he settled beside her on the swing.

"Patrick and I were preparing for our case," he answered. He placed the book on his thigh and shifted so he could look directly at her. "There will be a hearing."

Hope leaped in Alicia's heart. "Here in Sitka, you can't possibly doubt the outcome. Why, everyone knows what a well-adjusted, happy child Mariah is. They know you're the reason."

"The location favors us more than a Tacoma courtroom."

His agreement lacked conviction. "Why are you so morose, Caleb? What else is eating at you?"

"What the good folk of Sitka think and know has little to do with what will take place at the hearing. Judge Alphonse Wardel's decision is the only important one. For him to throw out Constance's petition, he must defy Judge Farrell of Tacoma. Farrell is a powerful man who could influence Wardel's future."

The bubble of optimism burst. Was there no haven for justice without politics? She hadn't expected the pervasive impact here, but she understood it too well to deny the significance. Perhaps it was part of the human condition and had nothing to do with any particular place in time.

"Is Judge Wardel the kind of man who puts his career ahead of his sense of right and wrong?"

"I don't know. Neither does Patrick, though he's pleaded a number of cases before him." Caleb gazed at the trees beyond the yard. "There isn't much in the way of court proceedings in Sitka to test a man in the way this does. You never know a man's true character until he comes to a crossroad."

"Or a woman's," she murmured, examining the calluses on her palms. During the long silence that followed, she felt the heated question of his gaze and began fidgeting.

"Are you at a crossroad, Alicia?"

The implications of the softly asked question seeped into the marrow of her bones. Her heart accelerated with the fury of a hummingbird's wings in flight. "I suppose I am where we're concerned."

"We have now come to the heart of the dilemma. You hold all the answers."

Startled by what sounded like an accusation, her gaze met his and found torment. She tried to look away, but could not. He hid none of his deep feelings in open conflict. The emotional honesty and the courage with which he invited her to see even the weak side of him daunted her. "I hold no answers."

"But you do, Alicia. Shall I explain?" Something in his demeanor promised she didn't want an explanation.

"Please do." The words spilled out in a whisper before she could stop them.

Mercifully, he remained silent for a long time. The struggle raging inside of him played out in the narrowing of his eyes and the grim set of his mouth.

"After Jed went off to college, I spent every waking hour building the sawmill and cutting trees. Every winter, I went to San Francisco for a month or two. The libraries and parlors of the gentlemen's clubs continuously opened new doors on my ignorance. When I came home, I tried to expand on what I'd learned and delved into the trunks of books I acquired on each trip.

"After Jed and Margaret eloped, they settled in San

Francisco. A year went by. Then they came to see me."
He stretched his legs and shook his head.

"They were like a warm hearth on a freezing night. I'd
missed them. Seeing them together, seeing how right they
were for each other . . ." He faltered, his eyes narrowing.
"Margaret belonged with Jed. Not with me."

"You forgave them," Alicia said, awed by the generosity of his spirit. "Because you loved them."

"Yeah. Funny thing was how much life improved for
me once I did. The three of us were closer than ever. Oh,
I still loved Margaret, but in a different way. She was my
brother's wife.

"Jed and I walked the floor the night Mariah was born.
After we took turns holding her, we went into Jed's study,
smoked cigars, and killed a couple bottles of fine brandy.
It was the happiest night of my life. Theirs, too.

"Six months later, Margaret and Jed were dead. An
electrical fire started inside the house. Jed got Mariah out
and went back in for Margaret. Neither one of them made
it out.

"I've been dealing with Constance and the courts ever
since."

Alicia's chin quivered under the stain of forced silence.
She ached to cry out to him that it wasn't necessary for
him to bare his soul to her. She had seen it, felt it, when
they made love, and knew the rare treasure of his heart.

"Mariah became my family. I had a child; I didn't need
a wife." A sudden, genuine grin erased the morose lines
from his face and brought a sparkle to his eyes. "I
wouldn't have had time for a wife. Maude was a pillar of
support, but she never changed a diaper or fed Mariah if
I was in the house. I wouldn't have had it any other way.

"Then you came out of nowhere, and everything
changed again."

Alicia's stomach rose to her throat. Was it possible he
knew she arrived in a cloud of fog?

"I discovered another kind of love, one that made me
question my sanity and permeated every aspect of my being."

The back of his fingers grazed the soft skin below her ear. A familiar flame of desire warmed her from the inside. His touch promised a wholeness to her being. Without it, she stood as an island of isolation with no hope of reaching the life visible on the horizon. Her head tilted in the direction of his touch.

"I love you, Alicia. Sometimes, I think you love me, too." This time his quick grin carried a sorrow she ached to dispel with the truth and a kiss.

Caleb's smile faded. "But you don't love me."

"Caleb, I never said I didn't . . ." She turned away, unable to see his confusion or confess the deepest emotions of her heart.

"I know. I've no wish to make you uncomfortable, Alicia. You do not want to wed me. I accept your decision. In time, maybe you'll change your mind. It is the interim we need to discuss."

"What's there to discuss? We'll go on as we have been." Even as she said it, the impossibility registered with heavy finality.

"We can't, Alicia. What you don't seem to realize is if there is an *us* without a marriage, there will be only two of us—until we have a child of our own."

"What are you talking about? Of course we'll have Mariah—"

"The rest of the world does things a bit differently than they do in Wyoming. Courts do not allow a child to live in a home where two of the inhabitants are indulging in the pleasures of marriage without legal sanction."

"But we aren't . . . At least we're not . . ." Alicia's voice trailed. They had made love. Knowing how they felt, it was only a matter of time and opportunity until they made love again. Lifting her gaze to meet his, any illusion she harbored to the contrary faded.

"Constance will argue Mariah needs a female role model more than a father figure. It nearly worked in San Francisco. If not for the friends who loved Jed and Margaret, Constance might have won.

"Mortimer has begun sowing the seeds of doubt and gossip concerning you."

"Then perhaps it's best for you and Mariah if I leave."

He paused. "Do you want to leave us?"

Tears stung her eyes at the thought of never seeing them again. "No! But I won't bring harm or give them an avenue to take Mariah by staying."

Caleb thumbed a tear from her cheek. "Should it become necessary, would you go to England with me and Mariah?" He cupped her head. "I won't insist on marriage, but we will travel as man and wife. You'll sleep with Mariah."

"Oh, Caleb, I—" The words refused to come. How could she explain she refused his marriage proposal for his sake, not for hers? She needed either less conscience or more courage and didn't have the right amount of either. If she had the courage to tell him the truth, he'd disbelieve her. No relationship survived long when one party thought the other a liar or delusional. If she had less conscience, she'd marry him and not worry about it. On the other hand, no relationship survived long when based on secrets and the inability to trust.

"I know this is asking a great deal. Will you think about it?"

Alicia nodded and stared into the long shadows giving the forest an eerie quality. When she looked beside her a long time later, she was alone on the swing.

Chapter Twenty-one

Taut hours stretched like elastic over the next two days. As though sensing the shroud of worry surrounding the Marker household, the sun hid behind rain clouds. The tension sizzling between Caleb and Alicia deepened the chasms of long silences. They spoke freely about everything except the topic dominating their thoughts and robbing their sleep.

At times, Alicia experienced an overpowering need to cram as much of Mariah's love and innocence into herself as possible. Regardless of what the future brought, she would cherish the time spent with little Miss Marker.

Caleb spent long days in Patrick Brown's offices poring over law tomes. The less predictable the outcome of any situation, the more prepared he insisted on making himself.

This morning, he'd waited until after breakfast, then announced Mariah would accompany him into town for the day. He'd delayed the inevitable as long as possible. Mariah had to visit with Constance, but not alone and not for more than several hours.

With forced optimism, Alicia helped the little girl don her finest dress and took great pains with her hair. She didn't want to leave room for criticism of the child's appearance.

The house seemed big and lonely after Caleb and Mariah left. Alicia paced the parlor, straightened the schoolroom, and offered to help Maude in the kitchen.

"You take no time for yourself, Alicia. The rain has stopped. Go for a walk, or take that gray beast you like so much for a ride," Maude chided. "You're too restless for your own good."

Alicia seized the opportunity by mounting Krakatau without a saddle. Caesar trailing her, she urged the horse into a gallop; a vain attempt to outrace the dilemma pressing her from all sides.

She slowed the horse to a walk as they approached the graveyard. In this place of eternal silence, she'd hoped to find answers, but even the solace of singing for the dead was denied.

A man in a finely tailored black suit stood before one of the moss-stained headstones. He held his hat in his hand as though the weight of it pulled the brim toward the long grass blanketing the grave. Although slightly built, his stance exuded a commanding presence. He faced away from her. Judging by the deep wrinkles weathering the back of his neck, she suspected the banners of age lined his face. A gentle breeze rising from the sea tousled his thinning gray-brown hair.

Not wanting to intrude, Alicia reined Krakatau away from the graveyard.

"Don't leave," the man said without turning.

"I've no wish to disturb you, sir."

"I didn't think it possible to disturb anyone in a graveyard."

Alicia hadn't either—until she and her sisters sang for Yolanda D'Arcy. "I'll come back later," she offered.

"No need. I haven't visited Prudence very often since she . . . died."

"I understand."

"Do you?"

Alicia nodded, though the man kept his back to her. For reasons she didn't fathom, her emotions rode close to the surface. "My people are buried very far from here. Even so, I feel closer to them when I visit this place. It's like . . . like a gateway to the afterlife. Maybe they'll know how much I miss them. I still need them in my life to talk to, to listen, then ask me questions the way they did when they were around." Suddenly aware of the tremor in her voice, she straightened. "I guess I got a little carried away."

The man nodded absently. "I well understand the desire for sage advice when troubled."

There was no sense denying she was troubled. If he turned around, he'd see what she no longer had the strength to hide.

"Do you often find answers in the peace of the graveyard?" He brushed loose twigs from the headstone he faced.

A faint laugh escaped Alicia. "Unfortunately, no. More often, I come away with a modicum of acceptance."

"Sometimes, that's more precious than answers. I've found that the most difficult answers are the ones inside us we'd prefer to ignore. They make life hard for a while, but when we listen and obey, they lead to solace. It's easier to remain busy and steeped in daily living so we can't hear them." The hat in his hand rose a few inches. "Here, you must listen."

"I agree, sir. This is also a place where I feel closer to my family. We spent a lot of time in cemeteries."

"Forgive my curiosity, young lady. Why?"

"My mother was the daughter of a minister turned mortician. She taught my sisters and me to sing harmony in a graveyard. She said if we sang from our hearts, the dead would journey with their souls lighter because someone cared enough to sing in their honor."

The man became so still, Alicia grew uncomfortable. Already she had revealed too much to the stranger. She started to rein Krakatau away.

"Miss? Would you do an old man a favor and sing for his daughter before you go?"

The emotion in his request moved her. "I'd be honored."

She straightened atop Krakatau and drew a cleansing breath. The first soft notes of the "Lord's Prayer," wafted across the graves.

Whether her morose mood won out or the distance from her sisters made her feel particularly bereft, she chose one of Caitlyn's favorites, "Pie Jesu" from Andrew Lloyd Webber's *Requiem.*

Slipping into the melody fit for this cathedral of giant spruce, she closed her eyes. The power of her voice carried through the high trees. Echoes of her sisters rose from her memory with a purity that sent tears coursing down her cheeks.

At the end of the song, she reined her horse away, unable to endure more of the sweet, painful connection reminiscent of all she had lost, all she stood to lose any way she went.

"Young lady?"

The lump in her throat kept her from answering. Instead, she sniffled in response.

"Thank you and God bless. I hope we both find answers."

As she rode off into the trees, she knew the stranger had a far better chance of finding solace than she.

"Judge Wardel arrived this morning." Caleb pulled a chair away from the kitchen table and sat across from Alicia. A summer rain beat against the windowpanes. The advent of night darkened the gray sky. Residual heat from the stove thwarted the damp chill seeking sanctuary inside the cozy home.

Alicia pressed her hands together. "I suppose Mr. Palmer and Miss Cunningham are eager to complete their business."

Caleb shrugged in concurrence. "The social life of Sitka

isn't up to their standards. It seems they haven't been invited to any dinners."

Alicia's gaze flicked in Caleb's direction. "Is the hearing date scheduled?"

"Not yet. Judge Wardel is reviewing the petitions for both sides. Patrick thinks he's being thorough and cautious. I suppose that's in our favor."

"At least he's looking at the whole case, not just the papers Constance brought from Judge Farrell." A faint smile tugged at the corners of her mouth. "An open mind can lead to enlightenment. What you discover in the process can be frightening."

"I suppose it can be."

"Do you have an open mind?" A burst of anxiety lifted her gaze to meet his. As quickly as her doubt flashed, it ebbed. Everything inside her stilled in anticipation of his reply.

"That is an easier question to ask than to answer." His slow response made her even more nervous.

She resolved herself and pinned him with her gaze. "Try." *Tell me yes, and mean it. Listen to what I must tell you without prejudice.*

"I suppose there are some subjects I'm more open-minded about than others. Can you narrow it down a little?"

"Unexplainable phenomena. Prophecies." The words barely escaped her lips. The decision she'd reached while riding home from the cemetery held fast. The stranger had been correct. The answers lay inside her all the time. All that remained was following the dictates of her conscience.

When she'd asked Caleb to join her in the kitchen tonight, she wasn't sure how she'd introduce him to her impossible circumstance, just that she had to start.

"I've read accounts—"

The anxiety of the great secret holding her hostage boiled over. She reached across the table and caught his hands in hers.

"Open or closed mind, Caleb?"

267

"Is there a reason I wouldn't have an open mind?" He looked pained that she'd doubt him.

"What I have to tell you isn't in any book or publication."

"Don't fence with me, Alicia. You've always spoken freely. Do so now."

"I'm trying." She released his hand, then laced her fingers in front of her.

"Then do it. Say what you have to say."

Her gaze remained locked with his. "And you won't shut me out before I finish?"

"I'll hear you out." Curiosity lifted his left eyebrow. "Does this have something to do with your aversion to marriage?"

Alicia swallowed hard, then nodded. Considering his preoccupation with the guardianship issue, she hadn't expected him to see through her so easily.

Braced on his forearms, he leaned onto the table. "I doubt what you'll tell me is worse than what I've imagined."

Her sad laughter filled the kitchen, then faded. She didn't want to know what sort of things he'd conjured. However, she would bet he hadn't come close to the truth. "I'm sorry for causing you anxiety." The echo of her mirthless laugh sounded again. "I'm sorry *I* have so much anxiety.

"With Judge Wardel here, things will happen quickly. After he renders his decision, we'll know what we have to do."

Unable to sit still any longer, Alicia rose and began pacing the kitchen. "The time has come," she said more to herself than Caleb. "I'll start at the beginning."

The curtain of years lifted. Clear, sharp memories rushed onto the stage in her mind. The words flowed in eager eloquence for freedom.

"Even before I was born, the folks around Drexel spoke of Yolanda D'Arcy with a sense of reverence and fear.

My sisters and I grew up with legends about her. Some called her the Witch of Wyoming. Others said she was a sorceress. No one went up on her part of the mountain.

"She lived alone up there. Part of her house went into the hillside. The front half or so was made of logs, stone, and mortar."

"Sounds effective against elements," Caleb said. "Tell me, if no one went to her house, how did they know how it was built?"

Alicia's heart beat in her throat. Apprehension brought fine beads of perspiration to her forehead. "*We* went up there."

"By we, do you mean you and your sisters, or the townsfolk?" The mild tone of his question sought only clarification.

She drew a breath, but failed to calm the thunder of her heart. "Fourteen years ago, I considered myself invincible. In a wild moment of bravado, I convinced my sisters to ride up Yolanda's mountain. It was a kid thing, you know? We were going to spy on 'the witch'."

"The dangerous or forbidden is the most tantalizing." The lift of his left eyebrow conveyed his understanding.

"Yeah, Bethany and Caitlyn nearly chickened out, and would have if I hadn't done some fast talking. I'd promised to lay down my life for them. The Witch of Wyoming wouldn't hurt them."

Alicia's eyes closed, and her sisters' young faces crystallized in the perfect vision of memory.

"I saw her house through the trees. I knew it was hers because it had a thatched roof, and no one else in the area had a roof like it."

Big-eyed, ashen-faced Bethany and Caitlyn had tied the horses up, held hands, and followed.

"I was the scout." A hollow laugh escaped her memory. "Because I'd promised to protect them, I had to go first, of course. In case Yolanda turned me into a frog."

"Sounds fair." The intensity of his gaze burned her heart with the fire of her own fear.

"We got close enough to see the front of the house.

Sure enough, the back was built into the hillside. We saw an old, stooped woman in a trench coat—"

"A what?"

"Trench coat. A double-breasted raincoat with big pockets." She waved the question off. Later, she'd explain the details he didn't comprehend. Right now, she needed to get through her tale before she lost her courage.

Although she looked at the floor, she saw Yolanda's ancient face. Age and hard living had turned her skin to leather. The web of wrinkles had parted around the glossy smoothness of scars along her left cheek.

"She had suffered severe burns at one time. On her face"—Alicia outlined the extent on her cheek—"down her neck, and lower. I have no idea how extensive, but it hurt something inside me to see the evidence of so much pain.

"Watching her became hypnotic. I'd never seen anyone do things with such deliberateness, so much economy of motion. I was terrified she'd see me and give me the evil eye. Then I'd be hopping for the rest of my life instead of walking. On the other hand, I was twelve and I could outrun a slow-moving old lady with a cane."

"The surety of youth." Caleb shifted in his chair.

"She was tending a garden bed. At first, I thought she was growing weeds. When I scooted closer, I saw it was an herb garden." She settled in the chair across the table from Caleb.

"Along the side of her house bloomed flowers in colors and varieties I'd never imagined. I had to have a better look. Bethany and Caitlyn whispered for me to come back. They wanted to leave. And so did I, just as soon as I got a look at those flowers.

"Ironically, that was the moment I knew I wanted to become a botanist. Even as I considered learning the secrets of flowers and the healing properties of plants, I knew some part of my destiny had solidified.

"When I checked on Yolanda, she was staring at me." Alicia's shoulders slumped. "I learned what it was to be paralyzed by fear. Inside my head, I wanted to run, to grab my little sisters and race to our horses. I just knew any second the old lady would point one of her gnarled fingers, and lightning would fly.

"I tried to yell at my sisters to run. To go home and stay there—forever." She reached across the table and took Caleb's callused hand in both of hers.

"Did they run?"

"No. Whatever happened to one of the James sisters happened to all of us in those days. They came up on either side of me." Her fingers laced through his from the back. "They held my hands.

"I remember looking at Yolanda as she leaned on a cane cut from a sapling and polished until it glowed. Then, when I looked into her eyes—blue eyes the color of cornflower—I stopped being afraid." She opened Caleb's pliant fingers and ran her fingertips over his heavy calluses.

"It was like she'd waited for us a long time. She took three flowers from her basket and gave one to each of us. She told us we were each others' greatest gifts and to keep faith in one another. Then she told us we sang like angels and asked us to sing for her when she was gone."

Antsy, Alicia released Caleb's hand and stood.

"We all promised. Caitlyn crossed her heart." Alicia turned away. "There was never a doubt we'd keep that promise."

Silence settled when Alicia finished the tale of the James girls versus the Witch of Wyoming.

Caleb said nothing, merely waited.

"In the years that followed, not once did we speak of Yolanda, not even amongst ourselves. And in my heart, I convinced myself she was just a self-sufficient woman who preferred solitude." She paused, exhausted by the tension of her body, and sipped her cold coffee.

"How could she be anything else, anything scary, when she grew the most beautiful flowers I'd ever seen?" She gazed into Caleb's rapt eyes. "*She* was the reason I became a botanist. I wanted to know the names of the beautiful plants and flowers surrounding her cabin. I wanted to learn how to grow them.

"Years later, after I'd filed for divorce from Chet, I went to see Yolanda again. The naïve romantic in me thought she'd decided to live in the way she did because of some tragedy involving a lost lover. I guess I'd changed. I hoped she really was mystical and had some words or a potion to make me hurt less.

"She didn't." She rubbed her palms together. "What she gave me was a prophecy I neither understood nor took seriously."

"You think she was a shaman or a seer?"

Alicia nodded. "Yeah, something like that, but I was a blind disbeliever."

"What was her prophecy?"

Suddenly, Alicia was bone-tired. Once she revealed her final secret, she couldn't rehide it. Her life, her future, hung in the balance. "I don't recall it word for word. In effect, she told me time was a river that twisted, turned, and occasionally folded back on itself. She prophesied I'd be caught in one of those folds, an eddy she called it, and I'd travel far from home. Alone."

Alicia closed her eyes. The full impact of the prophecy that she hadn't believed, hadn't wanted to acknowledge as possible, settled like a rock in her stomach. "She said the past was my future, if I were brave enough to accept it."

"Do you know what she meant?" he asked at last.

The doubt she heard forced her to lower her head in submission. "She came into town to die. No one knew why. They buried her in the Drexel cemetery. My sisters and I sang for her, as we had promised. When we finished, a fog thicker than anything I've ever seen came out of nowhere." Tears brimmed Alicia's lower lashes, then spilled in endless streams down her cheeks.

"I should have held onto my sisters. I should have taken their hands, as I did when they were little, and held on. The three of us could deal with anything together.

"But I didn't take their hands. Instead, I tried to lead

them through the fog. When it dissipated, I was standing in your woods . . . where you found me. I was thousands of miles and more than a century away from my home with no idea of how to get back."

Caleb didn't twitch a muscle. "You were what?"

Alicia lifted her head and looked him in the eyes. "I was here, thousands of miles from Drexel, Wyoming. Caleb, when my sisters and I sang for Yolanda D'Arcy, it was June Third, 2001. The reason I'm like no one you've ever met is because women from the future don't fall out of the sky like hail.

"I don't know what happened to my sisters. That gnaws on my heart every day. I pray they're still in Drexel."

Drained, resigned she had revealed all he needed to know, she pushed away from the table. An oppressive weight eased from her shoulders. Even her feet moved more freely. Whatever he decided, it was out of her hands. "I almost mustered the courage to tell you a couple of times. The timing never seemed right, or I lost my nerve.

"Ironically, time is the one thing in short supply. You had to know the truth, Caleb. If you accept this impossible thing that's happened to me, and you still want me as your wife, then yes. Oh, yes. I'll marry you. I want to have children with you. I'll never leave you willingly."

She turned away. "But if you can't accept what I've told you because it isn't in any book . . . or you think I've made this up . . . Well, I'm sure it will be best all the way around if I leave."

"I see." He hadn't moved since she embarked on her long tale. The whiteness of his knuckles betrayed the great restraint he'd exerted while he listened.

Alicia turned at the waist and looked at him. "No questions?"

The slow shake of Caleb's head told her more than she wanted to know. Whatever he saw wasn't in her favor. Without another word, she retreated to her room.

The parlor clock chiming the hour sounded like a death knell.

Chapter Twenty-two

The parlor clock chimed the passing of the hour twice more while Caleb sat at the kitchen table. Numbness gripped him from the inside out. Even his thought process had slowed to an infinitesimal pace.

Rivers of time.

Prophecy.

Fog.

An image of Alicia approached, then receded.

A black emptiness settled in with a loneliness so cold he shivered. The physical motion summoned a dull awareness of the present.

Gradually, the sounds of a storm penetrated his senses.

Of all the things his vivid imagination had conjured during his long, sleepless nights, not once had he delved into the realm of the supernatural. *Impossible!*

Why would she fabricate such a bizarre tale and tell him she wanted to be his wife in the same breath?

Unless it had really happened. Or . . . she suffered a form of dementia and thought it happened. That would explain the undeniable conviction with which she'd related the details of this impossible story.

Years ago in a San Francisco drawing room, he had listened to men of medicine discuss instances of traumatic events responsible for delusions in otherwise normal, sane individuals. Perhaps one of the books in his office held a key to divining the cause of Alicia's flight of fancy.

He left the table so quickly the chair tipped backward. The harsh bang on the oak hitting the floor startled him. In a gruff motion, he grabbed the seat and set the chair upright.

He had run in enough circles during the past week. His preoccupation with Alicia, the mountain of law books he'd pored over, and Constance's daily games and tantrums had hindered his ability to analyze the present circumstances.

He didn't question Alicia's desire to make love with him. In the small hours of the night, he conjured dozens of passionate lovemaking interludes. Now, she'd agreed to marry him, but . . .

Damn, why couldn't one thing be simple?

Seeking understanding, he strode down the hall to Alicia's bedroom. Light leaked from beneath the door. He opened it without knocking.

Immediately, he froze.

Alicia sat on the edge of her bed. One bare foot rested atop the other. A white lawn nightgown, open at the throat, flowed around her and clung to her breasts.

Desire roared through his loins.

It made no sense. The woman had given him the option of embracing the fantastic and supporting her delusion or losing her forever. And while neither was acceptable, all he thought of was being with her, making love to her.

"Did you think of some questions?"

The anxiety in her voice infused sanity through the haze of his confusion. Not much, just enough to realize the last thing he should do tonight was make love with her.

He eyed the bed fondly, certain they could lose themselves in passion until dawn. But the daylight would shine on their problems, too.

"Caleb? Are you all right?"

"No." The admission escaped as a croak.

As she rose from the bed, something fluttered to the floor. Neither of them moved into the chasm separating them.

Caleb's hands formed fists at his side. One emotion emerged from the maelstrom battering his reason: anger. He grasped it with the tenacity of a lumberjack clinging to a tree he'd topped. The whipsaw action of the top falling away threatened to shake him loose. If he let go, he'd tumble down the branches of logic into the chaos waiting below.

"Tell me you made up the story you told me. Then tell me why."

Alicia straightened, the tilt of her chin strong and implacable. "Are you asking me to lie to you?"

"No, damn it. I'm looking for the truth."

"I gave you the truth."

The anger flared, sending him forward a step. "What you told me can't be the truth. Nothing I've seen or read even hints at the possibility of a woman crossing the time and the distance you claim!"

"I can't help that. I have no explanation for what I can only call a scientific anomaly. Too bad Einstein didn't live long enough to figure out a time dimension theory." Her fisted hand rose to his chest. Without touching him, her fingers spread. After a brief hesitation, her hand dropped to her side.

"Don't you think I haven't contemplated how this happened a thousand times since I got here? Do you honestly believe I'd leave my sisters, my job, and my entire life behind if given a choice?

"Put yourself in my shoes for a few minutes, Caleb. How would you react if you walked out of a graveyard and into a place a century away from where you were moments earlier? Knowing no one? Without a clue of where you were, where you were supposed to go, or how to get there?"

A tremor in the questions she tiredly posed evoked a shred of sympathy. Part of him wanted to gather her in his arms and ease her agitation. Another part found fuel for his anger.

"What you claim has no logic, Alicia."

"Don't you think I know that? But it happened. To me." She pointed at the center of her chest. "I don't have the option of denial. I have no choice beyond acceptance."

She wheeled away, and crossed the room to the window. "At first, I thought all this was a dream. You were a fantasy too good to be true. I didn't believe I'd ever feel as deeply about a man as I do you. After we made love in the wood shop . . . If this was a dream, I didn't want it to end.

"But even dreams have a price. For me, that price is the truth. I had to tell you what happened to me . . . how I got here. I also knew how great a risk I faced in doing . . . the right thing. I won't dishonor either one of us by living with lies or secrets. Telling you wasn't easy, Caleb. You're not the freest thinker around."

She gestured toward the corner of the room. The worn travel bag she'd arrived with her first night leaned against the wall. "I'm packed. Under the circumstances, it might be best if I waited until Judge Wardel decides on Mariah's future. Then you can do whatever you need to do, and I'll quietly slip away."

The realization she'd anticipated his rejection spurred him into motion. Long, quick strides carried him across the room. In desperation, he gripped her shoulders. The heated contact imparted a burning awareness of how empty his life would be without her.

"Damn it, you're not leaving us. Where would you go? How would you live?"

"I'll make out. I've developed a flexibility and resourcefulness I never had in Wyoming. You've shown me what I need to adapt."

The resolve in her violet eyes left no doubt. The bitter

277

certainty that seeped through him stifled his wild anger. "You believe what you told me in the kitchen."

"It isn't a matter of belief. It's undeniable fact."

The wistful way she touched his cheek sent the fires of Pandemonium raging inside him.

"I don't want to change you, Caleb. And I can't make you believe something beyond your ability to accept. This isn't an ultimatum. It's just one of life's quirks neither of us understands. Maybe no one has all the answers. What it boils down to is trust, having faith in each other. We either have it, or we don't. How long could we exist without it?"

"If we never discuss it again, until we die of old age."

Alicia smiled and shook her head. "You believe that?"

He wanted to. Lord, how he wanted to, because he couldn't bring himself to lend an ounce of credibility to her story. "Give me a tangible reason to believe."

Alicia chuckled. "Like what? You want me to dazzle you with the history I know to be the future? What would it prove? There are no means to verify it. You may consider a spirited horse or a steel-hulled steamer fast, but they aren't. It would take months, perhaps years, before the proof you're asking for appears in a newspaper or a book."

"Alicia, I'm looking for compromise." He drew a slow breath. Hell, he'd settle for anything on the edge of reason. The need for a resolution summoned patience. "For God's sake, give me one tangible plausibility I can grasp.

"You tell me a story not even Mariah would accept without question and expect me to say, 'I have faith in you. I believe anything you tell me although logic decries it.' Then you tell me you don't want lies or secrets between us."

She leaned into the restraint of his hands. Unable to trust himself with her nearness, he held her back.

"You and Mariah own big pieces of my heart. But I can't stay with you believing I've fabricated this, and me knowing it is true."

"Why the hell not?"

"Oh, Caleb. How long would it be before we wound up in the forest or in the wood shop? If a child resulted from our lovemaking—"

"You don't know one hasn't. Neither do I. If you think I'll let you go anywhere as long as there's a chance—"

"That's my point! Can you imagine year after year of being married to me, making love, having children—"

"Yes, damn it. Every day and all night."

"—And looking at me, never sure whether I was lying to you? Or worse, maybe I was crazy because I thought I came from the future? Every time I said or did something that didn't fit into your orderly world, or I couldn't substantiate in one of your books, you'd question. It doesn't matter whether you kept your doubts or fears to yourself. We'd both know."

Alicia pushed against his wrists with the backs of her hands. "That path leads to destruction. I won't revel in the pleasures of the moment, then watch it disintegrate into the silent hell we'd create, Caleb."

"You're a hard woman, Alicia James. Hard and uncompromising."

Sadly, she shook her head. "No, Caleb. Just realistic."

She turned toward the bed and drew back the comforter. "You should leave now. It's late."

Damn, but he'd never felt so helpless and hopeless at the same time. Even his anger deserted him in the face of their impasse. He started for the door, then spied a scrap of white on the floor. He bent and picked it up.

When he turned it over, Alicia and two women smiled at him in vivid color unlike anything he'd ever seen. He flexed the palm-sized photograph, amazed the resilient image did not flake. "This is you."

"And my sisters. Bethany has the long chestnut hair. Caitlyn is the blond," she answered softly. "That was taken at the end of April, the week after Easter, when the three of us spent a day in Cheyenne."

"April?"

He stared at the picture, noticing tiny details that marked the three women as sisters and those that shaped

279

their differences. The whisper of his callused fingertips gliding over the strange surface disturbed the heavy silence. The vivid colors on the canvas paper danced in his vision. The artist had captured the joy the trio shared. A love of togetherness shone in their happy smiles and shining violet eyes.

"Together, the James girls could take on the world." Alicia's claim of solidarity with her sisters lay before him. They were a family, bonded by love and tragedy, strengthened by one another.

"Caleb?"

The sound of his name broke the spell cast by the strange rendering. Fatigue, and something he recognized as defeat, filled her sorrowful, violet eyes. The night's ordeal robbed all color from her delicate face.

"Take it with you, and close the door on your way out."

Realizing the impasse would not end tonight, he nodded and went to the door, then turned. She sat on the edge of the bed the same way she had when he'd entered the room. "I'm not willing to let you go."

"You would try to hold me prisoner?"

The pinch of her brow conveyed her doubt he'd succeed in doing so. "No. We will find a"—*cure*—"solution."

She opened her mouth, then closed it again.

In the hall, he held on to the doorknob. The solid barrier put her out of reach. He listened for a long time, but she did not lock him out.

For the next hour in his office, he searched the bookshelves for any mention of normal individuals suffering from a single delusion. Nothing on the pages bore a similarity to the fantasy Alicia embraced as truth.

Caleb tossed a book at the stack on his desk, then leaned back in his chair. In retrospect, she'd exhibited no other signs of instability. On the contrary, her judgment embodied a pragmatic soundness he admired. She did not slip from one persona to another.

Bone-tired, Caleb doused the office lights and went to

bed. Staring at the ceiling, he thought back to the day he'd first encountered his wood nymph.

Something had drawn him to that part of his woods. Even now, he could not define the urgency gripping him that sunny afternoon. As he had done often in the past, he had followed his instincts. Try as he might, he couldn't recall his reasons for venturing into the forest on foot— and without Caesar or Nero. Or perhaps he had never known. It wasn't important—until now when he questioned the reasons behind his actions.

The desperate call of two strange names had provided direction. He'd followed the sound until he found her walking backward and staring at the high canopy of tree branches.

From the moment he saw her in her strange attire, everything changed. She had irrevocably altered his life with a touch. A single poignant look from the depths of those violet eyes had reached inside him and unmasked the emptiness of abandoned dreams. In the same instant, he understood the isolation cloaking her from the rest of the world.

When he'd heard her calling in the forest, she had sounded frightened, almost panicked. If she had crossed through time and distance, her confusion was understandable. Any other woman might have succumbed to hysteria. And rightfully so, if she had experienced what she claimed.

Just when he discovered another hole in her impossible story, his knowledge of the woman thwarted him. From the beginning, Alicia showered open emotion and affection on Mariah. Her generous heart withheld nothing. The doors she opened for the child led to adventures he'd never considered—like teaching her to sing in a graveyard.

No one else would undertake such a shocking, controversial endeavor. Alicia had forged ahead as though teaching a child to sing in a graveyard was as normal as the sun rising each morning.

Caleb frowned into the darkness.

He'd once believed that children did not belong in cemeteries, not as residents or spectators. However, after hearing Alicia and Mariah sing, he'd begun rethinking his position on the matter.

The openness Alicia bestowed on Mariah carried none of the wariness that marked her dealings with everyone else. Not until the night they spoke of desire at the lumber camp had the heavy armor guarding the fragile side of her cracked.

That armor was in place now. The invisible barrier padded her heart with layer upon layer of protection. She had anticipated his reaction and fortified those defenses before he'd arrived in the kitchen.

He laced his fingers under his head, then closed his eyes. The burning sensation behind his eyelids had become as much a part of his life as breathing. Again, sleep eluded him.

"Dating," he murmured into the night. The strange word had bothered him the first time he heard it. The context in which she'd used it had alone made it comprehensible.

"Wyoming." The whispered word filled the darkness. She attributed so many quirks to her origins. Before Alicia, he'd never met anyone from Wyoming. What if they weren't as different as she let him believe?

His thoughts played hopscotch again.

A vision of Alicia building hillsides with mashed potatoes and washing the pea-trees away with gravy sent a tingle through him. She had known. Damn it, she had known what that mountainside looked like although she'd never seen it.

It wasn't in a book.

Not any book he owned, and his library on the subject of trees and logging was the most complete on Baranov Island.

She had said it wasn't in a book. She'd been so sure. So emphatic.

The thought of books jumped his memory to the day she sketched the garden cart in his office.

For a few moments, it seemed she was far away, remembering, mourning. Talking of her sisters. Wondering whether she was alone.

He recalled her anger when speaking about the drunk killing her parents at sixty miles an hour. While the image was impossible to fathom, he couldn't doubt the spontaneous sincerity of her conviction. When he questioned her, she had tried to slough off the reference. The injustice sparking her anger had showed him the truth in an unguarded moment. Or had it?

The multitude of incongruities began to blend. Through the melee, he relived her earnest conviction in her absurd tale. It felt like truth.

He shoved the images out. He couldn't analyze the paradox anymore. He summoned the memory of her standing on the veranda and singing to him as he stood in the rain. She had filled his senses with the beautiful, intimate song he was certain revealed her heart's sentiment.

When she sang, the naked light of her soul shone in her eyes and echoed in her voice. Nothing hid behind the armor then. Her love of song refused her all defense.

"The power of love," he whispered, reveling in the words of the song. At the time, he had hoped the song reflected her feelings for him. Now? he wondered—then wondered why he wondered until exhaustion forced his body to rest. He dreamed of all the beautiful, erotic fantasies they could make into sweet reality. The sorrow damping the sweet bliss the dreams imparted served as a constant reminder that that was all they were.

Dreams.

Flights of fancy.

Chapter Twenty-three

Accompanied by Caesar, Alicia rode off before the rest of the household rose. This morning, she sought to absorb some of the peace within the cemetery's stone boundaries.

Atop Krakatau, she listened to the world around her. Fat raindrops left over from the last night's storm dripped from the trees and splattered on the vegetation reaching for elusive sunlight. Birds called, then took flight, further disturbing the moisture collected in the trees' lofty branches. Below, fern fronds bobbed and waved under the playful assault. The fading dawn cast a heavily shadowed shroud over the gravestones and markers. It, too, seemed in a state of anticipation.

The courage she'd mustered to admit her impossible situation had caused her worst nightmare to come true. Of all the reactions she'd anticipated from Caleb last night, she hadn't expected silent shock to transfix him to the kitchen table.

Twice, she had returned only to find him rooted in place and oblivious of anything outside the prison of his closed mind. Each time the certainty of his judgment of her had grown heavier.

Later, he'd surprised her with an attempt to compromise.

But how could she compromise with the truth?

It had been difficult for him to suggest. She had not made it easier on him. Self-preservation had kicked in and she'd rejected him before he'd uttered the words that could break her heart.

In her room, she had stared at the picture of her sisters and relived their last trip to Cheyenne. Memories of the mall, silly fashion try-ons, the futile attempt to broaden Bethany's wardrobe, and the one-hour glamor photo studio flooded back. They had waited for the pictures over lunch. Even their food selections had reflected their differences and the tolerance that made them friends.

The memories of a carefree day had evaporated when Caleb entered the room. Then, her eyes had burned with unshed tears. Sheer determination had kept them from spilling down her cheeks.

The depth of his torment rocked through her, nearly loosening the tears welling on her lower lashes. The sensation of the searing anger engulfing him wrenched her heart. It had hurt even more to realize she was the cause. Within moments, guilt had raised its ugly head.

It stung this morning in the quiet company of the graves.

"I have nothing to be guilty about," she reminded herself aloud.

Caleb refused to understand that she couldn't stay or pretend nothing had changed. One of the many lessons her brief marriage to Chet had taught was the need for trust. Ignorance invited deception.

She and Caleb could disagree on a thousand things, but not this. Pretending it didn't exist was like trying to ignore a pimple on the tip of her nose while it grew into a boil.

"A leap of faith this big is a lot to ask," she whispered at the silent graveyard. Not just big, enormous. The realization formed a knot in her stomach. She wasn't sure who had the more difficult plight—the one needing the faith or the one who had to find it. Both seemed unfair positions.

As she usually did in troubled times, she retreated into the world of music; lyrics spoke so eloquently of pain. Knowing someone else had written the words echoing her angst made her feel less alone in her plight.

She hummed a song about a woman whose only hope was to call the man who mended broken lives and restored dreams. The hum became words sung with soft reverence and so private she didn't want even the birds to hear. Eyes closed, she finished the song so appropriate for her in this time.

As though answering the melodious plea, Caleb filled her vision when she opened her eyes. Her heart leaped and she almost cried out in protest at the thought of having to leave him.

"There is another way," Caleb told her in a shaky voice.

Choked by emotions, she stared at him. Had he followed her here?

"We'll find it, Alicia. God as my witness, we'll find a way to live with this." A nudge brought Vesuvius closer. "You want unquestioning, blind faith. That's damned difficult for even a saint to manage. I'm no saint. I don't know if I can find it within myself. I'll try. If it's there for anyone, it's you.

"I'm going to need a little of what you're asking for from you. I need your patience. Your help."

The ball of emotion in her throat grew. The depth of his love haunted his eyes. The toll of the battles he still fought showed in the dark traces beneath his lower lashes. Alicia gripped the reins in her hand to keep from reaching for him. She wanted to soothe his weariness, ease his doubt, and cast away his concerns. Yet she lacked the power to do even one of those things. He bore the invisible weight on his broad shoulders with a stoicism she admired. He was groping for direction she had no idea of how to give.

"I'm struggling, woman. Are you going to help me, or do I do this alone?"

She tried to speak. The words caught below the jumble of emotion constricting her throat. A rush of tears broke the dam of her lower lashes. They covered her cheeks like morning rain. She managed a nod.

"Is that a yes, I have to do this alone?"

Sniffing, she shook her head. Gradually, the lump in her throat eased. "I don't know what to do to help you. God help me, I love you, Caleb, but I don't know how to make you believe me." The words broke free without thought of consequence.

His eyes narrowed, then widened. "You love me?"

"With all my heart," she answered, her chin quivering. The last of her great truths stood naked in the morning light.

"It's a start."

"Of what?" For the life of her, she couldn't see how it did anything but complicate matters.

"Of convincing me miracles do happen. What else but a miracle would send a woman to love me? One I love beyond reason."

"Sometimes love isn't enough."

"Sometimes it is. Sometimes you make it enough."

"Enough to believe the impossible?" Dared she hope he could embrace what seemed so inconceivable?

"I'll work on it. With your help." He reined Vesuvius alongside of her. "Why don't we start with you telling me some of the things you haven't told me."

Caught off guard, Alicia squared her shoulders. "What do you mean?"

"Are there any other lightning bolts like last night's in store for me?" Caleb shrugged, his palms up in acceptance. "I just want to know how big a pill I have to swallow, that's all."

"No. I led a pretty boring life until the river of time caught me," she admitted.

Relief eased the fatigue lines around Caleb's mouth. "Boring is not necessarily a negative. The winter months are filled with boredom. Why don't you tell me about the ranch you grew up on? Your parents. Your sisters." He urged his horse forward, bringing Krakatau with them. "Then tell me why the hell Wyoming women wear trousers instead of skirts."

A surprised laugh escaped. She glanced at him and melted in the warmth of his smile. *Please, God, help us through this. I never want to lose this man.* Hope buoyed her spirits. A sudden optimistic giddiness danced in her blood.

"If you find that appalling, allow me to further shock you with the news that Wyoming will also have the first woman governor. Not for a while yet, but it will happen."

"When?" Caleb asked softly. Curiosity and a tinge of fear clouded his gray eyes.

"Thirty years from now, in 1925, Nellie Tayloe Ross's husband will die, and she'll serve out his term. As a child, she was one of my heroes. She lived for a century and a year. Imagine the changes she saw in her long lifetime."

They rode through the trees in silence for a while. "Have you digested that long enough for something a little closer to home?"

"Surprise me." A frown of regret accompanied a quick glance in her direction. "On second thought—"

"Too late. We filled the long Wyoming winters with hours of a game called Trivial Pursuit. All its obscure facts crammed into my brain are now gems of knowledge. Here goes.

"In 1900, just five short years from now, Juneau will replace Sitka as the capital of the Alaska Territory. Fifty-nine years later, Alaska will become the forty-ninth state. Women will have the vote here, too." She managed an apologetic expression. "Juneau will still be the capital."

Caleb swore under his breath. "That can't happen, Alicia. Sitka has always been the seat of government, even under Russian rule. Juneau is young by comparison, little more than a gold mining town."

"Ah, Caleb. Look at the broader picture history paints.

Government always goes where the gold is. Gold is money. Money is power."

Caleb shook his head, unable to accept her philosophy.

"Okay. Consider California in 1849. Sutter's Mill. Gold. Statehood. Oh my!" She put her hand against her cheek in feigned surprise. "Sacramento became the state capital. It was so much closer to the gold fields than San Jose or Monterey, two far more established and worthy candidates for the honor."

"You're a cynic."

"Guilty, with good reason." An easy camaraderie settled with the feather softness of fragile hope. The mood lasted until they reached home and found Patrick Brown waiting in the kitchen.

"It may be a couple more days before Judge Wardel schedules a hearing," the lawyer announced from behind the plate Maude had piled high with breakfast fare. He raised his cup for more coffee when she offered to pour.

"Why?" Alicia set down her fork and leaned forward with an intense interest.

Caleb watched her closely. On their way home from the graveyard, she had related bits of what she considered history, and he considered . . . what?

He didn't know. Her candid accounts of things yet to happen were as casual as a schoolroom recitation of something everyone knew.

Except him. There were no books to consult to prove or disprove her assertions.

"I'm not sure why the delay," Patrick answered.

"Does this work in our favor?" Alicia pressed.

"I wish I knew, Miss James. My dealings with Judge Wardel have shown him an honorable man. The action he takes in this matter affects him personally." Patrick fixed his gaze on Caleb. "Caleb explained the judge's predicament, didn't he?"

"Yes," Caleb answered.

"What predicament?" Concern drew Maude's mouth into a frown. "I have a stake in this, too."

"Caleb?" Patrick's raised eyebrows asked for permission to continue.

Caleb forced away the hundreds of questions concerning Alicia's assertions of traveling from the future and the things she related. He pushed away from the table and addressed Maude. "The judge who signed Constance's papers is very powerful. Apparently, he takes great offense at anyone who does not agree with his decisions. If Judge Wardel goes against him, the ramifications to his career could be enormous."

"You didn't think I should know this?" Maude demanded.

"What does it change? The outcome is all we have to deal with. There isn't anything we can do to influence the man's character." Caleb shoved his plate away.

"I rode out to inform you Judge Wardel is going to visit you this morning. In itself, his coming here is highly unusual, certainly not court practice. I can't recall an instance of any judge visiting a home, unless the case was criminal. He intends to spend time with Mariah."

"What the hell for?"

The touch of Alicia's hand on his forearm kept him from rising out of his chair.

"This may be a good thing, Caleb," Alicia murmured. "If his mind is open even a little bit, he'll see what I saw when I came here. He'll see a happy, healthy little girl raised by a loving father. Let's help him decide in our favor by cooperating."

Giving a stranger entry to his home was distasteful. Giving Judge Wardel access to Mariah was worse. The urge to protect Mariah by shutting the door on the outsider churned in his guts.

Maude set the coffeepot on the table and wiped her hands on her apron. "Listen to her, Caleb."

He swore under his breath, detesting the circumstances and resigned to the wisdom Alicia conveyed.

The mud room door banged opened. Mariah's giggles and Jeremy's stomping warned the end of the discussion.

"What do you suggest we do?" he asked through gritted teeth.

"Absolutely nothing," Alicia answered with the audacity to smile.

He bit off the retort that questioned her sanity, then stared at her.

"Crazy like a fox," Alicia said, still smiling. "There is no better salesman for keeping the guardianship issue the way it is than Mariah. She's five. She's innocent." Her fingers flexed on his forearm. "Caleb, she loves you with all her heart and never wants to leave. Let her plead her own case in a way no lawyers or self-serving adults can. If Judge Wardel is teetering on a decision, can you think of anyone more influential than Mariah?"

He didn't like it. Not one little bit. But, damn, it made sense. Not allowing the judge time with Mariah would hurt their cause.

He watched Jeremy lift Mariah to the sink and help wash her hands. "I'll tell her."

"No." The glide of Alicia's thumb along his skin calmed him enough to keep him seated at the table. "We tell her nothing. We let it happen as it happens. If we try to prepare her, he'll see it as coercive. Let her be herself."

"You scare the hell out of me sometimes," he said so softly, only she heard.

"I know. That's because men are such emotional creatures," she answered just as quietly, then grinned.

"Emotional, my—" he bit off the rest of the retort.

Mariah bounded up beside him. A few practiced climbs brought her onto his lap. Her small arms encircled his neck, then squeezed. "You looked like you needed a hug."

"I do." He cradled her against his chest. "I need more than one."

She buried her face in the crook of his neck and tightened her arms with all her strength. "I love you, Daddy. My hugs will make you smile."

"A kiss will make me smile even more."

Mariah planted a sloppy kiss beside his ear. The long, loud pucker did made him grin. He hoped Judge Wardel ruled in his favor. If not, they had a long sea trip ahead.

He set Mariah down. "Maude kept your breakfast warm. What were you and Jeremy doing in the barn?"

"I had to clean Edgy's stall." Mariah reached for her fork. "She's so glad it stopped raining. Now she can go outside and play all day and night."

"Her stall will stay clean, too," Jeremy added with a knowing wink.

Mariah's gray eyes found Alicia. "You were right. A horse is lots of work."

"And your pony is your responsibility. Your Daddy and I are proud of the way you're taking care of Edgy."

Mariah beamed under the praise. "When I get bigger, can I have a horse like a real volcano?"

"When you are much bigger, yes." Caleb's simple answer covered so much. Alicia was right. He'd allow Judge Alphonse Wardel time with Mariah. What could it hurt?

Three hours later, he had the answer. Most of the time, he'd tried to lose himself in his latest woodworking project. When his anxiety made concentration impossible, he went to his office and put away the books he'd rummaged through in the small hours of the morning. Finally, he joined Alicia in the parlor.

How the hell could she sit and read while Mariah chattered about anything and everything with Alphonse Wardel?

"Caleb, sit down and act like you haven't a care in the world."

He complied, staring at her all the while. How did she do it? She looked so calm, so poised . . . and the book in her hands was upside down.

"Turn the book over," he warned, reaching for the latest periodical from the National Geographic Society.

Alicia turned the book right side up. "It's not how you feel at times like these, it's how you look."

"Daddy, are you in here?" Mariah called as she skipped down the hall.

Caleb popped to his feet. The magazine tumbled to the floor. "I'm right here."

"My new friend wants to talk to you. Can I fix tea for a tea party?" Mariah waited at the parlor door for an answer.

"I'll help her." Alicia casually closed her book and set it aside. She rose from the couch with a regal grace. "If I'm not mistaken, Maude made cookies after breakfast."

"Oh good. We can have a real tea party with cookies."

Caleb caught the warning in Alicia's final glance, then waited until she and Mariah were in the kitchen before turning his attention to Judge Wardel.

Slightly built and a couple of inches taller than Alicia, Alphonse Wardel possessed the carriage of a large, powerful man. Deep-set brown eyes regarded Caleb from the hollows below bushy gray eyebrows. A neat gray mustache below his aquiline nose showed not a hit of color. Thinning gray-brown hair wound behind his ears. Carelines mapped his face. The quiet dignity surrounding the man promised fairness.

Judge Wardel took a seat on the couch. Caleb settled into his chair, then retrieved the publication at his feet.

"I'd like your permission to take Mariah into town," Judge Wardel said, resting his hands on his knees.

Caleb managed a shrug he hoped appeared more nonchalant than it felt. "I don't see why we can't take her to town."

"I meant to take her alone."

Caleb searched for a diplomatic response. "No."

A faint flicker of Wardel's mustache betrayed something Caleb lacked the patience to comprehend. "I am assuming you have a good reason for denying my request."

"Nothing personal, Judge Wardel, but I don't know you, only your reputation. While a lot of people I respect hold you in high esteem, I don't consider that sufficient reason to let you take Mariah out this door, let alone into town without me."

"You aren't going to make this easy, are you, Mr. Marker?"

"Easy? There's nothing easy about any of this. It was settled in San Francisco five years ago."

"Although it happens rarely, such matters can be addressed periodically by a court. Each jurisdiction exercises a broad scope of powers in dispatching controversies regarding the placement of orphaned children."

"Is that your way of telling me you can take Mariah to town without my consent?"

Wardel tipped his head slightly. "I'd prefer your agreement."

"Why take her into town—alone?"

"There is a great deal of tension between you and Miss Cunningham. I'd prefer your absence while I observe Mariah for a few hours with Miss Cunningham."

The small hairs at the back of Caleb's neck bristled. "What is this really about, Judge Wardel? You came out here and spent a couple of hours with Mariah. Neither Miss James nor I have intruded. Now, you want her with Constance for the afternoon. Then what? How do you determine anything about the way we interact with Mariah?"

A throaty chuckle brightened Judge Wardel's lined face. "By listening and talking with Mariah."

Mariah led Alicia into the parlor. When Alicia put the tray on the table, Mariah offered the plate of cookies to Judge Wardel. "These are very good," she confided.

Caleb welcomed the distraction of the tea party. The interruption afforded a few moments for examining what Alicia called the big picture.

The triumphant smile Mariah beamed at him after successfully delivering the cup of tea brought a responsive smile. "Thank you, Miss Marker."

"You're welcome, Daddy."

Her smile broadened and she resumed the role of hostess at the little tea party.

"Would you like me to sing for you?" Mariah asked Judge Wardel.

"Why, yes I would. Have you been taking voice lessons?"

"Oh, yes. Miss James and I go to the graveyard and she teaches me the notes using the gravestones."

Caleb felt the pit of his churning stomach drop to his toes. In total resignation, he met Alicia's unwavering gaze. The trouble with letting a five-year-old plead his case was that she had no idea of what might hang him.

Chapter Twenty-four

Alicia gripped the porch rail and prayed that letting Mariah accompany Judge Wardel was the right thing. Silently, she thanked Maude for the hundredth time since the housekeeper insisted on going to town for a few essential supplies. Judge Wardel may have seen through the spontaneous ruse, but he posed no objection when Jeremy and Maude followed him out of the yard.

The jangle of harnesses and the cadence of two buggies departing the Marker yard filled her ears. She listened until they disappeared down the road and took the last traces of sound with them.

"What did you say to Judge Wardel as he was leaving?" She looked at Caleb standing beside her and still gazing in the direction of the empty road.

"I told him to expect me if Mariah wasn't home in four hours." His head turned. Worry aged him the longer she stared up at his face. "How can you be so calm?"

"Calm?" A near hysterical laugh escaped her, sending the birds perched on the roof into flight. "Me? I'm as worried as you look. I don't have a clue about his purpose for doing this with Mariah. In my own time, I'd have a reason for optimism. But here? I have no idea how family court works."

"Family court?" He looked back at the empty road. "Never mind. I don't want to know."

A soft breeze rustled the trees. An eagle circled in the distance.

Caleb turned and leaned against the porch rail. The muscles in his forearms flexed as he crossed them over his chest. He stared at the wall when he spoke. "I've never had as much to lose as I do right now. The worst part of it is how little control I have over the outcome. The aftermath is another matter."

"What do you mean? The aftermath?"

A chill crept down Alicia's body. All hint of emotion fled from his gray eyes. The badges of worry faded from his expression and settled on hers.

"I know what you want from me, and I think I understand why it's important to you for me to accept the impossible. I'll need time—time we may not have if Judge Wardel changes the guardianship."

"You're going through with it, aren't you?" The statement rose from a calm certainty tinged with dread.

"I hope for the best, but I'm prepared for things to go against me. The arrangements are in place. Now I need an answer. Will you come with us?"

With all her heart she wanted to go with him. Doing so embodied the same commitment as marriage. Once she left, she couldn't return. Taking Mariah under those circumstances was kidnapping. Although the death penalty for that particular felony was years away, in the event of apprehension, the consequences were nearly as dire.

"What happens if you never find it within yourself to believe I came from the future?" The question escaped without thought.

"The door swings both ways. You're going to have to trust I can, aren't you?"

Realization dawned that it was her turn to stand on the abyss and make the leap of faith. If either one of them fell short, life would be hell. She'd be a fugitive with no place to call home.

"You do understand what kind of life we'd have if we took Mariah away under those conditions?" she asked slowly.

"You're right to question, Alicia. I have a better idea of what we'd face than you could. It's not all bleak. I have connections. We have plenty of money. The biggest change is leaving Sitka with no hope of returning here or anywhere in the Alaska Territory. We'd have to find a home outside the United States and its territories. Scotland is promising."

He turned away before continuing. "A true gentleman would never ask you to share in the adversity we may face."

A weakness in her knees made her sway. "Chivalry died with King Arthur," she murmured, grasping the porch rail tighter to keep from crumbling.

"Patrick will know where we are—after we reach our destination."

The strong pull of his hands carried her away from the rail and settled her between his legs. Reflexively, she snuggled against the heat of his chest.

"If we have to leave, I'll probably ask many difficult things of you, but never to abandon your watch for your sisters."

The solid thud of his heart against her ear lent assurance. The strength of his commitment seemed reflected in the hard muscle flanking his backbone. Her hands glided toward his shoulders, testing, relishing the assurance imparted by his presence.

"Will you think about it?" He placed a firm kiss atop her head. The heated sensation flowed down to her toes. A fiery wake of desire settled in all the places craving his touch.

She nodded, then raised her head. "It might not come to that, Caleb."

His mouth descended toward hers. "But it might. Just in case, my plans have included you."

The familiar scent of him fed her smoldering desire. The warmth of his breath as he spoke made her lips tingle. She straightened, bringing her top lip to the bottom of his mouth. "I won't allow passion to sway my decision."

"I never expected it would." The brush of his lips against her brought her to her toes.

She kissed him lightly while pulling the tails of his shirt free. "If it becomes necessary to leave, we go as man and wife," she whispered.

"You drive a hard bargain."

The gentle tease of his fingers against the side of her breast coaxed a subtle shift. He took advantage of the access to her aroused nipple begging for more excitement. The arousal straining his trousers promised even more.

"Not a bargain." Eyes at half-mast, she brushed her tongue over his lower lip. "It will be heaven or hell for us. Forever." The marvelous sensation of his skin against her splayed hands promised hell would wait. Heaven was at hand.

He captured her mouth in a slow, torturous kiss. Alicia savored every nuance of his exploring tongue, then took her turn with forced restraint. When the kiss ended, Caleb swept her up and carried her into the house.

Alicia freed the top buttons of his shirt. The provocative flesh she unveiled begged for kissing. She bent her head for a sample. He tasted of life and desire.

"Don't ask me anything important for a while." The flavor of his shaving soap lingered at his neck. She laved the spot, her tongue softening the whiskers reaching for the light.

Caleb paused at the bedroom door just long enough to throw the bolt. "This time, we'll make love properly. On a bed." He set her down beside the bed.

Alicia freed the last of his shirt buttons. "I wasn't aware of anything improper when we made love before."

Caleb removed her blouse and chemise between tantalizing kisses that made her heart beat more rapidly with each contact. Her skirt fell to the floor, followed by her petticoat, then her drawers.

Suddenly, he became still. Alicia's fingers faltered on the last two of his trouser buttons. She gazed up at him in question. A ripple of goose flesh traveled the length of her body. Through the haze of the desire coiling inside her, she felt as well as saw the adoration in his eyes.

Very slowly, his hands rose to her shoulders, then rested lightly. "You are more beautiful than I remembered."

A prickle of embarrassment made her smile. "We're seeing more of each other now than we ever have."

Caleb slowly shook his head. His fingers curled lovingly around her shoulders. "I memorized every curve and dimple of your body the night we made love in the wood shop. Still, you outshine the sun with your perfection."

Alicia looked away, suddenly uncomfortable with a man capable of memorizing the cellulite dimples sure to multiply with the passage of time.

Caleb drew her against him for a moment, then turned her to sit on the side of the bed. "Give me your shoes."

Alicia lifted her right foot, aware they were in her room.

As though reading her thoughts, Caleb grinned. "This one was the closest."

He stood after removing her shoes and stockings, and his boots. Confidence formed a knowing smile as he reached for the last buttons on his trousers.

Alicia rose from the bed and gently guided his hands away. Desire dilated his eyes and made her reckless. She freed him, then arched her breasts against his chest. With slow, exaggerated arcs her hands molded over his buttocks. The delicious glide of her breasts on his silken chest hair heightened his desire. At last, his trousers slithered down his legs.

When he reached to lift her onto the bed, she shook her head and smiled, her lips parted in invitation. "Kiss me." Her fingers slid along his ribs.

"Gladly." His dark head dipped toward her. "Everywhere." She caught his dangerous hands and entwined her fingers in his.

Caleb folded her arms behind her back. The jut of her breasts against him shortened the delicious game they played. He embarked on carrying out his promise to kiss every part of her by nibbling her earlobe. Between love bites, he stroked the sensitive lobe with the tip of his tongue. "Every time I kiss you, I know anything is possible. All the questions and doubts melt away."

The words sent a white lance of hope into Alicia's heart. Needing to touch him, she unlaced her fingers from his, but did not find the freedom she craved.

Caleb left a trail of burning kisses leading to the sensitive pulse point in her throat. "When you sing, the sincerity of your emotion touches me deeply. It's as though you're singing only to me. There's no doubt you were meant for me, Alicia." Reverent, gentle kisses covered her throat. "I hear you with my soul."

One by one, he untwined his fingers from hers. "Sometimes, when I see you across a room, all the dark places inside me fill with your light."

Alicia brought her fingertips to his face. How well she understood the dark places where Loneliness held hands with an old friend named Fear. Since arriving on Marker land, all the defenses she'd mustered against falling in love had crumbled. In a flash of rare insight, she comprehended the reason for being at this place and time. *Caleb.* A flicker of fear seized her, then evaporated into certainty.

"She told me about a gift waiting for me," Alicia murmured, caressing his cheek.

Caleb straightened and kissed her forehead. "Who?"

"Yolanda D'Arcy. She could have warned me away from the eddy in the river of time, but she didn't. She let me fall through time for a reason."

Caleb slid his hands over her shoulders and cradled her chin. "A reason and a gift?"

She searched his clear gray eyes. The path of her future emerged from the chaos. Whether Caleb embraced her truth or not, her place was beside him. Apart, life offered empty loneliness. Together, they shared a love stronger than time. "She gave me the gift of finding love and loving with all my heart, Caleb. She sent me to you. There is no one in all of time I could love as I love you. Whatever the future brings, it brings to both of us."

Her heart raced with an excitement rivaling her desire during the long moment he held them motionless. His eyes narrowed slightly. Tension filled the callused hands cradling her face. "Be sure the passion of the moment isn't clouding your thoughts when you speak these words."

"Oh, Caleb, I've never seen things more clearly." Suddenly, it no longer mattered if he accepted everything right now. He would. During the epiphany of understanding her heart, she'd crossed the great abyss with a silent leap of faith. Serenity replaced uncertainty. Doubt lay on the other side. She faced her destiny—Caleb and his generous love that made her complete.

Without warning, everything about him eased into an enigmatic smile. "Then she gave a gift to both of us. I accept."

Just what he accepted, she forgot to question when his mouth claimed hers. A fresh urgency marked the kiss. The thunder of his heart beat against her breasts. She rose on tiptoes, drawing them into a seamless embrace with the strength of her left arm curled behind his neck. The deliberately tantalizing forays of his hands along her body carved a need to explore the precious gift she accepted in her heart.

She eased away just enough to run her hands over his chest. The tremendous strength of his body quivered at her touch. "I want to know all of you," she whispered, then kissed the center of his breastbone.

Her hunger to experience the most subtle nuances of his flesh found no limits. The heat radiating from him infused her with confidence. She traversed the narrowing line of chest hair pointing the way down his abdomen to his erection. The line at his waist where the sun never kissed his skin fascinated her. So few things in life were defined as clearly.

She sank to her knees and filled her hands with the

fullness of his erect male flesh. His sudden intake of breath emboldened her. Testing, teasing, she memorized the changing textures revealed by sinuously gliding her hand along the length of him.

With deliberate slowness, she tasted him and inhaled the musk of their burgeoning desire. Caught in her own passion, she worshipped him without reservation.

Caleb lifted her to her feet. The wildness in his dilated eyes exposed how close she'd brought him to the edge of completion.

He laid her on the bed and settled between her thighs. The sound of his ragged breathing blended with hers in the otherwise silent room.

"The trouble with your best fantasies coming true is that it can be over too soon," he rasped, holding himself away from her.

Alicia reached down between them. "I want you now."

With a groan of ecstasy, Caleb filled her, then withdrew, only to enter her again and again.

Alicia drew her knees up, meeting each thrust with mounting urgency for the bliss awaiting them. The hunger coiling in her body quickened along with the pace of their lovemaking.

Lost in the passion darkening his gaze, she whispered his name.

In the instant of fulfillment, she experienced the beauty of his soul and felt his love in every cell of her being. She reveled in the rapture, feeling it flow through her with the glory of the sun exploding around her heart.

For a long time, they remained locked in a tight embrace eased only by the gradual return of regular breathing.

"I love you, Alicia." He kissed her lightly, then kissed her again.

"I love you, too, Caleb." She stroked his cheek, amazed anew at the wonders they shared. "It seems we are destined for togetherness." She grinned at the satisfaction lifting the corners of his mouth into a smile. "No refund. No return. As is."

"Dare I ask what you mean?"

Giddy from the joy they shared, she laughed. "Exactly what I said. You can't give me back. You're stuck with me."

"Lucky me," he murmured, shifting his hips.

"Don't tempt me—unless you mean it."

Again, he let his body provide the assurance. "I'll never get enough of you."

Her sated passion stirred with his kiss. She broke it, then drew a shaky breath. "We have to get dressed."

Caleb rested his forehead on hers. "You're right. I didn't think anything could take my mind off what we have ahead of us."

"Me neither." She chuckled. "Thinking and doing aren't always synonymous."

"Were you thinking earlier?" He raised his head.

She smiled at his uncertainty. "It was more like not thinking so hard I couldn't hear what I should have known for a long time. I meant what I said, Caleb. All the time I was lamenting what I'd lost, what I could yet lose, I didn't consider what she'd given me. She gave me you and Mariah. I love you more than I thought it possible to love another human being. We'll face whatever lies ahead together."

He thumbed a strand of hair from her cheek. "I believe you."

"Why?" The old fear sought a hold against her heart.

"Maybe because it's a helluva lot easier to believe myself the recipient of a miracle than to forgo the miracle itself."

Alicia laughed, then pushed at him. "Spoken like an analytically logical male."

Caleb rolled away and sat up. "What happened to your notion of men being emotional creatures?"

She rose to her knees, wrapped her arms around his shoulders, and planted a kiss on the back of his neck. "Sometimes you are emotional when it comes to those you love."

He shrugged and reached for their clothing. "Speaking

of which, you're right. Someone we both love is due home soon."

Alicia wiggled off the bed and dressed. After a few minutes in the bathroom, she joined Caleb on the veranda. He leaned against a support post, his left foot crooked on the rail. She settled on the swing and gave it a push.

They had said so much in the midst of passion, then reaffirmed their commitment in the afterglow. A comfortable silence settled over them. Gone was the tense uncertainty of separate paths.

Alicia drew a deep breath. A hint of a wildflower medley mingled with the tang of spruce rode the lazy breeze. The myriad shades of green in their surroundings took on a sharpness. High over the forest beyond the yard cleared for the Marker home, a hawk screeched in warning.

The occasional glances she exchanged with Caleb brought smiles. For the first time since leaving the Drexel cemetery, Alicia felt at peace.

Nero roused himself from his place in the sun.

The signal brought Alicia from the swing and Caleb off the porch rail. Hand in hand, they walked to the far end of the veranda, then separated as propriety dictated.

Judge Wardel's buggy emerged through the trees. Alicia leaned on the porch rail, just the way she'd watched it disappear. A pair of sturdy roans led the buggy into the yard. Judge Wardel brought it to a halt at the veranda.

Caleb leaped over the porch rail and landed easily. Several long strides brought him to the buggy. He reached for Mariah. The child surged into his arms and clung to his neck.

"Thank you for a very interesting day, Miss Marker." Judge Wardel bowed at the waist and tipped his hat.

"You're welcome. I had fun, too, but I'm glad we came home. I already saw Aunt Constance once this week."

Alicia caught the meaningful exchange of silent questions between the two men. She walked down the porch stairs and joined them.

"I'll expect you and Miss James at the courthouse at ten o'clock in the morning," Judge Wardel told Caleb.

"Is Mr. Brown aware the hearing is tomorrow?" Alicia reached up to take Mariah's hand.

"This isn't a hearing. Mr. Brown is aware I have some questions. Based on the answers I receive, I may schedule formal proceedings." He slapped the reins in the traces. "Good day, and thank you for sharing a most delightful little girl with me."

Silently, they watched him depart.

"Maude's coming home now, too. We saw her at Mr. Kratz's cafe when we went for ice cream," Mariah said. She placed each of her small hands into an adult's. "I like Judge Wardel."

"Why? 'Cause he buys you ice cream?" Alicia teased, swinging their arms.

"No. 'Cause he's nice."

Alicia met Caleb's gaze. Nice or not, tomorrow, they'd learn whether he was fair.

Chapter Twenty-five

At ten the next morning, Alicia entered the Sitka court-house with Caleb and Patrick Brown. She wore her best clothes, which appeared dowdy in comparison to Constance's mauve day dress.

Clad as he was in a dark business suit, Caleb's presence commanded attention. He seated Alicia at the table Judge Wardel indicated.

"Thank all of you for being on time," Judge Wardel said. He stood in the open area between the hearing tables and the judicial bench. "I'm aware you wish to sail for Seattle on Saturday's ship, Miss Cunningham. To that end, I am hopeful that by bringing the parties involved together we can settle this matter and avoid an official hearing."

Mortimer Palmer rose. "Judge Wardel, this is a waste of time. Judge Farrell has granted a change in guardianship to Miss Cunningham. We have no need of another hearing to ensure the legality of that change. I'm sure it is not your intention to challenge Judge Farrell's decision."

Alicia glanced at Patrick, expecting him to object or do something to argue the need for just such a challenge. Patrick remained silent and relaxed in his chair.

"I've known Judge Farrell for a long time, Mr. Palmer. I'm sure he thought the papers he issued concerning Miss Mariah Marker were in her best interests."

"I assure you, Judge, they are," Constance chimed in. "The child cannot continue living in this remote corner of the world. She needs the education her parents intended she have and would have ensured, had they lived, bless their souls."

Judge Wardel folded his arms and strolled to Constance's table. "You intend to give her that education?"

Constance's blond curls bobbed in emphasis as she nodded. "I do."

"In truth, Miss Cunningham, I find no fault with the education the child is receiving. She has an excellent grasp of numbers and can read simple words. Her penmanship skills are excellent for a child her age. Most impressive is her knowledge of geography and science. I doubt many schools could do more to develop her learning skills."

Caleb slipped his hand over Alicia's and squeezed. Her pride in Mariah should have eased the tension tightening the muscles in her shoulders, but she kept waiting for the next twist from the other side of the room.

Constance shot a fulminating glare Alicia met with jaw-tightened stoicism. "Although I deem Miss James's methods unconventional with a disregard for Mariah's welfare, I cannot argue with her success."

"Judge, I can't let that one go," Patrick said casually. "It is only Miss Cunningham's ignorance of children and personal bias that prompts her to make such provocative innuendoes concerning Miss James."

Judge Wardel nodded in their direction. "Your exception is noted, Mr. Brown."

"It is far more than the matter of who, how, and where Mariah is educated, Judge Wardel." Constance folded her gloved hands in front of her waist. "The Cunningham family has long been known as a pillar of the community. In order for Mariah to assume her rightful place in society, she must be exposed to the right people and the proper cultural environment."

Judge Wardel stroked his chin. "Tradition is important. How do you propose to accomplish that, Miss Cunningham?"

"By taking her to Boston. Generations of my family have populated Boston society. Mariah will receive an education in the best schools with her own kind."

"I see," Judge Wardel mused, glancing at Mariah's father.

Alicia felt Caleb's anger rise.

"I'm very glad you agree with Judge Farrell," Mortimer crooned. "Can we consider this matter settled?"

"No," Judge Wardel answered slowly. "There are a few things I need to get straight before putting this to rest."

"I'll be glad to clear up any question you have."

Constance smiled, then settled into her chair with the grace of a mauve cloud settling on a mountaintop.

Judge Wardel retrieved a sheaf of papers from a battered satchel leaning against the judicial bench. He wet his thumb and flipped through the array until finding the ones he wanted. He pulled them free, then arranged the pages on the table in front of Constance. "Is this an accurate picture of your assets, liabilities, and income, Miss Cunningham?"

A frown marred her pleasant mask as she studied the pages.

"It is," Mortimer answered on her behalf.

"How do you intend to finance the housing, clothing, education, and societal exposure you claim essential for Mariah's development?"

"Why, from her parents' estate, of course. She is their only child and certainly entitled to benefit from their assets."

Judge Wardel shook his head. "Mr. Palmer, did you not explain to Miss Cunningham the issue of Jedidiah and Margaret Marker's wills cannot be re-addressed?"

"Your Honor, under these circumstances, we felt—"

"What you feel makes no difference. We're discussing a point of law. The assets of the Marker estate belong to Caleb Marker. The San Francisco Circuit Court decision is final."

"How can you expect me to provide Mariah with what she needs without also granting me access to her parents' assets?"

"That is not a question I need to answer, Miss Cunningham. It is the question I'm asking you. Please explain this to me."

Mortimer gathered the papers. "Judge Wardel, you have at hand an opportunity to build your reputation and write new law by opening the question of a deceased parent's assets where support of an orphaned child is at issue." Mortimer's smooth delivery carried a hypnotic tone.

"I'm not interested in anything beyond the long-term welfare of a very nice, very happy little girl."

"She may be happy and healthy now, but what about when she comes of age?" Constance snapped. "Riding around in men's clothing like a heathen is hardly proper behavior ten years from now. Not even here.

"Instead, she should be attending tea parties, meeting gentlemen, and being courted by prospective husbands. If she remains in this remote place, she'll probably end as the wife of a logger and die an early death."

Judge Wardel turned his back on the proceedings and stared at the bench for a long moment.

Alicia straightened. Something in his stance was familiar. The slight tapping of his fingers against the side of his leg jogged her memory. He was the man in the graveyard who had asked her to sing for his daughter! Had she been less preoccupied, she might have recognized him sooner.

Slowly, he turned to address Constance. "I understand your concern. That does not change the law. Allow me to phrase my question in basic terms. Are you prepared to raise Mariah in the manner you've stated, in her best interests?"

"Yes, I am. I fervently believe returning to the Cunningham roots in Boston is to her benefit."

Judge Wardel nodded thoughtfully. "Financially, how do you propose to do this? Have you relatives in Boston willing to support your efforts in this matter? If so, I would like to see an affidavit or letter to that effect."

"Caleb, Mr. Marker, should support his niece. That is what his brother and my sister would have wanted."

Patrick pushed to his feet. "Jed and Margaret made their wishes concerning their estate and their daughter's care very clear in their wills."

"So noted, Mr. Brown." Judge Wardel nodded a silent request; Patrick resumed his seat.

"Mr. Marker has a moral obligation to support the child," Mortimer said.

"Which he has carried out without touching the assets of the Marker estate," Patrick said without rising. "He is under no obligation to do so if Mariah is removed from his care."

Mortimer faced them. His gaze softened with entreaty. "Surely, you would not want Mariah deprived of proper financial support, Mr. Marker?"

"You don't get another penny from me," Caleb growled in his usual eloquent style.

"I was referring to payments for her support from your brother's estate."

Patrick rose and tossed his pencil onto the table. "Mr. Marker no longer controls the Marker estate."

"What!" Constance lurched to her feet. The grating of her chair along the wooden floor sounded harsh. "What sort of ruse is this, Mr. Brown?"

Judge Wardel leaned against the judicial bench. "Who does control the Marker estate, if not Caleb Marker?"

"It was his to do with as he wished. Before attending this meeting, Mr. Marker made a gift of the estate in its entirety to his fiancée, Miss Alicia James." Patrick produced a sheaf of papers and offered them to Judge Wardel.

"You're nothing if not thorough, Mr. Brown. I'm sure

311

you left nothing to chance." Judge Wardel crossed the distance and picked up the papers.

"He can't do that, can he, Mortimer?"

"I'm afraid he can, my dear. And apparently, he has."

In the tense silence, Constance sank into her chair while Judge Wardel reviewed the papers. When he finished, he dropped them in front of Caleb.

"I'm waiting for your answer, Miss Cunningham."

Dazed, Constance raised her head. "I'm sorry, I don't remember the question."

"The question is how you are going to support this child in Boston."

"Might we have a moment?" Mortimer asked. Without waiting for an answer, he stood and held Constance's chair. The clack of their heels to the far corner sounded loud.

Alicia watched Mortimer whisper at length and wished she could read lips. The hiss of Constance's responses carried as much venom as the glares she shot Alicia. She felt the woman's animosity and continued staring back.

"I haven't got all day, Mr. Palmer." Judge Wardel collected his papers and arranged them in his satchel.

Red-faced with anger, Constance returned to the table. Mortimer appeared unfazed by her temper. He cleared his throat. "Caleb Marker's unwillingness to financially ensure his niece's rightful place in Boston society leaves Miss Cunningham no choice. Unfortunately, at the present time, she cannot support the child as she believes necessary. Mr. Marker's refusal to consider what is best for Mariah, coupled with his unwillingness to responsibly carry out Jedidiah and Margaret Marker's duties to the child, force Miss Cunningham to withdraw her petition at this time. However, her inability to financially shoulder the guardianship of the child does not lessen her concern for Mariah's future."

"So noted," Judge Wardel said. "Mariah will remain with Mr. Marker. Miss Cunningham, as in the past, you may visit your niece when it is convenient for you to travel here. That stated, we'll consider this matter closed.

Miss Cunningham, Mr. Palmer, you may go. Undoubtedly, you'll want to finalize arrangements for your departure Saturday."

Alicia turned her hand over and laced her fingers through Caleb's. She watched Constance depart, glad she wouldn't have to see her for another year or, with luck, longer. By then, the adoption she and Caleb discussed with Patrick would protect the Marker family from further threat.

"You three are very clever," Judge Wardel said. "You were right, Patrick. She wanted the money more than she wanted the child."

"Clever hardly covers your handling of this, Alphonse. You managed to resolve this without holding a hearing or overruling Judge Farrell." Patrick accepted the jurist's extended hand.

The lines in Judge Wardel's face deepened when he shrugged. "She changed her mind and dropped her petition. There is no reason for a hearing."

"Thank you, Judge Wardel." Caleb offered his hand.

"You don't fool me for a moment, Marker." He took Caleb's hand. "You and Kyle Larsen are limbs off the same tree. You would never have parted with that child any more than Kyle would let go of Prudence and Jackson."

"Kyle?" Interest arched Caleb's eyebrows.

"He was married to my daughter, Prudence." Unease deepened the lines in Judge Wardel's face. All hints of satisfaction disappeared. "I'd like to impose on you by borrowing Jeremy to take me to the lumber camp. It's time Kyle and I spoke of my daughter."

"Just tell Jeremy when you want to go." The way his eyes narrowed betrayed deep thought. "Kyle might be ready, too."

"Thank you." Judge Wardel gazed at Alicia.

She returned his sad smile. "Acceptance?"

He nodded. "Will you sing . . ." Judge Wardel's voice faded as though he lacked the strength to make the request aloud.

"Yes," she answered. "On the way home."

He nodded quickly, then turned away.

"Judge Wardel?" she called after him.

He paused, but did not turn around.

"Will you marry us when you return from the logging camp?"

"I'd be honored," he answered in a strained voice and continued toward the door.

"Bring Kyle with you?" Caleb called after him.

"I'll try." He turned the doorknob. "Yes, I'll bring him." Nodding, Judge Wardel left the courthouse.

"Congratulations," Patrick said, stuffing the estate transfer papers into his satchel. "I'll draw the adoption papers so we can file them the day after you're married."

Alicia gazed at Caleb. Disbelief flickered in his gray eyes. "It's over."

"Yes."

"What are we doing on the way home for Judge Wardel?"

"We're going to the graveyard, and I'm going to sing for Prudence Wardel Larsen. I saw him there once, but didn't recognize him until today. He never turned away from her grave while we talked."

"I'm not going to keep you out of graveyards, am I?"

"No."

"You still want Mariah to accompany you and sing?"

"Yes."

Caleb pondered the matter before answering, "All right."

Surprise jolted her. "Just like that? All right?"

"Call it an emotional judgment, not a logical one."

Alicia laughed until Caleb caught her up and kissed her soundly.

Alicia held Caleb's hand as they entered the cemetery. The first hint of autumn rode the sea breeze. The seeds for spring's fresh life scrambled across the ground and nestled among the long grass. A scattering of cut, fading flowers hugged the bases of two Larsen markers.

Since her last visit, someone had straightened the head-stones and scraped the moss from the inscriptions.

"How did they die?"

Caleb slipped an arm around her shoulders. "Fever. Kyle did everything possible for them. He succumbed to the fever after they died. I thought we'd have three graves here. He didn't want to live without them, but he kept on breathing. Eventually, he fought off the fever."

"He never recovered from losing them, did he?"

"No. He never will." Caleb heaved a deep breath. "Nor would I if we were parted for any reason."

She leaned into the warmth of the arm cradling her. "Neither one of us is going anywhere until we join Prudence."

"What will you sing for them?"

Alicia contemplated the question. "A song about angles singing." She glanced at him, and smiled. Another century would pass before the song appeared on a CD.

A cleansing breath filled her lungs with the heady scent of spruce. The song promised an end to the earthly worries of money, power, hunger, and lies. Instead, angels sang in a precious realm of kindness.

Silence settled over the graveyard at the end of the song.

"I've never heard anything so depressing and uplifting in the same song," Caleb murmured.

Laughter bubbled from Alicia's tilted head. "You've decided to become a critic?"

A lopsided smile accompanied a shrug of his shoulders. "You never cease to amaze me."

"Did you expect something conventional or solemn?"

"Not from you, my love."

Gazing into the window on his soul, she saw the depth of his belief.

"Take me home, Caleb."

Secure in the cloak of love, Alicia slipped an arm around his waist. Together, they walked out of the graveyard and into a future forged by the gift of love.

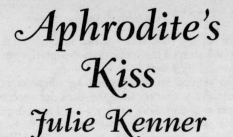

Aphrodite's Kiss
Julie Kenner

Crazy as it sounds, on her twenty-fifth birthday Zoe has the chance to become a superhero. But x-ray vision and the ability to fly are only two things to consider. There is also her newfound heightened sensitivity. If she can hardly eat a chocolate bar without convulsing in ecstasy, how is she to give herself the birthday gift she's really set her heart on—George Taylor? The handsome P.I.'s dark exterior hides a truly sweet center, and Zoe feels certain that his mere touch will send her spiraling into oblivion. But the man is looking for an average Jane no matter what he claims. He can never love a superhero-to-be—can he? Zoe has to know. With her super powers, she can only see through his clothing; to strip bare the workings of his heart, she'll have to rely on something a little more potent.

___52438-4 $5.99 US/$6.99 CAN

Dorchester Publishing Co., Inc.
P.O. Box 6640
Wayne, PA 19087-8640

Please add $1.75 for shipping and handling for the first book and $.50 for each book thereafter. NY, NYC, and PA residents, please add appropriate sales tax. No cash, stamps, or C.O.D.s. All orders shipped within 6 weeks via postal service book rate. Canadian orders require $2.00 extra postage and must be paid in U.S. dollars through a U.S. banking facility.

Name _____
Address _____
City _____ State _____ Zip _____
I have enclosed $ _____ in payment for the checked book(s).
Payment <u>must</u> accompany all orders. ❏ Please send a free catalog.
CHECK OUT OUR WEBSITE! www.dorchesterpub.com

the Mermaid of Penperro
LISA CACH

Konstanze never imagined that singing could land someone in such trouble. The disrepute of the stage is nothing compared to the danger of playing a seductress of the sea—or the reckless abandon she feels while doing so. She has come to Penperro to escape her past, to find anonymity among the people of Cornwall, and her inhibitions melt away as she does. But the Cornish are less simple than she expected, and the role she is forced to play is harder. For one thing, her siren song lures to her not only the agent of the crown she's been paid to perplex, but the smuggler who hired her. And in his strong arms she finds everything she's been missing. Suddenly, Konstanze sees the true peril of her situation—not that of losing her honor, but her heart.

___52437-6 $5.50 US/$6.50 CAN

. . . and coming
May 2001
from . . .

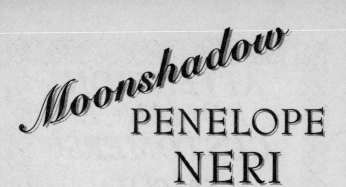

Moonshadow

PENELOPE NERI

"Lillies-of-the-valley," he murmurs, "the sweet scent of innocence." Yet his kisses are anything but innocent as he feeds her deepest desires while honeysuckle and wild roses perfume the languid air.

"Steyning Hall. It is a cold place. And melancholy," he warns, "almost as if it is . . .waiting for someone. Perhaps your coming will change all that."

Wedded mere hours, Madeleine gazes up at the windows of the mansion, stained the color of blood by the dying sun. In the shifting moonshadows she hears voices calling, an infant wailing, and knows not whether to flee for her life or offer up her heart.

___52416-3 $5.99 US/$6.99 CAN

Dorchester Publishing Co., Inc.
P.O. Box 6640
Wayne, PA 19087-8640